BLUE *THE CALLING*

KIAH CROSS

ISBN 978-1-63575-306-6 (Paperback)
ISBN 978-1-63575-307-3 (Digital)

Christian Faith Publishing, Inc.
296 Chestnut Street
Meadville, PA 16335
www.christianfaithpublishing.com

Printed in the United States of America

CONTENTS

To Teri Preiss and Dhia, who granted me permission to color outside the lines

"When we least expect it, life sets us a challenge to test our courage and willingness to change; at such a moment, there is no point in pretending that nothing has happened or in saying that we are not yet ready. The challenge will not wait. Life does not look back. A week is more than enough time for us to decide whether or not to accept our destiny."

—Paulo Coelho, *The Devil and Miss Prym*

FOR STARTERS, ME

The house was small, white, and ordinary—a 1940s bungalow with a blue front door. Had there been an orange-and-white cat on the top step, it would have been a greeting card. Proud shutters framed the windows. The planter boxes were appropriately bursting with petunias and geraniums. The windows themselves, small squares, reflected a cold white sky, though the sky behind me was blue and laced with clouds. It was not my house. I stood before it in utter silence, feet planted, arms at my sides. No cars drove by on the street behind me. No birds twittered or flapped in the trees. I watched, and waited.

Suddenly, flame spurted from the windows above the geraniums. Pieces of the roof shot skyward and seemed to hang in the air. Oxygen-hungry flames leapt up out of the roof hole. Fire moved in every direction. The planter boxes and shutters blackened, sagged, then disintegrated. Near the base of the house, where pieces of siding remained, the paint blistered and curled quickly in the heat. The roar was deafening. I tried to cover my ears but couldn't move my hands. I tried to scream, but my throat made no sound. The intolerable heat and the horrible smell of things that shouldn't be burning, but were burning nonetheless, assaulted my senses. My muscles were stiff and unusable. My legs rooted to the sidewalk. Not even my eyeballs moved when I directed them to. I couldn't look away from the yawning black-and-orange tear in the fabric of the neighborhood where the house had stood just moments before. Gathering every bit of strength I had, I managed to bend at the waist. I sat straight up in bed, gasping in the darkness, dripping with sweat. My dog, Chump, joined me on the bed and was desperately trying to gain access to my face with his tongue.

"I'm fine, Chump. Stop! Yuck! Enough, okay?" I said, fending him off.

He slunk to the floor, resting his chin on the edge of my bed, and stared balefully up at me. He had just been trying to help. I scratched his ears for a moment while I caught my breath and waited for my heart to return to its normal functions. I could still smell the acrid smoke and feel the effects of the heat on my face. It was the second night in a row that the same dream had awakened me. Vivid dreams weren't new to me. I'd been having them for as long as I could remember. Some were more disconcerting than others. Some left strong scents in my nostrils and strange sensations in my limbs. They ranged from pleasant to bizarre, ordinary to terrifying. This was only the second time I'd endured that particular dream, and I hoped it would be the last.

Sweat had soaked through my T-shirt and bedding. Gross. I crept out of bed, still shaking, and stripped the sheets, balling them under my arm. At least my mother would be pleased to find I'd done the laundry again without being asked. Quietly, so as not to wake my parents, I snuck downstairs to shower and start the wash. It was early Monday morning, and I had three exams to look, or not look, forward to: history, mythology, and personal finance. At least, Dad had promised to drive me to school so I could avoid an extended ride on the big yellow bus. Breakfast and school were up next.

My last class that day, algebra, was almost physically painful. Numbers tended to bounce around the inside of my skull like pinballs in a machine, never finding the proper channel to drop through... the channel that would rack up points in my column in the grade book. When the final bell rang to signal the end of the school day, I practically sprinted to my locker, then out to the parking lot to meet Millie. I stood on my tiptoes on the short wall that divided the grass from the sidewalk and scanned the crowded sidewalk for her. I spotted her siren-red head and wound my way through the crowd to join her. We didn't speak right away. We knew each other well enough to not have to.

We simply fell in step beside one another and headed down the street together, destined for her house. Sweet, smart, and loyal, Millie Gorse had the attention span of a fruit fly. She was my best friend. Almost my only friend, actually. She lifted my spirits when I got too serious—which was almost daily. I, in turn, regularly reminded her that her feet needed to actually touch the ground from time to time. Not just the tiptoes. The whole foot. She did almost everything at top speed and rarely toppled. I, on the other hand, toppled regularly—literally. I fell down quite a lot. Sixteen years old, running at full tilt across a field and *bam!* Face full of leaves. My mother blamed it on accelerated physical growth; my brain just never knew what size I was or how to maneuver me through space safely. I thought I was just a klutz.

September was giving way to October, and the summer heat had just begun to let up. The hills were still bare and brown, parched by the summer heat, the air devoid of moisture. The palms of my hands, and the soles of my feet felt itchy, and I scratched my initials in the dry skin of my arm. I had forgotten to apply lotion. We walked the eight blocks to Millie's house, using our feet to pop open the green spiky balls that littered the streets under the chestnut trees, rescuing the shiny brown nuts from the husks. The sky was clear, and there was a pleasant breeze. Millie was reporting on the new exchange student from Australia.

"He's gorgeous," she said. "You'll die when you see him."

I doubted that. My heart didn't tend to flop for the kind of guys that Millie's heart flopped for. The year before, Millie had been more like me... committed to her books and her thoughts. Over the summer, however, she had discovered boys. She loved the silly, fluttery feelings evoked by *just the right guy*. In contrast, the only thing I feared more than feeling wobbly and fog-brained at the very sight of a boy was the idea of someone finding out that I felt that way. A few guys at school held the irritating ability to make me feel weak in the knees, and I avoided them like the plague. I was convinced that boys were a weakness, an Achilles heel, an affliction of the horrible, sidelining type that keeps people from living out their dreams.

Straight down Cherry Street, right on Adams, left on Crestwood, left on Shane Avenue, I could almost have made the trip with my eyes shut. About halfway down street, still quite a distance from Millie's house, I stopped short and stared. There it stood: the little white house with the blue door and shutters, complete with flowering window boxes and neat green-shingled roof. A chill ran up my spine.

"What's up?" Millie asked, following my gaze to the little bungalow.

"Did this house just get painted, or has it always looked like this?"

"It's looked like that as long as I can remember."

"You know who lives there?"

"Just a young couple. They don't have kids. The lady takes good care of the yard, so Mom's impressed. Why?"

"I haven't noticed it before," I said, still staring. Even the little white bird painted on the front of the old-fashioned letter box beside the front door was familiar.

"Why would you notice it, Kiah? It's just a house." Millie moved on ahead of me. I didn't follow.

"Well, I dreamt about this house, Millie. I dreamt it blew up right in front of me. I've had the dream twice, as a matter of fact. The place was totally destroyed."

She stopped again and turned back, giving the cottage a second look. "Oh yeah? Well, that's weird. Are you sure it's the same house you dreamt of?"

"Yes, exactly the same, right down to the color of the door and the kinds of flowers in the windows."

Millie snapped her gum and shrugged. "You must have seen it before when you came over to my place, and then your brain just made up a crazy dream about it. It just means you're morbid, but we already knew that."

I still didn't move.

"The house is *fine*, Kiah. It was just a dream. Can we go now?"

She was right. The house seemed fine. But I wasn't so sure I'd seen it and then fashioned a morbid dream about it. There was more to it than that. I had the vague, nagging sensation that I needed to look close, pay attention, and remember. I'd had vivid dreams before—scenes that I'd later watched unfold before my eyes, as if from a movie I'd already seen. It was like a vivid form of déjà vu. I knew, for instance, when I was six years of age and Dad announced we were moving, that we would buy a house with three white columns and a pink flowering plum tree in the front yard. When I was nine, and an earthquake started shaking our house, I knew immediately that my mother's favorite vase would fall from the shelf and shatter against the antique iron at the base of the cabinet, into a thousand irreparable pieces. My dreams told me things to watch for, gave clues for me to follow. Most of them were relatively innocuous. An exploding house was another matter entirely.

"Come on… Let's *go*, weirdo," Millie said, pulling me down the sidewalk toward her house.

Before I go any further, I should introduce myself. My name is Kiah. I was dubbed Kiah Avis Adenauer at birth. And, no, I don't know what my parents were thinking when they named me—something exclusive and pioneering I'm sure. I'm not sure where to start my story, since people's lives don't have neat beginning, climaxes, and endings, like books do. At least, the beginning of *my* life isn't something anyone would find fascinating. It involved two nervous new parents, a trip home from the hospital in an AMC Gremlin, and a smattering of excited shirttail relatives that came to stand at the edge of my bassinet and admire the healthy newborn—at least that's what they tell me. I actually don't remember it myself.

By four years of age, I'd outgrown the bassinet and slept regularly in my big girl bed. I'd also learned to read and began to develop an uncommon fascination with words. I devoured adult level books by the time I was in the third grade. Words occupied a good amount of my thought time. I didn't just use them to communicate. I savored them—at least the good ones, anyway. I loved the tenor, the flavor, the meaning, and the origin of words. I rolled and sorted them in my head by category, root, length, flavor, even color. Many words carried distinct color connotations. I wholeheartedly believed, and still do, that the word *family* should be written in light brown; the word *class* in charcoal gray, definitely not black, and it carried a definite peachy flavor. *Frontage* was a decidedly green word, and *porcelain*, obviously, sported a light pink tinge. As a child, I gave my colored pencils a workout, rendering each word in its appropriate color. I tried, early on, to explain these intense feelings to my teachers but was met with blank stares, eye rolls, and impatient sighs. So I learned to write for others in black and white, the way they wanted me to, and keep my opinions on such important matters to myself. Their lack of understanding didn't dampen my resolve to chase down every one of the words and discover its source, to know its history. I found satisfaction in being able to pin down an initially elusive word... *Ha, I gotcha! I knew you started out as a mythological reference long before you entered the English language and made a pit stop at Latin verb along the way!*

My family moved multiple times when I was young—not for the reasons you might expect. My parents didn't even change jobs with most of our moves. Dad, like a hermit crab, loved the fresh start promise offered by a change of domicile. By the time, I was a third grader and had moved more times than I could count on my fingers. My mind conjured up a surrogate home and dropped it regularly into my dreams. At least I assumed that's how the stone cottage made its way into my subconscious. I'd be in the middle of an intense dream, sprinting down a dirty city block; and a cozy stone cottage would appear, incongruous, in the center of the street—or I'd find myself struggling, drowning in a large black ocean, waves sweeping over my head. The stone cottage would float into view on a large raft, windows warm and light, smoke drifting from the fireplace. When my grade school teachers instructed us to draw our own home, I drew the stone cottage, complete with three front steps and flowering climbing vines that draped low over the front porch.

I had my first waking vision during the fourth grade. I was staring out the school bus window at the endless rows of houses when the space between the road and the houses literally filled with horses. They thundered along beside us, muscles straining and nostrils flaring, jostling for position. I could hear their hoofs and smell their sweat. I somehow knew they weren't actually there, but they were *so real.* I stayed quiet and watched with utter delight. The vision lasted only a few minutes, then faded. I was disappointed. I immediately assumed everyone had such visions. The next morning, I shared my experience with a classmate, and she promptly repeated my words to everyone in class, adding her opinion that I was crazy. The look on the faces of my teacher and the other students made me wonder if she was right. My parents were called. They strongly cautioned me to keep my imagination to myself, and I heeded their advice; I kept subsequent visions to myself. Many of them came on like a migraine aura, sparkling around the edges of my vision, filling in slowly. The slow onset gave me time to get off by myself and sit down. A handful of times, they contained simple, pointed directions, like a road map for upcoming bend in the road. Those were helpful. Often they were complicated or downright bizarre and seemed to hold no meaning whatsoever.

My fifth-grade school year began in a tiny town on the Pacific Ocean. My mother turned down the school's invitation to the PTA board for the second year in a row—fairly citing a hectic work schedule as her reason. Her ensuing guilt led her to host a Chinese exchange student whose housing had fallen through. The girl's name was Ling. Barely taller than I, she looked, walked, and even smelled intriguingly different from anyone I'd ever met. Ling was shy and spoke very little English. She was a gift to me. From the moment she entered the house, I hung on every foreign, unintelligible sound that came from her mouth and made it my personal mission to draw as many precious syllables from her as I could. I designated a neon-pink locking diary I'd received from Grandma Margaret as my Foreign Language Journal, determined to unravel this new code called "Mandarin Chinese." I plagued Ling, begging her to give me words, words, and more words so that I could scratch out their sounds and meanings in my little book. She humored me. Soon we were gesticulating wildly to communicate the meanings of words she didn't know in English. It was much like the game I'd always played in my own head. For the first time, I had a partner to play it with. Soon, we were speaking back and forth in pidgin-type mix of Chinese and English that no one around us understood. When she left for home, I felt a pang of

15

loss I still can't quantify. I still wonder, with some degree of guilt, whether I missed Ling as much as I missed her words.

With Ling gone, I immediately searched for something to feed my newly acquired foreign-word habit. The public school didn't offer Chinese, but they offered an early learning pilot program in German. I signed up and drank in the language like a languishing camel at an oasis. I even bribed the local public librarian, who apparently adored yogurt-covered almonds, into ordering children's books in German. Mrs. Greeb was a prune-faced older woman with a permanent "hush" perched on her lips. The gift of almonds started an unexpected friendship. At Christmas, she gave me a surprise gift I would always cherish... a small foil-wrapped paperback copy of *Er Heiss Jan*, the first actual foreign language novel I ever owned.

Early on, I discovered I had an uncanny ability to read people—not their minds, of course, that would be downright bizarre... but people's feelings, their emotional *leanings* often struck me even more forcefully than their words. In one-on-one conversations, it was a perk. In large groups, the impact often overwhelmed me. At one of my father's work functions, for example, I was struck with the certainty that the woman in the red dress felt awkward and unwanted; her boldness was a cover-up for something crumbling inside her, and it brought me close to tears. The man in the blue hat had a secret, the kind of secret he hoped no one knew but feared everyone would see. The word *desperation* trailed behind the man in the green shoes like an unwelcome tail. People's emotional struggles and troubled psyches weighed heavily on me. I couldn't read everyone, of course. Some people hold their cards closer to their chest. My mother for instance: I'd never really been able to pin her down. Her walls were too practiced and well-fortified. I attributed it to her job as a lawyer. She made her living by being formidable.

With practice, it became easier to screen out the bulk of people's leanings. Every once in a while, however, empathy rose out of nowhere and struck me full force, despite my internal resistance. At fifteen years old, I was in the cold beverage aisle at the grocery store when empathy for the woman next to me rolled over me like a frigid wave, strong enough to make me gasp and stagger. *Lonely...* the word might as well have been tattooed in blue on her forehead. The woman narrowed her eyes at me, but it didn't lessen my empathy for her. It was apparent to me that she badly needed someone to hold her hand. I mumbled, "Excuse me," grabbed a few bottles of raspberry seltzer from the shelf, and fled as quickly as possible. I was mortified, not sure what to do besides retreat and wait for the intensity to pass. I kept such experiences to myself.

At sixteen years of age I was already *keenly* aware, that I did not fit the classic American teenage girl mold. And it wasn't for socially acceptable reasons; I was neither fabulously glamorous nor an extreme genius. I had been a gangly precocious child, and was growing into a gangly, offbeat young adult. My dark hair was cropped just above my shoulders, while the popular girls sported long, fuzzy boomerang perms. I pressed my nose into books, while most of the girls pressed theirs into each other's business. I read books and rode horses while my cohorts watched movies and planned parties. I was a classic square peg in a field of round holes, except that unlike many of the square pegs, I didn't even remotely desire to be round. I didn't enjoy talking about brand-name clothes or nail polish. I wasn't into designer lunch sacks. I never used the word *bogus*, and none of my clothing glowed in the dark.

The round pegs yearned for sameness. They jammed their legs into tight jeans, rolled their bangs into perfect curl tunnels on their foreheads, and traveled in herds, even to the bathroom. Anything "less than" made them feel superior; anything "more than" made them nervous. I tried not to hold it against them. They were, for the most part, nice people. Some weren't, of course, but for the most part… I tried to be polite, even tracking and holding conversations with some of them from time to time.

"So what did you do this weekend?" says Round Peg.

"Took a few early morning horseback rides and read a book. You?"

"Party as Tara's. She has a pool and an older brother!" Round Peg winks, as if to cue astonished approval.

"Oh, that's nice."

"Okay, bye."

"Bye."

My nonconformity seemed to make the round pegs, including some of my relatives, uneasy.

"Has she begun to, you know, *join in* yet, Lisette?" I overheard Grandma Margaret ask my mother. She spoke in the hushed tones a person might use to express concern about a coma patient who hasn't yet responded to stimulus.

"I'm sure I don't know what you mean. You should ask her yourself," my mother responded curtly.

Score one for Mom! Mom had, up to that point, supported my right to be exactly who I was, without explanations or excuse.

I attended the occasional school function, even tried out for basketball once... a complete disaster! (Why would anyone want the ball badly enough to *scratch* people for it?) I came to the conclusion that it was simply easier to be alone. It was also more lonely. My spirit developed a permanent ache, like a swimmer's cramp. I longed for something *more*... something I couldn't define... something no one else seemed to know was missing. I've heard everyone feels different from their peers. "It's a part of adolescence," they say. But I felt *really* different. There weren't many other girls my age avoiding large groups for fear of empathy attacks, and hanging out in the foreign language section of the local library.

Two friends, Millie and Nate, held me back from melancholy loner status. Even *with* their friendship, I grew increasingly restless and agitated, as if an invisible gnat buzzed around my head twenty hours a day—one I could swat at but couldn't escape. I'd like to tell you what the gnat represented, but I *didn't* know! Boredom? Desperation? They were certainly part of it. Something in me screamed that I, along with seemingly every other person on the planet, was *missing the point!* I just wasn't sure what the point was, or how to find it.

Then junior year dawned, and I caught a glimmer of hope. My mother sent me to Scotland for the summer to visit some distant relatives on her side of the family.

"To get you to stop moping and get your nose of your books for a while," she said.

It turned out to be one of her better ideas.

SCOTLAND

Boring old US of A
Scotland, June 1991

Departure day. I was flying to Scotland *alone*! I waved good-bye at the gate, heart thumping, and boarded the jet for what would be my first flight. *Commercial jets look so much cleaner than they smell. Which sense are we expected to trust?* Fourteen hours later, I landed in Edinburgh. Scotland was beautiful. The light was sleeker there than the light at home. The air felt weighty and valuable. Perhaps I was simply besotted by the newness of it all, coupled with the absence of the weight of expectation. I felt gloriously unfettered. The people looked at each other differently than they did at home. They carried themselves differently. They seemed less stiff somehow, and more free.

My mother arranged for me to stay with her cousins, Kade and Gwen Clacher, and their daughter, Elspeth. The Clachers lived on a thirty-acre spread in a country home the family had owned for as long as anyone could remember. Their home began its life as a tiny gray stone farmhouse, but several generations of Clachers had built onto it throughout the years—sometimes in wood, sometimes in brick, sometimes in rock. The resultant dwelling was squat, amorphous, and homey. It smelled of woodsmoke, mildew, herbs, and lye from the batches of homemade goat's milk soap that Aunt

Gwen made. The floors in the house sloped, and the ceiling dipped at unpredictable intervals. It wasn't unusual to hear a mild thump and a muttered expletive when Uncle Kade's head met up with a particularly low bend in the ceiling. Uncle Kade was a semiretired machinist who seemed twice as physically busy as my own father, but half as preoccupied.

Kade and Gwen were a quiet, peaceful pair. The scarcity of their words increased the value of those they did choose to utter. Their daughter Elspeth, on the other hand, was the most verbose person I'd ever met. When I got going on a subject I was passionate about, I could certainly fill the air, but Elsie put me to outright shame. Several years older than I, Elsie was home from college on break. She was more than thrilled to have a fresh pair of ears to listen to her ramble. She took it upon herself to personally acquaint me with every relative I'd never met and every square inch of the cold gray county. I visited thirteen separate family households in the area during my time there—all presumably my relatives, some barely hanging from the shirttail.

Barring Elsie, the majority of my Scottish family members weren't highly formally educated. I initially wondered if that had fostered mother's disapproval of them. They were mostly farmers, tradesmen, stay-at-home moms. The women milked goats and pinned laundry to lines in the yard. The books on their shelves were sparse but dog-eared, trusted treasures that told well-loved stories and gave much-needed instructions on recipes and gardening, wiring, and home remedies. In the evenings, the families gathered in their living rooms. The younger kids colored coloring books and poked each other in the eye; the older kids listened to music on their portable cassette tape players while doing homework, or pretending to. They seemed to simply enjoy each other's presence, a completely novel experience for me. I fell in love with all of them, in an unspoken sort of way. I also fell in love with their language. Not just the Scots language, a charming version of English but the Gaelic. Scots Gaelic is a treasure of a language connected to the heart and soul of those who speak it. Many of my newfound relatives spoke Gaelic at home, especially the older ones, and they were proud of it. They were eager to share it. I listened intently and hoarded their words. Within a short amount of time, I was fairly fluent, which delighted my great-aunts to no end.

One Friday morning, a week before I was slated to return home, Elsie and I visited the last new set of old relatives, just for the day. They were my second cousins. Their little greenhouse was in the countryside, far out of town, and the weather was clear and warm. Elsie had gone on a grocery run with the family; and I, feeling particularly sorry for myself about having to go home, begged off to explore the area alone on foot. Nature soothed my nerves. The endless hills and wide gray sky unknotted my shoulders and reminded me how big the world was, and how small my problems were in comparison. The hills were a quilt of mottled brown stone, green, and heather. I caught sight of an abandoned church and climbed the hill behind it. I perched at the top of the hill to take in the views. The only part of the little church below me that indicated the building's original purpose was a crumbling cross that had fallen and lying broken at the base of one of two remaining partial walls. The floor of the building was grass; the remaining windows held perfectly framed glimpses of the countryside.

I picked grass, heaping it into a tiny pile, and concentrated on breathing deeply. For a few more short days, there would be no expectations looming overhead, no math teachers rolling their eyes at my incompetence, no nosy American grandmothers wondering if my lack of boyfriend coupled with my short hair signaled an unnatural affection for women. It was just me and the air, and the ground... or so I thought. I leaned back against a boulder and closed my eyes. Suddenly, my field of vision filled with light and color. A waking vision, more startling and vivid than a sleeping dream, came on suddenly with familiar soft focused edges and glaringly bright central details. Directly in my center of vision floated a giant circular puzzle frame. The edges had been assembled completely, but there were no center pieces—only a deep colorless void inside the frame. The puzzle spun slowly, and I was able to read and identify some of what was on the individual edge pieces. It was a mish-mash of text, sketches and photos depicting people, animals, and even concepts. I recognized them as my feelings, my family, my thoughts. They were pieces of my life. Red for anger, blue for sadness, green for peace… I understood that I had yet to find and place the center pieces.

It's too bad there's no box lid to help me know what pieces I should be searching for, I thought.

As I watched the puzzle spin, I heard a woman's voice singing a passionate love song in Gaelic. The Gaelic for Dhia struck my ears and echoed in my chest. *Dhia* was the Gaelic name for God. I'd never heard anyone sing a love song to *God* before. In my mind's eye, a puzzle piece floated toward me and hung just above the center of the puzzle. The name *Dhia* was emblazoned on it in purple script. It hung in the air, seeming close enough to touch, as if waiting for me to take and place it. The raw passion behind the words being sung reached into my soul, beckoning and stirring, with a long, gentle, lavender finger. It sent a sliver of hope slicing through a dark place straight to my core. It was warm and electric, so strong it was almost terrifying—like nothing I'd ever felt before. My bones buzzed, my hands and feet tingled, my heart raced. I wish I could tell you what I hoped *for*, but I didn't know. I simply became aware that a reason to hope existed.

The vision disappeared as suddenly as it appeared, leaving me snuffling, panting, and mildly disoriented. I pressed my hand over my heart and willed it to slow down before it leapt out of my chest. The gloominess I'd felt earlier had completely evaporated; and I felt a grin, the kind I'd always associated with idiocy, plastered to my face. I knew suddenly that my return home wasn't an end to a precious reprieve as much as it was a bridge to something great and unknown that lay in my future. Whatever hope I'd glimpsed, I wouldn't be leaving it behind in Scotland… It was yet to come. I scrambled up from the ground and headed back toward the road. As I walked, I heard the love song again, but quieter this time and from far off. I glanced around, confused. The waking vision was absolutely gone. I scanned for answers and glimpsed a small black-haired woman through a window in the stone building. She stood on the far side of the church ruins near the broken cross. She waved and smiled, startling me since I only half expected she was real, and promptly disappeared from sight. I backed up to the edge of the road, scanning far and wide for her, but she was gone.

I stood for a moment in the street. My confusion existed on multiple levels. First, my visions usually had a solid framework… I'd certainly never before seen a character remain once a vision had ended. Second, and perhaps even more disconcerting, was the reference to God. I was not a religious person. My parents had been raised in Christian homes, like most Americans of their generation. My grandmother on my father's side, whom I called Oma, used to mention God occasionally. She even read me a few verses from the Bible when I was young, but whenever she did so around my mother, Mom put a sudden end to it. I caught the drift. Religion was not Mom's cup of tea. It wasn't for us. And yet, on that day, the name of God set an undeniable measure of hope and joy spinning in my chest like a silver top.

Clouds clumped together and began to spit rain at me. In a few minutes, the hillside would be drenched. I hurried in the direction of the little greenhouse. I reached the front stoop and shook the rain from my jacket. Elsie was there, waiting, just inside. She took one look at me and pulled me into the mudroom.

"What! What is it?" she demanded.

"You see it, right? You see something different?" I couldn't wipe the smile off my face.

"See what? What do you mean?" She sniffed me. "Have you been drinking?"

"No, of course not," I protested and began to remove my boots.

"Or maybe you've seen a ghost? A very friendly ghost, maybe tall dark and handsome? Where have you been, and what have you been doing?"

Elsie tended to deliver ideas and questions in rapid threes, expecting one immediate answer that quickly satisfied every query while she formulated the next three things that needed saying.

"I was just taking a walk and thinking, and then, well, I felt better about… things. I'm not sure why, but I feel really, really good. Maybe Scotland agrees with me." I grinned at her.

She narrowed her eyes at me, hands on her hips. "Or maybe you are getting sick." She felt my forehead with the back of her hand.

The next day, the inexplicable bubble of hope still hadn't dissipated. I felt the urgent need to make my outside reflect the strange change I'd experienced on the inside. Elsie took me to a little hair salon in the village nearest her house, and the sunny tattooed hair artist that owned the shop sheared my hair short. I felt so bold and free, in a "Daring Teen Gets Different Haircut from Everyone Else's, Not Just a Little Different, but Drastically So" sort of fashion.

The week drew quickly to a close. Everything has an end. I said my good-byes with stifled tears and boarded a plane back to the United States with a strange new hairstyle, a fair mastery of the languishing Gaelic language, the love of my newly discovered family, and some form of hope flopping and fluttering in my chest.

THE VISIT

January 14, 1992

Hope is a tenuous flame. Over the next year, it ebbed and flowed, sputtered and flared. I came home from Scotland with the conviction that my life wasn't just accidental or coincidental. I somehow knew that there was a divine being—not just out there somewhere, but actually available to me. I had the inexplicable feeling that this divine being had plans for me. It wasn't knowledge I'd gained by research… It was something I just *knew*! I felt it in my bones, and it whispered up and down my spine. I had no one with whom I could share my strange experience or conviction. Even if I had known someone who believed in God, I wasn't about to tell them I had come to know of His existence through a vision—*no way!*

Going home inevitably meant returning to high school (aka the Kryptonite of All Forms of Hope). I couldn't wait to graduate and get on with life. I lived in the small unforgettable Pacific Northwest town of Kenoa, in the center of a valley that always reminded me of a prehistoric salad bowl. The high walls of the bowl were crumbling rock, layers of reds, oranges, gray, and browns. A formidable river split the bowl in two halves. The Kenoa valley spent the winters under a deceptively cozy-looking blanket of snow, and baked to a crisp in the blazing sun of summer. Most of the year, it was devoid of natural green vegetation. There were, however, a few weeks in the spring when a dusting of light green velvet lay over the entire area offering a promise of loveliness it never kept.

The first half of December had been bare and cold, but by January 14, a good six to eight inches of snow had stacked up on the berms at the sides of the roads. The Kenoa road crew did a pretty good job keeping the roads passable. They had plenty of practice. On that particular night, I had volunteered to drive Millie home. We'd stayed after school to set up for the school's production of *Sound of Music*. The play had run late. It was almost 10:00 by the time we left the school parking lot. My father, having read an article about the dangers of distracted teenage driving, had arbitrarily removed the radio from my car. The silence suited me just fine. I found music intrusive and annoying unless it exactly fit my mood, which it rarely did. Millie was humming a Guns N' Roses song. *Yuck.*

"You are killing me, Millie," I said, easing the car onto her home street.

She grinned and hummed louder, then countered my complaint with her own. "If you drive any slower, the snow will melt before we get home. Is that what you are hoping for?"

I stopped the car in the middle of the road. My toes curled.

"I'm just kidding, Kiah. You aren't going to make me walk, are you?" Millie pretended to pout.

"What happened to that house, Millie... the little white house?" I stared through the driver's side window at a black hole in the snow, where the little white house with the blue door had stood, the last time I saw it. The car's headlights lit up the snow on either side of the black chasm. My heart was in my throat.

"There was a house fire. Last week. Didn't you hear about it?" Millie chirped, always excited at an opportunity to bear news.

I shook my head. No.

"They were lucky no one was hurt," she went on. "The couple who lives there was on vacation. There was a gas leak, in the middle of the day, and somehow it just kind of blew up. It shook the whole neigh..." Millie stopped midsentence and stared at me.

"Oh my gosh, Kiah, is this the house you had the dream about... ? Well, is it?"

I nodded.

"What does that mean?" Millie had a death grip on my arm.

"Ouch! It means you let go before you bruise me," I said, prying her fingers from my arm. "And it means you don't say anything about this to anyone, because they might think I'm crazy."

"Then you would be arrested because they would think *you* did it," Millie said. She had a flare for the dramatic.

"No, they wouldn't, Millie. You said yourself it was a gas leak. Now who's being morbid?"

I swatted lightly at her, then looked back at the blackened shell of the house. Almost all that remained of the house were a few charred beams reaching for the sky. The memory of the dream—the explosion, the heat, and the flames—made me shiver. I had definitely seen this house explode; I just hadn't been there at the time it happened.

"I think some things just can't be explained, Millie. Like mysteries. There just aren't answers for everything."

"Are you one of those things?" Millie asked.

"Of course not, silly. But dreams are. I've had vivid dreams where I could taste things, smell things, see things really clearly. They were so real. Haven't you?"

"I guess… maybe. But in my dreams I have to give speeches in my underwear, without my teeth, and then it doesn't actually come *true*!"

"Thank goodness!" I responded.

Millie snorted and pinched me.

"Ouch, be nice, or I *will* make you walk," I whined.

I pressed my foot into the gas pedal, and the tires spun momentarily before they caught. I dropped Millie off in front of her house.

"Seriously, Millie, I don't think we should tell anyone about my weird dream. Okay? Especially your mother." Millie's mom was a nervous wreck already. She was a fragile, worrying sort of person. Anything inexplicable or uncontrollable tended to send her over the edge. "If you say a word, I'll have to tell Jason Betz about that baseball card you stole from him in fifth grade, and still sleep with at night," I threatened, only half teasing.

"I do not sleep with it!" Millie declared. I couldn't tell if she was being truthful. Jason Betz was still one of her favorite crushes.

"I promise not to tell a soul. Scout's honor—and my cousin is a scout, so it counts, sort of." Millie crossed her heart. "But you have to tell me if you have any more of those dreams. Seriously. It's so exciting!"

"Well, I don't know if exciting is the right word," I hedged. "But keep it to yourself. Promise?"

"I promise. Seriously. I don't want to see you arrested. Who would I have to hang out with then?"

"No one. No one else would put up with your singing."

"Good night." She grinned.

"Good night."

I watched Millie pick her way through the fresh snow up to the front door and disappear into the house before I eased the car back onto the right side of the road and pointed it toward home. My nerves were on edge. Sometimes it felt to me as if someone, or something, was trying to tell me something. But I didn't know who, or what they were saying. The Gaelic word for *God, Dhia,* came to mind; but I pushed it quickly aside. At that particular moment, the whole concept of God seemed like a frightening romantic notion I'd entertained in a poetic setting in a faraway land. I wasn't ready to flirt with it further.

Calm down, go home, have a cup of tea, and go to bed, Kiah, I told myself, begging myself to heed my own directive.

Once my mind began to spin, I had a hard time stopping it—and it was going full tilt. Thankfully, my car basically knew its own way home. I was rounding one of the last, careful turns toward home when the hair stood up on the back of my neck. I had the strangest feeling that my name had been called, though I heard nothing. Every cell in my body except for those in my eardrums had registered the call. I had felt moments of heightened awareness before but in a subtle whispering sense. This time, it was more like a shout, a surging demand. I knew suddenly how my horse felt in the hours before a storm, when his instincts warned of danger; and he pricked his ears forward, every muscle tense, listening and watching—finally breaking to dash about the field searching wildly for signs that confirmed danger.

I slowed the car slightly and peered intently through the windshield, trying to hear over the pounding of my own heart. Snow fell in flurries, the flakes so light they swirled up as often as down. No immediate source of danger presented itself. I continued up the hill, but much more slowly— waiting, listening, then felt the fervent need to stop. *Just stop here!*

I spotted a turnout a few feet ahead, a wide space off to the right side of the road. The car suddenly felt like an airless tomb. I needed to get out. Hoping the snow was not too deep, I veered right, into the turnout. The tires bit firmly into the dry snow. I killed the motor and stepped out into the night. The moon was tucked out of sight behind the clouds, painting both the clouds and the ground a diffuse white color. The landscape was clearly visible. It was so quiet I could actually hear the snowflakes hitting the ground. *Plip. Plip.*

Now what?

Everything was still. Only the snowflakes moved. I waited, not sure what to do next. My spirit was definitely astir, gesturing wildly for my mind and body to join it in action. I just wasn't sure how. An incongruous image jumped to mind. It was the image of a small worn brown children's book, with illustrations wrought in full color on the miniature pages. It was a book I was familiar with; Oma had given it to me when I was a child, and I had hidden it under my bed, worried that my mother would find and confiscate it because it was a Bible story. In the story, a boy named Samuel was given into service at the temple of Jehovah God. Each night, Samuel slept on a flat mat in a desolate room. I had always wondered if he liked it there. He didn't look particularly happy or sad in the pictures. Just watchful. One night, as moonlight poured in the open window hole of his small room, Samuel heard his name called. He ran to the old priest, Eli, to ask what he needed. Eli said he hadn't called for Samuel and sent him back to bed, but the scene repeated itself several times. Eventually, old Eli caught on and told Samuel that God himself was calling Samuel. He told him to reply to the Lord, saying, "Speak, Lord, for your servant is listening."

But why did this story come to me now? I took a deep breath and concentrated, looking for a logical connection between the story and this situation. I felt the irony of looking for logic in a purely illogical situation.

Samuel. Samuel didn't recognize God's voice himself, but He answered it anyway, I thought. *Could that be the answer? Could God be trying to speak to me?* I wondered.

The only thing I could think of to do was ask Him.

Am I really considering talking out loud to God? The concept seemed more than a little frightening, and fully ridiculous. But I was standing alone in the dark, in a snowbank, with a serious case of the willies. It was worth a try.

What does a person say to a God who may or may not exist?

The Gaelic name *Dhia* came quickly to mind. It seemed more appropriate and less daunting.

"A Dhia, speak, for your servant is listening," my voice rang out in the night air, louder than I had intended it to. I felt foolish.

My heart began to pound again; and I felt, rather than heard, a direct answer. I felt it in my feet in the form of the insatiable urge to walk. I followed the urge, and it directed me to a towering copse of poplar trees at the edge of the turnout. On the far side of the trees was a small road, little more than a path. I had never noticed it before and doubted I would have noticed it even then, except that the path was completely devoid of snow. Snowflakes were piling up at the edges, but the path itself was bare; the flakes that landed there dissolved into the dirt. I swallowed hard and reached out to touch the dirt at the mouth of the road. It was reassuringly cold and hard, as it should be.

One might expect that I would note my own raised hackles and head back to my car. Hot tea and warm bed waited less than eight minutes up the icy road. I contemplated it but just couldn't. I had asked to be spoken to, and I had promised to listen. I didn't know *who* exactly I had made a promise to or *why* I had felt the need to do so, but I stuck to my word. I stepped determinedly onto the tree-lined path, following carefully as it wound right and left, then ended suddenly at an enormous tree at the base of a sheer rock wall. It was a strange type of tree—definitely not one I'd ever seen in the valley before. I couldn't tell if it had one ropy, gnarled trunk that split soon after it left the ground or many connected trunks that fused together to form one massive body. It bore dark diamond-shaped leaves. As on the path, the snowflakes disappeared into the tree rather than sticking to it; and the ground underneath it was cold, hard, bare, and dry. I stepped under the canopy of the tree, reached forward to run my hands over the trunk, and pitched violently forward.

I fell, or flew, or a combination of the two, in a graceless horizontal tumble. My brain sputtered, trying to process the new sensation, and quickly gave up.

As suddenly as the tumble started, it was over, and I lay in an unceremonious heap on the ground. Eyes still closed, I ran through a quick mental checklist of my body parts to see if anything felt painful or broken. Bruised? Maybe. Broken? I didn't think so. All my parts seemed to be in their proper places and functional. I opened my eyes, blinked against the light, and then blinked again. The memory and logic portions of my brain utterly failed me. I was no longer in a snowy field. Perhaps I had hit my head? I touched it gingerly. It seemed to be its normal size and shape. Perhaps I was dead? My knee began to throb. Minor pain was not rumored to be part of the after-life experience, but I hadn't known many people who actually died and then lived to share their experience, so I couldn't be sure.

A new landscape had sprung up around me. I found myself in an enormous, open, grassy field in the center of a valley. The valley was rimmed on three sides by impossibly high purplish rock walls, like a giant horseshoe. Most astonishing was the ocean shoreline that lay at the mouth of the horseshoe a few hundred feet to my right. The waves were slow and lazy, lapping up on the speckled pink-and-black sand of the beach. The sky was a hazy deep periwinkle color I'd never seen before. Layers of purpling clouds almost completely obscured the white ball of sun on the horizon over the waves. I couldn't tell whether the sun was just coming up or just going down. The wan sunlight struggled to illuminate the edges of the valley.

I sat for a moment, stunned and confused, my heart pounding insistently on my ribcage like a claustrophobic prisoner in a tiny jail cell. I rose to my feet and winced, my left knee decidedly sore. My skin vibrated, and my ears rang. I inhaled deeply and closed my eyes for a moment, trying to get my bearings. Adrenaline was surging through my body as if it had opened up a viaduct right next to my blood vessels and was in competition with my blood for how fast it could surge and how far it could reach.

Where am I? my mind screamed.

A Dhia, help me! That time, I didn't have to plan my words. At that moment, calling out to Dhia seemed the only natural thing to do. A phrase from a book I'd read drifted through my mind. "There are no atheists in foxholes," *or rabbit holes, apparently.*

Just breathe, Kiah, I told myself. I complied. At least my body, if not my mind, began to cooperate with me.

If I was *not* dead, and it was a dream induced by head trauma; then it was certainly the most intense dream I had ever experienced.

I turned slowly on my heel to look around me. The grass beneath my feet was short and cool, silvering in the waning light. There were clumps of taller grasses scattered here and there. Everything about the landscape was rugged and unfamiliar. It was shockingly beautiful. I felt a strange lightness that I had never felt, despite my bruises and general discombobulation.

The air was warm and smelled of full-on spring. I was overheating in my winter coat. I abandoned it to the ground and removed my bulky sweater, dropping it on top of the coat. I had an irresistible longing to remove my shoes and feel the grass between my toes. I paused. Common sense strongly recommended shoes and socks outdoors in grassy fields. But this experience wasn't common and didn't make sense. There seemed to be different rules here. Off came the shoes.

The grass was soft enough, and there seemed to be no rocks or pebbles to bruise my soles. The ground felt so very good beneath my feet. It welcomed me. In the distance, along the back wall of the canyon, directly opposite the shoreline, I saw a long low-slung building. It resembled a canvas tent jutting out toward the center of the field, like an arrow pointing to the sea. I set off for the building. Unfamiliar floral notes greeted my nose as I walked. My legs were wobbly, but curiosity and the darkening sky drove me to move quicker than my body wished me to go. It was growing darker.

Apparently, I thought, *it is evening, not morning.* I was pleased to realize that logic was beginning to return.

I reached the building and heard the soft buzz of voices from inside. They were not English voices. Two large curtains hung where the front door of the tent building should have been, parted in the middle, and lashed to the sides of the doorway. Soft light spilled out over the grass from the open doorway. I stepped inside the tent and caught my breath. The room extended even farther back than it seemed to from outside. It was filled with double rows of waist-high cots. The front half of the room was still and empty, but the back half of the room emanated human warmth and quiet activity.

Breathe out, breathe in, I reminded myself again. And my breath became uncaught. An ambivalent mix of pain and peace was palpable in the air. Healing was waging battle with fear and trauma inside that room. I could feel it. At the moment, healing seemed to be winning. The entire room was lit by strange vivid blue braziers: basic squares of bright bluish-white flame that hung at eye level on almost every wall of the room. The braziers, each approximately one foot in diameter, were unlike anything I'd seen before. I stretched my fingers toward the nearest square. It emanated no heat, and yet the flame wavered predictably as my hand passed over it. The floor seemed to be hard-packed dirt, somehow sealed so that the surface was tidy and dust-free. It harbored shiny specks, mica-like, that reflected the light from the braziers and gave the surface of the floor the odd appearance of a star-spattered night sky.

Several women, all dressed in dark blue, moved in and out among the cots at the back half of the room. One wore a long hooded robe; a few wore something that resembled hospital surgical scrubs. They took no immediate notice of my tiptoeing presence, giving me time to observe from behind a curtain that hung between a set of empty cots. I recognized another presence in the room as well, the invisible presence of the One who had stirred my heart on the moor in Scotland. It was a powerful presence, like that of lion. Intriguing and inviting, it occupied the entire space at once. I tiptoed unnoticed along the wall and took what I hoped was a covert position behind a gathered curtain beside an empty cot. The women were busy attending their patients, bruised and battered young men in various states of disquiet, occupying the cots.

A military hospital? I wondered for a moment. But no. There was no sign of anything military, and many of the young men were still boys, too young to have been in battle.

Several of the women were gathered around one particular cot. Its occupant, a boy in his upper teens, was in obvious distress. His tall, lank body ran the entire length of the stretcher. His jet-black hair was shaggy and unkempt, and he sweated profusely. His skin was horribly marred by multiple bruises and lacerations. A pair of deep, barely clotting cuts ran just off of vertical through the eyebrow above his right eye. His hands—translucent white, crisscrossed with lacy blue veins—plucked at the covers. His legs thrashed weakly. His dark, haunted eyes were wild and glazed, not comprehending what they saw, if they saw anything at all. A tall woman with sharp features and dark curly hair stood beside the cot, stroking the boy's arm and studying him intently. A surge of compassion filled my chest, and I ordered into the base of my belly as firmly as I could, hoping it would stay. Having my circuits overloaded with emotion would get in the way of my ability to see and process what was happening.

My heart reached out to the boy on the bed in a new way. I felt a burning, urgent need to help, but my feet were frozen in place. The tall woman answered the question of whether I was an invisible observer or an active participant in the scene by turning to look directly at me, beckoning me to the bedside with a sharp nod of her head. I took a few hesitant steps, and she motioned for me to hurry. I approached, unsure of what to do until the moment I reached the bedside, then placed my hand on the boy's cheek.

"Listen," I said. The boy did not respond.

"Can you hear me?" Still no response.

"Bioraich du chluasan," I said again, this time in Gaelic.

I made the language switch unconsciously, intuitively… trying to find a word, rhythm, or cadence that would elicit a response. His eyes flickered open, and I kept speaking. Clouds cleared from the boy's eyes, and he grasped my hand. Connection.

"We want to help you. You are safe now," I added, again in Gaelic.

The boy's breathing slowed slightly. The woman behind me came forward and nodded her approval. I continued speaking in low soothing tones. The woman briskly assembled what appeared to be IV tubing, attaching it to a pink glass bottle. She hung it over the boy's head on a hook. Tearing open a small folder of IV needles, she deftly inserted an IV in the boy's left arm. Stark fear flashed in the boy's eyes. His grip on my hands tightened, making me wince. His steady gaze, almost unnerving, locked with mine. His mind took flight and lit briefly elsewhere, in an ugly place, then resettled as I continued speaking in the language that had caught his attention.

A second woman, Asian and small, appeared beside me. She handed me a cloth, and I carefully wiped the sweat from the boy's brow, leaving the cloth on his forehead. Medicine flowed through the tubing, filling up the painful empty places in the boy's body and mind. As peace began to attend him, my shoulders unknotted. My breathing eased with his, as if the effects of the medicine flowed through the boy's veins, out through his fingertips and into mine, coursing toward my own heart. I held fast to his hands as his eyes drifted closed in sleep. I fought the urge to close my eyes as well. The Asian woman pulled a blanket up over the boy's legs. She seemed satisfied that things were under control and moved on to other patients. The tall woman noted and adjusted the speed of the drops as they fell from the bottle into the IV line, then began to run her fingertips lightly over the boy's face, starting at his temple. She moved on to his neck, shoulders, down his arms, chest, legs, and then his feet, leaving a wake of unconscious gooseflesh.

I watched intently, wondering whether she was assessing or comforting. Since the boy was sleeping so soundly at that point, the former seemed most likely. The woman was fully focused, her fingers pausing purposefully at each bruise, swollen area, and torn patch of skin. When she paused, I couldn't be sure, but I thought I saw, or perhaps sensed, a faint blue light between her fingertips and the broken skin tissue.

When she had finished her exam, the woman stood up to her full height and stretched her back, wincing slightly. She trained her gaze on me, as if assessing me as well. She smiled and gestured for me to follow her. I did. As we walked, I could see that the woman was well over six feet in height but walked languidly, as if her stature was not a burden to her.

The woman lifted the curtain at the back of the tent, and I ducked under and stepped beyond into a separate chamber. The second room was a long rectangle, hewn out of the rock wall behind the building. On one wall, a small blue brazier was burning. I blinked, allowing my eyes to adjust to the relative darkness. There were several more cots, along with various cabinets and small tables and chests of drawers. It was clean but cluttered, much less tidy than the large room that held the patients. Only one cot was occupied. The woman sleeping there snored quietly, her long blond hair spilling across the pillow. She started awake and sat up as we entered.

No one had yet registered surprised at my sudden, unannounced presence. I was hungry, a little dizzy, and my knee was throbbing. The tall curly-haired woman gestured for me to sit down on one of the cots: simple slatted frames each topped with a thick pad. She and the sleepy blond woman with the pillow lines etched into her cheek pulled up stools and sat down directly across from me. Our knees were almost touching. They gazed intently at me. I stifled an embarrassing, ear-popping yawn and tried to return their gaze.

The blond woman pointed to herself. "Hedi," she said quietly.

The taller woman, who was perhaps twice her age, pointed to herself in similar fashion and said, "Iva."

I followed suit and stated my name. "Kiah."

Iva and Hedi nodded and smiled, apparently pleased with the way things were starting out. I wasn't sure how the conversation would continue, since we didn't seem to share a language. Iva stood and fetched me a glass of warm liquid that smelled of lilies from a small wooden stand. It was some sort of tea. I drained it quickly.

Hedi began to speak.

At first, she used the language I had heard Iva speak in the main room. I shook my head, indicating I didn't understand. She tried another language—Mandarin Chinese. My face must have brightened for a moment. The women looked hopeful. But I shook my head again. No. I recognized it but didn't speak it well enough to make it worth the effort.

She tried again. "Wielleicht Deutsch?"

German. I nodded my head excitedly.

"Ein bisschen," I said, indicating that it was worth a try.

"Perfekt." Iva sighed in relief. She smoothed her skirts across her knees and continued in German, slowly, to gauge my comprehension.

"You have been Called," she said pointedly. "Now you must choose for yourself. If yes, then you have much to learn, understand?" German did not seem to be her first language, and it certainly wasn't mine, but I nodded, *yes*, signaling that I was keeping up.

I listened closely to her words, trying to commit them memory.

Hedi continued, "Learn languages. You are skilled with languages, yes?"

"Ja," I answered.

"Of course you are." She shook her head, as if she were foolish for even asking.

"You must know several languages. You can choose them. You will know the right ones," she continued.

"Also, study much… history, medicines, and most of all, you must learn to listen, learn to trust…"

Trust whom? I wondered.

I blinked, trying to process what she was saying, but my brain felt sluggish. Iva was waiting for me to indicate that I understood her. I understood her words, if not their precise meaning. I tucked her words into a safe corner of my mind for later sorting, and nodded.

"Most of all, learn to *listen*, Kiah," Iva repeated, slowing her words to make sure I caught everyone. "You must learn to listen, especially to the things that are not being said. Learn to hear the heart."

"Learn to listen to God."

Her mention of Dhia unsettled me. Something in me, though intrigued by Dhia, still resisted Him.

I waited for Iva to continue, but she seemed to have no more information to share. She leaned back and nodded at me, satisfied.

"Hungrig?" she asked, and my stomach growled. I was ravenous. I nodded in response.

Iva said something to Hedi, who rose and retrieved a strange pinkish fruit and a few patties of sticky rice from the nearest cupboard. Iva cut the fruit into slices and passed out the rice patties. We all ate in comfortable silence. I shifted my position and flinched, supporting my throbbing knee. Hedi noted my discomfort and pulled a small vial of oil from the nearby cupboard. She pushed up my pant leg, gaining access to my knee. It was notably puffy and misshapen. Even in the dim light, I could see lavender blotches forming under the skin. Hedi applied a few drops of oil to my skin, just over the darkest areas. The mellow woody fragrance of the oil filled the room. She ran her fingers over my knee, as Iva had done with the boy. When she paused over the most tender areas, I felt a strange tingly heat, like a low-level electrical current, radiate from her fingers. In the room's low lighting, the faint blue light I had noted before was more visible. I didn't understand what she was doing or how she was doing it, but the throbbing in my knee lessened considerably. She applied more oil and repositioned my pant leg.

The curtain rustled, and two more women entered the dormitory room. Both were medium height and slender. One looked Polynesian, and the other European. They acknowledged me with nods and proceeded to the far end of the room, where they prepared to go to sleep—brushing their hair and changing out of their clothes. Iva brought me a set of scrubs and a robe as well. Apparently, I was expected to stay with them. Since I had fallen to this place directly from the sky and didn't have a clue how to get home, I didn't protest. I was very tired. I took the clothing from Iva. The scrubs were much like the ones I'd seen surgeons wear, but softer, like combed linen that didn't wrinkle. The robe was made from a similar fabric, but a little thicker and more complicated in design. There were multiple ties inside the garment to keep it from gapping.

Once I'd dressed, Iva beckoned for me to follow her to the door. I tested my knee; it felt much better than before. Whatever Hedi had done was working well. I was able to walk with almost no limp. I followed Iva out of the building to a bath and toilet facility housed in a smaller tent just outside. There seemed to be no running water, but there were pitchers of fresh water and pats of soap for washing up. My bladder was ecstatic. It had been signaling me for some time, and I had been trying to ignore it. The toilet was a squatty-style hole in the ground with a stone surround. I hadn't used one before, but our exchange student, Ling, had once described the process to me. I didn't imagine at that time that I'd ever need the information, but was now glad to have it. I managed, well enough, without besmirching my clothing, then washed my hands and face in a basin of fresh water drawn from a nearby tank. Iva did likewise. We carried our washbasins around the side of the building and emptied them into a depression in the dirt beyond the tents.

I stopped and looked at the sky. Stars blazed, gloriously close, everywhere I looked. The air was crystal clear. Three moons, two silver and one purple, hung full and round in the sky.

"Beautiful," Iva asserted. It was a statement of fact. Not a question.

"Ja," I answered. It was truly beautiful.

We returned to the healing room. Only a few blue square braziers remained lit. The patients were sleeping. One woman, propped up in an empty cot under a brazier, was reading from a large book. Another ground something spicy and fragrant in a mortar and pestle on a high counter that ran along the back wall of the tent.

The boy I had been speaking to earlier was resting peacefully.

"What is his name?" I asked Iva.

"I don't know," she replied.

I was becoming accustomed to her broken German. It took me only a moment to input her words; translate them to English; and, having extracted their meaning, put them to rest. Neither of us, however, knew enough German to have the conversation I truly wanted to have.

Where am I? Who are these boys? How were they injured and by whom? Who are these women? Why am I here? The questions jostled for position in my mind, begging to be answered, but I didn't ask them. There was so much to see, feel, and hear that I didn't want to add my own voice and consequently miss anything. I laid my hands on one of the boy's feet. It was warm, and I could feel his pulse there: slow, steady, and reassuring.

We passed into the women's sleeping room. I was truly exhausted. Iva pointed to an empty cot at the far left side of the room.

"Go ahead and sleep," she said. "There is more to do in the morning."

I removed my robe and sat down on the cot, swinging my feet up. My head swam. Hedi placed a blanket over me, bringing it up to my shoulders as if I were a small child. My mind dove almost immediately down into sleep.

A GOOD APPLE

I slept hard and dreamt of moons and oceans that slid, singing and laughing, into one other. In the morning, my mind climbed onto the bridge between waking and sleeping, where the subconscious packs up shop and preps for hibernation, and the conscious mind yawns and blinks, readying itself for its shift at the helm. My eyes were not yet open.

It must be Saturday. That means barn cleaning, then heading to work. Wait, did I drive home last night? What is that smell? Something is Weird with a capital W... I smelled rice cooking and heard the rustle of human movements. Alarm bells went off in my head. I sat straight up and blinked rapidly, trying to process my surroundings. Suspicion confirmed. I was, in fact, not at home in my own bed. Through morning cobwebs, I saw three women. One crawling into the cot next to mine, another on the floor shuffling through a sheaf of papers. A third, the small Asian woman I had seen the night before, was dishing up black rice and spooning a sticky greenish sauce over it. She brought the dish to me.

My mind scrambled to find a hold on reality. My stomach, on the other hand, selfish as ever, insisted on tasting the food being offered. I sat up at the side of the cot and took the bowl. It tasted better than it smelled, simultaneously flowery, smoky, and sweet. Without asking or indicating her intent, the Asian woman hastily shoved my pant leg up over my tender knee. Obviously news of my injury had spread, and she planned to address it. She applied more oil to my knee and massaged it with short, swift upward strokes, then handed me my robe. I pulled it on, tying it as quickly as I could. The women gazed directly into my eyes, assessing me boldly as the women had done the night before. Her eyes were deep and kind but serious. I found her a little intimidating. Once she was sure she had my full attention, she pointed and turned to a cabinet mounted on the rock wall. Opening it, she gestured for me to peer into it with her.

The cupboard was deep and contained various random hygiene items. There were pats of soap, clean rags, little tubes and tins of what looked like lotions and toothpaste. I leaned closer. The Asian woman picked up a tube and handed it to me, indicting through gestures that I could touch anything I wanted. The tube she handed me was indeed toothpaste printed with Chinese characters. I returned it and picked up another tin: lotion. Its label printed in a Scandinavian language. Another tube of toothpaste, its label written in a language I didn't recognize. It was as if someone had traveled around the world collecting hotel toiletries and deposited them all into this cupboard. I wasn't sure what to make of it. There were also brushes, combs, toothbrushes, hair accessories. They seemed to be from different countries, and even different eras. Every item I saw posed more questions than it answered.

Satisfied that I had seen enough, the woman closed the cupboard and led me to a nearby wooden sideboard, opening its doors, gesturing for me to look inside. Cooking pans, utensils, and bowls, chopsticks, forks, spoons, more rags. Another cupboard held clothing and unmatched towels.

I wasn't sure why she was giving me such an intimate tour of their space or what she was expecting from me. I was certainly curious. When we had gone through all the cupboards in the sleeping area, we proceeded into the main room, where the patients were housed. Pink morning light was beginning to filter through the windows. My tour guide led me through the cupboards in this room as well. I noted medical supplies, bottles of pills, dried roots, ointments, herbs, and oils. I wondered where it had all come from. I was becoming impatient and a little worried. I didn't understand what was happening. If this wasn't some sort of dream, and I had been trying to get home before curfew when this detour happened, then that meant I was *extremely* late.

Suddenly, Iva appeared beside me.

"Guten morgen," she said brightly.

I was glad for the instant camaraderie of spoken word, even in a foreign language.

"I see you met Fa."

"Ah, yes. I did. Well, I didn't know her name," I stammered.

"Fa has much to show you before you go home," Iva continued.

Home. I was instantly relieved. This was the first time anyone had mentioned that I would be leaving. It kept me from having to search for the words necessary to broach the subject.

"You do not need words to hear, or sight to see, Kiah," Iva said, placing her hand on my shoulder.

Great, more riddles, I thought. *I don't need words to hear or sight to see?*

I disagreed, feeling certain that much of what I had already seen would, in fact take words... many, *many* words to explain; but I kept my opinion to myself and nodded.

Fa waved me toward the door, eager to take me somewhere. She led me out into the silver field. The air was comfortably cool and smelled of water on grass. Half the sky was clear and pink, the other half heavily clouded. The sun crested the rock wall behind us in the clear side of the sky. Salmon-colored sunrise flames of light danced across the top of the cliff. A flock of small birds swooped low over our heads and headed soundlessly out over the ocean where a strong mist was blowing in a bank of clouds from over the ocean. A heavy mist was dropping, soaking our hair and clothes, but Fa seemed unconcerned. I followed her across the field. For a woman with such short legs, she moved quickly. I rushed to keep up. My feet, not as used to being bare as hers, were recoiling at the mere idea of a hidden stick or thorn in the grass.

We jogged along the base of the rock wall along the right side of the horseshoe-shaped valley. My legs felt incredibly light and strong, as if they could run forever, despite my sore knee. We slowed at a grove of trees. Fa brushed aside a thick hank of vines that hung down the sheer rock wall, revealing a door. She grabbed hold of the sturdy rope latch and tugged hard. I joined her efforts, and together, we convinced the door to give way. Inside the door was a pitch-black space.

Fa reached instinctively for a torch on a ledge just inside the door. The torch held an incomplete circuit made of a white gummy substance that resembled rolled clay. She pinched the ends of the circuit together, and it sparked a blue flame identical to those in the braziers back at the healing tent. The torch flared bright, but not hot. We stepped inside the door into a tunnel. The ceiling was low, the walls close; and the scent of mildew and ancient water was strong. Fa was off and down the tunnel, headed into what seemed to be the center of the mountain. I set off after her, not wanting to stray too far behind her light. We climbed and twisted through a tunnel in the mountainside, sometimes climbing stone steps so steep they required midclimb resting periods. The blue light from the torch glanced off the walls, and the water that trickled in rivulets down the walls and the steps disappeared into cracks and crevices.

The tunnel finally opened into a large dome cave, completely empty except for two arched wooden doors along the right side and another (hopefully the *last*) set of stairs that curved along the left wall to a small door in the ceiling. We climbed up to the small door and together, heaved it open. Blinding light poured in. Fa extinguished the torch by pulling the ends of the gummy fuel source apart, effectively breaking the circuit. As our eyes became accustomed to the light, I could see that we were atop the cliffs overlooking the valley. The bank of clouds was now below us, continuing to drop mist on the valley. The tent buildings squatted far below us, and beyond that, waves rolled in on the shore. We stood on a ledge, just a few hundred yards across, that rimmed the entire valley, extending at least a mile into out into the ocean. The land fell away just as sharply on the outside of the U-shaped land formation as it did on the inside.

I gazed out across the newly revealed landscape outside the horseshoe. To our left, the ocean pounded relentlessly. A wild, rugged series of valleys, hills, forests, and streams spread out before us. A narrow river wound its way from the hills to the ocean like a fat silver snake. Just beyond the river, at the far side of a thick forest line, I saw what looked like a solid bank of thick black clouds. It extended upward as far as I could see and all the way to the ground, where it roiled and moved, trailing off in wisps into the trees. I didn't understand what I was seeing, but my soul recoiled. I felt strangely nauseous and even panicky.

I had forgotten Fa was even beside me until I heard she spoke.

"You did not look away. So is *good*," she stated matter-of-factly.

Already feeling quite nervy, I startled noticeably at the sound of her voice.

"You scared me! I didn't think you knew English!"

Fa shrugged slightly. She offered no explanation. She settled cross-legged on the ground, a few feet back from the edge of the cliff, and pulled me to the ground beside her.

"What do you see?" Fa asked me, keeping her eyes focused on the black cloud bank.

I looked back at the strange wall of clouds and didn't answer right away.

"Darkness," I finally said. It was the only word that came into my mind.

"Yes," Fa agreed emphatically.

"And here?" she asked, pointing the opposite direction toward the rising sun.

"Light?" I suggested, feeling like Captain Obvious.

"Yes," Fa agreed again, seeming unduly pleased with my powers of observations.

"I will tell you something now, and you will listen, yes?" Fa asked.

"Yes, of course," I answered. She immediately won all my attention. Perhaps I was about to learn something about where I was and why I was there.

"Iva said that you must learn to learn, yes?" Fa continued.

"Yes. She said learn history, languages, medicine."

"And Bible," Fa stated firmly.

"The Bible? She said nothing about that. I know nothing about the Bible," I objected. "I don't even own one."

"You will soon. God provides." She sounded exceedingly sure of herself.

"And you must learn it." She was adamant, stabbing at the air with her finger to drive her point home.

I had very little experience with the Bible—almost none actually, save the Samuel story tucked under my childhood bed. My family, to my knowledge, didn't even own a copy, though we owned what seemed like every other book on the planet. Our house was filled to the rafters with books, although I had never understood why. My parents rarely read them. They collected books, with the best intentions of carving out a free wedge of time and digging in but rarely followed through.

My mother read only briefs and affidavits, as well as her own notes, scrawled out on long yellow legal paper by her own hand. She seemed more comfortable redigesting her own ideas than entertaining anyone else's. Only then could she be sure what was inked was truly trustworthy. My father read endless documents relating to work, but I rarely saw him touch a book. To my parents, books were art or perhaps symbols of their well-educated status. To me, books were air. I couldn't imagine life without them. I even loved the dry musty smell of their pages. I had read every book in my house and every other book I could get my hands on, for as long as I could remember. If we owned a Bible, I was sure I would have known.

Fa ignored my objections. "Of course you will do all these things I ask you. That's why I picked you," she asserted, seeming pleased. I couldn't tell if she was pleased with me, or with herself.

"You picked me?" I wondered if being in a constant state of shock and surprise for a long enough period of time could render a person immune to it. I had the feeling that was one question I might get an answer to sometime soon.

"Yes, and no," Fa said helpfully.

"Yes, you were chosen. And then… yes, I picked you out. Like an apple from the bin. You are strong in the right ways, and you will be stronger. You don't think the same as others. You don't feel the same things. You *are* not the same."

She leaned back, eying and evaluating me.

"You are a good choice, I think. A Good Apple—ha! It is a saying in your country, I think?" Fa was delighted with her own pun.

"Yes, it is a saying."

She had said I was different from others. I definitely felt different, but didn't everyone feel different in some way?

"I don't understand, Fa, what you mean by 'chosen.' I was *chosen*? For what?"

"Chosen, yes. He chooses us, He calls us, and then it is our turn to choose. Some things you need to know and I will tell you. Some things you will not understand yet. Be patient. You will see."

Fa grasped my hands in hers, turning them over a few times, gazing at them. She examined my arms as well. She seemed to be looking for something I couldn't see. She gathered both my large hands in her tiny left hand.

"Now, a blessing. Put your head down," she commanded. She placed her right hand over the bony prominence at the base of my neck. She began to speak softly, urgently, in Chinese. She seemed to be either reciting or praying. Or both. My neck and my hands became warm, and my heart fluttered. She spoke with such urgency, such fervency. Tears rolled down my cheeks. I didn't understand what was happening, but I felt surrounded by something safe, something sweet. My head bowed all the way to the ground. I felt and saw, through my eyelids, a bright light. I opened my eyes quickly, and the light was gone. I closed them, and the light returned. Fa finished speaking, and the light vanished. She removed her hands from me and smiled as I sat up. Her eyes were moist with tears as well.

To say I didn't understand what was happening is the worst kind of understatement. I was in the center of everything incomprehensible, on the brink of something vitally important. I felt vibrant, alive, and filled with warmth. I felt a sudden surge of affection for Fa, as if we had grown very close in our tiny bit of time together.

"Now it's time to go," Fa announced suddenly. She rose to her feet and helped me to mine. We brushed leaves and dirt off our robes and headed back toward the door to the tunnel. The sun was shining brightly the morning mist had disappeared from the horseshoe valley. Outside the U, the black bank of clouds still stood, foreboding, in the same spot beyond the river. It sent a shiver up my spine.

"It stays there, always, not moving. This is its boundary. You don't worry," Fa reassured me. "Just remember."

We returned to the door and retraced our steps back to the dome cave. I shivered. It was much colder inside the rock. Fa removed a large cloth bag from a hook below the stairs. In it were my clothes and shoes. Someone had obviously assembled it for me and placed it there while we were out on the ledge.

"Time to go. Get changed." Fa gestured to my clothing.

Apparently, I was expected to undress and redress there in the dank cave. I obliged, shivering. The cool damp air made me thankful for the warmth of the winter clothing. Fa placed borrowed clothing into the bag and slung it over her shoulder, and we wound our way through the bowels of the mountain to the door at its inner base. Fa led us out into the grove of trees where we blinked against the brightness. I recognized one of the trees in the grove as the same type of tree I'd entered the horseshoe valley through. We approached the tree, and this time, a door opened at its base. Fa motioned for me to enter it. I took a deep breath and stepped through the opening into cold, snowy darkness. I was suddenly back at the base of the cliff just outside my hometown, this time, without the falling sensation. I turned quickly and saw Fa's face at the edge of the door.

"Listen, learn to listen," I distinctly heard her say as she pulled the door shut behind her. The door and the tree suddenly ceased to exist. I ran my hand along the ground where the tree had been. The ground was cold, hard, and seamless. Snow was falling steadily, and the flakes were beginning to collect there, as they should.

Stunned and shaky, I headed down the path to the place where I had left my car. It was still there, waiting for me, hunkered down in the snow like a brave old turtle. My heart was thumping wildly, and my knee ached. *What time is it? Are my parents searching for me?* I fished for the car keys in my pocket and crawled into the car. It started right up.

I looked at the clock on the dash—10:38 p.m. Seriously? Was it possible I had been gone a mere twenty minutes?

"Pointless question," I muttered to myself. None of the things I had just experienced hung in the realm of possibility. I muscled the car (manual steering) onto the road and pointed it toward home.

THE BOX

I drove home as quickly as I safely could. I rounded the last corner; and my house popped, warm and welcoming, into view. It was a modified craftsman-style home with vaulted ceilings, lights under all the eaves and manicured bushes in all the right places. My father designed it himself. I parked the car and hurried to the front door, eager to find out if I was a full day past curfew or fifteen minutes early. I nipped up the steps, and inside. My fifty-seven-sixty pound mud-colored mutt met me at the door. He was the kind of dog that seemed to be wagged *by* his tail. His body swayed back and forth exuberantly, paws hovering just off the ground as he vocalized in that excited, whiny, demanding way that happy dogs have.

"Hello, Chump." I scratched his poll affectionately. I had christened him with another name when I had gotten him as a pup, but somehow "Chump" fit him better, so we started calling him that, and promptly forgot his original name.

I headed to the kitchen in search of my parents. There were dirty dishes in the sink and an open bag of chips on the counter, indicating the recent presence of my father. My mother openly abhorred his habit of leaving food out and open. He knew it, yet persisted.

The kitchen was empty. I poked my head into my dad's office and found Dad. He hadn't bothered to change out of his work clothes, and the concentration line etched between his brows up on to his forehead appeared especially deep tonight. He was a good-looking man, blessed at an early age with a full head of thick silver hair.

"Hey, Dad," I said. No response. He was deeply absorbed in a set of blueprints and notes in front of him on his desk.

"Dad," I tried again. Not even a muscle twitched.

"Marshall!" I said in my best secretary voice.

"What?" he responded immediately. It was par for the course. Most parents become immune their parental monikers eventually. Mine were no exception.

"I just wanted to say good night," I told him.

"Okay, did you have a good time?" he asked, nosing back into his work. I could have told him exactly what I had been doing for the last eighteen hours, and he would have answered with a noncommittal, "That's nice, dear." When he was working, he dove deep and heard little.

"Oh, yes, it was good. Love you," I answered, staying in the doorway to watch him for another moment. His tendency to drift so completely into his own thoughts afforded me the opportunity to observe him closely. Something about his work was definitely vexing him that evening.

My father, Marshall Dillon Adenauer, was born to full-blooded Saxony German parents. So decidedly German were his parents, in fact, that I called them Oma and Opa, rather than Grandma and Grandpa. Their ancestors immigrated to the US while the ink was still drying on the Constitution. Oma and Opa were bakers—the serious kind that made only complicated breads and rolls, nothing sugary sweet and pointless. My dad grew up begrudgingly toting flour sacks and driving the family delivery truck with his twin brother. Dad worked his way through school, earning an architectural engineering degree. He inherited the work ethic of his parents, but preferred working with his mind over working with his hands. He had a determined, restless spirit. The temporary nature of the building projects suited his innate urge to be in constant mental motion.

My stomach growled loudly. I slipped back into the kitchen, grabbed a few chips from the open bag, and shut it away in the cupboard. I made myself a cup of tea and inhaled the steam. It was hot and wet but tasted of paper and perfume, rather like a greeting card shop. It wasn't near as comforting or delicious as the tea I'd had the night before with Iva and Hedi. Their concoction had obviously been made with real live flowers, tasty ones at that. I poked at the brown shreds lumped together in the tea sachet in the bottom of my cup, feeling skeptical, particularly as to whether they had actually been herbal and alive at some prior time, as the tea box claimed.

Just thinking of the experiences of the last day (or was it the last forty minutes?) made my mind lurch and reel. I leaned against the counter for support, feeling physically dizzy for a moment. *What had happened? Was it possible I had hallucinated? Perhaps I was going crazy?* I grabbed a banana and cruised past the doorway to the living room, where the fire was dying down to ash in the fireplace. I stubbed my toe on a newly placed basket on my way into the room. It was one of my mother's decorative baskets, recently placed, and filled with dried flowers and yarn-wrapped balls of various sizes. I wasn't sure how my mother found time in her busy schedule to shop for house decorations. Perhaps she was a member of some sort of ornamental-basket-of-the-month club.

My mother was somewhat of a mystery to me. Born Lisette Anne Bonner, she was of French and Scottish descent but reveled in her French heritage and downplayed her Scottish side for reasons I didn't fully understand. She was a litigation attorney—the type of woman whose very presence made people sit up and pay attention. She was my opposite in so many ways. Short and powerful with platinum blond hair, she spoke and even moved with a purpose; no motions were wasted. Meanwhile, I was tall and awkward, and spent more time in my own head than I did in my own common reality. Only my nose and my eyes were similar to my mother's, as if our Creator had started with the identical nose-and-eye stencil when He made each of us, and extemporized wildly from there.

When I was younger, I thought my mother hung the moon. She told stories, sniffed candles, and delighted in blueberries with a vivid spark of true enjoyment that fascinated me. *How could anyone take such utter enjoyment from such simple things?* As I grew, her spark faded. I searched desperately for ways to ignite it. I'd carve hearts and flowers in her soap or leave notes on her pillow for her to discover. She would reciprocate by dropping stickers and gum into my lunch sack or scenting my room with rose and lavender water while I was at school. By the time I entered my teens, those sentimental customs were mere memories. I wondered if I'd altogether imagined her joy and our closeness. Mother was a conqueror in her work and in every other aspect of her life, but even conquerors can't win every time. She carried her losses like cancerous growths—life-sucking, and hidden away from everyone in some secret internal part of herself. Her words and her expression hardened. Her powerful exterior was simply an excellent front for a glass, not iron soul. Glass is fragile and beautiful, but it can shatter. One must exercise cautious around broken glass.

I peeked around the corner into my parents' bedroom, rubbing my cranky toe. My mother's form huddled, small and reassuring, under the quilt on her side of the bed. I felt the knot in my stomach untwist. Unless my parents were truly oblivious, having missed the fact that I'd been MIA for an entire day, then it really had been only an hour since I'd left the school.

Not possible! The logic center of my brain screamed at me.

I considered then quickly discarded the possibility of waking Mom or calling Millie to chat over my experiences. Neither of them would believe me. There was nowhere to go but to bed. I needed to think. Or sleep. Or both. I climbed the narrow wrought iron staircase in the living room that led to the tiny loft bedroom tucked up under the crossbeams near the vaulted ceiling. It had a skylight and one forward-facing window, from which I could see all the way to the base of the canyon. Originally, the room was designed as a reading loft, but I had begged, pleaded, and promised to forgo my inheritance if I could claim it as my own. They had consented. My intended bedroom on the far side of the house became the guest room, and I moved into the loft. They found a shorter-than-normal armoire and fitted it into the corner for my clothing. On the hard days when nothing else made sense in the world—when I was angry, hurt, or overwhelmed—I curled up there like a bird in a nest, watching the stars through the skylight or losing myself in books. That night, however, none of my usual rituals promised to restore my normal sense of bored balance. My heart was still squirming irregularly, and I wondered if it would ever recover.

I set my teacup on the bedside table and dropped onto my bed. I felt jet-lagged and still hungry although my hasty snack sat stone-like in the bottom of my stomach. My thoughts spun as if my brain were a clothes dryer set on high. The sights and sounds of the horse-shoe valley tumbling endlessly. I tried to catch a few of the words Iva and Fa had spoken to me as they rolled by. I needed a focal point. *History, medicine, blue lights, listen! Bare feet, strength, Bible, chosen, Called. Called* and *listen* stuck out to me the most. I couldn't think of what to do with the concept of being Called. Called to *what?*

Listen. Both women had told me. *Learn to listen.*

But how? What am I supposed to be listening to?

I made a conscious effort to clear my mind and listen. It wasn't easy. The snow clouds reflected the light of the moon, making midnight brighter than I felt it should be. I heard power in the furnace, water in the pipes, and the sound of my own breathing. I drifted off to sleep.

"Kiah!" Mom was yelling my name from downstairs.

"Front and center! The barn is calling your name. I can smell it from here!"

My head was pounding, and her voice was just shrill enough to intensify the throb. When my parents had purchased my first horse for me, they made it clear that they would buy the animal and I would be responsible for all the upkeep. I eagerly agreed. At ten years of age, with stars in my eyes, I was ready to move into the barn and become the permanent stable maid in order to get my hands on my own horse. In reality, the deal wasn't nearly as sweet as it originally sounded. Saturday mornings were generally reserved for barn cleaning.

That particular morning, I didn't relish the prospect of donning muck boots and hauling hay in the freezing cold. My horse, however, remained my closest confidant. I knew that once I got to the barn and saw his sweet, gentle face, I would cave and linger past feeding and cleaning time for as long as the cold weather would let me stay. I padded barefoot downstairs to the kitchen. Mom was wearing her weekend wear: chinos and a pastel seersucker blouse... tucked in, with a belt.

"You sick?" she asked. "You're always up before the sun. It's almost 11:00."

"No," I mumbled. "I just have a headache. I didn't sleep well. Do we have a Bible?" I asked quietly, trying to slip that last part in without her really noticing.

She stared at me as if I had asked her if she had a third nipple.

"Why do you ask?" she asked, cocking her head and staring at me.

"No reason. I just wondered," I said, trying to sound casual. I busied myself with the cereal box. The last thing I wanted was to have my sanity questioned by an attorney who also happened to be my mother.

Mom left the room, and I figured the conversation must be over. She and I didn't have a bad relationship. We just didn't seem to speak the same language anymore. I tried to be obedient, and she tried to be fair, but the older I got, the further apart we drifted. That morning's conversation was typical of our usual exchange: short and abrupt with no real information exchanged.

I sat down at the kitchen bar to eat my cereal. Outside the window my horse, Dresden, was stamping his hooves in the snow and bobbing his head. His communication skills were excellent; he was displeased with my tardiness. Dresden was a big, rangy caramel-colored warmblood. I watched him dash powerfully around the entire pasture, kicking up fresh powder, and return to the gate to stare balefully at the house. I was chasing the last soggy flake around the bottom of my cereal bowl with my spoon when my mother reentered the room. There were cobwebs hanging from her hair, and she carried a large box. When she cleared her throat and spoke, she avoided eye contact, and her voice had an edge to it that pricked up my ears.

"This is yours, Kiah. I was planning to give it to you when you moved away to college, but I suppose now is as good a time as any. It's nothing really... You may not want any of it. But you mentioned a Bible. I think there is a Bible in there."

The box was large. It obviously held more than a Bible.

"What is it? Where is it from?" I asked.

"It's just stuff... family trinkets from the Clacher side of the family," she answered. The Clachers were the Scottish relatives on her mother's side, the ones she preferred not to discuss. That fact alone boosted the conversation upward of 7 on the 1–10 "Sensitive-Subject-o-Meter." To say that my mother was reticent to discuss the Clachers was an understatement. When she had initially suggested I visit them in Scotland, Dad and I both had to lift our jaws off the ground. I still don't understand why she arranged the visit. I never really pressed the subject. Mom didn't respond well to pressure.

Listen, sounded a voice in my head. The word came to me so clearly that I almost jumped.

"Okay, Mom. You want to show it to me?" I asked.

Mom maintained her death grip on the box.

"No. You can just go through it yourself. I have no interest in it and wouldn't be able to tell you anything about it anyway." I sensed that she was being less than truthful with me.

We had a momentary tug-of-war with the box before she finally released it to me. It was cold and gritty under my fingers. I noted the old, uneven tape marks visible beside the current tape job. It had been opened and resealed at some point in the past.

"Has it been in the garage?" I asked.

"Yes," she answered brusquely, "for a very long time." She spun on her heel and fled the kitchen, leaving me alone with the heavy package. I wanted to rip it open immediately, but Dresden was still loudly demanding breakfast. I wrestled the box up the circular stair-way and deposited it on the floor inside my room, then dashed out-doors to feed the horse and clean the barn.

Dresden was in a rare wretched mood when I got there. He pinned his ears and wiggled his lips at me, snorting as I tossed his hay into the pasture rack where he preferred to eat.

"I'm so sorry, boy," I told him sincerely. Animals love their schedules. My tardiness had messed with his internal clock in an inexcusable way.

"You and me *both* this week, big guy," I muttered, still feeling jet-lagged.

I decided to make it up to him with an extra scoop of grain. Opening his stall door, I grimaced. Normally, he did his business outdoors, differentiating himself from most other horses. That day, however, he had relieved himself on the rubber matting inside his stall. Twice. The steam rising from the piles on the floor told me he had quite recently executed his revenge.

Touché, Dresden.

I cleaned up as quickly as possible and refilled the water trough. A frigid wind was clearing the snow clouds from the sky, and the temperature was dropping. I hurried back inside, dropping my barn clothes and boots at the garage door. Curiosity was eating a hole in my brain. I grabbed a pair of scissors and a damp rag and raced to my room. Chump was still stretched out on the floor in my room, snoozing. I scratched his ears affectionately and began to wipe down the mysterious box. The rag was soon black. I set it aside. The shipping label on the box was extremely faded, the date completely obscured. I could tell it was sent from Scotland, but the name of the sender was illegible. It was addressed to my mother. Ms. Lisette Bonner. I couldn't make out the full address.

I slit the tape with the scissors and opened the flaps. The top of the box was layered with wads of old newspaper. I smoothed a sheet and inspected the headings. It was a Scottish newspaper dated January 1968. It gave the details of a great storm that moved through central Scotland the preceding week. If the newspaper was current at the time the box was sent, it meant my mother was about my age when she received the parcel. Under the packing, I found several bundles of handwritten letters, tightly bound with assorted silk ribbons. The ribbons were brittle with age. The paper, fragile and yellow, was coming apart at the creases. I carefully cut one ribbon and unfolded one of the letters. It was written in Gaelic. The handwriting was lacy and loopy. It was addressed to Shae from someone named Ailsa. The script was faded, and my Gaelic was insufficient to comprehend the whole message at a glance. From what I could gather, Ailsa had taken a trip and found herbs and flowers that excited her. She was sharing her findings with Shae. She hoped that Shae would consider making the trip herself at some point. Simple directions to the site of her discovery were included.

I returned the letter to its bundle and rifled through the other stacks of envelopes. There must have been more than forty letters in all. I set all the bundles beside me on the floor and returned my attention to the box. The next item I lifted out was, itself, a simple wooden box: dark and unpainted, with a locking latch on the front lip. The latch was broken and the box opened easily.

Inside, on a simple silver chain, hung a delicate silver cross etched with Celtic knots with a large, flat opal at its center. The inscription in the back of the cross read simply, *Iona*. I replaced the necklace in the box and closed the lid, setting it aside as well.

Excitement fluttered in my belly. There was something special, something important about the box and its contents. I felt it in my bones. I couldn't believe my mother had such disregard for it. She wasn't a natural historian, and frankly, neither was I. History had always been my least favorite school subject, but the contents of the box were compelling. They weren't just general history; they were *our* history. *My* history. I couldn't imagine simply setting them aside for decades without a very good reason.

The next item I extracted was an old leather journal. I thumbed carefully through its pages. Some of the entries were date with the month and date, but none noted the year. I looked back at the letters. They were hand addressed and not sent by post. I opened the top envelope and carefully removed the letter.

"May 29. Dear, Shae," the heading read.

Again, no year was listed. I returned my attention to the journal. The flyleaf revealed that the journal belonged to Ailsa. I flipped through the little book. It was completely full of journal entries, lists, recipes, and sketches. The sketches seemed to be mostly of plants and landscapes. Whoever Ailsa was, she was a passable artist. There were two more journals belonging to Ailsa in the box. I made a mental note to get in touch with the Clachers and ask if they knew who Ailsa was. I was relatively sure my mother wouldn't be volunteering that information with me. There were two tightly wrapped items left in the bottom of the box.

I unwrapped the first item. It was indeed a Bible. The leather binding was deteriorating, and, like everything else in the box, it was written in Gaelic. The Bible was completely handwritten. *Who hand-copies a Bible?* I wondered. I also wondered whether it was the

Bible Fa had referenced when she told me I would soon receive one. Unfortunately, it didn't promise to improve my biblical knowledge. Not only was it not written in my first language, it was also so old and fragile that I was afraid to even leaf through it.

One item remained at the bottom of the box, a large, heavy securely wrapped package. I unwrapped it. It appeared to be the cover of a book, but was unlike any book I had ever seen. It was heavily encrusted with gold and gems. The gold etching was laid out in a regular pattern of loops, lines, and whorls. A large red stone nestled in its center, smaller jewels trailing away from to the cover's edges. There were random indentations in the gold, divots from which some of the gems had apparently come loose. It was exquisite. I sat back and stared at it, wondering what in the world it could be and, again, why my mother had relegated it to a box in the garage.

"Beautiful, isn't it?" My mother's begrudgingly appreciative voice emanated just behind me.

I jumped.

My mother had entered the room at some point, was standing behind me, silently watching.

"You scared me! How long have you been here?" I asked.

"Just long enough," she answered evenly. "I can't tell you what you will want to know about these things, Kiah. It might disappoint you, but I don't have answers for you. No one had answers for me when I got this box either." Her words were distinctly bitter.

"But I can tell you that you must not discuss these things with anyone, not even the Clachers. They can't answer your questions. I promise you that. You believe me when I say that, don't you, Kiah?" My mother was as serious and sincere as I had ever seen her.

"Yes, I believe you, Mom."

I had no reason not to believe her.

"I can trust you to keep these things to yourself?" She leaned close to me, reading my face like a book, the way she did her clients. It was unnerving and more than a little irritating.

I stared back at her and ignored her question. "Why didn't you open any of those letters? Did you look at the journals? I mean, did you even find out what any of them said?"

Mom held up her hand to stop me.

"No, Kiah. I didn't read them. I didn't choose them."

"What do you mean you 'didn't *choose* them'?"

She ignored my question completely, as I had hers. Fair enough.

"I didn't plan to pass them on to you either, but I realize now that I don't have the right to take that choice from you. These things, this history, it belonged to your family... part of your family anyway. You are a Clacher woman, technically. So the choice belongs to you as well." Her voice dropped off abruptly. She was close to angry tears, and I had no clue why. I watched her push her feelings back down under the surface, and the usual hard placidity returned to her face.

"That's all I'll say on the subject, Kiah. You are a smart girl, and a good girl." Her voice was steady and held a note of finality that told me the conversation was drawing to a permanent close.

Her head whipped up, and she squared her shoulders.

"Well, that's done." She sighed, relieved, as if she had finished one of those "birds and bees" conversations that parents dread.

I shared neither her sense of relief, nor her sense that anything was "done." Quite the opposite, I felt like something big was just beginning. I momentarily considered telling my mother about the Calling, the tents, women, and the injured boy in the valley; but just as quickly as the idea came to me, I shot it down. Something kept me from speaking. We stared at each other for a few seconds. I wondered if she was holding more back from me, or I from her in that moment. She broke the gaze first.

"Dinner," she declared and turned to go.

"Thank you, Mom, for the box... and for giving me the choice," I said to her back.

She stiffened and nodded almost imperceptibly.

The next day dawned early. Much too early. I had slept fitfully, dreaming fractured dreams of screaming, bleeding young men, women searching frantically through piles of ash, and falling from jagged high cliffs, never landing. I woke up trembling and cranky. As a young child, after a particularly rough nightmare, I would creep quietly down the hall into the bathroom with my blanket, past my parents' room, careful not to wake them. Turning the water on, to a slow audible trickle, I would lay on the floor with my ear pressed up against the furnace register and listen to the concurrent sounds of wind and water. It had been comforting. That morning, I wasn't sure what exactly to do to calm myself.

I fumbled for the clock. 5:24 a.m. My heart was pounding, adrenaline coursing through my limbs with no real purpose.

Am I going crazy? The unwelcome thought crept into my head.

"*No, you are just waking up,*" said a clear voice. It was a voice from inside me, but it was not my own. I slipped from my bed to the floor and, for the first time in my life, knelt to pray.

"A Dhia, what do you mean I am waking up? Are you with me now? Have you been with me all this time?" I whispered quietly, feeling awkward about speaking alone in a room to someone I wasn't completely sure existed. I wasn't sure what kind of answer to expect.

I never left you, came the answer, inaudible, but sure and strong. It resounded in my gut, reverberated up through my chest and caught in my throat. I blinked back tears, a little frightened. Somehow, acknowledging Dhia's presence in my own home, kneeling beside my own bed, made it real.

"Help me, help me understand," I pleaded in a whisper.

I felt an answering sense of peace touch down on my shoulders and sink slowly to my center.

SAM

I awoke early in the morning on April 25. It was my birthday. Again. It just *had* to happen every year. That year, there were supposed to be eighteen candles on my cake… and yes, there would be candles no matter what age I was. Mother insisted. I wasn't fond of birthdays. Birthdays meant too many people taking too much notice of me, asking inane questions such as, "So eighteen, eh? Do you feel older?" So far, being eighteen actually felt exactly like being seventeen. I lay on my back on my bed, idly working a feather through the fabric of my pillow and adding it to the pile of feathers I'd already extracted and dropped behind my bed. I was dreading going downstairs. A marked sense of restlessness woke me early most mornings since my visit to the valley. It was a sense that something required my immediate attention, but I had no idea what the something was. That day, it was stronger than usual.

Get up, now and go! the silent sense urged.

Okay, but where am I supposed to go? I wondered, unable to think of a single destination that would satisfy the urge. I found the lack of direction extremely irritating.

The sky through the skylight above me was a clear deep shade of blue. Only one star was visible. It's light still stronger than the early morning sunlight. I'd never seen anything like it. The phrase *bright and morning star* popped into my head, and I wondered where I had heard it before. The stars had stood out to me recently too, as if perhaps the answers to my questions lay out there somewhere, beyond my reach. I tried to order myself back to sleep. No luck.

My mother had taken note of my restlessness and my early rising. She mused that perhaps I was done growing. My friends noticed a difference too. I was more restless, angsty. I felt like I was treading water in the fog, waiting for it to lift so I could see where to go. Doubts still plagued me; and as time passed, it was easier and easier to believe that I had imagined the visions, voices, and strange trip through the disappearing tree. I wondered if there was there such a thing as transient teenage psychosis, and if so, would it pass? Thankfully, my friends and family chalked my moodiness up to PMS and took it in stride. Sometimes I wished I could do the same.

With little else to do at 5:00 a.m. (which I affectionately call the butt crack of dawn), I had taken to early morning horseback rides. Dresden responded with true internal conflict. As much as he loved exploring the countryside with me, it concerned him that these excursions were regularly occurring before breakfast. He paced the fence line as I approached the barn, head held high, ears pricked forward. The night had been unseasonably cool. Dresden's breath showed in visible puffs in the cool air. I brushed and saddled him quickly and gave him a treat, which he accepted, though I got the feeling it didn't change his feelings about the questionable nature of prebreakfast rides. I had been working on perfecting my ability to mount him from the ground. Owing to his size, it was no easy feat. That morning, I bounced up and onto his back with relative ease. Perhaps my restlessness translated into strength, determination, even grace? Well, grace was a bit much to hope for.

We left the pasture at a lope and headed up the steep canyons walls. It took twenty minutes or so to climb the hills to the ledge above the canyons. The shale and sagebrush of the hill gave way to long dry glass on the flat hilltop ledge. There was a stiff breeze, and the sunrise was golden. Dresden huffed and pranced, catching his breath after the climb. Normally, we headed east from the flats above my house, met the top of the canyon, and wound back down to my house along the roadside. That day, however, Dresden urged us westward toward the reservoir. It was the first morning of my adult life. I was in the mood for something new.

Dresden pulled hard, and I let him lead. Soon we were sliding downward through the deep steep shale and sand toward the bottom of a long hill. I hadn't been that way before; the descent was steep and quick. By the time we reached the bottom of the hill, I was as out of breath as the horse. Dresden still had a definite idea of where he wanted to go. It was unlike him. We wound around boulders and clumps of bitter brush, and stopped short at the base of a familiar sheer rock wall. Dresden had returned me to exact spot where the tree had appeared, where I had fallen through to the strange valley by the beach. My insides began to jump and tighten.

Dresden pawed the ground and snorted restlessly, not trying to move on, but not fully comfortable staying still either. He was responding to something I wasn't perceiving. I slipped off his back to the ground, muttering soothing things to him, and felt my way hesitantly along the wall toward the spot where I'd fallen through. The wall was solid. The path was grown over and barely visible. I wouldn't have recognized it as a road had I not known to look for it. The air was still and empty.

"A Dhia, I am waiting for you!" I cried out. "I have heard you, I have listened for you, and I am still confused! Why am I here? What do you want from me?"

There was no answer.

Dresden whickered softly.

A strange new thought came to me all at once, out of the stillness. *The teacher is always silent during a test.*

Teacher? I mused. *What teacher? And how could this be a test?*

Again there was no answer.

Great. Now I'm talking to myself. I leaned back against the rock and sighed. At least it was a beautiful morning. And I was old. Eighteen years old. *So old.*

I scratched absently at the mildly itchy, vibrating sensation at the base of my neck just above my shoulder blades. I'd felt a similar odd buzzing before and chalked it up to being the nervous system equivalent of a short circuit. Just then, however, it was especially strong and radiated along my shoulder blades accompanied by a strange, warm pressure. I began to wonder if I might be having a heart attack. Panic brought with it a flood of adrenaline. My palms grew clammy. Blood began to pound in my temples. There were no homes or roads in view, no one to call out to if I needed help. If I lost consciousness there, it would be a long time before I'd be found. The sensation grew stronger, until suddenly my entire body shot up into the air. Dresden's reins jerked out of my hand, and he sprang back in alarm and dashed down the path toward the turnout. I stopped moving rather suddenly about forty feet off the ground. I could see Dresden standing alone, legs spraddled and ready to bolt again, at the mouth of the turnout.

The pressure and vibration along my upper spine and shoulder blades continued. I felt ridiculously like a kitten being held by the scruff of the neck from its mother's mouth. I didn't have time to gather my thoughts before I began to move again. I spun sixty degrees and felt myself being pulled even higher, up and over the plateau and toward town. If I hadn't been having a heart attack before, I was sure I would have one now. I was instantly worried about leaving Dresden. I knew he preferred not to be alone but was in no position to do anything for him.

I'll take care of him, a quiet voice said.

I wasn't entirely sure if the voice was audible, but I recognized it absolutely as a voice of truth, and I trusted it. I shifted the horse's well-being out of mind and concentrated on what was happening to me. At least Dresden was on the ground. I was continuing to gain speed and altitude. It was frightening, exhilarating, awkward, and almost painful all at once. I tried to straighten my body and found I could manage a somewhat more agreeable boardlike position, arms at my sides, legs straight out behind me. It seemed to take some of the pressure off my shoulders and neck. Far below me lay the valley spotted with houses, square green yards, and aqua bean-shaped swimming pools. The people and cars looked like ants and beetles scurrying this way and that, completely unaware of my bizarre predicament.

I forced my muscles to relax and sensed a slight gain in personal control over my trajectory, though I still moved along under a power not my own. My neck continued to vibrate; and I felt, if not exactly heard, a consistent rustling behind me. I turned my head cautiously to see if anyone or anything was above and behind me and saw dizzyingly blue sky through what looked like a thin film of food wrap, the type my mother used to wrap my sandwich when we ran out of the little bags that zip shut. I turned my head back toward the ground quickly, feeling mildly nauseous. It seemed impossible that I was being hauled along by sheets of plastic food wrap, but the number of items on my personal List of Things I Deem Impossible was dwindling by the moment.

I quickly reached the center of town where I felt a strong pull toward Kahn Street, a quiet, older business strip in the heart of town. I leaned in that direction. The alley behind Kahn was devoid of people. It seemed a safe place to come down, if I could manage it. I veered right and dipped, uneasy at the prospect of landing. As the alley rose to greet me, I put my feet down, squealed a little, and shut my eyes. My feet skidded across the asphalt; and I slid to a hard, fast halt, landing on my back in the center of the alleyway.

Out of breath, I sat up cautiously and checked out the condition of my body. An abrasion on my left elbow was seeping blood slowly but steadily through my shirt. I put pressure on it with my right hand and climbed to my feet.

If I'm going to do this more than once, I need to work on my landings, I thought wryly.

My heart was thumping loudly, and I took a few deep breaths, trying to regain composure.

"A Dhia, I need your help. Which way now?" I said under my breath. The air was chilly, and my sweater was still attached to Dresden's saddle.

Left.

I headed left. The businesses along the alley were closed. A tavern, a martial arts studio, a secondhand shop… The buildings were old and dilapidated, the brick and concrete disintegrating and mixing in with the dust at the level of the street. It occurred to me that everyone and everything was on a constant journey toward dusthood. At the end of the block, incongruous with its surroundings, stood an old stone church. One of the first buildings built there was practically a Kenoa monument. Tall and proud, its steeple and bell had brought an air of civilization to the early, newly settled version of Kenoa many years before. I had driven or walked by the church a million times. I'd even heard the bell ring for special occasions but had never gone inside. I mounted the steps and reached for the latch on the red wooden door.

As a young child, I had attended a few weddings and funerals at churches—the ones Mom couldn't avoid taking us to. Her uneasiness around churches was contagious. I hadn't much liked any of the American churches I'd visited either. They were musty like libraries but without books and carried the added odors of stale weak coffee and urinal cakes. Only the stone churches in Scotland, stone sentries of bygone grandeur, had garnered my interest. Standing on the steps of Kenoa's stone church, I felt a stir similar to the one I'd felt at the ruins on the day of my puzzle vision. The door was unlocked. The smoky scent of lit incense greeted me as I entered—not the cheap perfumey kind, but the real thing, the kind that smelled like burning leaves and good pipe tobacco. I saw no one in the dim hallway nor in the offices to the right or left of the small foyer. I proceeded to the main chapel, where stained glass windows extended floor to vaulted ceiling on either side of the room. The double rows of wooden pews faced a raised dais with wooden kneeling benches at the front of the church. The worn carpeting matched the faded velvet padding on the oak pews.

A man rose from the front pew to greet me. He wore a plain charcoal-gray button-up shirt with a clerical collar. I was surprised to see someone so young looking so formal and religious. He appeared no more than thirty years old, with close cut dark hair and a kind square face. I had always imagined priests and reverends as older men with more wrinkles than hair follicles, but that man blew my theory. Apparently, clergymen had to stop over at youth on their way to fulfilling my stereotype.

"I'm Kiah. And I'm not sure why I'm here," I stammered to him as he approached. I stuck my hand out for him to shake.

"Good morning. Welcome. Call me Sam," the man replied, reaching out to take my outstretched hand in both of his. I wondered momentarily why *he* was there so early on Saturday morning. The feeling of his warm hands on mine unexpectedly broke something inside me, and I felt wobbly and teary. The aching that drove me and pushed from deep within sprang suddenly to the forefront and demanded to be taken seriously. My eyes were leaking, and the insides of my nose were swelling obnoxiously. I had carried something for a long, long time and couldn't carry it any longer. I needed to let it go.

"Have a seat," Sam said, directing me gently into a pew.

He probably saw plenty of emotionally unwound individuals in his line of work. It was comforting to think that I was somehow in his job description. Sam sat in the pew in front of me and waited patiently for me to speak, but I wasn't sure where to start.

"Are you sure I shouldn't call you Father? Or Reverend?" I asked him. For some reason, it seemed very important that I address him appropriately.

"It's just Sam," he replied, "I tried the proper titles, but they just don't fit me."

That made sense. Sam emanated warmth and light, not unreachable formality. He fell silent again, waiting for me to find my words.

I had no idea where to start. "I've never really been to church. Well, just when people usually go, when someone dies or gets married. My parents… they don't go to church. I don't think they ever have. I guess my grandparents did, but they are old now. Not so old they don't have teeth or anything… Well, I guess you don't care about their teeth. That's not the point…"

I could feel a flush climbing up my neck. My mother's voice sounded off in my head. *Kiah, really, you don't have to tell everything you know.* I took a deep breath, refocused, and started again.

"Anyway, I don't really know anything about church. I never had a Bible. We have every other book in our house, but no Bible, and honestly, I really don't know why I'm here."

I paused and tried to gain some measure of thought direction. I certainly couldn't tell him I had been deposited on his doorstep by an invisible hand. If I told him the full truth, including the visions, the flying, the visit to the valley through the tree… he would think I was entirely bonkers. I didn't feel right about lying to him, however. I wanted to tell him how I felt inside, about the voice that spoke to me, the feelings I had that didn't seem to originate with me. The weight I carried, my longing for more… *but how and where to start…?*

He waited patiently, hands folded on the back of the pew as if we had all the time in the world.

I finally settled on a safe place to begin.

"Last year, my parents sent me to Scotland to visit some relatives. Have you been there?"

He shook his head. No.

"I loved it there. I wanted to stay," I sniffled, and Sam produced a small package of clean tissues, seemingly out of nowhere. I was impressed. Perhaps they taught that skill in seminary school.

"There's a lot of old churches in Scotland. Some of them are kept up, and the rooms are mostly roped off. You can only go through with a tour. Look and no touch, you know."

Sam nodded, listening intently.

"I don't even think anyone really goes to those churches anymore, you know? Like for worship and services? And actually, that made me kind of sad. Someone built those buildings, right? With their hands, they laid the stones. They carved the wood. It wasn't easy. And I heard the guides talking about how many people died for their beliefs there. They died for their right to practice their beliefs. They worked and bled and died for something. Their beliefs must have been real to them… not just an idea, but something they felt like they were supposed to do. They must have had a reason, right? A really good reason." I fell silent, thinking, remembering. I suddenly wasn't sure where I had been heading with my story.

"What do you think was their reason?" Sam asked.

I thought about that for a minute.

"Love, I guess," I answered.

Love seemed like the only possible reason for that kind of work, that kind of sacrifice.

"One of the guides told a story about a builder at a cathedral. The guy was carving a bird into a rafter, but the rafter was going to be covered up by the roof, eventually. Someone asked him why he would spend so much time on something that no one would ever see. The builder said 'because God will see it.' That was enough for him. He didn't care if *people* ever saw his work. He just loved his God enough to make something just for Him. That's real love, right? The kind of love that people don't really talk about anymore? The kind of love people are willing to do anything for. Where did that kind of love go?"

Sam's expression remained passive.

"The churches are still there, but the people who loved that way are gone, I think. The churches are just shells now, like those decorative glass eggs that grandmothers have on their shelves… Beautiful on the outside, but nothing on the inside. Just empty and sad."

I sighed, blew my nose, and continued, "I was on a walk, though, by myself, in the valley of the Abhainn na Braghad—that's North Scotland… Anyway, I was walking and found the ruins of an old church. Just a few walls and parts of doorways and windows were left. The floor was all grass and flowers. I sat down on a stone in the middle of it, and I felt like I never wanted to leave. Have you ever been someplace like that? A place you just didn't want to leave?"

"A few times," Sam answered. "Not very often, though. Why didn't you want to leave?"

"I don't know how to explain it," I said, wanting to convey what I felt that day. "I guess… warm inside. Safe. And known. I felt like someone was with me. Someone I didn't know, but who knew me, if that makes any sense."

He nodded again.

"And I heard something, like a voice inside my head that wasn't my own." My cheeks flushed again, and I glanced at Sam, trying to gauge his reaction to my admission that I had heard voices in my head.

"What did it say?" he asked, unruffled.

"Just that I was not alone, that I had never been alone. And actually, when I heard it, I knew it was true. Even when I am by myself, even when I'm lonely, I never feel truly alone. I actually feel more alone in groups of people than I do by myself. So do you think that's God talking to me? Could He have been with me all along?" I asked. It was a question I had been afraid to ask anyone for so long.

"I think you know the answer to that," Sam replied. "Who do you think that voice belongs to?"

"Dhia," I confirmed. Emotion began to well back up inside me. It was such a relief to be talking through these things with an actual person.

"Eeya?" Sam asked, puzzled.

"Oh, that's Gaelic for God," I explained. "It's spelled D-h-i-a, but in Gaelic you drop the *D* sound when it's followed by an *h*. You don't really care about the spelling, though… Anyway, I once heard a woman singing a love song to Dhia, and the name just *sounded* right to me. So when I talk to Him, that's what I call Him. Dhia. I don't talk to Him often, really. I don't know really how. Honestly, I never really believed in Him before, but there's some things that happened recently that have made me think, made me believe. I've seen some things that I think… I think are from Him. Things I can't explain." My face and neck were red and radiating heat. I was talking too fast. I felt so vulnerable and foolish saying such things out loud.

"Sometimes I kind of feel crazy," I admitted.

"Well, I can reassure you on that point. I don't think you are crazy. Lots of people hear from God." Sam laughed a little.

"Do you? Hear from Him, that is? Does He talk to you?" I asked.

"Yes. Not aloud… not yet anyway, but I do hear from Him," Sam went on, "when I'm very still, very focused, very quiet. Often when I'm praying, I will get a feeling or a thought I know is not from me. That's how I know He is speaking to me."

"But if Dhia is real, then why doesn't He just speak straight out? So we can *all* hear Him? So we don't have to guess and wonder what He means?" I blurted.

"Well, there are a lot of things about Him I don't totally understand," Sam admitted, "and that's one of them. I think that He wants us to look and listen for Him. He wants us to really search. His heart is *for* us, and He wants us to seek His heart."

That made sense from what limited experience I had with Him. How often had I heard His voice say, *Listen?*

"But how can we know anything about Him if He isn't always clear, and some people don't hear it at all?" I asked.

"Well, the Bible, for starters," Sam answered, "it contains His voice."

I thought of Fa and Iva, of their adamance that I study the Bible.

"How do I know if the Bible is true? I mean, people say it's pretty accurate historically speaking… places and people and times… but what about the part we can't verify? The parts about miracles and stuff?" I queried.

"You mean the part about visions and people hearing God's voice in the wilderness? Let Him verify the truth of that Himself. It sounds like you already know His voice, Kiah, so read His words and ask *Him* your questions. He will teach you what is true."

It sounded so simple. Naturally, If Dhia was real, He could confirm His own words. I suddenly wanted very much to know what the Bible said. Perhaps it did contain answers to some of the thoughts and feelings and experiences I had been having, but the mere prospect of finding answers didn't dispel the weight I carried.

"What else is bothering you?" Sam asked.

"I feel so heavy. Like I'm carrying something heavy with me. Something I can't see. Something I can't get rid of." A sense of desperation physically squeezed my heart, and I gasped. I shut my eyes; and an image, a vision, enveloped me. I was moving through the halls at my school, covered in what looked like gray paint or mud. A few of my schoolmates, also encrusted in drying gray mud walked the halls with me. It cracked and wrinkled at our joints, flakes drifting to the floor. The flakes were beginning to build up along the hallways like sawdust. The other students trudged on, unaware of the gathering mud.

"Kiah, are you okay?" came Sam's concerned voice.

"Yes," I answered quietly, "I'm just seeing something. Sometimes I see something like a movie in my head."

My own voice sounded far away and hollow in my ears. If I'd opened my eyes and focused on Sam, perhaps the vision would have disappeared; but I kept my eyes tight shut, not wanting to miss whatever was before me.

"Is Dhia showing me something?" I asked Sam.

"It could be." Sam sounded uncertain yet willing to entertain the possibility. "Can you tell me what you see?"

I described the halls, the students, and the peeling mud.

"What does it mean?" I asked.

Sam paused before he answered, "I don't know for sure, Kiah, but could the mud be sin?"

"I don't know much about sin," I said. Desperation was camped out just behind my breastbone, pushing its way up into my throat. "Explain it to me," I demanded.

"Okay, well, Dhia is one hundred percent good, right? He defines righteousness. He is holy." I continued to watch the desperate gray people wander through my mind, oblivious to the dangerous gray accumulation. I kept my ear trained to the far-off sound of Sam's voice.

Dhia is good, all good. Yes, I could agree with that.

"And?" I asked, realizing I sounded impatient but wanting to know more.

"Do you know the Bible story about Adam and Eve?" Sam asked.

I had heard of it. "Tell me," I said.

"God created the Earth and everything in it. Then He created man and woman, Adam and Eve, to be his companions. He wanted relationship with them... companionship, friendship. The Bible says He walked with Adam and Eve in the garden of Eden, the perfect place He created for them to live in."

Again, this rang as deeply true. I knew one thing for sure: Dhia wanted me. It wasn't just that He wanted something for me or something from me... He actually wanted *me*. The knowledge of His wanting had been planted that day on the moor when I'd heard the woman sing His name. It was incomprehensible and undeniable.

"He loved us enough to give us choice, Kiah. We can choose to walk with Him, or we can walk alone. If He forced us to follow Him... well, where would the love be in that? God asked Adam and

Eve to obey one rule: they were not to eat from a certain tree in the garden. It was the way He presented them with the choice between good and evil." Sam's voice continued. He knew the story well. "We have an enemy, though, Kiah. He is the sworn enemy of God."

At that, a chill shot through me.

In my mind's eye, a small hole opened up in the school wall beside me. Peering through it, I saw a single tree in the distance. I could hear and smell the small, steady, tearing sound of a distant sulfurous rotten wind heading my direction. "That enemy, also created by God and given the same choice, wanted to *be* God. He still covets God's throne."

"Satan, then?" I asked.

"Yes."

"So what's with the tree?"

"You see a tree?"

"Yes, one tree."

The tree in my vision was small and far away, with vivid green leaves and plump purple fruit. I squinted, quickly realizing that squinting doesn't improve vision within a vision. I could just make out a single beautiful, dragon-like creature talking to a woman under the tree. Horror, revulsion, and fear welled up in my chest as the woman bit into the fruit. I clutched the wooden pew.

"Satan told Eve a lie mixed with just enough truth to make it sound acceptable," Sam said. "He told her that she would be like God, knowing good and evil, if she bit the forbidden fruit. Eve already wanted to be more like God, so she bit. She disobeyed. She sinned. She chose the *only* sin revealed to her as an option. Then Adam came along, and she shared the fruit with Him. He chose to sin as well."

As Sam spoke, the woman in my vision was joined by a man who also bit the fruit. Juice, like blood, dripped from their chins. A mud hole appeared under their feet, a dark smudge in the lush green grass. Tendrils of mud snaked up their arms and legs, but they didn't seem to notice the change. They were too busy searching frantically for a place to hide. They seemed heartsick and terrified. I felt faint and sick. The hole in the school wall closed. I couldn't see the tree or the couple anymore, but my desperation and revulsion remained, now accompanied by a deep sadness.

Sam's voice, gentle and firm, continued. "God defines righteous, Kiah. He's one hundred percent good, right? There's no evil in Him. Adam and Eve chose to turn against Him, against His goodness, against His provision for them. They were cast out of the garden because of the choice they made. The relationship with Him was broken."

Suddenly, I understood. I understood the horror and sadness of the choice they made. They chose to walk away from Dhia—to break relationship with Him. They chose sin, and I keenly felt their loss as my own. They had disobeyed the one thing Dhia had asked of them, and I... *I* had followed suit. I also had chosen to disobey Dhia in my heart. I was not raised with knowledge of the Bible or been taught about Him, but in my heart I knew what was right and had gone against that many times. I suddenly had a name for the weight that was on me, the gray sludge that sluiced its way up my body and clogged my path was not just a figment of the vision. It was the visual manifestation of the sin I carried, and it left a sickening residue, an ugly stain. I also knew I wanted to be rid of it.

"It's not just their sin. It's mine," I said aloud, acknowledging my sin as much to Dhia as to Sam.

"Yes," Sam agreed, "it's all of ours."

"Am I supposed to just learn to *live* with this knowledge?" I asked him, my teeth on edge. I couldn't imagine bearing the weight any longer.

"No. God made a way for us to be free of sin. He sent hope. He sent an answer. He sent a path to freedom from sin." Sam's voice was kind and resolute.

"Jesus," I blurted as the name sprang to mind. I had heard the name many times, mostly as an utterance of frustration and hopelessness by the kids at school. I knew from the history books that Jesus had definitely lived on the Earth and caused quite a disruption, but I had never considered the claims that He was the son of Dhia. I knew Christians relied on Jesus as their Savior. Until that moment, I hadn't understood how that all worked, nor had I desired to, but my desires were changing.

The moment I uttered the name "Jesus" aloud, hope shot through me; a shaft of light directed to the darkest place in my soul. My hand rose impulsively to my cover my heart.

"Yes," Sam confirmed, "God sent His son, Jesus, to Earth as a man. God's own people killed God's own perfect Son, and Jesus let that happen because He loved you enough to die in your place."

Truth. The word rang out in my heart. In that moment, I knew Sam was speaking absolute truth.

Meanwhile, the vision continued. The mud thickened along the school hallways, making it difficult to move. I dragged myself through the knee-deep mire, barking my shins painfully on a set of buried steps. I sank to a sitting position on the steps, rubbing my aching legs. No one else was in sight. From where I sat, I could just see some sort of liquid was beginning to seep through the cracks in the double doors at the end of the hall just above me. I squinted, trying to identify it. Water? More mud?

Again, squinting in a vision didn't increase my visual acuity one bit. The trickle grew steadily larger, and I was able to identify its color. It was red.

Blood red.

Blood.

"What's with the blood, Sam?" I asked, a little alarmed.

"You see blood?" Sam asked.

"Yes."

"Well, God is a righteous judge, a good judge, and the penalty for sin is death. Long ago, He demanded animal sacrifices from His people, to remind them of their need for Him and of the death they had chosen when they chose to sin. He didn't abandon them to their consequences. Instead, He paved the way back to Himself. The people sacrificed animals to show they understood the consequence of their sin and their need for forgiveness, but the animal sacrifices were only a symbol that pointed to the perfect sacrifice that was yet to come. Jesus was always a part of God's plan, Kiah. God's own people killed God's own son, Jesus. He was the perfect sacrifice. It was *His* blood that finally freed God's people from the consequences of their sin."

"But I'm not free, Sam. How, how do I get free?" I cried out. My heart was still heavy, and I longed to be free of the mud. The sulfurous rotten odor of it was growing stronger.

"Do you believe that God sent His son to die for your sins, on the cross, the only perfect sacrifice that could and did set you free from the righteous consequence of your sin?"

Did I? I asked myself.

Yes. I did. And I knew what I needed to do, what my heart wanted to say.

"A Dhia, I'm sorry for ignoring your voice for so long. You have always been with me. You have called my name. You have spoken to me. You have shown me things that I haven't understood. You have given me so much. I have heard you, but I ignored you! I have been embarrassed that I even heard from you. I know, now, that you sent your Son to die for me, for all of us. Please forgive me? I choose to accept your forgiveness. I want you. I need you. A Dhia, be with me. I need more of you!"

Tears ran down my face and dripped from my chin, but I didn't bother to wipe them away. I kept my eyes closed and waited to see what Dhia would do next. I didn't have to wait long.

The trickle of blood coming from the doorway at the end of the hall swelled to a rush, as if an enormous vein on the other side of the doors had broken and blood was pouring from it into the building. I watched the blood swirl in whorls and eddies toward me. The patches of mud sizzled, hissed, and dissolved the moment the blood reached them. The red flood quickly reached my feet. My skin throbbed and stung as the level climbed quickly up my legs and then knees, thighs, waist, belly, chest until it was at my neck.

What now? I wondered, *Swim?*

I felt no answer to my question, but knew I was not alone. I felt Dhia's presence, familiar, and yet new, distinct somehow... What was here with me was a distinctly different part of Him, a part I had not experienced before. Jesus was there, giving me a very important gift. I stood perfectly still and waited. I felt the hot blood enter my ears; my skin continued to sting as the mud pried loose and whirled away. The level rose above my head, and I was surprised to find I could actually see through it, though the light was dim. Looking left and right, I saw the contours of the hall. My feet were free of their clay confines, but I didn't feel the need to move, not just yet anyway. A ruddy light shone down from above me. I looked up and saw a single bright star. I inhaled, unable to hold my breath any longer, and my mouth filled with the coppery tang of blood. I felt strangely eager to let it fill every part of me. I wanted no trace left in me of the sour rotting mud that was sin.

The blood seared my lungs as it entered, but it was no more painful than it had been on my skin. I felt vibrantly alive.

"What is the star, Sam?" I asked. It seemed strange to experience the blood so strongly and yet still be able to talk to Sam so easily.

"A star? Well," Sam hesitated, thinking, "the Bible refers to Jesus as the 'bright and morning star.' That might be it." He wasn't sure.

"That's it," I confirmed. It was the same phrase I'd woken up to that morning.

As quickly as the torrent came, it subsided. First the level dipped below my chin, my shoulders, my belly, my waist, rapidly draining to a trickle before vanishing altogether. The floors and walls returned to their original off-beige hue. I was alone in the hall, and no trace of the mud remained. My skin was pink and raw. I touched a particularly reddish spot, where the mud hadn't given way as easily as it had in others, and winced.

"Sam?" I called, "Are you still there?"

"I'm here." His voice sounded a little closer again; and I felt, though I could not see, his fingers grasp my left hand. At his touch, the school halls faded and were replaced by the stained glass windows and stone walls of the church.

Sam's kind, concerned face swam into focus a foot or so in front of mine. He looked rattled.

"Are you all right?" he asked.

"Yes," I said. "Well, no. I mean, I think I might be. Just give me a minute." I gasped and tried to catch my breath. "What was that? What did I just do?"

"I'm pretty sure you just placed your faith Jesus Christ as your personal Savior." Sam smiled. "Though I've never seen anyone do it in quite that manner. God is new all the time. He is new every morning."

"It's not always like that, for everyone?" I asked him.

"Well, I don't know what you just experienced, but I can pretty safely say, no... it isn't like that for everyone. He meets us all differently. He meets us all where we are. You were seeing something I didn't see. Do you want to tell me what you saw?"

I hesitated, not sure how to respond. I wasn't in the habit of discussing my visions with anyone. Of course, I didn't usually experience them in the presence of others either.

"Have you see visions before?" I answered Sam's question with a question of my own.

"No, no I haven't," he admitted. "But I know some people do. I believe God communicates with a few people in that special way."

"So I am odd," I stated flatly.

Sam laughed a little. "Not odd, exactly, but you may have a gift. If you see and hear God in a way that most people don't, then maybe that's a part of his special purpose for you. He has a different plan for everyone. The Bible says that many are invited, but few are chosen. I think that may apply to you."

I thought about the word for a moment... Not long ago, Fa had told me I was chosen, and my mother had told me I had the right to choose.

It was all still as clear as mud. (Pun acknowledged but not intended.) A chill ran up my spine. Even the memory of the mud was unpleasant.

Free of the vision, my skin and lungs no longer stung. My mind was still swimming in the deep end, but my heart soared, and my fingers tingled. I momentarily feared I might rise up out of my seat. The freedom gained by the loss of the heavy clay that had clung invisibly to every inch of my skin was tangible and electrifying. I purposefully slowed my breathing.

"How are you feeling?" Sam asked.

"Joy, I feel joy, Sam. I don't feel joy often and certainly never like this. I feel so light! I feel so light... Is that normal?" I wasn't sure I was making sense, but honestly, at that moment, I didn't much care.

"You are making sense." Sam grinned. "Welcome to the family."

He extended his arms toward me, and I accepted his hug, realizing just how shaky I really was.

Temporal reality tapped me on the shoulder, and I realized it was probably time to head home.

"Oh, I'm sorry, it must be getting late. My parents don't know where I am. I really have to go," I announced reluctantly. There was so much more I wanted to ask Sam, but I urgently felt the need to go. "Can I come back sometime and talk to you more? Ask more questions?"

"Yes, of course. I would love for you to come back. Any time," Sam said. I sensed that he full meant what he said, which was refreshing.

"Do you have a Bible?" he asked.

I thought of the handwritten Gaelic Bible... That was too long a story to launch into.

"Yes and no," I answered, "unhelpfully."

"Okay." Sam wasn't sure how to respond. "Well, you are a puzzle. How about I give you a Bible anyway? And if you don't need it, you give it to a friend."

Another Bible. Fa was doubly right.

Sam rose and offered me a hand, for which I was grateful. My legs were wobbling like those of a newborn colt.

"You sure you're feeling okay?" Sam asked, waiting for me to stabilize.

"Yes, just a little discombobulated," I responded, feeling more sturdy once I was on my feet.

"Discombobulated?"

"Yeah, well... me and my big words. I read a lot...," I explained.

"I like big words," he reassured me. "I may have to find a reason to use that one this week."

I followed Sam unsteadily to his office, where he pulled a Bible off a stack of identical thin green paper volumes on the bookshelf, then hesitated, changed his mind, and replaced it. Instead, he pulled opened the bottom drawer of his desk, withdrawing a thick leather-bound volume with gold-leafed pages.

"This is a study Bible," Sam said. "I have a feeling you might want to read some of the notes that scholars have added on the bottom of the pages. Just know that those notes are nothing more than printed opinions. The important part is to get to know the inspired words of God Himself."

"This looks expensive," I protested. "I can get it back to you soon."

"No. I want you to have it." Sam's firm tone left no room for discussion. "I wasn't sure why I bought it when I did, a few months back. I already have another one like it, but God asked me to get it. Now I'm pretty sure He meant it for you."

"Thank you," I said quietly. My eyes felt moist. The kindness of a stranger, rare as it was, often stirred my emotion. That day it almost tipped me into tears. I cringed at the prospect of turning into a crier. I'd always prided myself on my emotional control and logical analysis of facts and situations. I felt the security of having it all together slipping away from me like sand through my fingers—along with almost every other notion or illusion I had of who I was. I glanced at the clock on the wall—7:16. I probably still had time to get home before they knew I was gone.

"You have a ride home?" Sam asked.

"Ah, yes… At least I think so," I answered, suddenly not sure whether I did or not. "I'll be back if I don't."

"Okay…," Sam said, still not sure what to make of me. That made two of us.

"Thank you," I said, and I meant it. "I'll think I'll remember this day forever."

"Happy birthday," responded Sam.

"How did you know it was my birthday?"

"I meant your spiritual birthday. The day you were adopted into God's family. You mean it's your actual birthday too?" Sam asked.

"Yes. I guess it's both," I answered. "I really have to go. It was nice meeting you, Sam."

"You too, Kiah. Come again, anytime."

I left the church feeling as if I had gained two friends.

BIRTHDAY GREETINGS

I retraced my steps back to the alley. The sun was waxing, but the dirty little strip of street was still empty.

Now what? I wondered.

As I reached the end of the alley, I felt, rather than heard, Dhia prompt me... *Are you planning on asking Me?*

Asking for what? I wondered. Then it dawned on me. Dhia had gotten me here, albeit in a rather unorthodox, terrifying way. He might want me to ask Him for a ride home.

"Dhia, please show me the way home. Would you like me to call for a ride? Or return the way I came?" I asked in a whisper, still feeling strange about speaking out loud to someone I couldn't see. Honestly, I would have preferred a nice, relaxing automobile ride.

Immediately, my neck vibrated, and my palms broke out in a sweat.

Crap! Definitely not a car ride!

The vibration spread again along my shoulder blades, and I was jerked into the air, this time even higher than before. The air at the higher altitude was chilly. I shifted back into plank position and concentrated on taking deep breaths. Nausea gripped me again. I would have been much happier flying closer to the ground, but perhaps too many people were out and about. A few small clouds scudded by beneath me as I moved swiftly through the air.

The buildings below quickly gave way to row houses, then larger homes, then acreage with only the occasional house dotting the landscape, until the steep canyons walls loomed before me. I cleared them by a good forty feet or so, and breathed a sigh of relief at being somewhat closer to solid ground.

"Slower?" I asked aloud as I reached the familiar plateau above my house.

The word *feet* sprang to mind, so I experimented with the position of my feet. First, I pointed my toes and felt myself speed up. That was not what I was hoping for! I immediately drew my toes up toward my body and extended my heels and felt myself slow drastically. Almost giddy at having found the brakes, I slowed even more and banked over the edge of the plateau into the canyon above my house. I was relieved to see Dresden in his pasture, contentedly munching hay. The prospect of landing still made my palms sweat, though I was no longer over concrete and traveling more slowly. I tucked my feet under me, reversed my body position, and landed gently on my butt in a pile of dirt and rocks a few feet up the hill behind my house. I took a moment to collect my nerves, then slid the rest of the way down the embankment toward the house.

Dusting off as best I could, I entered the back door of the house and called out, "Mom? Dad?" as I shed my boots and shut the door.

"You have a good ride?" Mom asked as I entered the kitchen.

That answered one question… Obviously, she and Dad had not returned Dresden to his confines. So who had?

"Yes, really good ride," I answered. "Whatcha making?"

Mom didn't answer. She was busily whipping a sticky sweet-smelling whitish substance in a bowl. She always made homemade cakes for my birthday, insisting that every good mother did. She must have read that in a parenting guide somewhere. Mom's cakes didn't look quite like those on the glossy pages of her cookbooks, perhaps owing to the fact that for Mom cake making was merely a semi-annual endeavor. Secretly, I didn't even like cake, but I always ate a slice. I did appreciate the effort.

"Happy birthday, Tiddlywink." Dad called from the direction of the living room. He didn't call me Tiddlywink often anymore, only dusting off the term for special occasions such as birthdays and… well, pretty much just birthdays.

"Thanks, Dad." I gave him a hug.

"What kind are you making?" I asked again, peering over her shoulder into the bowl.

"It's supposed to be double vanilla." Mom sighed. "But, honestly, I think it's just sugar flavored."

"My favorite," I declared.

Obviously, Mom was in a rare maternal mood. Dad was in the kitchen calling me pet names, and Mom was covered with baking flour. I felt inordinately grateful for the normal moment, especially considering the happenings of the morning. I blinked back tears—*again?*

"What's wrong?" Dad asked, concerned.

Mom swung around to face me, registering worry as well.

"Ah, nothing. Really, I'm okay. I think I'm just getting old."

They both relaxed visibly. They loved a simple answer to what could be a potentially emotionally sticky situation.

"You are allowed sentiment in your old age," Dad joked, relieved that the moment was passing.

I excused myself, showered, then climbed the stairs to my room and collapsed onto the bed. I didn't know how much more change my heart could take. I felt confused but hopeful—on edge yet strangely peaceful. The day before I'd seriously questioned my own sanity. A day later, I knew without question that I was not crazy and Dhia was real, but the reality of Him was more frightening than I couldn't have imagined. Everything seemed new.

There's nothing new here, Kiah. Nothing surprises me. Dhia's words rose, resonant and comforting, inside me. Maybe I didn't need to understand everything that was happening. Maybe I just needed to learn to trust the One who *did* understand what I did not. I just honestly didn't know how. I was used to trusting only myself and my own knowledge.

I opened the trunk at the end of the bed and examined the family items Mom had given me. Their meaning was a mystery, but when I touched them, I felt their promise. They were solid reminders of my history and my future, simultaneously. I laid the letters and journals aside. Opening the small wooden box, I ran my fingers over the silver cross, wondering again what Iona referred to. I made a mental note to research it as soon as possible. I picked up the Gaelic Bible and stared at it, pondering the morning's events. *I flew?* The Bible felt heavy and important in my hands. I opened a page, and the name *Dhia* jumped off the page to greet me. This book was about someone I now *knew*. I wished there was a way to know all His words and messages at once. I hoped that the pages might hold some answers to my questions. It was a very old book, however.

How are old stories and ancient references going to help me figure out my life today? I wondered.

I unwrapped the bejeweled book cover. I usually left that piece alone. It seemed more fragile and valuable than anything else in the box. I felt the need, though, to lay eyes and fingers on it. It seemed even more beautiful than it had the last time I'd seen it. I gingerly turned it over and examined the inside cover. It was lined with thick stained fabric that was torn in places and fraying badly at the edges. I noticed, for the first time, a small but unmistakable smudge of blood that could have been a partial finger or thumb print near the cover's bottom edge.

Theme of the day—blood.

I sighed impatiently and rubbed my hand over the details on the face of the cover, willing a new clue to reveal itself.

Now, answers now would be nice! I thought.

"Can't you tell me, Dhia, what this is—or what it's for? Or what I should do with it, or any of these things… Why flying? Why falling? Why Chosen? Why me? What does this all mean?" I whispered aloud to the silence. The silence remained silent.

My mood was deteriorating. I suddenly wanted nothing more than to lock the door and curl up with a book and pretend I lived on a deserted island. Friends and family would be arriving soon, however, and I would be expected to be fully engaged in conversation. I needed to, as my mother often told me, "*get my head out of the clouds and on straight.*" I replaced all the items in the trunk and fastened the new lock I had just purchased to its clasp. I didn't think anyone would disturb them, but I wanted to be sure.

Millie arrived. She was such a fixture at our house that she never bothered to knock. She appeared unannounced at my door and flounced onto the bed beside me.

"Okay, tell," she demanded.

"Tell?"

"Yeah, tell! What does eighteen feel like? I mean... you are an adult! Come on! Bye-bye, childhood! What's it like?"

"Exactly like being seventeen. There's no difference whatsoever," I responded.

"Untrue. That just can't be!" Millie insisted. "Because seventeen sucks, and you, as my friend, are fully responsible for offering me hope!"

"Okay, I hope eighteen is better for you than it is for me."

Millie punched me in the arm.

"Ow, careful!" I whined, rubbing my arm, which bore a few more telltale signs of my clamorous morning than I had initially realized.

Millie grabbed my elbow and inspected my bandage, abrasion, and fresh bruises.

"Ow, not helpful!" I said again. Millie was a miniature bull in the china closet.

"What did you do... fall off that enormous beast again?"

"No! I did not. Dresden is not a beast. He's very sweet, and I don't fall off him. I just took a header while I was on a walk this morning. It's no big deal." I retracted my arm.

"You fell down while you were *walking*? What are you, seventy?" Millie remained skeptical. She was scared to death of horses and fully convinced that Dresden was evil and would someday be the death of me.

"Okay, well something's different about you," Millie announced. "You are smiling, and you never smile."

"I smile," I protested.

She looked skeptical again.

"Okay, point taken. I don't smile much compared to you. I have to balance you out so we don't look like a pair of grinning idiots."

She punched me in the arm again.

"Ouch, stop that, or you can't have any of my cake!" I threatened.

We both giggled then, thinking the same thing. We had both eaten my mother's cakes and knew my threat didn't carry much weight.

"So what is up? Did you meet a man?" Millie wasn't willing to let the subject drop.

"Sure, yeah, I met a man. He's in his thirties. Good-looking too. I spent the morning with him," I answered glibly but truthfully.

"No, you didn't. Get serious. What's up?"

"Okay, something is different," I admitted. I wasn't sure exactly what to tell her.

"Tell," she demanded again, turning toward me and gazing at me intently.

"I'm not sure how to say it, Millie. I'm not sure I understand myself. I've just been changing on the inside lately."

"Yeah, I know, and you never talk about it. We don't even get together much anymore. You've changed... So tell me the truth, are you secretly dating?"

"No! Of course not!" I answered indignantly, as if she had accused me of wetting the bed.

"Okay, then what is it?" she went on. "It can't be that big of a deal."

"I'll tell you, but please don't tell my family this. I just don't think they could handle it... I think I might have become a Christian, a believer in God... I mean, I have. For *sure* I have. I mean I am... for sure," I stammered and looked sideways at her, waiting for a response.

"Phew, is that all?" Millie flopped onto her back. "I thought you were going to tell me you were gay or something."

"Well, honestly, I thought you would be more open to me being gay than religious." I was relieved that she hadn't flipped out. I wasn't sure if I could take being vehemently chastised after the emotional morning I had.

"So are you religious, or are you a Christian?" Millie asked.

"Isn't that the same thing?"

"Not always. Sometimes people believe in something, and they just live it out, you know? It's a part of them. And then other people wear it like a hood ornament, point to it constantly, and run over everyone who doesn't have it… that's being religious."

"You sound like you've thought about this before."

"Well, yeah. I believe in God."

"Really, you've never said so," I said, wondering how we could be so close and miss something so obvious.

"Well, with how your mom feels about church…" Millie gestured with her hands as if to the silent elephant in the room.

"How do you know my mom's not into church?"

"The first time I came over to your house, I was alone with your mom for a minute, and I mentioned a church my mom was thinking about taking us to, and your mom kinda freaked out." Millie shrugged.

"What do you mean 'freaked out'?"

"She gave me the third degree and told me your family didn't do church and that wasn't about to change. She told me not to take you anywhere near a church. It was super weird."

"Why didn't you tell me?"

"I didn't know you that well back then. We never went to church anyway. My parents could never agree on which one to try. Besides, I just figured your mother been in a cult or something. Was she?" Millie asked.

"Not that I know of," I said. I honestly didn't know why Mom was the way she was. "Sorry she was so weird."

"That's not your fault," Millie said.

We looked at each other for a minute, then Millie sighed. "Okay, look, let's make a deal. We can talk about anything, even God… no limits, okay?" I hesitated a moment before answering. There were some things I would *never* be able to share with Millie. I could definitely agree to share more than I currently did.

"Okay, we share our hearts and not just on the safe topics," I said, extending my hand so we could shake on it. Millie responded by giving me a quick bear hug instead.

"Sheesh!" she said, flopping onto her back once again.

"So do you talk to God often?" I was curious about this side of Millie that I hadn't known existed.

"Talk to God? You mean pray? I guess so, sometimes… when I think of it. Mostly, I just know He's up there somewhere, and I hope that He remembers me."

"And you find that comforting?"

She thought a moment before answering, "I guess."

"Does He talk to you?"

She blinked a few times. "Um, no… not really. I mean, sometimes I think I know what God would want me to do in a certain situation. If something is a really bad idea, I can tell. I don't feel good about it. I think that's God telling me to be careful. Is that what you mean?"

I shrugged. "I don't mean anything in particular. I just wondered how it worked for you."

"Does He talk to you?" Millie eyed me suspiciously.

"Yeah, I think so. I think maybe He's been talking to me a long time. I just didn't recognize His voice." I didn't explain further. I already felt like I was out on a ledge.

"So why did you become a Christian? Did someone tell you about God?"

"Well, yes, sort of," I said, thinking of Sam.

The doorbell rang downstairs, and Millie hopped up from the bed, ready for a new topic and activity. "Apparently, eighteenth birthdays *are* serious business. Let's go see what kind of food your mom made before Nate gets here and eats everything."

I trailed her down the stairs and to the door.

Nate Mancini rounded out my pathetically small group of friends. A year younger than both of us, but a bona fide genius, he was graduating with us in the spring. The birthday dinner was good. As predicted, Nate had third helpings of everything, including Mom's cake, which pleased her to no end. Nate's own mother served mainly store-bought prepackaged meals, and he wholly appreciated eating anything he didn't have to thaw before eating. Dad's twin brother showed up and gave me fifty dollars in typical "uncles-give-birthday-cash" fashion. I received the usual barrage of questions about my college plans. What major I would choose? Where would I be attending college? I surprised even myself by answering honestly, "I'm thinking about nursing school."

Nate's fork stopped halfway to his mouth.

"You're kidding, right?" Nate asked. "I didn't think you liked people that much."

"Hey, that's uncalled for. I like people… in general. It's just the individuals I'm not always crazy about."

"Don't nurses actually have to work with individuals?" Millie asked.

Well, maybe you don't know me as well as you think you do," I told Nate.

"Apparently not, Nurse Rachet," he joked.

My mother's face was slightly pinched but purposefully expressionless. My father looked momentarily bewildered but got over it quickly. He was generally supportive of whatever I wanted to do, even if he didn't understand it. Everyone knew I loved books and probably assumed I would pick a studious, theoretical career—not something personal in nature. A year before, they would have been right, but holding the injured boy's hand and feeling his fear and pain surge instantly changed that. The experience sparked in me an unquenchable desire to help people. It felt like a longing, a calling. Sitting at the dinner table, I looked at my hands and knew they were built for serving. It was a strange new awareness growing inside me: I was created with a plan in mind. I didn't have to follow that plan; Dhia wasn't in the business of forcing anyone to do anything. Something told me that fulfilling the purpose I was created for would satisfy the yawning, plaguing restlessness that consumed me; and I was willing to do anything, even hard things, to see what that meant. I did get the impression that to follow Him would entail the doing of hard things.

Eventually, the birthday gathering broke up, and everyone went home. My mother tackled the dinner cleanup, and Dad retreated to his office to work on a project. I was exhausted but happy and peaceful. I didn't even mind the ache of my bumps and bruises; they were solid reminders to myself, if no one else, of who I was becoming. The night was chilly. I slipped on a jacket and let Chump out of the laundry room. He appeared momentarily disgruntled at having been locked away from the guests but forgave quickly, following me out the door to the barn for evening feeding. As I approached the stable, I heard Dresden whicker in the darkness. It was past feeding time. I flipped on the barn lights, delivered to him a generous amount of grain, and threw a few flakes of hay into his feeder. As I sat waiting for the water trough to fill, I noticed the door of the tack locker was ajar. Propped up on the saddle just inside was a sealed envelope. I opened it and pulled out a thick folded sheet of paper. A dried pressed flower was glued to the front of the handmade card. The inside read:

Happy birthday, Kiah!

With love,
Fa

MOM

The last month of school went by quickly. Graduation plans took over what little bandwidth that existed in the minds of the seniors at Kenoa Valley High School. I had trouble joining in the excitement. My mind burned with questions about my future in light of every-thing that had happened. Mine weren't the type of questions my guidance counselor, kind and helpful though he was, could answer. I borrowed a Gaelic dictionary from the public library and began to translate the journals and letters belonging to Shae and Ailsa. It was tedious work, but I loved it. It made me feel like Nancy Drew, the girl detective. The library didn't originally have a copy of a Gaelic dictionary. They had to mail order it from a larger city. I checked and rechecked the book out several times before the librarian stamped the inside of the cover with the word *Discard* and told me it was mine to keep.

Nate's mother had gone into full meltdown at the thought of Nate leaving for college and had barely let him out of sight the whole summer. She was a single mom, and he was her only child. She rented a private park carved high in the hillside and hosted a combined graduation party for me, Nate, Millie, and all our friends and family. It was an earthy, punchy, free-flowing event; and though I normally avoided large groups of people, I actually enjoyed the party. The lack of walls somehow relieved people of the pressure to "say the right thing." We sat in the heat on the edge of the hill and watched the lazy little valley. For a moment, I almost felt sentimental about leaving it... almost. I keenly felt that I was at end of one thing, the beginning of another. It was the first good-bye of a summer of hard good-byes.

I didn't mind change. It kept life exciting, but I was starting to understand why people say change is hard. The prospect of leaving behind every single daily routine and every person I knew was more than just a bend in the road ahead; it was a precipitous drop. It occurred to me that I'd probably never live in that little town again. I was taking a leap, wondering where and when I might land.

Millie worked long days in her father's orchard all summer. We stole evenings in the library as often as we could. We talked about college, philosophy, boys, even a little about Dhia. She was giddy at the prospect of spending as many years as she possibly could in her university of choice in Southern California. She planned never to live anywhere that required the wearing of sweaters or coats—*ever again.* Nate's scholarship and its accompanying summer internship took him to Boston the week after we graduated. One day he was there and available to us; the next day he was simply gone. His absence left a bigger hole than I imagined it would. It made me sad, cranky, and a little impatient. I felt left behind.

I had previously applied and been accepted as an international student at a college in Scotland and was scheduled to start classes there in the fall. Luckily, they had a nursing program. The school officials assured me it would be simple to switch majors, but encouraged me to obtain some sort of health care job experience before I began nursing classes. I reluctantly quit the job I loved, riding problem horses for a local horse trainer and secured a summer job transporting patients at the local hospital. Honestly, I missed the horses. They were so much less complicated to care for than people... and often, less stinky.

One of the hardest things I had to do was to give my horse to Mary, the horse trainer I had worked with for the past five years. She offered to buy Dresden, but I adamantly refused. She demanded to pay. I refused to accept any money. Finally and surprisingly, she gave in. Knowing he would be with her gave me peace of mind. I took pride in "out-stubborning" her until I opened the graduation card from her and found five thousand dollars. She said it was a graduation gift and completely nonnegotiable.

I tried attending a few churches that had youth groups, activities for young people, but wasn't interested in endless games of Capture the Flag and Human-Hungry Hippopotamus. The people were mostly nice, but I was looking for something that fed my soul, not merely filled my time in an arbitrarily acceptable manner. I gave up quickly on the idea of finding a peer-based group and settled for stealing quietly into the back of a few services at the stone church to hear Sam teach. It was so obvious to me that he didn't just know *about* Dhia. He *knew* Dhia. So many Christians spoke of Dhia as if He were an intriguing concept. They wore Christianity like a bulky coat, pulling it on and off to suit their comfort. It was discouraging. Sometimes, after work, I stopped by the little church to chat with Sam. He would brew Lemon Burst tea and relax in the wingback office chair while we "swapped notes." I asked questions about Dhia, and he told me what he knew of Him, referencing the Bible often. I even described a few more of my visions. Sam listened but didn't have much light to shed on their meaning.

"If God has something more for you to understand, then He will show you, eventually," Sam would say.

It was what I expected him to say and what I had already told myself, but it was still irritating to hear. I wanted to know *right away*. Unfortunately, Dhia didn't bend to my whims. He didn't follow my timeline. Instead, I got the feeling He was teaching me to trust His timeline. There were still many things I chose not to share with Sam. I didn't go anywhere near the subject of my strange fall through the tree or the flight that landed me at his doorstep on my birthday. Even if he had believed me, which I doubted he could, I had the feeling those were forbidden topics. I kept my eyes open for supernatural encounters or notes from Fa and the other women from the valley but was disappointed.

"Hurry up and wait... Hurry up and wait," Grandma Margaret used to mutter when she was impatient. Those were my feelings exactly.

A few times I sat at the base of the cliff at the turnout and prayed, hoping the tree would appear but it didn't. I didn't fully expect it to. The space at the base of the cliff where I'd entered the tree was ordinary, not sacred or peculiar in anyway. It held only dust and memories. I knew Dhia well enough to realize He was of character and value, but not necessarily of habit. He didn't feel pressure to do things the same way every time for my comfort... obviously. Maybe He was trying to teach me patience. Ha!

Before I knew it, summer ended, and it was time to leave for college. The week of my departure, Mom grew silent. She tried to pretend she was jammed with work, but I knew it was more than that. Change was a beast she couldn't control, and that made her nervous, even angry. I wasn't focused and driven enough to gain entrance to a prestigious university, but I didn't settle for the closest hometown community college either. I chose the University of Aodhagan (pronounced "Eggan"), a small university in Scotland named after the castle on the college campus. Aodhagan billed itself as an international school. Students attended there from almost every corner of the world. It was Tuesday evening, and I was set to fly out the following Friday. I was sorting my clothes for the umpteenth time, trying to make a final decision on what to bring and what to leave behind, when I sensed Mom's presence in the doorway behind me. She didn't come to my room often, only when she wanted something. I didn't turn to greet her.

The first one to speak loses, I thought. I'd heard that somewhere.

Finally, she spoke. "The box needs to go with you."

There was no need for clarification. I knew she was speaking of the family items she'd given me.

"Are you sure? I have been wondering about that stuff. I'm not sure that a college dorm is the best place for it..."

"It can't stay here, Kiah. It needs to not be here anymore. It needs to go with you," she continued quietly but firmly.

It dawned on me then that maybe Mom hadn't given it to me because she thought I should have it, but because she couldn't stand having it anymore herself. If so, why didn't she just get rid of it?

"Okay, I'm staying in a dorm, though. I'm not sure that's the best place for…," I started again.

"You'll manage," she barked, then continued in a softer voice. "You always do. You are strong, Kiah. And you are getting stronger. I know I don't say it often. But I see it. I see you." Her voice broke, and she fell silent.

I held my breath, not sure how to respond. Mom expressing sentiment was an occurrence rare enough to change the very quality of the air.

"I know you deserved more than I gave you," she said in a voice just above a whisper.

An admission of wrongdoing? That was new. I impulsively searched for a way to shield her. "That's not true, Mom. I don't think that," I objected. "You and Dad gave me everything I needed."

"I'm not talking about what *you* think you needed, Kiah. I'm not talking about the things you can touch. It's the things you can't touch…" She hesitated, contemplating continuing, then clamped her mouth shut.

It seemed like it might be the only opportunity to say it, so I took a deep breath and plunged headlong.

"I believe in God, Mom. He talks to me." I studied her face, watching for her left eyebrow to rocket toward her hairline the way it did when opposing counsel said something absolutely inane. Her expression didn't change, however. She didn't even twitch.

I continued, "He always has, I think… talked to me, that is. I just haven't always listened or understood. And this year I started talking back, well… answering, I mean. That's the choice you were talking about, wasn't it, Mom? Choosing to listen to God?" My heart was thumping. I wasn't sure how she would respond. She didn't.

"You heard me, right, Mom?" I tried again.

"I'm processing, Kiah. Give me a minute," she answered, her voice abrupt and odd.

I gave her a minute. She still said nothing.

Feeling unexpectedly piqued, I continued. "I don't understand why this is such a big deal, Mom. People all over the world are Christians. People have Bibles that aren't locked up in the attic above the garage either. They are on their bookshelves. People all over the world believe in God. Just because our family doesn't..."

"I never said I didn't believe in God, Kiah. Have I ever once said that to you?" she spoke quietly through clenched teeth.

I pondered for a moment, trying to remember.

"No, I guess not," I answered. "You never said anything at *all*. Oma talked about God and church when I was little, and I asked you about it, but you said nothing. There is a God, you know about Him, He loves me, and He has a plan for me... and you never tell me? You tell Millie never to talk to me about it? What is *that* about? It's like you're trying to hide God from me? Why? I don't understand!" My words spilled in a torrent. "Do you believe in God, Mom? If you do, then why? Why wouldn't you tell me? You just..."

"It's different for you, Kiah," Mom interrupted again. This time her voice was filled with pain.

Did she know something—something about my experiences that she wasn't telling me? My mind raced.

"Why? Why is it different for me?"

She didn't answer. Her lips were drawn so tight they had gone white, and I realized she was afraid.

"Mom?" I asked, quieter this time.

"Maybe I should have told you, Kiah, about God. I never wanted to lie to you. I just wanted to protect you, but hiding the truth from you, that was wrong. You have the right to choose for yourself, and I wasn't fair with you. I should have given that choice to you." Tears stopped her words, and she struggled to regain control of her voice. I had never seen her so emotionally undone. These were uncharted waters, and she seemed to be drowning.

"You know now, though, despite my efforts. He asked for my help... to get his work done... He never needed me, but He wanted me and I... I knew He wanted you too. I just couldn't..." Her voice trailed off, and she clamped her mouth shut tight.

Is my mother talking about Dhia? I wondered. She wasn't making much sense.

"I *don't* know, though, Mom. I *don't* know what I need to know. You want me to know the truth? Tell me, because I don't know! I know about God and Jesus now, yes. But you just said that believing is different for me? I don't know what you mean by that. Why do I hear God in ways other people don't? Why did you say this is different for me? Tell me the truth about that! You have to tell me. Please tell me what you mean!" I begged.

I watched her eyes as she contemplated my request, then drew a mental line in the sand.

"No," she said firmly.

"Not telling you about the truth about Him in the first place… that was a mistake. I will own that. But I will not be part of what happens if you choose…" Her voice broke again, and she cleared her throat before continuing. "The rest of that, Kiah. I won't be a part of that. I can't be part of that." Her eyes glittered again with their usual stony resolve. Whatever had opened in her heart for a few precious moments was closing back up.

"Mom, please. You have to tell me what you mean. Please!" I implored, reaching for her hand, trying to keep the walls from going back up. She shrank from my grasp.

"It sounds like you already know some, don't you? You have already chosen, Kiah, haven't you?" she asked.

I thought about that for a minute. *Had I chosen something?* I had accepted Jesus's gift, certainly, but that wasn't what she was speaking of. I hadn't resisted learning what Fa asked me to. I'd begun to listen in history class. I'd answered the call to help people and switched to a nursing major. I was eagerly waiting for my life to take a drastic turn in another new direction.

"Yes. I have chosen," I said. My yes was just as firm as Mom's no had been. It resonated all the way through me to my toes.

"Tell me, Mom. What have I chosen? You have to tell me more," I said—but she was already shaking her head.

"No. I won't be a part of this, Kiah. I can't. I promised myself, and I promised you, when you were born… I made myself a promise. I won't discuss this again." She spoke from the far side of the invisible line she'd drawn. The line was tangible, and the chasm it created was widening. I felt a deep pang of loss.

"I do love you, Kiah. I'm so proud of you. I don't say that enough," she continued, her voice tinged with regret. "I wish you had said no, but I imagine that didn't even cross your mind, did it?"

I pondered a moment then answered, "No, I guess it didn't."

Everything in me wanted to plead with her again to tell me she knew, but Lisette Bonner was as stubborn as I was. Maybe even more so.

"I love you," she said softly, briefly stroking my brow with her forefinger the way she had when I was very young. "I'm sorry. I'm not strong enough to do what you want me to do."

Her expression confirmed the truth of her words.

"I don't believe that at all, Mom. You are the strongest person I know."

"Well, you don't know me, Kiah, like you think you do," she clipped. There was pride in her tone. She was right. My mother had always been a bit of a mystery. I just hadn't realized exactly how much of an enigma she truly was until that moment.

"What children know of their parents changes when they aren't children anymore… and you are no longer a child. You will begin to see the world now with different eyes." She stood on her tiptoes and placed an unexpected kiss on my cheek. It felt like a kiss good-bye, and it sent an icy chill up my spine. I pulled her into a quick hug, warmer from my side than from hers.

She retreated wordlessly down the stairs, leaving me to cry silently in my pitiful pile of half-packed belongings. I didn't know what to do. Follow her? Beg her to talk to me? It wouldn't help. Instead, I sank to the bed and sifted through what I remembered of our fragmented conversation. My mother was afraid of what I'd chosen when it came to following Dhia… That much I knew. At the very least, it confirmed that my feeling, beliefs, and experiences were real and valid. My heart stood still for a moment at the prospect of what that could mean for the future. I'd seen things that broke the laws of nature, and there was obviously more on the horizon. A wave of apprehension washed over me, and I felt completely alone. My knees and hands shook uncontrollably. With some difficulty, I peeled off my clothing, donned a sleep shirt, and kneeled at the bedside. I begged Dhia to meet me there and restore my hope. I decided not to climb into bed until I felt at least somewhat better about things. I fell asleep there, arms stretched out across the bed, knees numb, in a soggy patch of my own tears.

The rest of the week went quickly. Friday morning brought a scramble of last-minute arrangements, luggage checks, and a hasty trip to the airport. Those were the days before stringent airport security, so my parents trailed me all the way to the gate. Dad kept busy checking my passport and tickets, intermittently asking if I was sure I had everything I needed.

"I have everything, Dad. I'm sure of it," I reassured him for the umpteenth time. My carry-on was heavy. I stashed the book cover and the Bible inside and the remainder of the items from mother's box in my carry-on luggage, trusting Dhia to help them end up at their proper destination. My paranoid side imagined them endlessly circling an airport conveyor belt in Mazatlan.

Mom stayed quiet. Everything that was going to be said between us had already been said. She had already said her good-byes and checked out. The boarding announcement for my flight came on over the loudspeakers, sending little lightning bolts of anticipation through my middle. It was time to go. My chest hummed with anticipation.

I hugged both my parents. We each stifled our emotions for the sake of each other's comfort.

"I love you, guys," I said.

"We love you too," Dad answered seriously. And I knew it was true. They did.

ACROSS THE POND

Eleven hours and forty-five minutes. That's how long it took to fly from my corner of the US to Edinburgh. Normally, I would have been ecstatic at the opportunity for hours of uninterrupted reading time. That day, things were different. For so long, I'd been looking forward to getting away from Kenoa and back to Scotland. Now that it was actually happening, fear of the unknown was setting in, and the conversation I'd had with Mom at the beginning of the week was still nagging at me. The idealistic promise of a great adventure was turning into an unnerving reality. My insides buzzed.

A few hours into the flight, I checked my watch for the seventy-third time. My hands were clammy, and my knees kept bouncing of their own accord. The old man in the seat next to me kept throwing me half-sympathetic, half-annoyed glances.

"Nervous about flying?" he finally asked.

"Not really, no. Sorry, I must be bothering you," I answered ruefully, pushing my left knee down, tangibly urging it not to jump. "I'm headed to college. It's my first year. It's scarier than I thought it would be."

He nodded his head in understanding. "I remember the first time I left home. I was fourteen years old…"

"Wow, fourteen. That's young."

"Yeah, well, I didn't know I was leaving for good. I thought I was just running away from home for a while, to teach my folks a lesson, y'know?" There was a note of sadness in his voice that made me really look at his face for the first time. He was perhaps seventy years old. His skin was well wrinkled and well tanned, except at the corners of his eyes where it was almost translucent. He stared vacantly out the window.

"So what happened?" I asked.

"Nothing. Everything. I don't really know… I met some bad people, made some bad choices. One little decision led to the next, and by the time I decided to go home, thirty years had passed. When I finally got home, they were gone—my parents, everyone… They were all gone." His voice trailed off as he journeyed through his memories. He resurfaced suddenly and realized I was there. "Now I'm sorry. Here you are nervous about going away to college, and I tell you that story." He clucked his tongue and shook his head. "I'm not used to talking to people, I guess. I've lived alone a long time."

"Oh, that's okay. Everybody has strange conversations on airplanes," I said, but he didn't hear me. He was wandering through his memories again.

"Everybody my age yaks about going back and doing things over and what they'd do with a second chance. That's a bunch of crap." He snorted forcefully. "You can't change what you've already done. You can't go back. But I can tell you what I wish I *had* done differently. Maybe you can learn from that. Maybe that makes it worth saying, eh?" He waited for my permission to continue.

"Sure, I think so," I agreed.

He took a moment to choose just the right words. "Gratitude," he finally said, then smiled, pleased with himself for putting his finger on precisely what he wanted to convey.

"I didn't have any gratitude. Gratefulness, you know?"

I nodded.

"I should have taken the time to be thankful for what I had. There's always something to be thankful for, if you look. The good Lord always gives us something, and you gotta hang on to that something, even if it's small. That'll get you through, you understand?"

I nodded again.

"You know the Lord?" he asked as an afterthought.

"Yes, I mean… I'm getting to know Him."

"Well, that's good, then, right? I mean, too many young people don't respect God anymore." He shook his head regretfully.

"Thank you for telling me that," I said, wanting him to know I was grateful for his shared words. "I will remember it."

I felt the urge to reach out and squeeze his hand but didn't have the nerve. He reached out instead, patted my hand awkwardly, and I grasped his fingers for a moment before he returned to his crossword puzzle. The physical touch of another person had a stabilizing effect on my nerves. I leaned back in the seat, closed my eyes, and drifted off to sleep. Before I knew it, the flight attendant was waking me and offering a meal.

"Last chance for a meal before we land," she apologized.

I had slept most of the flight. My neck was stiff, and my mouth felt cottony. I accepted one of the pitiful meals (chicken, I think, though I'm not entirely sure) and a ginger ale. I checked my watch. Two hours left. It was nighttime. I pulled up the window shade to peer out and caught my breath. I watched the Northern Lights dance, dipping and swaying across the sky. Just as the lights began to fade. A bright star appeared just over the wing of the jet. It flashed strong and bright for a mere moment, then winked out entirely.

"Thank you," I whispered into the darkness.

THE CALLING

Elspeth, my second cousin, met me at the airport. I recognized her by her frizzy mop of cinnamon-brown hair. I braced for impact when I heard her squeal her greeting and head my direction. As usual, she practically bowled me over. Life seemed bent on pairing me with exuberant, demonstrative people. Elsie was six years older than me. I'd lived with her family on my last visit and planned to spend the next week with them to get adjusted to the time difference and visit until the dorms opened. Elsie had just polished off her sixth year of study at a London university, graduating with a degree in philosophy of music. I had no idea what she planned to do with it, and for the time being, neither did she. Graduation cap in hand, she had returned home to work at a coffee shop and search out a venue for her musical abilities.

"Kiah, how are you? No. First, let's talk about me a minute. How's my accent?" she bubbled.

She had been working hard on losing her Scottish accent and adopting a British one. She seemed to have landed somewhere in the middle.

"Fabulous," I declared. "I almost mistook you for the queen of England."

She rolled her eyes. "So how are you?"

"Good, Tired. Stressed. Excited. I need a shower. That about covers it."

"Sounds normal. So… straight home, shower, and to bed then?" she asked. It was nearing midnight. I nodded. Bed sounded like a fabulous idea. After gathering my luggage, we headed to the car and took on the task of inserting a year's worth of my provisions into the tiny backseat and trunk of Elsie's miniature car. By the time we finished arranging, pushing, pulling, and even cursing, her car looked like a bloated tick ready to pop. My legs and back were complaining vehemently at having been stuffed sardine-style in an airplane seat for so long, but I was able to coax them back into a cramped position in the passenger seat.

"You are tired, so I'll talk," Elsie offered, even though we both knew she would carry more than her share of the conversation no matter what condition I was in. It was actually comforting to listen to her chatter. I occasionally inserted a "Wow," or "Oh really?" and sometimes, a "That's amazing." She prattled on about school, the bands she had been in, and a marvelous Spanish boy she had met. Apparently, his voluminous American-style pants were adorable. I felt tired and numb. I had expected my return to Scotland to feel like coming home, but it didn't feel like that at all. I felt strangely removed from everything I saw and heard, perhaps due to fear of the unknown. Perhaps I just needed to adjust to the change.

Elsie's parents, Gwen and Kade Clacher, lived in the country on thirty acres of farmland. It had started out as a tiny gray stone farmhouse, but several generations of Clachers had built onto it throughout the years. The resultant dwelling was squat, amorphous, and homey. Inside, the floors sloped, and the ceiling dipped unpredictably. It smelled of woodsmoke, mildew, and laundry soap, just as I remembered. My uncle Kade was a man of extremely few words. He welcomed me at the door with a gracious smile and a pat on the shoulder then brushed by us and out the door, presumably to retrieve my luggage. I knew I should offer to help, but I was just too tired. I went straight to bed that night in the makeshift bedroom under the stairs that I had occupied on my previous visit.

The next week was jam-packed with small, happy reunions. I visited more cousins, aunts, and uncles than I care to recount. One thing nagged at the back of my mind every minute: I wanted desperately to ask someone in our family about the box of Clacher family items, to see if anyone knew anything about Shae and Ailsa, the women referenced in the journals and letters. I just wasn't sure whom to ask. So I asked Dhia to point me in the right direction, then waited and watched for an opportunity. Late in the week, I sat at the table of my great-aunt Moira Clacher, along with nine other family members, having my fifth family banquet in as many days. Cock-a-Leekie soup, bannocks, pan-fried sea bream, and barley pudding. The waistband of my jeans was soon strained, and I felt sure I wouldn't have to eat at all for the entire pursuant school year.

Moira's old farmhouse was reminiscent of Kade and Gwen's home but smaller. Moira, the matriarch of the family, stubbornly refused to give up the farm when her husband died of old age a few years before. Her grandson Evan felt obliged to move his family in and help her run the farm. Evan had seven children, and they all lived virtually atop one another in the tiny house. The place teemed with life, as well as the sticky patches and general moisture that go along with the presence of children.

The table that night was set formally with the best china (brought out only for guests), candlesticks, and a worn but freshly starched linen tablecloth. The children were repeatedly warned, a few even threatened, not to break the dishes or set fire to the table. They had a million questions about America. For instance, they had heard everything was bigger in the USA, and they wanted to know exactly what that meant—pencils? Toothbrushes? Dogs? They seemed mildly disappointed when I produced my toothbrush, and it very much resembled their own. As much as I loved answering their clamoring questions, I was also hoping for a chance to talk to Moira alone. I'd felt a nudge, presumably from Dhia, to bring along the box of books and letters from Mom with me. I was eager to discover why. As the dinner meal wound to a close, Evan's youngest daughter, Kenzie, careened in from the barn, pink cheeked and breathless.

"It's the cow, Nan!" she chirped. "She's at it! It's time!"

Everyone at the table except for myself and Moira quickly scooted their chairs away from the table and dashed for the door. I must have looked bewildered.

"She's pregnant and due," Moira explained.

Everyone jostled and flapped by the mudroom door momentarily, donning boots and coats, then headed for the barn to view the much-anticipated arrival. I was invited to go along but declined, citing inadequate shoes. Once they were gone, I pushed back from the table and began to collect dishes, wondering just how to broach the subject of the box and its contents. It turned out that I needn't have worried. Moira broached it for me.

"Set down, Kiah," Moira demanded quietly.

I complied immediately, as everyone did when Moira spoke.

"So ye are the one, are ye? The Lord has called ye? Ye have the items from yer ma?" I was taken off guard.

I had been prepared to uncover the subject cautiously, but my great-aunt had deftly laid it bare.

I managed a nod. "I think so."

"Ye think so? Does thet mean ye have them in yer possession, or nae?"

"I mean, I do. I absolutely do," I clarified.

"Well, thet's thet then," she said with finality as if the subject, just begun, was already closed.

"That's *what* then? I haven't a clue what any of this means. You know about the box? You know what's inside? My mother gave me the box. She said the things inside were my inheritance but that I shouldn't discuss them with anyone. I can tell there's something else, something big that she's not saying. I told her God spoke to me. She didn't even blink. I asked her to tell me what she knew, but she seemed afraid. She refuses to discuss it with me. She just refuses. I just don't understand why. Do you know what any of this means? You have to tell me what you know!" I paused, surprised at the amount of words and information I'd spilled out on the old woman. I really had planned to proceed with greater caution.

Moira sighed and set her chin. "I'll speak of this today, with ye, and just to ye, but yer ne'er to repeat a word of it to anyone else, ye hear?" Moira was used to laying down the law and having people follow it. "And ye'll call me Nan, like all the others?"

If it meant she would talk to me further, I was prepared to call her anything she liked.

"Nan it is," I quickly agreed.

She pushed her chair back from the table and crooked her finger at me, indicating I should follow her. I trailed her into the living room and sat on the sofa opposite her favorite setting chair.

She settled in and got straight to business. "Yer ma, now... what did she tell ye, precisely?"

"Precisely nothing. Honestly. I've told you everything she told me. She didn't even tell me Dhia was real. I had to find that out on my own. But she doesn't deny it," I said firmly.

Well, she was trying to protect ye. I can see thet. Ye canna blame her fer that," Nan said.

"Protect me from *what*?"

She held up on finger to silence me and sighed, trying to figure out where to start. "So there's a woman in almost every generation, a woman thet's 'Called.' Well, thet's the way it is wi' the Clachers. I dinna ken how it is wi' other families. But I dinna think most families have the Callin' at all."

"Called?" I asked.

"Called by the Lord for a higher purpose."

"Do you mean called to be a Christian?" I asked, puzzled.

"Aye, thet, but more than thet as well... It's a call to serve the Lord in a very special way."

"So you were chosen then? You were Called?"

Nan shook her head adamantly. "Nae. I wasna called. I thank the Lord fer thet! My sister, Gaira—she was, howe'er. I heard the rumors that she was mebbe called, e'en before she left. I didn't believe 'em at first." Nan shook her head sadly.

"Left? Where did she go?"

"I dinna ken, do I? All I ken is thet the Lord called Gaira into His service, and then she was gone. Nae one's seen her since. That's how it works, isna it?"

The word '*gone*' shot straight me.

"I don't know, Nan. That's why I'm asking you. God doesn't call people to disappear, right? That makes no sense! Your sister was

Called, whatever that means, and then she was gone? Gone where? Where did she go?"

Nan sighed again, realizing I truly was clueless.

"I'll start ye back a bit. Gaira was seventeen the lest I saw her. I was thirteen years old. Ma raised us all to fear the Lord… and Gaira did, more than anyone else I've known. Saw visions, she did. But that ye must already know." Nan nodded at me, obviously assuming I saw visions as well. My palms began to sweat.

"And she heard the voice of the Lord an' all… and she didna keep quiet about it. Thet's when the rumors began. They said she was 'Called,' called by God. And they said some Clacher women had been called afore her. I dinna believe them at first. Folk here are superstitious." Nan choked up a bit, cleared her throat, and spoke again.

"Then Gaira came to me, in the wee mornin'. She woke me and had me set up to hear her well. She gave me the box an' told me to keep it safe nae matter what—to show nae a body. She said it was important. I wasna to look in the box at all. I promised, but I did look anyway, naturally. I saw letters, books, and something else, big and heavy, wrapped tight. I opened a book, a diary with names I dinna ken. I opened nae'thing else. I didn't want to damage anything and make Gaira angry… or the Lord, fer thet matter, ye ken?"

I nodded and asked eagerly, "The names, Shae and Ailsa, from the books and letters, do you know who they were?"

Nan shook her head. "Family relations, perhaps, but none I ken. I hid the box well… protected it, as Gaira asked. It's all I had of her. The day she left, she kissed me on the head, like Ma always did, and said I needed to be good, learn to listen to the Lord, and obey. She said she loved me. I dinna ken what she was saying or why she was saying it at the time. I thought she was mebbe meetin' a lad. Then she left. And she was gone. She was just gone." Nan dabbed at her tears with the hem of her skirt before she continued. "They looked everywhere for her. But she was gone."

I was rooted to my seat, scared, almost speechless. My first thought was that Na's story *had* to be part of what my mother didn't want me to know. My second thought was that I might know exactly where Gaira had gone. Perhaps I had already been there myself. It had never occurred to me that I might disappear from my current life, never to be seen again or that I could have disappeared the night of the visit to the valley and never returned. That thought raised gooseflesh over my entire body. I gripped the flowered sofa cushion.

"I'm so, so sorry, Nan," I stammered. I wasn't sure what else I could say to comfort her. I didn't want to prod an emotionally tender subject, but I had so many questions. I steered toward what I hoped would be safer ground.

"If you had Gaira's box, then how did my mother get it?" I asked.

"I sent it to her," Nan said simply.

"*You* sent it to her? Why?"

"I was forty-seven years old. It was a cold Tuesday. I found a note under my pillow directing me to send the box to Lisette Bonner in America. It also said how much I was loved and had made my family proud. It was signed by Gaira. She was the only one who knew of the box, so it couldna been anyone else. I dinna want to part with the box. It was all I had of Gaira, but I did as I was told."

"Gaira? How could that even be? She wasn't dead?" I blurted.

"Och nae. Some folk said she must ha' died. I kent different all along. I felt her life in my bones." Nan patted her own chest confidently, just over her heart.

"I just didna expect to hear from her after so many years. And I dinna ken about your mother either. I ne'er heard back from her when I sent her the books. She didn't take the Call, 'course... I kent that once I saw ye." Nan eyed me thoughtfully.

I shook my head. No. She obviously hadn't.

"What is the 'Call' that you are talking about, Nan? It seems to be more than just believing in Dhia."

"Och aye, an' much more," Nan agreed. "I havna had the call, so I canna tell ye much. Nae many *do* have it. I've known only Gaira, and she jest ne'er seemed to belong to us from the start, if ye catch my meanin'. She was the Lord's from birth, lent to us until she could tie her shoes and nae much longer. She was a different sort."

Nan paused, smiling, remembering her sister. "The Callin' runs strong in the family, thet much, I *can* tell ye. There have been others."

"How many others?"

"I dinna ken." Nan shrugged. "I asked about it when Gaira left, but nae a body could say anything but the rumors, and ye ken how rumors are. Everyone says a different thing. Most folk now think the Callin's just a legend, and legend goes there's mebbe one in each generation. It's a call to serve, Kiah, but in an unusual way, for sure. I dinna ken where, and I dinna ken how, but it's in the service of the Lord, and there's nae wrong with thet. The Lord can be trusted. It's hard on the family, though. Servin' the Lord is nae simple task. Ye have a choice, naturally, so think well on it… or have ye already chosen?" Nan asked.

"I think I have already said yes," I replied. "I just don't know exactly what I have said yes to."

Nan's eyes twinkled. "That's life, ye ken? Ye must commit before ye see what ye purchased. The Lord's nae different. He writes our stories, and we can say yae or nae to some parts, but we fool ourselves if we think we ken better than He does. Aye is ne'er the wrong answer. Whatever He has for ye, it willna be boring. I can tell ye thet."

Her eyes filled with young wonder, and she leaned forward, clasping my hands in hers. "He's offered ye a gift, Kiah. It's a gift given to only a handful o' women, special women… women like Gaira. Ye were made for a special purpose, and there's nae a body can take that away from ye, e'en if they try—and they jest might try! So be warned. It's a good choice ye made. A strong choice. Though I havena seen Gaira since, I ne'er thought she made a wrong choice. The heart knows, ye see? My heart knows. Yer heart knows."

Nan had said the words I needed to hear. I needed to hear aloud that I'd made a good choice even though the road I was choosing might lead into incomprehensible wilderness. My mind reeled, and tears dripped freely from my chin. Nan blotted them with her sleeve.

"Can I bring the box back here? Can it stay with you? It might be safer here than in a college dorm room. I think Dhia asked me to bring it along."

"Dhia?" Nan asked. "I notice ye prefer the Gaelic name for the Lord?"

"I guess I do. I used that name the first time I prayed, and it just sort of stuck."

"And who taught ye to pray, Kiah?"

"No one… Well, I guess that's not really true. I'd say Dhia taught me Himself."

Nan nodded. It made perfect sense to her. "I can see thet. Yer a listening soul. A' course ye can leave yer box here. I'll keep it in the attic, and ye can visit it whenever ye like."

"Thank you."

"Yer welcome."

Mindful of the advice of the old man on the plane, I noted the gratitude I felt for Moira Clacher and silently thanked Dhia for it.

"Now listen well. As I said before, folk dinna take as kindly to the Callin' or the things of the Lord as they used to around here. Some are hostile. So ye'll keep this to yourself, ye hear?" Nan made her point firmly but kindly.

I nodded. I certainly hadn't planned to say anything to anyone.

"Thet's a good girl, then. Gaira dinna need to say anything either, but it dinna keep her quiet. She was bold. She figured if ye have a mouth, ye use it whene'er ye like. Thet made trouble." Nan tsk-tsked and waggled her head back and forth. "Ye have a head on your shoulders, though. I knew that the first time I met ye. I thought then thet ye might be Called." She seemed pleased with her own intuition.

"Thet's thet, then, right?" Nan rose from her chair and placed a hand on my shoulder.

I nodded my head, not trusting myself to speak.

I retrieved the box from the car and followed Nan into the back hall where she pulled down a set of retractable attic steps.

"Up the stair, on the right. Ye'll see a large trunk with a broken latch. It's empty. I'll have a lock put on this week and have the key for ye."

I mounted the stairs and followed her instructions. Parting with the box felt strange, like leaving an old friend that I somehow barely knew. I desperately wished I knew more about the items and what they meant.

Patience, whispered a voice inside me. The voice was definitely not my own. I was feeling far from patient.

I pulled the string that hung from the single bare bulb on the low attic ceiling, and the light winked out. I heard the clatter of tiny feet and chatter of many voices from downstairs. I shut up the attic steps and joined the family in the kitchen where they were prying off their dirty boots and coats and removing hay from each other's hair. The shaggy red cow had given birth to a pure white female albino calf.

They christened the calf "Milk," an appropriate name on several counts. We all gathered around the wood stove in the living room and listened to the children tell us everything they knew (and in a few cases, I suspect *more* than they knew) about the great event.

My heart felt full and warm. Nan hadn't answered all my questions, but she had confirmed that I was on the right track. I had what I needed for the moment, and I felt at peace.

BERT

This first time I set foot on Aodhagan's campus the sky was gray and cranky. Adrenaline hummed through my veins, and if I wasn't trying so hard to act casual, I might have skipped across the parking lot. It felt very much like the first time I boarded the big yellow school bus in kindergarten. *Well, world, it's just you and me now.* Equal portions of pride at being a grown-up and childish excitement clasped hands and danced in my chest.

Elsie had offered to help me move in. We parked in the main lot, left the luggage in the car, and went in search of directions to the freshman dorm.

"I see you were in a dreary Dracula sort of mood when you chose this place," Elsie declared, hands on hips. She gazed up at the administration building, a castle in its former life.

I rolled my eyes and feigned offense. "I didn't choose it for its buildings. I chose it for its programs."

"Och, ye did not!" she responded, slipping momentarily into her native Scots.

"If you were choosing a college for its programs, you'd have stayed home. You came here for the ambiance. Tell the truth. You were looking for spooky and decrepit, and you found it." She gestured toward the administration building.

She had a point. The gothic building, tall and mossy, was flanked by several other ancient stone buildings and surrounded by old trees with gracefully bending, heavy branches. The other buildings on campus had been added sporadically throughout the years as the college grew. The result was a hodgepodge of construction from almost every era except perhaps the modern era. The only aesthetically unifying force on the campus was the landscaping. The mature vegetation and well-kept flagstone walkways held everything together like the cohesive finishing stick on a crazy quilt.

Elsie, hands on hips and brow furrowed, had more to say. "There are two types of people in the world: those who think their home is better than anywhere else, and those who think anywhere else has got to be better than home. The former group sits at home, terrified of change. You are the latter. You'll find out it's not better here than anywhere else and either keep searching or go home," she declared, fully convinced she had the world and everyone in it precisely pinned.

"That's a cynical view, Elsie. Did you wake up on the wrong side of the bed? I'd like to think there's more than two kinds of people in the world… three of four, at least. What about the kind of people that aren't afraid to explore? Or those who don't feel at home anywhere? What about the people who just like to roam? I'll admit to looking for a change of scenery from home, but I don't expect this place to hold all the answers for me. Besides, I didn't actually think it would be quite this…"—I searched for the right word—"original."

"Original?" Elsie exclaimed. "You've been reading the recruitment pamphlets. This whole place is plain *old*!—and not in the charming way. You'll need extra socks. I seriously doubt they have indoor heating. I'll get you some of Da's stockings. He can spare a few pair."

"Oh, great. That will be attractive," I added.

Elsie's rant about the probable lack of indoor heating was likely not much of an exaggeration. I added extra clothing layers to my mental list of things to buy soon. We stopped in at the welcome desk to ask for directions to the freshmen girls' dorm. The brassy-haired woman at the welcome desk informed us that brand-new residence halls were recently built at the south end of the grounds. *New dorms*—that sounded promising. Then she added that the freshmen girls were still housed in Cannon Hall, inexplicably called "Bert" by its occupants.

"Bert is one of our more original buildings," she added.

Elsie gave me an I-told-you-so look.

Bert turned out to be a sagging ivy-covered brick saltbox on the fringe of campus, and my room very much resembled a monastic cell done over by Spartan Ikea enthusiasts. Bert's common living area was its saving grace. It housed a good-sized sink, new white cupboards, a refrigerator, large dining room table, several glaringly bright golden-rod couches (who *ever thought* of that color for a couch?), and a few scattered beanbag chairs.

Elsie pulled her car around and parked close next to Bert, and we unloaded my bags. It didn't take long to unpack and put every-thing away since I had only as many belongings as I could bring on the plane. Finally, I spread my newly purchased mint green com-forter with its clear vinyl stitching over the bed and threw my pillow on top. Done. I lay awake in my unfamiliar bed that night, listen-ing to the sporadic dripping of water in the ancient plumbing echo through the bowels of the building. I pulled the covers tight around my head until just my nose stuck out and waited for sleep. New bed, new country, new faces, uncertain life plans… I felt as if I'd signed up to run a marathon in a brand-new pair of untested shoes. I felt very far from home and very small.

The whirlwind of the first week of school quickly gave way to predictable routine. The dripping plumbing became just another background noise, and Bert became home, sort of… as close to home as it could be, at any rate. I pondered Elsie's views on people who stay home versus people who search for home. Maybe part of her theory was true… maybe home, for me, would always be elusive. I developed a few virtual "new shoe" blisters in my first weeks at Aodhagan, but they were minor. Routine and classwork eventually soothed the pres-sure points. Fresh setting notwithstanding, school is just school… and I was relatively good at school. Drag out of bed, attend early classes, have lunch, attend afternoon classes, have dinner, study, grab snack, study, fall into bed, sleep, repeat. It was an unseasonably cold September. The leaves on the Wild Crab trees threatened to turn color even as they clung to their fruit. I called Mom and Dad weekly to give an update. Dad usually answered the phone.

"Hi, Dad, it's me."

"So it is! How are you?"

"Good. You?"

"Good, really good. How are classes? You studying?"

"Yep. I'm studying."

"No parties, right?"

"No parties, Dad. You know me better than that."

"Right. Just making sure. Your mother's not here again, Kiah. She's had a very busy run at work since you left. I'll tell her you called."

"Okay, tell her hi."

"Of course. Take care of yourself."

Okay, you too. Love you."

"Love you too."

The calls home never lasted long.

Letters from Millie were frequent and newsy. The regularity with which she wrote made the daily stop at the front desk enjoyable. Her letters reminded me someone somewhere was thinking of me. That felt good. Millie begged me to come to my senses and join her in the California sunshine. She was concerned that I was rusting away in a castle beside a stack of books. Her fears weren't wholly unsubstantiated. I didn't tell her I'd adopted an abandoned office in an unused section of the administration building. The hallway that led to it was cordoned off, and a sign stated the area was slated for eventual reconstruction. The stairway was extremely steep and narrow, and the rooms were small. The heat was iffy there, as it was in many of the buildings, but the peaceful silence and the view from the high windows was unparalleled. I had my pick of six empty rooms. The one I chose housed a dusty old desk and a broken wooden chair, which I shored up and spit cleaned. I took Elsie up on the offer of her father's thick stockings and wore them over top of my own pathetically thin cotton socks for warmth. I fashioned long armed gloves from a few pair by cutting away the heels and toes. I'm sure I looked like a hobo, but no one besides the occasional mouse was there to complain. I used the space for studying, reading, praying, and escaping my dorm mates. I had heard that normal roommates were rarer than unicorns. I can confirm that as fact.

Before my strange visit with Fa in the horseshoe valley, my future had been a frustrating blank canvas. What to study? Language? Research writing? Blah! Nothing sounded interesting. I cringed every time my uncle asked, "So do you know what you want to do when you grow up?"

If I answered "No, not yet," I'd sound aimless or lazy. I was convinced I would do something meaningful with, or at least during my life. I just had *no idea* what it was! Working in offices with endless reams of numbered papers, adjustable chairs, synthetic air fresheners, stale donuts, and staler conversations—being subjected to the same personalities and scenery day after day had always sounded *torturous*. I loved books, but books were a portal I wanted to crawl through. I didn't want them to become my job.

Try explaining all that to Uncle George. He won't understand. Uncle George (who might be your aunt Esther, uncle Roger, Mrs. Wilson, or any one of a number of assorted adults) wants you to say, "I'm going into computers," or "dentistry," or "teaching," or "I want to illustrate children's books." That way, Uncle George can fit you snugly into his preconceived notion of how the world *is*, and how it *should be*. If you give him a clear, clean answer like "I was thinking of dentistry," then he can shove his hands in his pockets, smile wide, lean back, and say, "Yep, that's what I thought. You looked like a dentist to me from the moment I saw you." Wink, wink.

Really? I look like a dentist? Do all dentists look like me, or just yours? Perhaps it's time for you to switch dentists. (I don't recommend actually saying that. It's not worth it… That's why it's in italics. Just think it and move on.)

The visit to the horseshoe valley gave me my first real glimpse through the wall that separated me from my future. The crack was tiny but let in just enough light for me to see the next step. I was learning that that's how it was with Dhia. He didn't provide a road map, but He lit up the next step, in His time. I can pinpoint the exact moment crack appeared: it was the moment I touched the injured young man. A thousand images flickered through my mind simultaneously, converging into a single point of light. A thousand rooms, each holding a solitary soul, each hanging onto the line between life and death, wellness and illness. I was at each bedside simultaneously, delivering the same message. *You haven't been here before, but I have. I won't leave you here. No matter what happens, I'll stay with you.* It wasn't my message. It was His. They weren't my words, but He was delivering them through me. I'd since come to know that the "He" was Dhia. Even without knowing who had sent me, I'd felt I was where I was meant to be doing what I was meant to do exactly when I was meant to do it. It was a completely new feeling. It felt right. It felt solid. It felt good.

That flash, brief as it was, gave me several important things: a sense of purpose, a glimpse of Dhia's heart for his people, and a new definition for the word *beauty*. Dhia's heart for his people was the most beautiful thing I'd ever experienced, and I was willing to do anything just to experience it again.

I don't think we get many glimpses of true beauty or the heart of Dhia. Or maybe we do... We just don't recognize the glimpses for what they truly are. Maybe we catch Dhia's reflection in the face of a brand-new mother, exhausted and torn, leaning wide-eyed over her newborn baby, listening to its ragged, unsteady breath, living from breath to breath until a regular rhythm is established. Maybe we catch a hint of Him in the sweat on the brow of a surgeon in the operating theatre, his hands inside a fragile heart for twenty hours straight, knitting it together and willing it pump again. When a homeless man shares his sandwich... when a poor woman donates her last penny...

Dhia set fire to a latent part of my soul that day. It wasn't a new thing He gave me at the valley. The desire to love people in His way was something He'd built into me from the beginning. I just didn't know it was there until He lit it up. I wondered if He planted that desire in me before or after He created my spleen? Did He infuse me with an overactive dose of empathy at the exact same time He formed my heart? Maybe someday I'll ask Him. Discovering a calling is different than finding a new hobby. It's like drinking sand for years, then getting your first taste of water. *Wow, this stuff is awesome! Why haven't I noticed it before? I'm just* never *going back to sand.*

There were moments in the first few months of college when my Calling stood so tall and exciting that I couldn't wait for the next chapter to unfold. I looked for Dhia around every corner. I also had my share of dark panicky moments where self-doubt took over, and I wondered if I was living fully inside a delusion of my own making. When doubt crept in, I stole away to the little office in the administration building and prevailed upon Dhia to remind me who I was and who He was. I was placing my trust in someone I couldn't see or touch. It was frightening. I was learning to *choose* hope. The part of me that wanted amazing, earth-shattering things to happen warred with the part of me that knew I needed to glean more knowledge, understanding, and patience before I could move on.

Chemistry, Gaelic, German, anatomy and physiology, and Introduction to Nursing. My school schedule was full. Even so, I managed to meet a few friends. (Millie was proud!) Apparently, being a book nerd was much more popular at the university level than it was at the high school level. Most of the teens who had fought so desperately to fit into the same mold for the past four years reversed course, frantically trying to differentiate themselves from pack and find their niche in the world.

I adopted two friends rather quickly. Or rather, two friends adopted me. Aggie and Donal were without pretense. They were the sort of people in whose presence I was instantly comfortable. Donal was the only freshman boy registered as a nursing major. The opportunities for teasing on those grounds alone were truly endless. He didn't seem to mind the attention. Perhaps that was *why* he had chosen the nursing program. He was a tall fair-skinned lanky Irish boy who chose Aodhagan almost entirely to spite his purely anti-anything-Scottish parents.

Aggie was Hungarian and atypically gorgeous. She tried unsuccessfully to hide her poise and beauty in boxy sweatshirts and old running pants. Aggie was a double major: nursing and natural sciences. She didn't know what she wanted to do exactly except that it would involve trees... not hugging them but not burning them all down either. She thought trees were the key to answers to ecology, economy, oncology, philosophy, and pretty much everything else except perhaps marital issues. Aggie didn't plan to date or get married; then she met Donal. Aggie and Donal hit it off early in the school year and were soon inseparable. Before the end of the first quarter of the school year, they were finishing each other's sentences. They swore they were only friends but squabbled like an old married couple. Maybe some couples are like that… They skip the romance and go straight to the heart bond, and then hopefully, at some point, they come back around to the romance part of the equation, and it knocks their socks off.

For some inexplicable reason, the pair of them enjoyed having me as their third wheel. They dragged me to concerts. (Have I said yet that I really hate large venues packed with sweaty, loud bodies?) They took me to parks, free lectures, and even a few pubs where I would sip at a glass of cheap red wine or bitter lemon and people-watch. I kept busy with school, but my heart was still restless, its eye on the horizon. In early November, Aggie, Donal, and I were lounging in the back row at an Intro to Nursing lecture. The speaker was so boring, despite her charming Irish brogue, that a full third of the class was snoozing. Donal's head was tilted back, his neck at an impossible angle. He was fully asleep. I watched a little pool of drool collect on his freckled chin and wondered exactly what Aggie saw in him. Aggie was trying to talk me into taking an extra credit local history course.

"It's supposed to be an easy credit, Kiah, history or no… It's a one-day field trip, and then you turn in a paper afterward. Plus, it's a mostly deserted island, meaning lots of opportunity for you to indulge in solitude and introspection…" Aggie dangled the dearth of human interaction in front of me like a carrot. I suspected that I was being teased.

"Give me the specs."

"What are specs?" Aggie gestured to Donal's reading glasses with one eyebrow raised.

"No, not spectacles. Specifics, specifications. Details. What are the details?" I clarified.

"Oh, the details. It's a mystical island of some sort. They call it the Cradle of Christianity. Iona… have you heard of it?"

My head snapped up. The word *Iona* garnered my full attention. Iona was the name on the silver cross in my mother's box.

"Iona is an island?" I asked.

"Yeah, apparently." She shrugged. "Have you heard of it?"

"No. Yes. Sort of… I'll go with you, guys. At any rate, count me in."

'Seriously? Just like that?"

"Absolutely."

I didn't know how common the name Iona might be, but it was worth checking out.

IONA

The day of the history field trip dawned crisp and unexpectedly clear. The three of us bundled up in scarves, sweaters, and boots appropriate for day hiking. Just off the Isle of Mull in the Inner Hebrides, Iona was two hours by train and boat from Aodhagan. The island itself was small. The landscape was rangy and bleak, dotted with scrub grass and sparse trees. Low-slung stone and Earth hills undulated behind a small row of quaint houses and buildings just off the bay at the boat dock. The water was crystal clear and uncharacteristically calm. The shadows of the rocks that jutted into the water played across the shallow bay floor.

My breath came easier on Iona, and that seemed true for others as well. I watched the other students sigh and their shoulders relax as we exited the ferry and stepped onto the island.

Our eager guest professor greeted us at the information building. An assistant curator on loan from a museum in England, she was dressed in '70s secondhand shop semiprofessional style with matronly shoes and an olive drab cardigan. She ushered us into a small conference room that held less chairs than it did occupants. Aggie, Donal, and I stood against the side wall near the front. There were too many people in a small space. I felt like I could smell every single one of them... bad aftershave, a hint of fried onions, toothpaste, the body odor of someone who'd recently had too much to drink... I hoped the lecture didn't last long. The professor was completely enthralled with her topic.

"The island of Iona has so much to tell you. You must listen to her stories!" she gesticulated wildly as if she were reading a fantastic children's book to a rapt group of first graders. "She is shrouded in mystery but so important historically. She's one of my favorite places in the world, and it is my privilege to share her with you," she gushed.

Donal gave me a dubious sidelong glance.

"It is rumored that before AD 563 this island was a sacred site for druid worshippers, but exactly what they did here and when exactly they began doing it remain a mystery. Druid worshippers today are still drawn to the island. The earliest confirmed happenings on the island were in AD 563, when the Irish monk Colum Kille and twelve of his followers established a monastery here. Colum Kille is known today as St. Columba. He was somewhat of a character. He banned women and cows from the island, citing as his reason that 'where there is a cow, there is a woman, and where there is a woman, there is mischief.'"

"Well, thet part is true," Donal muttered.

Aggie glared and shushed him.

"Despite his idiosyncrasies, Colum Kille was well respected and vastly influential. He was instrumental in helping Christianity spread successfully from here throughout Europe. This island has often been called the Cradle of Christianity. As such, Christians still come to this island to remember her past and hazard a brush with the divine."

She went on to say that Iona was repeatedly and brutally attacked by the Vikings. Many monks were killed. The Vikings didn't settle on the island, however, and the monks not killed during the raids created a special book containing the first four Gospels of the New Testament of the Bible in Latin.

"The book was an elaborate and artistic work with a golden, jewel-studded cover. In AD 807, we believe due to the repeated raids, the book was moved to the Irish island of Kells. Sometime in the eleventh century, however, the book was stolen. The pages themselves have since been recovered. The cover was never found."

The tiny hairs on my neck stood suddenly erect, and cold sweat beads formed at the base of my spine. All the moisture in my mouth evaporated, and I couldn't swallow.

I have it! I thought, clapping my hand over my mouth to make sure I didn't actually say the words aloud.

I was quite certain that the cover to the book of Kells was sitting in the trunk in Nan's attic.

"Are you all right?" Aggie's voice came to me as if from a long distance and through a layer of cotton. I made a concerted effort to connect my gaze with hers. Her face swam into focus.

"Are you sure you are all right?" she asked again.

Everyone in the room was staring at me. The professor, standing quite near me, stepped quickly backward. She probably hoped I wouldn't vomit on her sensible sturdy shoes. It was likely a smart move. Someone stowed a chair under me, and I sank into it.

"Dizzy... sorry, just dizzy," I managed to mumble, feeling embarrassment flush my neck.

"Water, though. Water would be nice," I added.

"I have ginger," the professor offered. She meant soda. "Perhaps you could use the sugar..."

"Please, and thank you," I accepted the soda and sipped at it. It was too sweet.

"Please, go ahead with your talk. I'll be fine," I assured her. I still felt shaky, but the soda was helping, and I needed time to gather my thoughts. Everyone returned their attention to the guide, only occasionally glancing at my direction.

Get it together! I told myself forcefully. *A Dhia, why? Why do I have that book cover?* I asked silently.

Just listen, came the clear answer. *Just listen.*

Listen... there was that word again. I began to realize my pattern of begging Dhia to communicate, then freaking out when He did. That was something I needed to work on. I took a deep breath and tried to focus.

"Columba's original abbey was destroyed completely, but in the twelfth century, a Benedictine Abbey was established. One building remains from that time—St. Oran's Chapel. During the Reformation, the island was razed again. All but three of the many Celtic crosses were destroyed. It is important to note that Celtic Christianity is different in some ways from Roman Christianity. Many people wanted the Celtic version of Christianity done away with. Even today, Iona remains a testament to changing religious winds. In 1938, George MacLeod came to Iona and founded a Christian community dedicated to social justice and mercy. This community still exists and today endeavors to live out the Gospel of Jesus Christ in a new way that meets the needs of the world's people. But remember, this is *not* a place belonging to just one religion. Many seekers come to Iona from many walks of life and many faiths. Iona is well-known as a 'thin place.' This means some people believe the separation between the heavens and the earth, or the real and the spiritual, seems thinner here. Of course, that is a matter of opinion. I'll give you a few hours to explore the island and see for yourself. There are walking maps on the front desk. The island is small so it's hard to get lost, but please take a map anyway. I would like to meet you back here just past lunchtime. Does two o'clock sound good?" She tapped her watch, and most of the students looked reflexively at their own watches, nodding assent. The lecture was over. Chairs scraped and bags rustled.

"Are you feeling better now?" Aggie asked again, turning to me. "You looked awful."

"Sorry, I'm not sure what that was. Maybe lack of sleep, but I'm better now. Where to?"

"I was going to suggest a hike," Donal hedged, "but are ye up for that?"

"Totally. I could use the air."

It was chilly outside but not raining, and the smell of dirt and sea far outshone the smell of too many bodies in one tiny room. As stunning as it was to learn about the book of Kells, I got the getting the distinct impression it wasn't the sole reason for my presence at Iona.

Listen, I heard again as we filed out of the building. The professor had called Iona a thin place—a place where people experienced the divine more easily. I could see why people found peace and spiritual meaning there. The quiet, the lack of stimulation, the waves, the ruins, and the greenery—it all felt uninterrupted, uncluttered. It was easier to slow down and tune in without the bright colors, intrusive noises, and flashing lights of regular life. Perhaps Iona reminded people to listen to what had already been there all along… their hearts, their consciences, and Dhia Himself.

We chose the southern trail toward the back side of the island. Aggie and Donal were soon embroiled in one of their usual conversations. The spoke in shorthand, finishing each other's incomplete sentences sometimes verbally, sometimes with facial expressions, eye rolls, and hand gestures. It was mostly unintelligible to others including me. I tuned them out and lagged behind, trying to clear my mind, silently asking Dhia to speak clearly and not let me miss anything He was saying.

I have the cover to a historically important book? Really? And what's up with Iona? What is my connection to this place? Why am I here? Questions bounced around inside my skull like popcorn in a popper.

"Wait and listen!" Dhia's words rang out clearly enough that I wondered if they were audible. I glanced at Aggie and Donal to see if they'd heard them. They hadn't.

Aggie had brought her camera along and was soon busily snapping pictures of plants and fungi. We seemed to be the only students to have chosen the southern route. We climbed the gentle hills with minimal effort. I'd been walking quite a bit lately—taking long walks off campus in the countryside regardless of the weather. My legs, especially my calves, had definitely benefitted. They were rock hard and reliable.

As we walked, I got the niggling feeling that my feet were taking me somewhere important. The hair on my neck stood on end in a familiar way. We rounded a corner near the back bay, and Donal nearly trampled a small Asian woman sitting in the middle of the trail.

"I'm so sorry." Donal leaned over to help the woman up, but she jumped quickly to her feet.

"My fault," she said and turned to face us, brushing the dust from her jeans.

It was Fa. Unmistakably.

For a moment, I wondered if Donal and Aggie could actually see her, but of course, they could. Donal had tripped over her. I felt my worlds collide.

"Hello, Kiah." Fa smiled. I hugged her impulsively. She was real.

"You know each other?" Aggie asked.

"Well, yes. Fa, this is Aggie and Donal. Aggie and Donal, this is Fa. She's a, um… friend. An old friend," I finished lamely. *Was I old enough to claim that I had old friends?* I wasn't sure how to explain her presence. I looked to Fa but could tell by her expression that she wasn't in the same quandary I was. She didn't feel the need to explain anything.

"Hello, Kiah's friends," she said briskly, hands in the pockets of her jeans. Her oversized pink sweatshirt looked as if it had been machine washed repeatedly, and I wondered if that was possible. I was having trouble reconciling her clothing and her location with what I knew of her. Still surprised, more than a little excited and totally not sure of what to say next, I waited for someone else to speak.

"Since I see you now, I am hoping to talk with you more. 'Catch up with you' is maybe what you say?" Fa said.

"'Course," Donal answered for me. "Ye can talk and walk together, and Aggie and I will go on. Meet you at the village after lunch?"

"Good," Fa answered, nodding agreeably.

I nodded as well. My tongue was tied to the floor of my mouth.

Aggie leaned close and whispered, "I'll see you later, okay? We will talk." She was hungry for an explanation. So was I.

She and Donal consulted the trail map and continued on, glancing back over their shoulders at us a few times. Once they were out of sight, Fa climbed wordlessly up over the hill to the left of the trail, and I followed. We crested the hill, and Fa started down the other side toward a small deep bay. She glanced around, confirming we were alone, then began to remove her sweatshirt.

"Heavy shirt off," Fa demanded. She began to unbutton her pants as well.

"You swim, yes?" she continued.

"Well yes, but wait…," I started.

"No time for wait," she said, pointing at my shirt and gesturing for me to remove it.

"Your shirt, pants, too heavy. Take everything off. You will need it dry later."

Skinny-dipping in the cold ocean? Fa was certainly well on her way to her birthday suit. There didn't seem to be any choice but to join her. I had waited too long and had too many nagging questions, to pass up this opportunity; but it was *cold*, and I didn't relish the idea of removing my clothing. I was soon naked, shivering and feeling ridiculous. Fa stuffed our clothing into a cloth bag and stashed it in a deep hole in the rock under a nearby ledge. She scrambled over the last few rocks and into the water.

"Come, come," she urged.

"You hold breath. We go deep."

"Ah, I don't dive. We have to go down?" I objected. My toes curled, grasping the rock. "I stay afloat and swim, okay? But I don't dive, and I don't really swim well underwater."

"No problem, I pull you down." Fa smiled as if her words should reassure me. She grabbed my arm and hauled me into the water. It was frigid and took my breath away. I felt my blood vessels shrink, instinctively conserving their heat. My bones cringed. Fa let me catch my breath for a few moments.

"Okay, now you take a deep breath. Hold it. I pull you down. You follow me. You will be okay."

I was becoming numb, and my mind was in full fearful revolt. The water was deep enough to obscure the ocean floor under our feet.

A Dhia, help me, I can't do this without you, I'm so afraid! I prayed silently.

I felt a small measure of calmness, like a steadying hand on my shoulder. I stopped treading water, took a deep breath, and nodded at Fa. She kicked down hard, and I followed her. She was stronger, much stronger than she looked. She continued downward, leaving the light at the surface of the water. My lungs screamed insistently, but the calm still accompanied me, overruling my body's impulse to gasp.

Down, down, fast and steady, until the darkness gave way again to light. I was confused. Had I somehow missed us reversing course and heading back the way we came?

We broke the surface of the water, and I gasped, lungs burning. Fa was pulling me toward land but not the land we'd left. Instead of gray rocks, the bay was lined with soft pinkish sand. The sunlight was warm on my face. My knees dragged bottom as we reached the shore.

"See, you did good. You are strong. Next time, not so hard."

"Next time?" I protested, gasping.

Fa didn't seem to hear me. She was on her feet again, bounding across the sand, wringing out her hair as she went. We were not in the horseshoe valley.

PETRA, AKA THE ROCK

Fa retrieved a package from a crook in a nearby willow tree and extracted clothing one small set and one large set of clothing like that I'd worn on my last visit. Fa had obviously anticipated my arrival. I was regaining tingly sensation in my limbs and beginning to shiver. It seemed to be early morning. Three moons (yes… three,) two silver and one lavender, hung full and round in the periwinkle sky. A white ball of sun snuck over the horizon to join them. The bay was a gentle wide arch, and creeping vines covered in delicate blue flowers crept all the way to the water in many places. Small flotillas of vines and flowers bobbed on the surface of the water. Inland, the creeping vines gave way to soft short grasses and more scattered willow trees. The tree branches, heavy with lemony green and white flowers, draped all the way to the ground. They swayed in the breeze and gave off an earthy sweet fragrance, like vetiver and clove. The terrain stretched for many miles with a low-slung lazy green mountain range far in the distance.

"You dry?" Fa asked.

"Mostly, I think," I answered.

She handed me my clothing, and we dressed. It felt strange to wear what amounted to hospital scrubs in such a rugged environment. Of course, there wasn't much about the situation that *didn't* feel strange.

"Iona's gate, *this* gate, is a permanent gate," she explained.

"Gate? What gate?"

"Your gate, in your town, the one you came through before... was it last year?" She counted in her head, using her fingers for reference but gave up quickly. "Any way, no matter... whenever. That was a temporary gate, but Iona's gate is always open. So it is harder to get to. No one can find it. It must be hidden."

"No wonder no one finds it. They'd have to be crazy to dive deep in that icy bay. Who would ever think of that?"

"Exactly." Fa nodded in agreement.

"We have only a few days. We must be quick."

I sorted her meaning from her words before I responded.

"Oh no. I need to be back in a few hours. If I'm not back, they will go looking," I protested.

"No matter. The time is different—remember? A few days here is a few minutes on Earth. So no problem." She waved her hand dismissively in the air.

My heart thudded. Confirmation: I was no longer on Earth. I felt my eyes grow to the size of saucers. Going with the flow had been easier on my first visit, when it seemed quite possible I was merely dreaming. I no longer had that reassurance. Fa was real. The beach was real. My logical mind felt stretched to the breaking point. Fa reached for my hand and pulled me to my feet. I didn't understand where I was or why time didn't seem to work the way it was supposed to.

"Come, we talk at the tree," Fa said.

We walked up the beach a ways and turned inland toward an enormous tree whose branches grew in a large low *U* shape, forming a natural bench seat. The bark was covered with dark thick moss. There was plenty of room for Fa to sit on one bend of the *U* and *I* on the other. We nestled in.

"You just said that time is different on Earth. As if Earth was there, and we are here. If that is true, then where is *here*? And how can *here* even possibly be *not* Earth?"

"You listen and don't worry to understand everything, okay?" I nodded.

"Here is not Earth. Here is, well, maybe you can call it the Rock. Petra." She paused.

"And?" I prompted.

"And, well, it's not Earth." The conversation was chasing its own tail.

"Okay, well, if it isn't Earth, then exactly what is it? Where am I? Why am I here?"

"So many questions but there are no simple answers. Please have patience. I will tell you, but you must be patient. Slowly, hm?"

I took a deep breath.

"Yes! Better." Fa approved. "Okay, so this is a planet. You know, Himself made many planets. Many have no life, and they are beautiful in other ways. A few are special, beautiful, with life. Human life. Earth is this way. Petra is this way." She smiled, stroking the soft moss absently. I wanted to prompt her to continue, but remembered her request for patience and bit my tongue.

"Petra was meant for humans. These doors, God's gates, were meant for humans, so they could live in either place. Petra or Earth. But humans on Earth… you know the choices we made." Fa's eyes softened. "So when He closed the gates to the garden, He hid the gates to the Rock."

"Which garden?" I blurted.

"The garden of Eden."

I had read about the garden of Eden. When Adam and Eve sinned, God had sent Adam and Eve out of the beautiful garden He had made for them, then stationed an angel with a flashing sword at the entrance to bar them from returning. I had seen a glimpse of it during my visit with Sam.

"Is Petra a part of the garden of Eden?" I asked, but Fa didn't answer my question.

"There are many gates that lead to Petra, all over the world. They are hidden. Sometimes, someone falls through a gate… an accident. When this happens, we return them home. Long ago, people did not fall through so very often. Maybe there are many more people in the world now, so we stay busier with the rescues than long ago."

"Who is 'we'? Who returns people to Earth?"

"The Called," she answered, simply.

Called. There was that word. It gave me goose bumps.

"And I am Called," I stated flatly, feeling weight and truth in the words.

Fa nodded in agreement. "You are Called."

"Called to what?"

"That answer is long and wide and deep. It will take a lifetime to know. But it is a call to serve."

"Do many people who are Called live here?" I asked.

Fa shook her head. "Not many. Petra was meant for a shelter, a haven for those who needed rest and healing for a long time. At one time, the people who came here did not fall accidentally through the gates. God chose carefully who would come to Petra for healing. The Called had the job to bring them here for a time, then send them home. The difference in time is good for this... long here, short there. There is much time for healing. Anyway... that all worked well for a very long time, I think. Then a group of people with evil in their heart found a gate, and they came through." Fa's face clouded over.

"Couldn't Dhia just close them out?" I asked.

"*Dhia* is Gaelic for God, yes?"

"Yes," I said.

"Your name for Him?"

"Yes," I said, feeling self-conscious.

"Do not worry. Your name for Him is close to your heart. It is a good thing. Of course He could have closed them out. He can do anything... but He did not."

"Why?" I asked.

"I do not know why. He loves us, and He wants us to love him in return. He made us this way... to love, but not everyone chooses well. He asks us to love Him, but He lets us choose. He does not stop choice. So sometimes bad things happen, and then not everything seems good. Those are the bad consequences of sin. He does not always stop them. What He does not stop, He can always redeem. His best is still possible... This I know." Fa laid a fist over her heart with firm resolve.

"This group that's given over to evil, do they have a name?"

"Their names are Kress. They came here long time ago. He gave them their choice, but He gave them a boundary too. They have land for themselves, and they do not leave it," she said adamantly.

"They never cross the boundaries?" I asked. I knew the nature of people and boundaries. It was hard to believe that they fully respected them.

"Never. The boundary means death to them. Our side of the boundary is ugly and scary for them. They are afraid of God. They are afraid of the Blues. They do not want any part of us."

"How many Kress people are there?" I asked.

"Many people, thousands maybe now."

I drew my face into a question mark. "Do they keep coming here from Earth?"

"More Kress? No. They live only here." Fa shook her head sadly. It wasn't a topic she relished.

"Sometimes, though… someone who is *not* Kress falls through a gate." She shuddered and continued. "When a person falls through, we get them back home. This is a part of our Calling. The Kress people have chosen every evil. *Every evil*, Kiah. God has given them over to their choice. They are very dark. They hug the darkness."

"But you said they fear God? People usually deny God when they just don't believe in Him. Is that what you mean?"

"No," Fa responded. She was contemplating, choosing her words carefully.

"God is more easily seen here. Here, He moves in ways to be heard, seen, smelled, felt. It is hard to explain this until you see it. But you will see it. You will understand. The Kress… they know God is real. They believe God is real. They hate Him, but they do not deny Him because they cannot. They see His power. They are very fearful people, very strange. Sometimes, almost not like people at all… so evil and so dark. The Kress cannot return to Earth. That is part of their boundary. The gates at Kress territory only work one way, only to the Rock, never back."

"Why? Why didn't God close their gate all together? I don't understand."

Fa placed her fist over her heart again in what seemed to be a sign of faith—her way of showing that, though she didn't understand what Dhia was doing, she trusted Him.

She shook her head. "I don't know why."

Just then, something dawned on me.

"The wall of dark clouds, by the mountain, from when I came here before. Is that the Kress boundary?" I asked.

"Yes." Fa nodded.

"In the Kress country, sin is stronger, even much stronger than on Earth. Like ink, like a stain… sin is this dark. On Petra, the dark is darker, but the light is lighter. Sin and goodness are both stronger. If Earth is gray space, Petra is black and white."

Fa jumped down from her perch and drew a map in the dirt on the ground at the base of the tree.

"Here is Kress," she said, scratching lines across a medium-sized area at the center of the map, which, delineating the space from the rest; then she gestured to the rest of the map. "The other space… this space is clear. Light. It is our space. We can go freely anywhere. Here, there, wherever there is no dark cloud boundary. We have many places." She jabbed her finger into the dirt at various sites on the map, leaving a myriad of dots. "There, there, even there. Many places," she repeated.

"You said the Kress are afraid of the Blues… Who are the Blues?"

"The Blues are another name for those who are Called. A nickname given to us by the Kress."

"Why Blue?" I asked.

"For a long time, we have worn only the blue robes when we go into Kress territories. They see us, they see we are wearing blue, and they are afraid," she explained.

"Wait a minute." I was confused. "You said 'when we go in' to their territory. I thought you said we don't go in there."

"No, I did not say that at all. I said they do not come out from their territory," Fa clarified. "You see sometimes, someone falls through a gate, and the Kress take them as a slave." She climbed back up in the branches of the tree beside me and looked me in the eye.

"The Blues go in to rescue them, to take them back. We rescue the men and boys that they take, then bring them to the healing rooms. They need help. They need healing before they return to Earth. This is hard but *so* important. Do you understand?"

"Maybe a little. I'm beginning to," I answered. "But why boys? Men? Why not rescue the women? Don't women fall through the gates sometimes?"

I wasn't sure I understood the gates completely—how they worked, where they were—but there were only so many questions I could ask at once.

"Sometimes, a few women come through but not so much trouble with the women. The Kress do not keep women. They throw them clear of the boundaries. We find them and return them to home, so this is no problem."

"But why would they keep only men and boys?" I was still confused.

Fa obviously didn't want to answer, but she pushed on. "The Kress men use their own women for breeding. They think women are necessary but repulsive. The women also hate the men. The women live separately. They have separate camps, separate lives from their men. They make food, and they make babies. They share only one thing… They share their hate. Kress men place a high value on healthy, strong men from Earth. Valuable for slave labor, for hard work, and, well, for"—she shuddered, repulsed—"for pleasure. You understand?"

"Then why don't they just date each other?" I asked.

"It's not about love and caring, Kiah. This is different than that. For the Kress, this kind of slavery is very much about domination and power. Do you understand?"

Her eyes pleaded with me to understand, so she wouldn't have to explain further.

I understood, suddenly and fully, as if a veil had been lifted from my eyes; and I saw what I didn't want to see. Given over to hate in every way, the Kress valued evil domination in every sense of the word. I felt sick to my stomach and pitched my head to the left, vomiting behind the tree. I remembered the fear in the eyes of the young man in the Valley, and my heart ached. I felt dizzy, and the world spun. I didn't have a clear picture of what the Kress were or how they lived, but I caught a taste of the depth of their evil, and horror and utter sadness racked me.

"In the Kress, true evil has run its course and does exactly as it pleases with no restrainer. There is total separation of men from women, heart from heart. Total hate. This kind of evil is not new. They have taken evil as far as it will go, but each sin itself is not new."

I nodded. I completely understood what she meant. There were so many references to evil deeds in the history books, and the world seemed to grow just a little darker every day. I wondered how long it would be until the world followed in Kress' footsteps.

"Remember, though… the goodness of God is always more than the evil of the Kress or the evil on the Earth. Even when we see only the darkness, we always remember the goodness of God."

"But I don't understand why Dhia allows that! Just… why?" I grappled for a possible answer.

"He allows choice, Kiah. You know this. You see this. Choose Him or not choose Him, you always have this choice to make. You can love Him and love what is good, or you can hate Him and choose evil. Kress have this choice too, and they have made their choice for darkness. God is respecter of person's choice. Bad choice makes bad consequences. The Earth shows us many bad consequences. You see this all the time. Bad things happen to good people. Such bad things. Until God returns to Earth to judge this evil, it will be this way and worse." Fa shook her head sadly. "But God gives hope too, yes? He asks us to love and to be His hands, His feet. He calls us to serve. His word says, 'Harvest is plenty, but workers are few.' Many are called and few answer. But you… you have said yes not just to His gift but to a special Calling. He made you for this Calling, Kiah. He gave you everything you need for this work, for this life. He built it into you. You will help us. Help us heal them and send them home."

I felt drained. It all seemed so far beyond what I could handle. I felt completely inadequate.

Fa responded as if she had heard my inner self-doubt. "You feel not ready, not prepared, like you can't do any of this, right?" she asked.

I nodded. That was exactly what I was feeling. "Good. That means you are perfectly ready… because Blues can do nothing on their own. We need to know we can do nothing on our own. The things we do can only be done through God. We depend on His strength. We listen. If you are strong on your own and rely only on yourself, this is not good. You will fail."

"Then I'm your girl… because I have plenty of experience falling on my face," I quipped.

"If you know you can do nothing, then He can do everything. You are perfect person for this job because you know you are not perfect on your own. You learn to listen, to lean, and He will be strong through you, okay?" Fa leaned close and studied my face.

I must not have seemed reassured.

"I give you so much information and no time to process. We can have lunch. Then you will feel better. We can talk more after," she announced, jumping to her feet.

I looked around, bewildered, wondering where lunch would materialize from. The back of my neck began to vibrate, and I immediately experienced equal parts dread and anticipation. Apparently, we would be headed to lunch by air.

"Again? Do we ever get to travel along the ground around here?"

Fa grinned. "Oh yes, *lots* of walking. Just not today. There are no cars or trains and not many roads. The land is big, and the Blues' places are very far apart. Remember, He is more visible here. He takes care of what we need. Like manna for the Israelites, right?" I thought of the food that God provided in the desert for His people when no food source was available. It fell straight from the sky. I looked up, half expecting manna to fall from the sky just to prove Fa's point, but the sky was empty.

"I don't remember the Israelites being yanked off their feet into the air very often," I whined, palms sweating.

"Maybe not very often. But remember Phillip and the Ethiopian?"

I drew a blank. "I must have missed that story."

"God told His servant Phillip to go to a certain place where he met an Ethiopian man. God had special plans for that man. He sent Phillip to explain the story of Jesus to him. The Ethiopian man heard and believed that day. Phillip took him to the river and baptized him. The man was very important. Have you heard of the Coptic Christians?" she asked.

I nodded.

"The Coptic Christians descended from this man."

"And how does that explain my need to travel above the ground... ?"

"Patience! I am not finished with the story! Phillip was needed somewhere else, right away. God took straight into the air from the river, and He disappeared. God delivered him to the next place he needed to go. So... like that"—she waved her arm skyward—"that's the way we go."

I made a mental note to read that story. Knowing some guy in the Bible traveled this way didn't make me feel better about flying. I was still nervous.

Suddenly, we shot straight up, high above the tree. My stomach lurched.

"This way... feet pointy," Fa instructed. She was a sure straight arrow headed for its mark. I was more of a sky octopus.

"More practice, then you will feel better, okay?" Fa tried to suppress a giggle.

I crossed my unruly arms and legs, adjusted my position, and felt the tension on my neck lessen. Then I stared at Fa. Extending from the base of her neck, almost invisible, was what looked like an enormous pair of wings. They only barely blurred the view of the horizon, as if they were made of water. I started to wobble and redirected my attention forward. We were moving fast, much faster than I had gone on my previous trip, more than one hundred feet off the ground. The landscape was a blur below me, and I quickly learned that looking straight ahead lessened my dizziness.

Fa banked left, up and over the low hills I had seen in the distance. I followed, pleased to managing to bank without wobbling. Progress! I was pleased. More empty hills spread out before us. There were no buildings, no dwellings—only flocks of birds that dispersed, alarmed, as we passed. After a while, the hills melded into mountains, and the foliage became denser.

"Up," Fa shouted. We nosed up at a forty-five-degree angle, barely clearing a large tree-covered hill. What I saw on the other side took my breath away. It was the single largest mountain I had ever seen. We continued climbing but not fast enough to clear it. I looked at Fa, who seemed to be slowing, pulling her toes up toward her body. I followed suit.

Fa pointed at a small dark spot in the cheer cliff wall before us. "Cave."

I nodded and fell in behind her, hoping I wouldn't bowl her over as we entered the opening.

The mouth of the cave plunged us from bright daylight into utter darkness as we entered it.

"Okay, down now, arms in," Fa shouted from her position just ahead of me. I pulled my legs under me and subconsciously clenched my eyes shut. Miraculously, I came to an almost complete stop before my feet touched the ground. I skidded a few inches and landed on my butt. My eyes adjusted to the darkness, and I could see the outline of my friend standing a few feet in front of me.

"Good landing. You didn't smash me." She gave me a thumbs-up. We apparently shared the same concern about my flight skills. We were in a cavern of some sort. I couldn't see the ceiling or the walls in the darkness, but the echo of Fa's voice told me it was quite large.

"You stay," Fa directed, jogging ahead into the darkness. I sat on the cold stone cave floor, trying to catch my breath. I could hear water trickling all around me, but the ground below me seemed dry. I was starving! A few minutes later, a familiar blue square of flame appeared before me in the distance. Then another and another as the braziers, set end to end, basically lit each other. Soon light flickered all over the cavern walls. It looked like a giant tic-tac-toe board. Stalactites hung from the ceiling far above us. The cave floor was crisscrossed with small rivers. Some of the rivers steamed.

"Careful, some are hot," Fa warned.

"Come." She waved me on in her direction. I gingerly crossed the cave floor to join her. We entered an open mouthed tunnel that ran upward at a mild angle and to the left. Fa touched the wall that ran the left side of the tunnel; and blue flame shot ahead of us, down the track, lighting out way. The rock walls of the tunnel were fascinating. Mildly shiny, they looked and even felt more like metal than stone.

"What is this place?" I asked Fa. We were almost at a jog.

"This is the cave,'" she said.

I needed to learn to be more specific with my questions. I reloaded my words and tried again.

"What is the cave *for* exactly?"

"For emergencies. We really don't use the big room for much, but I wanted you to see it. Only one time, I remember we used it for protection from a storm that lasted over a month. That was a long time ago. We use these tunnels sometimes when we stop over on the way somewhere else. You are paying attention to where everything is, yes? In case you need to come alone some time."

"Wait a minute," I objected, "I didn't know I was supposed to be memorizing things, places… Why would I need to come here alone?"

One step at a time. Just listen, came Dhia's voice from within.

Lord, help me listen. Help me pay attention, I responded silently.

Fa made a small impatient sound and stopped abruptly, turning to face me.

"You never know what you will need or when you will need it. You must *always* learn, Kiah… every day, in every place. This is true here, and it is true on Earth. Your mother taught you this, yes?"

"Well, yeah. I guess she did." My mother never missed a word, a beat, or even a nuance. She was always learning, always recording, just in case she needed to use it in an argument later on.

"You listen to your mother. Mothers are very smart"—Fa turned back around and headed down the tunnel again, then threw another word back over her shoulder at me—"usually."

"If I had listened to my mother, I wouldn't be here," I muttered.

We finally stopped in front of a nondescript door. The latch opened smoothly, and we entered. Fa lit the lights, and the room was bathed in a soft blue glow. The space was simple. Hewn into the walls on both sides of the long narrow room were wide bench seats lined with simple tickings stuffed with materials unknown to me. Someone had hung loose linen curtains on the walls. It made the room feel strangely cozy. I sat down on the nearest bench seat. It was surprisingly comfortable. The far end of the room housed a rudimentary kitchen. Fa retrieved fragrant rice patties, two bread rolls, two jars of water, and a few pieces of fruit from an icebox and joined me. We ate in peaceful silence.

After we ate, Fa showed me to the makeshift toilet, little more than a bucket in the next cavern over. Quite a hefty flow of water rushed through a depression in the rock at the back of the small room. It served as a rudimentary gray water system.

Once we had eaten and cleaned up after ourselves we were on the move again. We put out the lights and closed the doors and continued down the tunnel.

"How far does this tunnel go?" I asked Fa. I wasn't in love with the close quarters.

"All the way through the mountain," she answered, "but we won't go that far."

I waited for further explanation, but none came.

We came to a Y in the tunnel. The left fork continued downward. The right fork ran sharply upward a few feet and ended at a wooden door. We climbed the right fork, opened the door, and stepped outside into the base of a deep crater in the central peak of the mountain. The sky was clear, and the sun was straight overhead. The floor of the crater was stone covered in silt that plumed up behind our feet as we walked. I followed Fa to a man-made ladder, which we climbed almost to the top of the crater wall to reach. I was out of breath by the time we reached the landing and opened the door in the rock wall. We entered a small hospital room of the sort you might find in a Beatrix Potter children's story. I half expected to see a large rabbit pop in through the ceiling, bearing carrot soup and castor oil. I heard the sound of rushing water, quite a lot of water, but couldn't identify its source.

"Help me open this." Fa motioned for me to help her pull a thick rope, part of a pulley system attached to the thick wooden doors that made up the entire ceiling. We pulled the ceiling doors open, and sunlight flooded in. Central to the room was a tall flat cot with a sturdy handmade mattress atop it. Cupboards flanked the head of the bed. Fa opened the cupboards, revealing medical supplies of all sorts: IV tubing, medicine bottles, dressings, oils, herbs, and many things I didn't even recognize.

"This is healing room," Fa explained, "very far away from the other stations, so not used so much. You remember Hedi?"

I nodded, remembering the young blond woman with pillow lines on her face.

"Hedi stocks this room and others. Such a hard worker and so quiet. She likes to work alone."

Fa moved toward a recessed bench seat hewn into the wall. This bench seat was quite wide, extending a few feet into the wall and formed a niche about the length and width of a full-sized bed. The ceiling of the niche was just high enough to allow a person on the bed to sit straight up. I could see a few square braziers and some recessed shelving along the back wall of the niche.

"Blues sleep here"—she gestured to the sleeping niche—"and here." She pointed to an identical alcove at the far side of the room, then opened the cupboards above the alcove. "Blankets, towels, clothes all go here."

Pulling back a large curtain, she revealed an adjacent alcove that ran at a right angle to the main room.

"Kitchen. Be careful of the hole," she said.

At the far side of the kitchen alcove was a large hole in the floor, at least five feet across, that led straight down into darkness. A waterfall ran down the back wall. Fa picked up a glass from the counter and filled it from the waterfall.

"Clean water," she assured me, and drank. "No pollution here, and no animals up this high. Very safe."

She lit the light squares in the kitchen and prepared a basin of soap and water. We both washed our hands in it. Then she poured the remains down the near side of the large hole in the floor.

The soap made my fingers buzz and immediately turn slightly red.

"Best soap ever," Fa informed me. "Comes from a tree here. Antibacterial. But be careful… Don't eat it."

I hadn't been planning to eat it. I opened my mouth to ask what would happen if did eat it; but Fa stopped me, shaking her head, and pointed me back toward the main room. "Not much time. So maybe you can look at supplies, to become more familiar with this area."

"Time for what? Is someone coming?" I asked, puzzled. Fa, busy heating water on the kitchen cupboards, didn't answer. I had been under the impression she was giving me a welcome tour. Apparently not. I wondered what was coming next.

A STITCH IN TIME

I didn't have to wait long for my curiosity to be satisfied. As I stepped past the kitchen curtain, I heard a loud rustling sound, and a shadow fell over the bed. I pressed myself against the wall and watched as a Blue I didn't recognize dropped flat, facedown into the room and hovered over the bed. She resembled an eagle clutching a motionless body, one bigger than her own, to her chest. The legs of the man she carried were strapped to her legs, his body strapped to her chest. Fa rushed over and undid the straps. They carefully lowered the man to the bed. Another Blue dropped into the room immediately behind her, and they set to work on the seemingly lifeless form.

The patient was apparently still alive. He was covered with dirt, blood, and bruises—some fresh and some obviously old; but I saw him shift slightly. The scent of infection, like impending death, hung heavy in the air. I wanted to help but felt totally useless and paralyzed.

Fa swung to face me and pointed at my nose.

"You watch and pray," she directed.

Relieved to have some direction, I climbed up onto the sleeping niche behind, tucking myself out of the way, and began to pray fervently as I watched.

The women worked seamlessly together, barely speaking to each other. One woman, short, stocky, and blond, busied herself with IV supplies and medicines and instruments. She quickly cleaned a patch of skin on his arm and inserted an IV, then hung a large pink glass bottle of fluid and Yed in a small glass bottle of orange liquid.

Satisfied that the fluids were flowing, she stepped away to adjust the pulleys and close the ceiling doors, darkening. She lit the braziers.

The willowy woman who had carried the patient captured and held most of my attention. She couldn't have been more than ten years older than me, but her long silver hair hung far past her shoulders. Free of her human cargo, she stretched her back, pulled a clean smock on over her clothing, and quickly gathered her hair into a twist and tacked it to the top of her head. Fa and the other women donned similar smocks. Fa brought hot water, washcloths, and scissors to a tray near the man's bed. The woman set to work, praying quietly under her breath. I can't say for sure how I knew that she was praying except that I felt it. Sure and steady, her prayers filled the room like sweet perfume that battled the smell of death in the air. Fa checked his pulse and smiled, surprised and pleased. She nodded reassuringly.

The silver-haired woman wiped a thick layer of grime from the man's face, uncovering his eyes, nose, mouth. Fa ferried the dirty washcloths away and brought back fresh ones whenever they were needed. The man was breathing on his own in a ragged sort of way. Fa and the silver-haired woman checked him over quickly, turning him gently to the left and right.

"No large bleeding." Fa glanced in my direction, making sure I was listening. A blue glow played under the other woman's fingers as they moved, assessing and cleaning. I couldn't draw my eyes away from the gentle, confident movement of her hands. The man's shirt, laden with filth and blood, was pulled and cut away from his shredded chest. He would need stitches. Many stitches. The shorter woman opened a suture tray and readied it.

Fa and the silver-haired woman washed every bit of dirt from his chest, scrubbing in a way that made me wince. The man never roused. Fa brought a small bottle of silver fluid from the cabinet and carefully poured it into a laceration on the man's chest. Both of the other Blues held the man's chest and arms down to the surface of the bed, bracing him in case he flailed while Fa lit the silver fluid. Flame flared up suddenly, quickly, along the angry furrow, then went out.

The man groaned slightly; his eyes fluttered open and then closed again.

The short woman adjusted the flow of the orange medicine, and they repeated the therapy, pouring and lighting the silver fluid repeatedly until every laceration on his chest had been seared. Then Fa and the silver-haired woman began stitching the wounds closed.

"Come." Fa motioned for me to join them. I approached the bed and stood beside the silver-haired woman who didn't seem to register my presence. She stitched quickly and deftly, still muttering prayers.

"Here. We start here." Fa pointed to an untended wound and explained what she was doing as she worked.

"See? Start here. Bite with the needle, all the way through. If too shallow, it pulls through. No good. Pull to here, then cross and bite here. Pull until you have short on one side, long on the other. Loop, loop, grab short side, and pull. Then loop, grab short side again and pull. Then one more time. Pull tight. Simple."

I nodded, fascinated, watching her work. I fought the urge to wince every time the curved needles bit into the raw tissue.

The short blond woman handed me a smock, and I put it on. She also gave me a paper package, which I opened. Inside I found a pair of super thin, translucent gloves. She motioned for me to put them on, and I did. I glanced at the other women's hands and realized they were wearing the same gloves. The silver-haired woman beside me passed me a small curved needle that resembled a shorn fingernail. She pointed to a laceration running horizontally across the man's abdomen. My heart was pounding. *Did she expect me to stick needles into this man?* I hadn't even finished my introduction to nursing course yet. I'd done little more than change adult diapers.

I hesitated and looked at her. Her gaze, steady and sure, reflected the light of the braziers on the opposite wall. She pointed back to the wound and put her hands over mine, directing them toward the gash. I borrowed her confidence and took a deep breath, plunging the needle through the skin at the close end of the wound. Fa narrated, giving directions and verbal pointers, as the silver-haired woman guided my hands, pointing, applying pressure, nodding her head in approval. Soon my shoulders relaxed. *Shallow to deep, cross, deep to shallow, pull, loop, loop, pull, loop, pull, loop, pull.* There was something reassuring about the methodical bite of the needle and closing of the wound. Jagged angry flesh became a neat, straight line of stitches.

The blond woman pulled out another suture tray and arranged it before me. Fa fell silent, and I set to work stitching the shallow wounds, while the silver-haired woman stitched the deeper wounds. She bound the deeper tissues together before closing the surface of the wound with a second row of stitches. I'm not sure how long we worked. It felt like time stood still. When the man's chest and arms were entirely tended, we rewashed the area with the tree soap and applied salve to each wound; then we moved on to his legs, back, and feet. Some of his wounds were shocking and horrible. I couldn't imagine how they had been made and didn't want to. Thankfully, the work and the prayer stopped my mind from wandering too far.

There was a particularly deep wound across the man's lower back and buttocks; the muscle there was torn. Fa immediately lit sharp smelling incense stick in censures around the room. The smoke was thick, and our eyes burned. "This kind of smoke is antibacterial," Fa said.

The silver-haired woman cleansed the deep wound. They poured the silver fluid into it and lit it, and the silver-haired woman went to work trimming and stitching muscles and sinews. She was highly skilled. Sweat dripped from her brow, and tears caused by the smoke streamed from her eyes. Fa handed me a washcloth, and I wiped the woman's face as she worked. When every wound was cleaned and closed, the short blond woman cleared the clutter—needles, gloves, cloths, papers, packaging—gathered it, and stowed it in a wooden box.

"We will burn it," Fa explained.

The women gathered around the injured man and laid their hands on him. Fa began to pray aloud, first in English, then in Chinese. The other women followed suit, each in their own language. The prayer wasn't just a ritual. They were pouring their hearts out. There was something powerful about the collected prayers all going up at once. I joined them. As we prayed, the incense remained lit, but the smoke cleared entirely from the room. The light from the square braziers brightened measurably and turned white. A presence I can only describe as completely pure and holy entered the room. We all dropped to our knees exactly where we were, surrounding the bed, still holding tight to the man arms and legs. My chest burned, and my breath came in gasps. My forehead felt heavy, and the floor beneath my knees felt hot. I pressed my head into the cot, still holding fast to the man's elbow. My fingers were vibrating just like my shoulders did while I flew. I forced my eyes open and looked at them. Blue light glowed under my fingers just as it did under the fingers of the other Blues. Startled, I almost let go. As quickly as it came, the presence lifted. The braziers returned to their normal blue color, and everyone returned to their feet. The women wiped their eyes and returned quietly to work as if the experience wasn't the single most overwhelming experience of their lives; meaning it probably wasn't new to them. Meanwhile, my hands trembled and my knees wobbled.

"Sit down," Fa directed. "It will pass." She nudged me toward the niche behind me, and I sat.

"I told you, remember? God is more easily seen, felt, heard here. You will get used it. Now you rest. Just rest," she reassured me.

"That is going to happen more than once?" I asked.

She didn't answer but helped me lie down in the wall niche.

"Just rest," she said again. Emotion welled up inside me and threatened to spill over. I was grateful for the relative privacy of the dark sleeping niche. I wasn't sure I could ever get used to what I'd just experienced. It was the overwhelming kind of thing that neither my body nor my mind understood. I tried willing my hands to stop shaking, but it didn't work. I decided to concentrate instead on what was the Blues were doing. The smoke from the incense had begun to drift through the room again. The Blues put out a few of the braziers, dimming the lights. The silver-haired woman sat down on the mattress beside me and held a cup of tea to my lips. I tried to take it from her, but my hands were still entirely uncooperative.

"Don't worry. I will help you," she said in Gaelic. I looked at her, surprised to hear a familiar language. She held the cup to my lips as if I were a small child. I drank... toasted rice and chrysanthemums... It steeled my nerves.

"You will get more used to His presence. It will become easier," she promised.

"You speak Gaelic, don't you?" she asked me.

I nodded.

"You did well today. You are a quick learner."

I didn't feel I was doing well at all. I felt completely wiped out.

"S'mise Gabije," she said, "but you can call me Gabi."

"S'mise Kiah."

"That's a beautiful name. It means 'of the Earth, the start of the season, with the strength of God.'"

"Really? I had no idea. I thought my mother just picked it because no one else did, and she likes to be different."

"Maybe she did," Gabi responded.

"Does it really matter what a person's name means?"

"I think so." Gabi pulled her legs up onto the bed and stretched out beside me just as Millie would have, as if we had known each other for years. I watched the blond woman hustle around her patient's bed, cleaning the floor and checking his breathing. He looked peaceful, so very different than he had when he arrived.

"What does your name mean?" I asked.

"Gabije means 'to cover, to protect.'"

I'd just watched her drop into a room clutching a broken body to her chest. The name fit her. She covered and protected well.

My name, on the other hand, felt like a stretch. *Of the Earth, start of the season, with the strength of God.* I was from the Earth, so that part was easy. And a new season was definitely dawning, but my arms and legs still felt like jelly. I certainly wasn't feeling in possession of the strength of God.

"You don't have to feel strong to have the strength of God." Gabi followed the train of my internal musing unnervingly well. I glanced in her direction. She was staring at the rock just above our heads; her hands clasped over her chest.

"You just have to know where your strength will come from when you need it."

Dhia, give me strength. I have none on my own. I need you! I prayed silently.

I closed my eyes and let my mind float. In my mind's eye, I placed my questions, my doubts, and my shortcomings like so much firewood onto a raft. I untied the raft and let the current pull them downriver. I knew I would see at least some of them again, but for the moment, there was relief in letting them drift. I sighed, relieved, as the raft floated out of sight. I took one small step into the cool water. Even though the river was only in my mind, an instant cooling calm immediately moved up my legs and all through me, even to my fingertips and the roots of my hair. I drifted off to sleep.

When I opened my eyes again, I heard only the sound of the waterfall in the kitchen. Gabi was rolled tight into a ball, fast asleep, just beside me. I crept down to the end of niche, careful not to bump my head on the rock ceiling that hung low above me, and eased out of the alcove. I stretched and checked my legs for strength. They had regained solidity. With only one lit brazier, the light in the room was dim. The air was chilly, but a small heat draft emanated from somewhere, sliding through the room at waist level. Fresh incense, the kind that fought infection, filled the room with helpful haze.

The man was propped now, on his right side, covered in blankets. His breathing was regular but heavy and a little labored. I was surprised to see oxygen tubing in his nose. The tubing ran to a large brown jug beside the bed. Something inside the jug glowed green.

I studied the man's face for what was really the first time. His hair, the color of fall leaves, was long and shaggy. Someone had caught it up into a ponytail at the base of his neck. His eyes were sunken. In the dim light, I couldn't tell if bruising or extreme fatigue darkened the sockets. The sun had etched deep lines into his forehead and cheeks. Silver scars crisscrossed the sun lines, and beads of sweat stood out on the bridge of his well-tanned nose despite the chill in the air. Still, the face under all those lines was youthful, younger than I had previously assumed. It felt strange to have spent such intimate time with a person, even touch the inside of his skin, and still not know his name.

The blond woman was kneeling at the foot of the patient's bed on a pillow, praying. She nodded at me as I passed. It felt strange not to know her name either. I ducked under the curtain that hung in front of the kitchen alcove and found Fa stoking a small fire in what looked like a small pizza oven. Apparently, Petra had two kinds of fire: blue heatless flame that didn't smoke and a more familiar kind of fire that burned much as Earth's fire did but more vividly. The kitchen was smoky, though most of the smoke was heading out and up the waterfall hole. Fa was flushed with exertion.

"Can I help with something?" I asked.

"You scare me! No sneaking up on me, or I fall in the hole!" she scolded mildly.

"The wood is very hard, like iron, and it's wet. The fire doesn't want to go. I'm trying to make bread."

I glanced at the countertop into a bowl of something dark and purple, mashed, speckled with small yellow seeds. It smelled like skunk.

"Um, what kind of bread are you making exactly?" I asked, wrinkling my nose.

So far I had enjoyed the food on the Rock, but what was in that bowl didn't seem promising.

"Oh, not that. That is a, well, it's a"—Fa searched for the right word—"poultice. Is that the right word?" she asked, still coaxing the fire.

"Yes. What is it for?"

"Infection. That man is fighting an infection. I'm not sure where. This is cosh. Smells bad and works good. It draws out infection better than Earth's antibiotics. Works best over the site of infection but does fine on the feet too. You place it on the feet. The blood vessels pull it into the body. Works very good." The flame in the oven flared, and she stepped back, grinning triumphantly.

"Ha! Good."

"Now we make bread. Then we go," she said. She opened a jar of dark-brown flour and pointed to the lower cupboards.

"Two bowls, please," she directed.

I opened the cupboards and rustled around until I found the bowls.

We combined eggs with startlingly orange yolks and some sort of animal milk from the icebox. I crushed herbs and added them. Fa everything into a large, sticky dough. She divided it into four loaves and set them on a stone cooking surface that she popped into the oven.

"One nice thing about making bread here is there's no need to rise first. It rises in the oven." I watched the bread. It was already doubling in size. "Everything cooks faster."

"Why?" I asked.

Fa shrugged. "I don't know. Maybe you should ask Him."

It was yet another example of Fa's faith. She seemed to trust Dhia with *everything*.

Maybe my stress level would decrease if I would simply surrender my need to always "know."

I dutifully switched topics. "Hey, you said we were leaving soon... Isn't it the middle of the night?"

"Yes and yes." Fa pulled two rosy pink pears from the icebox and handed me one.

I waited, hoping she would volunteer more information about our destination. She did not. Instead, she looked me up and down. "You are a mess," she declared.

That was true.

I followed Fa into the main room. She stopped at the empty sleeping alcove, opposite the one where Gabi rested and retrieved a stack of jumpsuits like those Gabi had worn when she dropped into the room earlier.

"No robes?" I asked.

"Not today."

Fa held one up to me for sizing. It seemed too short. She returned it to the pile and rifled through until she found one that fit me, then took another for herself. She grabbed undergarments from the shelf and headed for door. The blond woman was back at the man's bedside, arranging medication and taking notes in a tablet. Fa

153

spoke to her in Chinese, and she nodded, listening. I remembered a few Chinese words from my time with Ling the Chinese exchange student but not enough to understand what they were saying. I made a mental note to add more languages to my school course list.

We left the room and returned to the landing that overlooked the mountain crater. Two silver moons bathed the coast in silver light. The stars seemed close enough to touch. The floor of the crater shimmered and seemed to move. I leaned over the edge of the small wooden platform and saw that the ladder disappeared into a steaming silver lake.

"A natural hot spring runs through here at night. It fills the crater and makes a really good bath." Fa stepped out of her scrubs and shimmied naked down the ladder, then tied a small bag to the lowest visible rung and eased herself into the water.

I noted that Blues didn't seem overly concerned about modesty. Granted, there didn't seem to be many men about. I removed my clothing and followed suit. The air was freezing, but the water was extremely warm, almost hot. It smelled of sulfur. Fa dipped below the surface of the water, wetting her hair entirely. She reached into her bag and pulled out a small bar of soap and broke it in half, giving half to me. It smelled like pitch. We both washed up, then swam out toward to the middle of the lake. Bubbles, accompanied by faint green glowing streams of light, rose here and there from the basin floor beneath us. I stopped to tread water and watch one of the larger bubble streams.

"It's an organism that gives oxygen. Phosphorescent is the word, yes? For the glowing?" Fa asked.

"Yes. Phosphorescent. Is this what was in the jar beside the man's bed? Do those things really give off enough oxygen to make a difference?"

"Oh, yes, quite a lot. The big ones we cannot seal in jars or the jars explode. If you dry them out, they are very light. Easy to carry. They are called sporna." She looked up into the sky as if she could tell the time by looking at the stars. Perhaps she could.

"I think it is time to go," she said, heading for the ladder. I was reluctant to leave the warm water and didn't relish the idea of walking anywhere in the middle of the night. Suddenly, it occurred to me that we might not be walking, and my stomach sunk. I lagged behind. By the time I reached the ladder, Fa was already dry and mostly dressed.

"So slow," she chided.

I climbed out of the water into the frigid night air and accepted a thin piece of fabric to dry off with. The jumpsuit was a complicated but surprisingly comfortable garment. There were several panels in the pants that wrapped tight and tied around the thighs, knees, and legs. The shirt was comprised of four separate flaps that wrapped and tied securely around the waist and chest. Sturdy canvas straps buckled across the chest and hips and around the thighs and ankles. I recognized the straps. They were the same type that held the injured man fast to Gabi the day before. I sincerely hoped I wouldn't find myself strapped to anyone anytime soon.

We slipped back into the smoky healing room. The braziers had been lit, and the room was once again filled with light. Gabi was repacking his deep wound, applying the skunky cosh substance to its edges. She applied a clean cloth bandage over the entire area and stepped back, motioning for Fa and I to join her. Gently, she turned the man's right arm outward and pointed at his upper forearm. There were several lines of stitches there that extended past his elbow, like the tines of a rake. Strangely, the raw red stitch lines were interrupted in a regular pattern just below his elbow by what looked like small sections of fully healed silver scar. I was puzzled. Gabi took my hand and held it over the top of the stitch lines. My fingers lined up perfectly with the healed sections. I still didn't understand.

"What does that mean?" I asked in Gaelic, so Gabi would understand.

"It means Dhia healed the parts of the skin you touched."

"But why? Why would He do that? Did He do that anywhere else... where you put your hands?" Gabi shook her head.

"No, only here," she said. "Did Dhia tell you anything, Kiah? Did He say anything to you when He was with us?"

"No. I heard nothing. I only felt him, and the lights changed color. They turned white. And my head was so heavy I could barely lift it. Is that the same as you saw, you felt?" I asked.

"Yes, that was the same." Gabi nodded her head.

"You are a healer," Fa said.

"Aren't all Blues healers?"

"In a way, yes, but some are more gifted in other areas. For instance, we are all communicators, yes? But some people communicate better than others. We all walk, but some people fall down often, while others move with style."

The last part I understood. I tended to fall down more often than the majority of people with two functioning legs.

"I think Dhia is telling you something about who you are. He gifts a few with an extra ability for healing, Kiah. Maybe you are one of these. You should pray about it. Remember it. Thank Him for it," Gabi said.

A memory sprang to mind. When I was five years old, I accompanied my uncle to the dam where he worked. We had stood outside at the top of the dam, behind a narrow railing, and looked down at millions of gallons of water pounding and roaring out of the floodgates beneath us. The spray saturated my shirt and hair. I felt the power below me vibrate up through the metal floor of the platform. It was powerful and frightening but magnetic. I never wanted to leave. I felt the same way, staring at the silvery scars on the man's arms. Dhia had healed those patches of skin in a way that made me aware of His proximity. I felt His strength surging just out of sight.

Gabi startled me by kissing me on the forehead as if I were, indeed, five years old, then turned and hugged Fa, kissing her on the forehead as well. Fa picked up two knapsacks full of fresh bread, dried meat from sources unknown, fruit, bottles of water, and a few oxygen-producing sporna disks. She added a small metal locking box to her knapsack, and we set off. My neck began to buzz. We wouldn't be walking.

THE STONE CABIN

We exited the healing room through the waterfall hole behind the kitchen. Fa pointed her toes and sped ahead of me high into the air above the mountain. I brought my limbs underneath me and did likewise. I was beginning to get the hang of flying… sort of. Fa dropped back and pulled up alongside me.

"They aren't our wings," she said, as if answering an unspoken question. "I think they are maybe angel's wings. We aren't angels, and these aren't our wings."

"Does that mean we borrow them?" I asked, not sure how someone could borrow someone else's wings.

"Maybe, or maybe angels fly with us."

I glanced again at the watery shape extending from just behind Fa's shoulders. There might have been a space between Fa's shoulders and the wings; at high speed and in the dark, it was hard to tell. I wasn't sure how I felt about being carried by unseen beings or about borrowing someone's wings either, for that matter. I wasn't sure if it was disconcerting or reassuring that we might not be flying alone. On the other hand, angels or no angels, we were never really alone anyway. Dhia was always with us. I was beginning to realize how limited my perspective had always been. I'd lived generally unaware of the spiritual realm. Many people denied its existence altogether simply because they hadn't experienced it or because it made them uncomfortable. I'd never given it much thought, always ignoring the things I couldn't explain… the visions, the dreams, the dejavu. If it wasn't logical, I set it aside. Everyday life was hard enough without fussing over the things I couldn't understand.

"Do the other Blues know whether we fly alone on borrowed wings or if we are carried by angels?" I asked Fa.

"I don't know. I never asked anyone."

The two silver moons hung in the sky behind us. The purple moon hung before us. We cleared the mountains and headed out over a dense forest or jungle—I couldn't tell which. It was cold, and my teeth began to chatter.

"We will be down soon," Fa reassured me. We dropped down, side by side, and streaked along just over the treetops. It was warmer near the ground. I smelled flowers. The forest was enormous, but eventually the trees thinned out, and the land began to rise again. We crested a hill and slowed over a small sparse collection of stone huts, landing in the middle of a road. Fa landed delicately while I skidded to a stop in a cloud of dust. I brushed the dust off my jumpsuit and followed her down the road to its end. Tucked into the hill was a small stone cottage, *my* stone cottage—the one that had been a staple in my dreams for years. My heart leapt, and I pulled up short.

"What's the matter?" Fa asked.

Three steps to the plain wooden door—two narrow, one wide. One small window on each side of the door. It was exactly as I remembered it, exactly as I'd drawn it.

"I know this house," I told Fa. "I've seen it in my dreams."

"Really. God has shown it to you before now? Do you want to go in?"

I did want to go in. It felt like coming home. Shaking slightly, I mounted the steps and went inside. The smells of dried herbs, dust, and smoke met me at the door. It was small inside and definitely cozy. The stone floor looked recently swept. There was a large fireplace and well-stocked woodbin at the center of the left wall in front of a large wood-framed couch. The couch was like a handmade futon with huge throw pillows. Beyond the living area was a closed door to what I assumed was the bedroom. Fa set to work starting a fire while I explored the open kitchen. I ran my hands along the scarred butcher block countertop and explored the items on the open shelves above. There were glasses, dishes, and silverware, all mismatched and well used. Many were bent and chipped and hailed from seemingly all over the world.

"The Blues bring things back on their trips. Many years, many countries." Fa was keeping an eye on me as I explored.

Tears were welling in the corners of my eyes. I had a strange sense of nostalgia along with a healthy dose of unidentified emotion. Sadness? Fear? Confusion? A touch of anticipation and excitement maybe?

"You say this is all mine?" I asked, searching for understanding.

"Yes, yours."

"How can that be?"

"The Blues in your family have all stayed here. Now it is your turn, if you want it. Not much resale value, anyway." She smiled, pleased with her little joke.

"This is *my* house?"

"Yes."

"And where is yours?" I asked.

"Not here. I sleep in a room in the big house down the road, but I will stay with you tonight. We have much to talk about and not much time. Your friends must be heading back toward the abbey for lunch by now."

Thinking of Aggie and Donal, still walking along the path on the little Scottish island, made me dizzy. I still didn't understand how time and space contorted, shortening and lengthening, between Earth and Petra. I continued exploring the kitchen. A large sink basin, complete with drain hole, sat on the counter. Above it hung a huge tank with a spigot extending from its base.

"Water heater heats with wood," she explained. "The tank refills from outside. It's nice to have hot water."

At the back corner of the kitchen was a narrow door that led outside. Fa opened it and pointed a short distance to a stone building almost entirely hidden by climbing vines.

"That is the bathhouse. Toilet, sinks, hot water tank for bath. You share this with your neighbor." Fa pointed toward the next cottage. "Right now, no one stays there." She pulled the door closed, and we returned to the living room.

"This door here leads to the bedroom."

The bedroom was very small, ten feet across at most. A large wooden bed dominated the room. Open shelving partially filled with books, clothing, blankets, and other items circled the room. Unlike the other places I'd visited on Petra, the room was personalized and homey. A massive colorful quilt topped the bed. Parts of it were faded, a few pieces worn thin, and it had obviously been repaired and repatched in places. The fabric patterns seemed to hail from multiple eras. At the foot of the quilt was a label hand-embroidered with the name *Ailsa*.

I recognized the name immediately from my journals and letters. Excited, I swung around and faced Fa.

"Who is this? Who is Ailsa? I know this name!" My pent-up questions made a hole in my restraint wall and spilled out. "She made this quilt? I have letters and journals from her! They were in a box my mother gave me. Who is she?"

Fa held up her hand to stop me.

"Tea first. *Then* we talk. But *one* question at a time, okay?" She patted my shoulder and headed to the kitchen to make the tea.

Fa's ability to focus completely and take things as they came, while admirable, was sometimes exasperating.

My feet and head were buzzing, and my body was heavy. I threw myself on the bed and buried my head in a pillow. It smelled of lilacs. A scant few minutes later, Fa returned with the unidentified meat jerky, herb bread, and hot tea. She climbed onto the bed with me, set the tray between us, and sighed.

"There is so much to tell you. Why don't you first tell me what you know? You have a box of things from your family, you say? Tell me about that." Fa tore into a piece of jerky and gazed expectantly at me.

I told Fa about the letters, journals, and the box with the Celtic cross charm.

"The cross has the word *Iona* engraved on the back. It has to mean this island, right? Maybe the gate?"

Fa nodded. "Probably."

"I didn't recognize it at first. I hadn't even heard of this island before this weekend."

Fa handed me a slice of bread, but I was too preoccupied to eat it. "The island has its own history that is separate from Petra's," she said. "People think there is something mystical about Iona. They call it a 'thin place.' Have you heard that?"

I nodded. I had heard it from the guest professor.

"That means people feel pulled to the island, and not just for the scenery or history. They think maybe they will hear from God more there. I think it is maybe more about the gate. People can sense spiritual things. They are drawn to what they don't understand. A part of them longs to draw near to God, even as they reject Him. They don't understand that God is available to them always, anywhere, in their homes, in their cars. They don't see it. So much smoke. People just don't understand." She shook her head sadly.

"What do you mean 'there's so much smoke'?"

"Smoke. Τυφλός. It's Latin. Do you know this word?"

"Typhoo? I know the word. It means to be blinded by smoke. I think it's the root for the word *typhoon*."

"Exactly. This is the kind of smoke that Mogui likes… He likes to make a smoke screen."

"Mogui? Who is Mogui?" Fa had lost me somewhere between islands and spirituality. I was unsure whether the smoke she was referring to was real or theoretical.

"Ah, I mean Sadan… you call him Satan? In Chinese, he is Mogui," Fa clarified. Her eyes lit up with an idea, and she scrambled off the bed to a standing position.

"Mogui tries to hide truth from people. He wants to keep people from connecting to God. If he makes God seem hard to find, hard to reach, he wins. Like smoke. A house catches fire, and you are in your room. You wake up, sense fire, look for the door, but you can see nothing. The smoke is everywhere. You are confused and become lost, even in your own familiar room. Where is the door? The walls?" Fa pantomimed confusion.

"The door is, maybe, open, but you do not see it… so you die. This is Mogui's plan. Smoke. Τυφλός. He cannot take God away from people, but he can confuse, lie, make his smoke—and so he does. Especially on Earth. He has won so much ground there. People have given it to him. He roams the Earth making smoke, causing fear and confusion. He brings death any way He can and *still* people give Him more of themselves all the time! They give Him so much ground! But you can say no to the smoke. Blues are smoke fighters… like firefighters, but not. We fight the smoke. When people visit Iona, they think they are closer to God, so they listen. Then the smoke clears a little. If they just listen to Him when they go home, the smoke would clear there too! But they don't understand. They so easily forget." Fa huffed, frustrated. "Do you understand?"

"I think so. So the more people tune in and listen to God, the more the smoke clears. When we give in to our fear and confusion, we give Satan power, and the smoke gets thicker."

A clear picture sprang to my mind of smoke so thick it turned to ash. The ash piled and congealed into gray mud. I recognized it as the mud that clogged the halls and caked my skin in the vision I had in the little stone church on my eighteenth birthday.

"So the Blues… by healing, by listening to Dhia, following Him… we fight the enemy? We clear the smoke? Even though it's only a few of us and we aren't out preaching on the streets?"

"There are many ways to fight the smoke. Anyone who seeks God and His truth, anyone who believes Him, I mean really *receives* Him, fights the enemy. This clears the smoke. Anyone who truly loves with His selfless love clears smoke. Blues are a tiny group. Maybe we hear more because we *listen* more. We see more because we *look*. Every believer can do something powerful with God, because the power is God's. It does not belong to any one of us. If only they will listen to Him, receive Him, and walk with Him." Fa's voice was filled with more emotion than I'd ever heard from her. "Some people are called to preach, Kiah. Some are called to heal. Some are called to help, to teach, to build. All are called to love." She dropped back down onto the bed beside me. She looked surprisingly fragile and tired with her long silver-streaked hair unbound and splayed across the pillow behind her head.

"I guess I understand. I just don't feel like I know how to fight... not in the way you are saying."

"You have everything you need. We fight by knowing Him, trusting Him, looking for what He is doing, and joining Him in His work."

"But how am I supposed to know what to do? I don't always know what He is doing."

"You can look for His work by seeking God's virtues. Find what He is doing, and He leads you out of the smoke."

"Virtues?"

"Even people who don't know God can display goodness. You can recognize God's hand in this. Watch for goodness. Truth is another virtue. Think about this... Do you ever recognize truth with your heart but not with your mind?"

I nodded. I'd felt that way a few times.

"The more you listen to God, the more you will recognize truth," Fa promised. "There is also beauty."

"Beauty?"

"Absolutely! Beauty. Mogui knows beauty is one of God's greatest virtues. It draws our hearts. God made it that way, and Mogui does his best to twist this to serve himself."

Evil twists beauty? I thought about that for a moment. False unreachable standards for modeling, pornography, eating disorders... the distortion of beauty to take its power away from Dhia. Evil *had* done an excellent job of trying to steal beauty away from its Creator.

"Beauty isn't always easy to find." I thought of the boy in the horseshoe valley, of his injuries and the look of terror on his face. Where was the beauty in that?

"That is sometimes true, but there is always something to find... even glimmers or slivers of beauty are important. You just have to look harder. Think of this... How would we recognize true beauty if we never saw the lack of it? God can use anything, even our sin, to reflect something beautiful. And you can choose to reject the ugliness that you find. Embrace beauty instead." Fa paused a moment to let that sink in before she continued.

"Think of the cross. It is a tool for torture, right? It was a means of death, pain, and agony. It represented all things ugly. God fully changed its meaning. He made it into a symbol of the single most beautiful act in human history. This is His redemption. Will you choose to see the ugly or the beauty? You can always choose what to seek, Kiah. It is a choice that Blues must make every day. We see the ugliness so easily, but will we choose also to see the beauty, the truth, the goodness in dark places?"

I was following Fa's train of thought, barely. I recognized the truth in her words, but it seemed somewhat theoretical and unusable. It was hard to see truth through the lies, goodness through evil, and beauty beyond the devastation of sin. There was so much I didn't know and didn't understand. I was being Called to live a life I could barely grasp.

"I found someone in my family that knows about the Calling, Fa. It's my great-aunt Nan. Her sister, Gaira, was Called. She told me the Calling goes back in our family for generations. When Gaira was Called, she left the box of books and letters with Nan. She swore her to secrecy about it, then disappeared. She totally disappeared! I've heard of missionaries that live in huts and risk malaria and diseases. I know they are willing to sacrifice their comfort to obey God… but to *disappear altogether*? Have you ever heard of that? Is that going to happen to me?"

I glanced at Fa, trying to gauge her response. She was listening but didn't answer. If my story surprised her, it didn't register on her face.

"Her family didn't hear from her for thirty years. Then she sent a note to Nan asking her to ship the box of stuff to my mother. My mom got the box, but I don't know what happened after that. I think she must have known she was Called, but she said no. She didn't even want me to know about the Calling or about God. Mom just won't discuss it with me at all. Is it because everyone who is Called disappears? Is that what she is afraid of? Is that what will happen to me?" I was talking too fast again. Fa put her hand up to stop me.

"No, of course not everyone who is Called disappears. Some move to Petra. They live here. Some live on Earth. A few go back and forth. They live in two places. This is more difficult, I think… living in two worlds, but maybe this is the Calling for you. Remember, there is always choice. If your aunt's sister moved to Petra to serve, then she chose it from her heart, from obedience to her God. Your aunt is right, many women from your family have been Called. Sometimes they say yes, and He Calls them to serve in this special way, to serve on the Rock. Ailsa was one of those women. From the generation of your great-grandmother, maybe? Your great-aunt didn't know her?"

I shook my head. "No, she didn't recognize the name."

"Maybe earlier then," Fa concluded. "I haven't heard of Gaira either. But the Blues do not keep records, I think. There is no real way to know who served where and when. Sometimes God calls many women, generation after generation, in the same family. I don't know why this is. Only God knows this." Fa placed her fist over her heart again, indicating that she took this on faith.

"Maybe it is like the priests of the Bible. Many men called from the same tribes and families whose inheritance was not on Earth. Their inheritance was the temple. Maybe the women in some families are Called to serve as Blues, and their inheritance is also not on Earth. This is how I think about it." Fa sat up and sipped her tea.

"So Blues were made to be Blues from the time they were born? Maybe even before they were born? Is that how it works?" I asked.

"All people are built with a purpose from Him. He chooses us, and we can choose to follow Him, or we can choose our own path. He does not abandon us, Kiah. He gives us choice. He gave your mother choice."

"Could my mother have said no to being a Blue but still yes to Him in her heart? She could still live her life with Him?"

"God gives us all choice. Perhaps her heart felt too heavy with His asking? He does not force our actions when He calls our hearts."

"That doesn't really answer my question, though. I just wonder if she could still love Him even if she said no to the Calling. Could she still have taught me about Him even if she didn't want to follow His Call to be a Blue?"

165

"Do you mean can people follow Him in their heart but not obey in action? It is a question that I cannot answer so easily for you. What God accepts and what people feel they can do are two separate things. Can you go against the most important voice in your life and yet feel close to Him? God does not force us, Kiah. He judges our hearts for Him, not our actions. It is our heart for Him that He desires. Ask yourself this question: could you say no to this Call and still yes to Him?"

Could I? Could I imagine saying yes to believing Dhia for what is true and yet say no when it came to the plan He laid before me? It was a question that makes my head ache and my heart burst. I didn't know how to answer it.

"Your mother's heart is something no one, but God can see and know. It is such a relief to know that He alone judges. Come... I think we should walk." Fa rose from the bed and headed for the door.

THE NEIGHBORHOOD

The day was warm but not hot. The sky was streaked with layers of dark-gray and sherbet-colored clouds, and the light shining through them made a kaleidoscope effect on the ground. We walked in silence for a while, just taking in the view. I wondered how many of my family members had walked the same road—women who were born to but largely unknown by the Earth. I also wondered how my mother could have turned it down. *Did she know about this place?*

The dirt was rich brown, almost black, and soft. The trees lining the little road were enormous and willowlike. Their branches bent and trailed to ground so that we had to part them like bead curtains in order to pass underneath. Small gray birds with pink chests flitted in and out between the branches. Some of them followed us as we meandered down the road. The cabin next door was similar to mine except that a tree or bush of some sort had grown up and over it, engulfing it almost entirely in lemon-colored flowers and bluish leaves. Someone had trimmed it back from the doors and windows.

"No one lives there now?" I asked Fa.

"No. Not now."

"Does that mean someone in her family said no to the Call?"

"I do not know… maybe. Or maybe she just hasn't come yet."

"Would it be okay to pray that she does?"

"It is always okay to ask, as long as you don't expect to get your way every time. He longs to hear us say what our heart desires."

We walked away from the village toward the hills. The short gnarled trees there were much less elegant than the willows on the road. Their trunks were knobby and spiny. Their diamond-shaped leaves had gray-green tops and flashed peachy-silver bottoms when the wind turned them. The wind stirred up as we climbed the hill, and the branches clacked together. We peered over the top of the hill, and I caught my breath. The hill sloped gently downward, and the scrub trees continued for miles in a long channel straight ahead of us. To the east lay a valley flush with fruit trees, gardens, vineyards, and arbors draped with flowering vines.

"Is that where you grow your food?" I pointed to the gardens.

"Yes, much of it."

"Where do you get your meat?"

"Some hunt deer. Some of the men who do not return to Earth help with that, as well."

To the west lay a large coral lake.

"Pink algae," Fa explained. "There's a lake like this on Earth too. Have you seen it?"

I shook my head no.

"This lake is always this color. The water is healing."

The trees around the lake were different than the trees dotting the rest of the landscape, as if the quality of the water, or the algae, was allowing entirely different foliage to grow there. The leaves on the trees were broad and shiny; and multicolored fruits and flowers, unlike anything I'd ever seen, adorned the branches and littered the ground beneath the canopy.

As wild and new as all that was, something intrigued me more. Beyond the tree line straight ahead of me, so far I had to squint to see it, was what looked like an enormous castle.

"What is that, over there beyond the trees?" I asked Fa.

"A sort of a castle," she confirmed.

"Does anyone live there?"

She shook her head.

"Who built it? What is it for?"

"I think no one knows. At least, no one remembers. Petra has more questions than answers. There is no written history. There are cottages, the castle, bridges, old roads that lead to nowhere… No one remembers who built them."

"An entirely forgotten history? That can't be right. Someone knows. Someone *always* knows, right?"

Fa pointed skyward.

"I mean *besides* Him…," I clarified.

"Maybe," Fa said, continuing down the hill.

We reached the entrance to the gardens. There were strange vegetables and fruits growing on bushes, hanging from trellises and trees and growing up from the ground. They garden wasn't laid out in lines as Earth gardens usually were. Rather, everything grew in clumps in concentric circles. Rows of veggies and flowers ringed nut and fruit trees.

"Why not in rows? Wouldn't that be easier?" I asked Fa.

"Some plants like to grow together. They help each other better that way. They are like people. Sometimes we need a certain person to help us be our best."

"Can I eat something?"

"Sure, everything here can be eaten." She smiled.

I picked a long shiny purple bean-like fruit (or vegetable, it was hard to tell which) and bit into it, then spat it out immediately. It was the most bitter thing I'd ever tasted.

Fa laughed as if it were one of the funniest things she'd seen in a long time.

"This is for medicine. It is very good for helping the body heal fresh wounds. Maybe not so good for flavor."

"Thanks for warning me," I said, scraping pieces of the sticky fruit from my tongue and spitting. The flavor seemed to be spreading down my throat despite the fact that I hadn't even swallowed. My lower lip was beginning to feel a little numb.

"Maybe you could recommend something?" I mumbled.

"Maybe you should have asked me for suggestion in the first place," she chided.

An object lesson… great.

Fa picked a green spiky fruit about the size of a ping-pong ball from a nearby tree and expertly popped the orange fruit out from the skin, handing it to me.

"Just eat the whole thing?" I asked.

"Yes, the seeds are small."

The flesh was smooth like mango but with rows of pulp, like an orange. It tasted like grape and rhubarb. I let the juice run off my chin, hoping it would rid me of the remnants of the nasty purple bean thingy. Fa was still smiling.

"Okay, you had your fun. Where to now?" I asked.

We wound through the gardens for a few miles, eating our fill of fruits and veggies and watching for wildlife. We spotted all kinds of birds, small groundhog-like critters with long ears, and several silver deer.

"I've wondered something else about Blues... Is there something different about all of us? I mean, *really* different?"

"How do you mean 'different'?"

"Seeing visions, knowing things before they happen... that sort of thing. Does that happen to all Blues?"

"Describe to me what you mean." Fa settled herself on the ground under a tree.

I joined her and told her about my visions and the colors I saw when I thought of words.

"I can smell disease on people, sometimes. I can smell death. I go into groups of people, and I smell *everything* I do not want to smell. Their deodorant, their Chap Stick, their shampoo. Sometimes, I smell fear, jealousy, even hate."

Fa listened thoughtfully. I told her I'd know before we moved what our new house would be like... about the earthquake and my mother's vase... about the little house exploding first in my dreams, then in reality.

"I wonder, sometimes... If Dhia is telling me these things, does He mean for me to *do* something about them? Should I have told someone about the house? Was I supposed to prevent it from happening somehow?"

"At the time it happened, did you feel the need to do something about it—deep inside yourself?" Fa asked.

I tried to remember. "No, not at all. I just felt the need to notice, to watch, to listen."

Fa shook her head. "Then no, I don't think He meant for you to do something about it. He may be teaching you to listen to Him and to pay attention. Sometimes He gives us proof that He is there, to let us know to listen for Him. This way, God teaches us. He sometimes tells us, 'See here… I'm speaking. I'm moving. Watch me. Take note. Do you hear me? Do you hear my voice and recognize my hand?"

"So this is typical stuff for Blues?" I asked.

"Maybe… no. Not typical. But not rare either. Some see visions even from the time they are very young. Some hear His voice and know it as well as their own. Some hear from Him in dreams and visions. Some do not. He speaks to different people in different ways. Some people who are *not* Blues experience these things as well."

"But why? Why doesn't He speak to everyone so clearly in every way He can? And why not all the time? Why only sometimes?"

"Maybe someday you will ask Him."

"So you don't know either," I said, feeling a little disappointed. "Maybe you know this, then… What is the blue light that comes from the hands of the Blues when they are healing?"

Fa wrinkled her brow. "Blue light?"

"Yeah, the blue light under the Blues' fingers when they help heal someone."

Fa shook her head slowly. "I've never seen this blue light you are talking about. Perhaps it's also something He is letting you see."

"Seriously? No one else sees it?"

"I have no idea, Kiah, if anyone else sees it. I have not heard of this, so I have not asked. You have seen it many times?"

"Yes."

"Perhaps it is a gift for you to see it."

"But *why?*" I asked.

"I don't *know*, Kiah. You know who to ask for that." Fa's tone signaled that her patience with me was wearing thin. "He will show you if it is important for you to know. Just let Him show you. Be patient," she chided.

A small cloud passed over us; and mist, like the kind in the produce section of the grocery store, began to drop. It struck me that Dhia was tending the garden Himself. He knew exactly what the garden needed and exactly when it needed it. We got up and began to walk again. By the time we had reached the edge of the garden, the mist stopped. We didn't return the way we came, but took instead a double-rutted road that looked as if it had been made by horse-drawn wagons. Sure enough, we passed piles of road apples. My father's term for horse poop. Thinking of Dad made me miss him.

We ran into a few women and one man. The man's face was scarred, and he wore long sleeves despite the warmth of the day. They all smiled, but no one stopped to talk. They were all busy, heading wherever they were headed. One woman pulled a cart full of produce behind her, assuaging my curiosity about what her business was. The rest of them remained a mystery. I wondered if I'd know them some-day; if I'd ever be able to predict where they were going just by their clothing or the direction they were headed, the way I might be able to at home.

Will I ever live here, really, truly live here? I silently asked Dhia.

There was no answer.

Do I even really want to live here? I asked myself.

I had no answer for that either.

"So how many Blues are there, in total?" I asked Fa.

"Not many I think, when you know how many people live in the world. Right now, here on Petra, maybe there are a few hundred? No one counts. We are not so organized. I think. some Blues work here, on the Rock. You have met some of them. Some grow food, make clothes, blankets, tend the animals. They each do their own work. Some work on Earth… helping, watching the gates, bringing people He asks them to bring here for healing. Some are waiting."

"Waiting?" I asked. "Waiting for what?"

Fa shrugged. "I don't know. Maybe they don't know either. Or maybe some do. They are waiting for something He is asking them to wait for and getting ready in the way He is asking them to get ready."

"Where are they waiting?" I asked.

"That way mostly," she answered, pointing to the northeast. There were low hills there that lead to mostly bare medium-sized hills, behind which stood a ridge of mountains.

What must that be like? I wondered. *Leaving Earth to wait on Petra for something yet to come, something that you don't understand?* I wondered what they did while they were waiting. I couldn't imagine it, but it wasn't long ago that I couldn't have imagined *any* of what I was experiencing.

"Fa, you said you still bring some people from Earth for healing, some who don't fall into Kress?"

"Yes, sometimes there are others from Earth. God may give one of the Blues a picture of whom to go to, when to go, where to go. Sometimes they are in Kress, and several of us go together to get them. Sometimes they are on Earth. Some Blues get many pictures. Some, not so many," Fa indicated a small amount with her fingers.

"Your family, Kiah—they are known for hearing God's voice, feeling His heart, then doing His will. Your family seems to sense His presence well. This is why I chose you to train. I am curious." She smiled and bumped my arm with her elbow.

I tried to smile back at her, but my smile felt lopsided and forced. My heart was pounding. I had assumed that the things that made me different from the people I knew at home were things that I shared, at the very least, with the other Blues. It didn't seem, however, like Fa had very many answers except to just listen, just pray, just be patient…

Dhia, I still feel different, even here. I still feel like I don't fit. Where do I fit?

He didn't answer.

The road wound around a hill covered in scrub trees. We circled the hill and found ourselves back in front of the row of stone cabins. I was growing hungry again and tired. I realized, then, that we'd walked and talked all day long. Perhaps it was jet lag had warped my sense of time; or perhaps in Petra time itself was elementally different.

The sky, light just moments before, was growing dark fast. It was nearing nighttime, but night didn't normally gather so fast, even on the Rock.

"A small storm," Fa said just as hot pink lightning forked across the sky.

A SMALL STORM

Purple clouds bunched and roiled overhead. The wind picked up speed, rattling the branches on the scrub trees behind the cabin like so many dry bones. The sound was deafening. If that was a small storm for Petra, I wondered what large storms were like. I remembered Fa telling me they'd once spent a month waiting out a storm in the cave in the mountain. We hurried inside the cabin, depositing our shoes on the mat inside the door. Fa stoked the stove and lit the braziers while I set the tea to boil. We retrieved the herb bread and jerky from the kitchen and settled in on the couch in front of the fire. The electrical storm raged, loud and dry, outside. I waited for the sound of rain on the roof but didn't hear it.

"So what happens to the people you help, Fa? Once they are healed, where do they go?"

"We send them home again," Fa said simply.

"But how does that work, exactly? Don't they tell people about their time here? Once they go home?" I asked.

Fa shook her head. "You might think so, but no. Not so many talk about it. Some people are so sick, so tired, they think they were dreaming. Some people just can't believe anything they can't understand—and they can't understand this place, so they say nothing at all. They don't want to sound crazy!" Fa laughed.

I could see her point.

"Also God helps guard our secret, Kiah. He helps people forget. He helps guard the knowledge of this place. Once the Healed return home, there are Blues on Earth to help them if they need it."

"Fa, were your family Blues?" I asked.

"No, my family did not know of God. My family lived in Mongolia. Do you know this place?"

"I've heard of it." I didn't know much about it.

"Mongolia has open plains, many sheep, horses, and a very big sky. We lived in a tent there. I did not even go to school. I helped my mother wash clothes and train eagles to hunt."

"Seriously? Eagles?" I interrupted.

"Why would I lie about that?" Fa asked, then continued. "When I was nine years old, a woman, not Chinese, moved into a tent near ours. I had never seen a white woman before. Her nose was smooth and sharp like an old bone, and she had yellow hair. Most of the kids were frightened of her. They told me that only Nats had yellow hair." Fa smiled at the memory.

The tea pot whistled, and Fa rose to make and pour the tea. It was an earthy, almost goaty brew as dark as coffee. She added a few shavings of a spicy root to it and a rather generous spoonful of honey.

"What is a Nat?" I asked her.

"A spirit, like a ghost. The children had never seen white people before, so they thought she was a Nat. I wondered myself. The woman lived like us, near us but in her own tent. She helped people with their jobs and gave out food when people were hungry. No one knew why she would do this, so they were suspicious. I watched the woman. I followed her. I was so curious. She took me into her tent one day and gave me little cookies covered in chocolate. My first chocolate! They were so good. The woman prayed many hours every day. She hung a cross on the wall in her tent, and she kneeled there, praying, singing. It was so beautiful. I thought she was an angel. My mother told me to stay away from her, but I disobeyed." Fa fell silent for several moments. I wondered if she had fallen asleep, but when I looked over at her, I realized she treading water in her own memories.

"Then what happened?" I prompted.

"One night I heard the sound of engines. I was eleven years old. It was the sound of many engines and yelling… so many voices yelling and talking all at once. Everyone was running outside. I was in my sleep clothes, but I got up and ran outside the tent. There were trucks, vehicles coming toward us over the field. They were shooting the sheep, shooting the people."

I sat straight up on the bed. "Oh, Fa! What did you do?"

"I didn't know what to do. I could not find my family. Everyone was talking, yelling at the same time… shouting, running. Then I saw the blond woman. She took my hand and told me to come with her. She started to run with me. The engines were getting close. I heard people screaming, dying. Then we lifted off the ground. We flew. God picked us up and took us to a gate, to Petra, to the Rock."

"The woman was a Blue," I said.

She nodded, and we fell silent, each processing her story in our own way.

"She kept you safe. Dhia sent her there for you because He had a plan for you," I told Fa, feeling the truth of it all the way to my toes.

"That's true," Fa agreed.

"The woman was a Blue, and now you are too, even though your family is not? How does that work?"

"God does whatever he wants to do, Kiah. Many Blues have a family tradition of the Calling, but some do not. I used to wonder if maybe long ago my family was Called, but the history of that was forgotten. I do not know. What I know for sure is that there is no 'for sure.' Usually, Blues work on the Rock, but not all do. Usually, Blues have a special gift or two, but some have more and some have less. You try so hard to find a box to put yourself in, Kiah. Maybe you are trying to put your Dhia in… something you can understand and always predict. This is not how He is. God is big. He does not fit in your box, or mine."

"You are saying I should throw away my box, then? Does that mean I have to stop trying to understand?"

"No, of course not. You were made with your questions, and you should ask them. Just remember that the answers are so much bigger and so much different than you think they will be, and they may come so much slower than you want them to."

"And what about the woman who brought you here? Was she from a family that knew the Calling?"

"Yes. Her name was Tess. She trained me here. She spoke Chinese to me and taught me English and Kress. I lived with her in the main house at the end of this road. She took me on jaunts behind the cloud, into the Kress territory." Fa shivered a little.

"Jaunts?"

"A 'jaunt' is what we call a mission, a rescue."

"So what happened to your family back home?"

"Gone, all of them. They were all killed that day," Fa said quietly.

"Who killed them, Fa?"

"I don't know. What I know is God saved me. He knew what would happen, and so He brought me here."

"But have you ever asked Him why He didn't bring your whole family? Why He didn't save everyone? Why just you?"

"At first, I asked this question, but He did not answer it. He just cried with me."

"Cried with you? What does that mean?" I asked.

"I lay in a field on a hill not far from here, and I asked my questions, the questions you just asked about my family and why they died, why I lived. The sky opened up, and God cried with me. There was lightning and thunder. It was only Him and I. He grieved with me. He told me He had a plan for me. He did not answer my questions, Kiah. He changed my questions."

Fa smiled at me. "Oh, don't cry for me, Kiah. His people are my family now. Tess was my family. You are my family. I don't want to be anywhere else. I am where I am meant to be." She squeezed my hand.

I touched my face and discovered it was wet. I hadn't realized I was crying.

"Is Tess gone now?" I asked.

Fa nodded. "He took her home to heaven last year. She was happy. She was ready. She was very peaceful when she left." Fa smiled softly then sat up and headed for the door.

"I think we need more tea."

I stretched carefully. Every one of my joints felt stiff, and my legs were aching. I hoped it wasn't the flu. I didn't think it was. I hadn't ever felt so sore, so tired, so peaceful, and so unsure all at the same time. Fa returned with her tea, and we sat for a while, sipping and listening to the thunder and lightning shake the Rock. I tightened a blanket around my shoulders and pulled my toes in under it in a subconscious effort to protect myself from the storm, though it wasn't cold.

"So Ailsa was a Blue from your family. She belonged here just like you do. She made the quilt on your bed," Fa said.

It still felt strange to hear her say that it was *my* bed and *my* cabin. I ran my finger over a frayed blue chambray square on the quilt and wondered again when it was made.

"The letters I found in the box were written to someone named Shae. Who is Shae?" I asked.

"Shae was a Blue as well. She stayed in the next cottage over."

"When?" I asked.

Fa shrugged. She didn't know.

An image much like a moving photograph sprang to mind… that of a young redheaded woman sorting herbs in the tiny kitchen, writing excitedly, sealing the page into an envelope, and running to the cottage next door to slip it under the door for the occupant to find once she returned. Perhaps Ailsa and Shae were like the proverbial ships that passed in the night, seeing each other when their Callings happened to bring them to the same place at the same time—leaving notes for each other whenever one happened to be on the Rock without the other. That would explain the lack of dates in the letters and the journals. What good would dates do if they were traveling back and forth between Earth and Petra?

"But then why doesn't anyone at home know of Ailsa? Why didn't my great-aunt know her name?" I asked Fa.

Fa shook her head. "This I don't know."

Lightning forked again, and I felt a deep ache in my bones. Uneasiness flitted across Fa's face.

"What is it?" I asked.

"He is angry, I think. I told you Dhia shows himself to us more easily here. This storm… He is angry."

"Angry about what?" I asked, borrowing Fa's uneasiness.

"I don't know. Maybe something on Earth. Maybe something has happened somewhere."

Fa dropped to her knees and began to speak to Dhia fervently in Chinese. Tears ran down her cheeks as she prayed. I caught a familiar word here and there. She seemed to be grieving with Dhia over whatever grieved Him and reminding Him of His goodness and her devotion. She pled for His will to be done on Earth.

I slipped off the couch, meaning to join her, but had the sudden urge to find paper and pencil and write something down.

I rummaged through the drawers in the kitchen and located a leather-bound paper tablet, returned to the couch, poised the pen above the paper, and waited. One word came to me. I wrote it down, then another came, and another… I wrote each one in turn. My eyes were hot and blurry with tears as I wrote. My chest filled with a heated mix of sadness, anger, and regret. I wrote until they stopped coming, then looked back to see what I'd written.

Oh, to break, to build, to yield,
To hold dear and not to turn
Blind, bloody, staring at the past,
Judging right from left, right from wrong, with stupid eyes,
Cursing, hefting, sordid camps of "what we do,"
Lines drawn
Holes dug,
Faces painted,
Eating dirt to satisfy our souls
Thirst slaked with bitters,
Hunger satiated with ash,
Mute by choice.
Mouths yawning.
Vocal cords hoarse from striving
Never heard.
Emptied out, drained bloodless with no recourse,

By Choice.
Oh, to see
To break, to build, to yield,
To know, and never return.

I felt stark remorse as I read what I'd written—not for having written it but for the choices we, people, had made. It was a desperation like nothing I'd ever felt before, and I didn't fully understand it. It was more of a reflection of Dhia's feelings than it was my own, but I felt it as if it were my own grief. I started to remove the page I'd written on from the tablet, planning to return it to the kitchen drawer, then remembered this was my cottage. It was my tablet to keep. I wrapped the leather laces around the little book to secure it and pocketed it.

Fa finished with her prayers and rose from the floor.

"I think it's time to sleep," she said. The length of the day showed in the lines on her face. I hadn't seen her sleep at all the night before, though it was possible she stole a wink or two while I napped in the niche.

I'd spied and coveted a few fresh toothbrushes in the kitchen drawer. I retrieved them along with a small vial of toothpaste. Fa and I brushed our teeth in comfortable silence at the kitchen sink, listening to the wind howl. The lightning had died down a bit. The thunder was more distant and less frequent. We had talked so much and so long that there seemed to be nothing left to say. Fa gathered a few blankets from a shelf along the living room wall, and I headed to the bedroom.

"Good night," I said softly.

"Good night," came her muffled reply.

I pulled the bedroom door closed, lit the brazier, found a pair of pajamas, and pulled them on. The pants, which seemed to have had blue pinstripes at some point in the past, were too short and too wide. Luckily, there was a drawstring waist. The shirt was light and breezy, almost threadbare. I reached for the brazier, planning to put the light back out. I hesitated a little as my fingers closed on the blue sap. I didn't have much experience lighting and extinguishing the braziers. I had to talk my fingers into closing on open flame. It was barely warm to the touch. The sap felt like stiff prechewed gum between my fingers. I separated the two ends of the fuel source at the right corner of the square and watched as the flame went out and the room went dark.

There was just enough light to make out the dim shape of the bed. I felt my way there and climbed under the quilts. My limbs were sore and weary; my heart still heavy. My mind raced, churning bits of the day's conversations and the questions that remained unanswered. I tried to picture Aggie and Donal in my mind. They seemed so far away. They *were* so far away. Were they walking along the hiking trail? Or stuck in some sort of strange slow motion time warp because of the time difference between the Earth and the Rock? I didn't think it was the latter, but I gave up trying to wrap my mind around it. How many of my ancestors, faithful women, had slept in this room? Surely they were more sure of themselves, stronger, more ready than I was for whatever lay ahead. I suddenly felt very small.

A Dhia, teach me! Teach me to not to worry about what is beyond my control. Teach me not to lean on my own understanding. Teach me to trust you. Teach me to be fully present in the moment. Teach me to wait for you. Please give me Your peace, tonight. I need Your peace.

The rain finally came, beating steady drumbeats on the roof.

SPITTLE

The return swim through the Iona gate wasn't quite as challenging as the initial trip had been. The absence of stark terror made it much more manageable. As I powered through the water, I felt the temperature change… from the warm Petra currents to the frigid gray waters of the Bay at the Isle of Iona. Lungs bursting, I broke the surface of the water into the cold gray light. A stiff briny breeze blew across the surface of the water.

Relieved that there were no tourists walking the trail above the bay, I hauled myself onto the rocks. My body seemed heavier than I remembered, and I wondered if it was an effect of the cold or if the gravity was somehow different on Petra. Small bluish bruises dotted my knees, a reminder of my time in Dhia's presence at the bedside of the unconscious man. I began to shiver violently.

Fa burst out of the water right behind me. I had expected her to see me safely to land and pop back under the water, disappearing into the deep like a dark darting seal. Instead, she joined me on the rocks. She retrieved our clothes from the ledge, and we dressed quietly and quickly. I followed her, with some degree of difficulty since I was still shaking and numb, to the top of the hill. We turned in the opposite direction of the village. Away from the shelter of the bay, the breeze lessened, and the air felt cold and clammy. The trail wound back and forth a short while before it *Y*ed to the right, marked with a gate and a sign that read *Restricted Access*. We moved onto the private path and followed it to a shabby little cabin in an old stand of yew and oak trees. Wisps of smoke rose from the chimney. Fa bounded up the steps, opened the door, and waved me inside.

"Shine! We are here!" Fa called out as she entered the tiny living room. The overly warm room felt heavenly. A fire blazed in the tiny fireplace. It was a room owned by books. Books were jammed into every nook and cranny and into the shelves that lined the walls. They spilled out over every surface. There were books on end tables, the overstuffed chair, and the sad little couch, and stacked in piles behind the rocking chair. I felt instantly at home.

Fa relocated one such stack and planted herself on the couch, wrapping up in a blanket.

"In here, I'm coming!" came a muffled voice from somewhere down the hall.

"Shine?" I whispered to Fa. "Is that someone's name?"

"Yep, mine. My parents were hippies." The answer came not from Fa but from Shine herself, who appeared suddenly in the door behind me. I noticed her eyes first. Large and inviting, they were almost colorless, like an overcast sky. She wore a prairie skirt and an incongruous old blue T-shirt that said Bay Crest Finals 1986. Setting a tray full of baked goodies down on and end table, she hurried over to us, grabbed my upper arms, and rubbed them briskly.

"Good grief, Fa. Did you try to freeze her as well as drown her?" she asked. Her accent was unmistakably American.

"Of course. This is how I always do," Fa answered.

"I stoked up the fire to 'skin melt' level. Maybe it isn't enough. You are an ice cube! So let me guess… You were here to see the island and decided to swing by the Rock on your way?"

Shine was obviously a Blue.

"School. I am with a school group. I'm here today taking an extra credit class," I explained. Shine edged me into the nearest chair, dislodging a book that hit the floor with a loud thud. Shine disregarded it and fetched a worn quilt from the back of the couch and tucked it all around me.

"So you are getting the official history of the island, then. Come back again sometime when you don't have to rush off, and I'll fill you in on the rest. Oh, I've been hoping to meet you!" She grinned and sat on the couch opposite me.

"How did you know I would be here? Or who I am?" I asked.

"Oh, I just knew. Grapevine. Actually, Fa told me she would be bringing someone by today. Tell me a little bit about yourself. Oh wait, I forgot… cookie first?" She leapt up to grab the tray and held it out to Fa.

"Super healthy, I promise. Flax and honey mostly."

Fa peered at the cookies on the tray as if they might be dangerous insects. "Just one, I think," she said, taking one and biting into it. She looked less than thrilled with the experience.

I shook my head. "No, thank you. I am headed to lunch soon."

Fa mouthed the word *chicken* at me from behind Shine's back.

"Okay, so? Name? Age? Stats?" Shine planted herself in front of me again, tucking her long blond hair behind her ears.

"Oh yeah. Sorry. I'm Kiah. I'm eighteen. I'm from Washington State. I'm going to college at Aodhagan. I'm new, *very* new to all of this."

"Nice to meet you, Kiah. I'm Shine, but you heard that part already." Shine leaned back in her chair, fanning herself with an envelope, and proceeded to fill me in. Originally from Philadelphia, Shine was twenty-four years old. Her name actually was Shine… Shine Silk Marceau. She had studied history with an emphasis on genealogy at Yale University. She lived and worked at the Iona Community: an ecumenical group on the island that worked for social justice and peace.

"That's my day job, anyway. I also tend the gate," she said, holding her finger up to mouth as if to remind me to "keep that part secret."

"Are there Blues who tend every gate?" I asked.

"Oh no. Most of the gates don't require a towel and a fireplace." She leaned forward, gesturing at my huddled, shivering form. I was exhibit A for her point. "I think there's been someone at the Iona gate for a long time, though. Centuries, maybe… Do you know, Fa?"

Fa, picking the remains of Shine's health cookie from her teeth, shook her head. No.

"Anyway, I've only been here a few years, and I don't just stoke the fire and provide dry clothing. There are other things to do. Deliveries, keeping track of the rumors, that sort of thing."

"Rumors?"

"People in Scotland and Ireland have heard rumors about the Calling for years. Most people just think the Calling is a legend, superstition."

"My great-aunt said something like that," I said.

"Yeah, well, for the most part it's just people just like passing on tales and its harmless gossip. There are some, though…" Her voice trailed off, and she knit her brows together. "Recently, there are some people that take it more seriously than that. And their intentions aren't good."

"Who are they?"

Shine shrugged. "I'm not sure, but a few Blues have run into some really hostile individuals lately. It's a relatively new development. You will know if you meet them."

"And what do I do if I meet them?" I asked, mildly alarmed.

"Pray! And don't talk to them long. There's no point in conversation. They are dangerous. Maybe not physically but definitely spiritually. Some of their demons recognize us even if they don't know us themselves."

"Demons?" I snorted. "You are kidding, right?"

I glanced at Fa, who was placidly following along with the conversation. She had nothing to add. I had only just begun to consider the power of Dhia. I hadn't given much thought to the darkness having power as well. It seemed incredible that Shine was discussing demonic forces in the same tone most people would use to talk about a difficult chemistry teacher.

"Just remember, the demons can't handle hearing about the blood of Jesus Christ. The blood of Christ has defeated them. It holds power over them. Talking about that will end any conversation that gets too ugly. Guaranteed," Shine tried to reassure me. "You warmer yet?"

I nodded. My teeth had ceased chattering. My feet and toes were beginning to tingle.

"You will be working in the healing rooms?" Shine asked, switching subjects abruptly and offering the tray of deformed cookies once more. I deferred as politely as possible.

"The healing rooms? Yes, I think so. I mean, actually, I don't know exactly," I stammered a little, wondering if I should already know.

"It's okay, of course you aren't sure yet. You are taking it on faith, one step at a time."

"Honestly, I feel more clueless than faithful at this point," I blurted. "I don't know what I'll be doing yet because no one's told me. I feel like I'm on a scavenger hunt without clues. And I'm barely keeping up."

"You may not know exactly where you are headed, but you are strong. You are stronger than you know. I can see that about you." Shine grasped my hands in hers.

"And you have a healing gift. A strong healing gift. I feel like I should tell you that. Is that something you know?" she asked, her clear eyes probed mine.

I tried not to shy away from her gaze, but the directness and intimacy commonplace among the Blues still unnerved me, especially when it came from someone I barely knew. In my own home, when directness came into play, intimacy often evaporated.

"What makes you think I have a healing gift?" I asked.

"It's just something I see about you. Is it something you know?"

"There was something that happened on the Rock that made we wonder about that... about being a healer... but I don't know for sure what that all means."

The term *healer* excited and frightened me a little.

Shine smiled and gripped my shoulders. "You don't have to understand everything right away. Just listen. Know what He tells you. Wait for the next step. He will show you."

"Have you heard that before?" Fa smirked.

I rolled my eyes at Fa.

"Are you a healer?" I asked Shine.

"No. I'm not. I mean, I've helped out when I needed to, but I'm more of a speaker and a listener than a healer. I love to listen to the Lord. I'd spend all my time with Him if He would let me. I love sharing what He has to say with other people too, though…" Her face lit up in a pure, almost childlike way. Hearing someone speak joyfully and plainly about God was completely foreign to me. My first instinct was borderline disbelief, though I could tell she meant every word. It made me wonder what it was about the world that made me shy of such bold passion for God. If she'd said she spent hours a day watching soap operas or gushed about football, somehow that would have been more easily acceptable.

Smoke, came the silent answer from inside me. The kind of smoke that Fa had talked about. Evil benefits when goodness and purity are discounted and not believed. It was more acceptable to scream and cheer at ball games than it was to openly show our love for Dhia. *Why was that?*

"Hey, how do you calculate the time difference between here and Petra?" I asked Shine. "Last time, I was only gone five minutes in one day. This time it was several hours in three. I don't understand the math."

Shine shook her head and rolled her eyes skyward. "It's harder than calculus. Don't even bother. The season and the time of year make a difference. Sometimes even the weather changes things. Just listen to God. He keeps us on schedule."

Just listen to God… She said it as if it were just that simple.

Can people really hear from God that clearly, that well? I wondered.

"Yes," came the answer in a low but audible voice.

I jumped and quickly scanned the room for the source.

"What's the matter?" Shine asked. "Did something bite you?"

"Nope. I just asked a question in my head and got an audible answer."

"Makes me jump almost every time," Shine concurred, grinning.

Just then, Fa rejoined us. "Time to go," she said, scooping up a tightly wrapped plastic parcel from a cubby on the shelf.

"Is this the only thing that needs to go back?" she asked Shine.

"Yep, that's all," Shine answered. "It goes to Cara at the Dragon Bridge."

The mention of a bridge piqued my curiosity. I assumed it was on Petra, but there was no time to ask. Fa was already halfway out the door.

Shine hugged me firmly.

"You guys made my day. I can't wait to see you again. Come anytime."

I nodded, more than a little disappointed to be leaving so soon. I had a million more questions for Shine and no time to ask them. I hurried after Fa. Shine waved at us from the front window as we left. It began to rain as we descended the steps and headed for the main trail. Fa had pulled a tattered red umbrella from the bench seat on the porch and handed it to me.

"For the long walk," she said, not taking one for herself.

"Are you headed back to the Rock?" I asked her.

She nodded.

"I don't suppose you know when I'll see you again?"

"Of course, no… but soon, I think." She smiled.

We walked together in silence to the back bay where we parted ways. I shuddered just thinking of the chilly swim that lay ahead for Fa. The rain was getting serious by the time I reached the edge of little village. The wind drove the water in at a horizontal angle, rendering my shabby umbrella useless. I abandoned it to an umbrella stand on a nearby porch and walked the rest of the way to the visitor's center without it. I seemed destined to spend the day soaked to the bone. I stopped off at the visitor's center to retrieve my paper bag lunch and rejoin Donal and Aggie. We lunched under the awning at the back of the building, watching the sheets of rain pound and darken the hillside while I sidestepped their questions about Fa. Just as I finished the last bite of the sad little sandwich I'd packed for myself, the professor stuck her head out the side door to call us back inside. We followed her on a walking tour of the Abbey, St. Oran's chapel, and the burial site of ancient kings. Her exuberance about ancient raids and skirmishes seemed to render her impervious to the water. Her words ran together in my brain like the pureed macaroni casserole the hospital served to toothless patients. My arms felt heavy, my fingers puffy, and my thoughts sloshed back and forth, side to side and corner to corner in my brain. I powered through the remainder of the afternoon in low-power-automatic-pilot mode.

Finally, we arrived back at the ferry dock where the professor said her good-byes and thanked us for being good listeners. I lagged behind the group slightly, last in line to board. As I stepped onto the ramp that led to the small waiting ferry, the professor stepped directly in front of me. Her face hovered inches from mine, and her expression slid from professional to cold and razor-sharp. Her dark eyes glittered.

"You're not welcome here," she said and spit in my face.

I froze, momentarily unsure whether I had experienced or imagined the bizarre interaction. An invisible band tightened around my chest, and the muscles in my forearms flooded with something heated—blood or adrenaline, maybe both. The line of cooling spittle down my left cheek told me I hadn't imagined the offense. Slowly, without taking my eyes off the professor, I reached up and wiped the dampness from my cheek with my sleeve. I wondered if I'd just met one of the hostile women Shine had warned me about. The professor's expression returned suddenly and completely too professional, as if a shadow had passed through her for a moment, then moved on. I wasn't sure she even realized what she had just done. She turned on her heel and marched away while I boarded the boat.

MO CHARAIDH, MY FRIEND

One of the first lessons I learned in nursing school was that people are messy. People are messy even when they don't mean to be and sometimes *especially* when they don't mean to be. The first section of clinicals for the freshmen nursing students occurred at a local nursing home. We basically took over the role of the nursing assistants, the personal caretakers for the residents. We weren't paid for our services. Instead we paid good money (college tuition) for the privilege of observing various fluids and solids that had been expelled from our patients and deciding if said effluents needed to be documented, returned to the patient, or simply washed away. Then most of the time we also got to do the washing away. There were some activities that didn't include bodily fluids, but they seemed few and far between.

Initially, I wondered if I would ever get used to seeing things outside my patients that were inside my patients only moments before. Urine, feces, emesis, spittle, blood, dentures and a variety of unidentifiable and sometimes unspeakable things. We, of course, spoke of even the aforementioned unspeakable things, sometimes in great detail. The physical mess is really just one category of messy, however. There's also the emotional mess category, which is even harder to get used to. Maybe that's because we aren't built to accustom ourselves to pain and death. Some things are supposed to be hard. They are supposed to hurt.

It was Friday afternoon, a few short weeks since my initial Iona visit. I sat at the bedside of Cumina, a woman who very much resembled a milky white raisin. She was one of my first patients. She was also, thus far, my favorite. While fear of death hovered in the nursing home in general, it didn't seem to penetrate the doorway to Cumina's room. Cumina didn't speak and rarely even moved on her own, but something drew me to her room. *Goodness* permeated the air there. I could feel it. I could almost smell it. My primary task was to put Cumina's limbs through a series of passive range of motion exercises. I stretched her legs and arms gently away from her body, but they drew back in, curling tight like the wings of a baby bird whenever I let go. Her skin was fragile. It tore easily, and bandaging the tears was difficult because the tape itself caused tearing. Even with moderate pressure, dark bruises spread under her translucent skin like blue ink stains. I did my best to handle her with my palms rather than my fingertips. I suggested wrapping her skin tears in rolls of gauze rather than applying plasters. Surprisingly, the nurses took my suggestion. Cumina wore a fixed vacant expression. I had worked with her a handful of times and had yet to see her register awareness of her surroundings or my presence. I talked to her as if she understood me, but she never responded.

Sometimes a particular song from an elderly senile person's past can spark thought and shed light into a darkened corner of the mind. Just that morning, a nurse's aide had taught me a simple Gaelic folk song that sometimes reached through Cumina's fog and roused her for a short time. I memorized the first few lines; and while I flexed the old woman's fragile fingers that day, gently rubbing oil into the joints, I watched her face and began to sing. Her unfocused gaze shifted from somewhere above my head to my meet my eyes, and her voice joined mine. High-pitched and squeaky as a rusty hinge to begin with, it mellowed quickly, and I heard traces of a once-beautiful singing voice. I stopped singing and listened to her as she sang through the song a few times, wondering if she would lapse back into her unconscious state or stay in the world for a while once her singing stopped. Her voice trailed off, and her eyes focused on mine.

"That was beautiful," I said in Gaelic.

Cumina smiled and grappled for my hand.

"You are as beautiful as ever. I've missed your voice." Cumina smiled at me. Her Gaelic was much smoother than my own.

"I didn't know you remembered me," I told her, wondering if she did actually remember me from last week or if she mistook me for someone else.

"I'll always know you, mo charaidh," Cumina scolded. "I'd know your face anywhere. Where has your hair gone?" She attempted to reach for my face; but her arm, weak from disuse, fell back to the blanket. I grasped her hand and brought it to my head, letting her touch my hair. I wanted to sustain her awakening for as long as I could, no matter whom she mistook me for.

"I cut it a few years ago. It's easier this way. I needed a change," I answered truthfully.

"I'm so tired, Elly. Will it be time to go soon?" she asked me, eyes searching my face.

"Time to go? Where do you want to go, Cumina?"

Who is Elly? I wondered.

"I'm just so tired, Elly," she repeated, murmuring like a stream. Her eyes drifted toward shut, then fluttered open again. "And why are *you* calling me by my first name?"

"What would you like me to call you?" I asked.

"No one's called me anything but Cumina for so long now. Cumina sounds like an old woman's name!" She smiled a little at her own tiny joke. "I think maybe the world's forgotten my name… has forgotten me… everyone but the Lord, so that's all right. You remember me, though. Of course you do…" She patted my hand and smiled. Strands of her white hair fell out of the loose bun atop her head and lay across her face.

Her voice dropped lower, and she began to sing the folk song again, but it deteriorated quickly. She was lapsing back into unawareness.

"What can I call you, Cumina? What can I call you instead?" I asked, but the lights in her mind were dimming. Her mind slipped back out of reach. I took the loose hair tie out of her hair and refastened her bun. She had a remarkable amount of hair for a woman her age, whatever that age was. I tucked her in to bed and turned out the light, then headed for the nurse's station. The hall had fallen quiet, and the overhead lights had been dimmed. The strip lights at the edges of the hallways twinkled like runway markers.

The nurse at the front desk snored in her chair. She looked older than most of the residents. Her head was cocked back at an unnatural angle, one of her eyes half open as she slept. It was disconcerting. The name tag pinned to her rumpled uniform read "Fionulla." Except for Fionulla, the nurse's station was empty. My cohorts, Aggie, Gillian, and Christie, were all still out of sight and busy with their patients. I tiptoed past the nurse quietly, though the sound of her snoring would have allowed me to pass by undetected in medieval armor and snow skis. I entered the chart room and pulled the charts for my patients. I needed to record my interventions on their permanent records and write up a nursing care plan for my own schoolwork. We were required to write up nursing care plans on every patient we saw. They were the bane of the nursing student's existence. They were long, involved, and never, as far as I knew, used in the field. I became easily frustrated with pointless paperwork. Perhaps it built character. *Is monotony-induced hysteria a positive character trait?*

I flipped open Cumina's chart, hoping to find the nickname she was speaking of so I could call her by it the next time I visited her. It jumped off the page at me like hot grease, raising gooseflesh on my arms rather than burns.

Name: Cumina Shae Hedley   Birthdate stated: August 15, year unknown
Age: estimated 100+ years   Next of Kin: unknown

Her name was Shae. My mind spun as I tried to calculate possible dates. The letters written between Ailsa and Shae had no dates to work from, however. I had no place to start.

Could Cumina really be Shae... Ailsa's neighbor on the Rock? Cumina had called me Elly. Or maybe she hadn't. Maybe she'd called me Aylie. Aylie was short for Ailsa. That would mean she mistook me for one of my own relatives. I abandoned my charting and searched instead through the chart instead for clues to Cumina's background. The personal history section of the chart was sketchy and devoid of anything useful. She had transferred from another facility in Edinburgh six years before. The insurance section was also strangely empty. Where the insurance company or payer's name should have been, it simply read *Paid in Full*.

"Have ye seen a ghost?" rasped a loud voice from just behind my left ear. I jumped and dropped the chart. Fionulla had rolled her chair silently up behind me. She cackled and slapped her knee. I had been so deeply engrossed in my own thoughts I hadn't noticed that she'd stopped snoring.

"She's our mystery, thet one. Nae a'body comes to see her, nae a'body asks after her. Lots of folk have nae kin. It's sad. But did ye see her account's been paid? I've ne'er seen thet afore. They say a large donation must 'ave been made in her name. I havena notion if thet's true or nae, nor of her history. All she does is sing the one song and then babble a wee bit about her past."

The nurse rubbed her chin, and I couldn't help but notice that she hadn't bothered to pull the whiskers that grew there like slender black-and-silver tree trunks. Perhaps there were simply too many to fuss with. I decided not to tell her about Cumina's short awakening. I didn't want to prolong the conversation.

"It is strange," I said to the nurse.

"Aye, it is." She bobbed her head up and down in agreement.

"I guess I should finish my care plan," I told Fionulla, glancing at my watch. I had less than a half hour left of my shift.

"They're still having you do that guff then, are they?" She shook her head. "I'll leave you to it."

I forced Cumina to the back of my mind and finished the care plans as quickly as I could. They weren't well done, but they would have to do. Before I left that night, I stuck my head into Cumina's room. She was asleep, propped up on her side just as I'd left her. I adjusted her position again—knowing that, with almost no fat under her skin, the edges of her own bones could easily cause her bedsores.

"Good night, Shae. Sleep well," I whispered softly in Gaelic into her ear. Her eyes fluttered.

My carpool was waiting for me outside, and they weren't a patient bunch. I hurried to the door and barely caught her quiet reply.

"Good night, Aylie, mo charaidh."

A VISITOR

Ar n-Athair a tha air neamh, gu naomhaichear d'ainm.

Thigeadh do rioghachd. Deanar do thoil air an talamh, mar a nithear air neamh.

Tabhair dhuinn an-diugh ar n-aran laetheil.

Agus maith dhuinn ar fiachan, amhail a mhaith-eas sinne dar luch-fiach.

Agus na leig ann am buaireadh sinn; ach saor sinn o olc;

oir is leatsa an rioghachd, agus an cumhachd, agus a' gloir, gu siorrhaidh.

Amen

Matthew 6

I woke up early the next morning facedown, soaked in cold sweat. My neck muscles were knotted from sleeping long and hard in the same position. I knew a dream had awoken me but couldn't remember the details. It was something cold, dark and twisting, fraught with streaks of orange and strange unearthly screams. I breathed deeply, trying to steady my nerves and rose up on one elbow. I tried shifting my legs toward the edge of the bed but only managed to move only a few inches. Something was holding me down. My limbs felt useless and rubbery. General sleepy malaise turned quickly toward panic. Someone was in the room with me. No, not someone… something. I turned my head as far as I could toward the ceiling and glimpsed a dark haze above me. It shifted visibly and purposefully not with the air movement but of its own accord, sliding and swirling. I had the vague notion it had followed me out of my dreams, but that wasn't possible. *Was it?*

"What now?" I muttered.

I was having trouble holding onto any purposeful thoughts. Dread and profound hopelessness had as tight a hold on my mind as it did my body. I felt as if a heavy fog had settled in my brain, impeding my thought traffic. My thought highways were Interstate 5 at 5:00 p.m.

Think, Kiah! Think! I told myself. I blinked rapidly and, with massive effort, managed to shift onto my side. My wobbly elbow was aching. I was tempted to drop back down, face-first onto the pillow but was honestly afraid I might suffocate. It struck me suddenly that the something might be there not only to scare me but to kill me.

Be still! Don't move! Don't think! Just listen a minute! I told myself. I took a deep breath and tried to focus.

You need to speak. I heard a small voice whisper somewhere inside me.

Speaking…that was one thing I hadn't tried yet. I cleared my throat and heard faint sound emanate from my vocal cords. My voice seemed to be working, but what should I say?

A Dhia, Help me! What do I say? I prayed silently.

That was the other thing I hadn't tried yet… prayer… the thing I should have tried first.

I listened for Dhia's voice. My elbow and shoulders were cramping up, and pain shot through them in a continuous circuit. I heard no answer, but a prayer sprang to mind, one suggested by Jesus Himself in the sixth chapter of the book of Matthew… the Bible. I cleared my throat and began.

"Our Father in heaven, hallowed be your name. Your kingdom come, your will be done, on earth as it is in heaven." My throat was dry, and my voice squeaked. I felt the presence over me move but not lift. I continued.

"Give us this day our daily bread, and forgive us our debts as we forgive our debtors, and lead us not into temptation, but deliver us from evil."

At that, I felt the presence shudder. It seemed agitated, disturbed. So I repeated the phrase "deliver us from evil," even louder, half hoping it would rouse my sleeping, grouchy neighbor, but Bert's old walls were solid and thick. I could probably lose my voice screaming and still not be heard a few feet down the hall.

"For yours is the power and the kingdom and the glory forever."

I finished and twisted, shifting toward my right side. I managed to rest on my left hip and relieve most of the pressure on my right elbow. I still needed it to brace me, to keep me from falling flat. The haze above me was swirling. Small wisps of orange flashed at the edges. It was definitely what I had been dreaming about. *Or had I been dreaming?* I didn't have time to sort that out.

"My situation has not improved, Dhia! Help me!" I cried out.

I suddenly remembered something Sam, the man of God at the little stone church in my hometown, had once told me. *There's power in the blood of Jesus Christ, Kiah. There's power in His name. The demons shuddered at His voice, and they left when He commanded them to.* Shine had mentioned that as well.

The haze shifted direction again, roiling, and beginning to make a hideous wheezing sound. I mustered as much authority as I could and shouted.

"By the power of the blood of Jesus Christ you are defeated, let me alone! Leave now!" The fervor and volume of my own voice startled me. The pressure on my body released instantly, and I felt so light that I momentarily wondered if I might rise up off the bed entirely. The haze lifted toward the ceiling, condensed until it was almost black with yellowish-orange tinsel-like glints then shot toward the window and exited through the uppermost pane, shattering it into a million tiny shards.

I was alone once again. The air was still except for the cold night air now seeping in through the hole in the window. The palpable fear and despair had exited with the unwelcome guest. I could hear normal noises again. The numbers on my digital clock clicked and flipped, and the pipes creaked as a toilet flushed somewhere in the building. I lay back, trying to catch my breath, feeling weak and shaky but safe. I moved my legs toward the side of the bed, easily this time. I slid over the edge of the bed onto my knees and rested my forehead on the carpet.

"Tapadh leibh, Dhia," I whispered. Thank you.

Peace arrived, and I closed my eyes, taking in the quiet. I had no idea what had visited me, but it was gone. Dhia had vanquished it. For the first time, I truly understood the meaning of the word *vanquish*. I had always thought of evil as a theory, a characteristic connected to people's behavior. I had just witnessed proof that evil existed also in a tangible nonhuman form.

Breathe. Just breathe, I reminded myself. I complied.

I lay in the dark, feeling the cold night air stream in through the new hole in the windowpane and chill the room. I wasn't sure how I would explain the damage to the maintenance staff. The glass shards had flown out of the room in the direction of applied force rather than in, leaving me with no good excuse for how it happened. I would probably have to pay for the damage. That was the least of my concerns.

My limbs were feeling more solid and reliable, and it was time to move. I rose from the floor and pressed the desk lamp switch. The light didn't respond. The room stayed dark. I tried the lamp on the bureau. It flashed but burnt out immediately. I started to think my visitor may have damaged more than just the window glass. I tried the overhead light switch and received confirmation. Every bulb was blown. I opened the door to the hall; but the only light in the common area, the nightlight by the toaster, was barely helpful. I abandoned the idea of seeing what I was doing and searched mostly by feel through the back of my desk drawer. Retrieving a roll of packing tape and a pair of scissors, I removed a cardboard box from the back of my closet and dumped its contents onto the closet floor. With some difficulty, I managed to tear and cut a flap of the box into a square large enough to cover the hole in the window, sealing it entirely shut.

I hastily gathered clothing and headed for the bathroom. The hallway was much warmer than my room. I wondered if the broken window was completely responsible for the lack of heat or if my visitor itself had contributed directly. I shuddered at the thought, then shuffled into the bathroom, rubbing my throbbing elbow. I locked the bathroom door behind me, dropped my clean clothing onto the toilet, flipped on the light, and looked in the mirror.

I looked ghastly. My oversized Hypercolor sleep shirt, which was designed to change color with my mood and body temperature, had given up on its job and turned dark gray. It clung damply to me. My hair, similarly soaked through with cold sweat, was plastered to my forehead. I peeled my wet shirt off and turned to see my shoulders in the mirror. Fresh bruises were blooming along my shoulder blades. I shrugged my shoulders and winced. That would be sore for a while. My elbow was swelling and stiffening. It was still the wee hours of the morning, and my dorm mates were all asleep. I figured I could probably escape chastisement for exceeding my shower time limit…Bert's house rules dictated a ten-minute maximum. I took a restorative twenty-five.

The warm water restarted my mental process and my metabolism. My stomach began to growl. I needed to find out more about what had just happened and whether the thing might return. Shine was at the top of my list of people to ask.

Should I go see Shine? I asked Dhia silently.

I felt a definite yes response. I wasn't sure it was from Dhia or my own rattled psyche, but either way, I needed to go immediately. I headed back down the hall into my room. The furnace was clanking away, trying to reheat the small space. I appreciated its considerable effort, but it was still chillier than the hall. The clock read 4:00 a.m. Buses didn't run that early, and I didn't have money for any other form of transportation. I wasn't willing to simply sit in my unlit room until daylight. I bundled up with leg warmers and an extra scarf and slipped my warmest coat over my sweatshirt. I jotted a quick note to Aggie, letting her know I'd be away for the weekend and slipped it under her door. I knew she would assume I was spending time with family.

I penned another note that explained my intention to pay for the broken window and considered slipping it under Big Bert's door, then changed my mind and crumpled it up. Big Bert's real name was Marta. Marta was the residence hall assistant, thus the nickname Big Bert. She was the official den mother for all of Bert's residents but more closely resembled the profile of an overbearing stepmother. She took her job much too seriously. Rather than invite Big Bert's scrutiny, I chose to hope no one noticed the damage right away and take it up with someone once I returned.

I locked the dorm room door, zipped the key into my pocket, and headed for the front door of the building. The night air outside was cold. *Really*, really cold. I wrapped my scarf over my head and twice around my neck, tucking the tails into my coat while I picked my way down the path toward the center of campus. Heavy mist settled often in the campus valley, freezing quickly, coating everything outdoors in a thin sheet of clear ice. Even the homely weeds became things of beauty, glistening like miniature glass statues. I had heard somewhere that the ice coating actually insulated the weeds, grass, and trees against the cold, protecting it from frigid death. Ice that gave warmth, life, and beauty. It was just like Dhia to make things work that way. He was an instigator of miraculous, sometimes ironic extremes. When I took the time to look and listen, I saw his fingerprints everywhere. I took a few moments just then and thanked Him for his beauty.

The icy footpaths shone in the moonlight. Student workers, still unconscious in their beds at that hour, would soon drag themselves out into the cold to salt the walks. I chose to walk on the grass instead of the concrete to keep from upending. It would be just like me to survive a supernatural attack and then knock myself out falling backward on the sidewalk. Every step I took made a loud crunch, and I left a trail of broken blade footprints behind me.

I had planned to turn right at the main campus road, but something drew me further on, past the decrepit old forestry building to a part of the grounds I hadn't visited before. There, a high fence surrounded a large arboretum dotted with trees. The garden extended all the way back toward the far edge of the campus. I followed the path along the edge of the arboretum to its end. Much of the campus was surrounded by high rock walls or iron gates, but there was no need for fencing along that particular edge. The land sloped sharply into a gulch, impassable with thick gnarled foliage, forming a natural barrier. The sky was crystal clear and perfectly still. Only the wispy evidence of my breath moved. I half expected it to freeze and hang, suspended in glass. It didn't. I was standing on the embankment, waiting, not sure what to do next, when I felt a familiar buzzing at the base of my neck.

I immediately registered concern. Being lifted by my freshly bruised shoulders wasn't a pleasant prospect. I took a deep breath and braced myself for the abrupt tug upward. When it came, the pain was sharp and radiant. I winced and tried to breathe through it. I flattened out, trying to ease the pressure on my shoulders as much as possible. The pain settled into a dull throb. I whisked along, high above the ground, wondering what I looked like from below. Bundled in layers of coats and scarves, perhaps I resembled the Flying Purple People Eater. I was actually wearing my only purple shirt. The entire countryside was asleep. Only a handful of cars crawled carefully along the slippery roads. It was *so* cold. I hunched my shoulders gingerly and tightened my scarf.

Okay, Dhia… tell me which way to go, I prayed silently.

Right, straight, up over the hills, down, left slightly, straight ahead. I didn't hear the words but felt His gentle insistent guidance. After what seemed like forever, I saw the fog-laden ocean ahead on the horizon. The land below me was no longer encased in ice. I came up on a thick fog bank and wondered whether to go over, under, or straight through.

Under, came the answer.

Under turned out to be very low indeed. I skimmed along, just above the black sheet of water below me, and under a white sheet of clouds. We had studied frostbite in nursing class the week before. I wondered if I would soon have to treat it firsthand. My nose felt frozen solid. The clouds rose, and I rose with them. I could see Iona ahead. It was starting to rain. Well, rain was a mild word for it. The water came down in constant, slanted, needling sheets. I scanned for Shine's cabin and saw a wisp of smoke in the small grove of trees near the back bay. Sweet relief flooded my chest. I slowed automatically, drawing up my toes and turning my feet under me. I landed softly but gracelessly on my backside on the muddy mush that was the front lawn. Picking myself up off the ground, I headed quickly for the porch. Shine—smiling, dressed in her Saturday comfies—opened the door before I had time to knock.

TO LEAN

"Well, get in here, Silly!" Shine urged, beckoning me in off the porch. I noticed she had a stack of towels over her arm.

She didn't have to say it twice. I came inside and wincing, peeled off my coat as delicately as I could.

"Are you injured?" Shine asked, alarmed.

"Oh, no. Well, sort of, I guess," I answered. "My shoulders are sore."

Shine took my soggy clothing. I wrapped myself in a bath sheet and settled onto the floor in front of the woodstove. I wondered if violent shivering was bound to be my state of being every time I visited the little cabin. I certainly hoped not. Shine returned with an armload of oversized dry clothes. I began to reach for it, but she held out her hand.

"No, no. Just wait until you stop shaking. You have to get warm first," she insisted.

"I'll get hot tea. Are you hungry?"

I shook my head. My stomach, awakened by the warm shower earlier that morning, had shut down again on the cold trip over land and sea. I didn't think I could eat anything.

"Warm up first." Shine nodded and disappeared into the kitchen. I wondered how often she got shivering visitors. I certainly wasn't the first.

It was lavender tea that she brought back with her, hot and calming, with local honey. Shine wrapped another blanket around my shoulders and waited, content, until I was ready to talk. The hot tea did its job. I stopped shaking.

"Okay, I think I can get dressed now."

I dropped the blanket and towels away from my shoulders and reached for the clothing.

"Oh my!" Shine blurted. "What happened to you?"

She was staring at my exposed shoulders.

"Well, that's the main reason I'm here," I said, wondering how dark the bruises must be since they'd had a few hours to set in. "Something attacked me… sat on me, actually. This morning while I was in bed. Wait, did you know that? Did you somehow know I was coming?"

"I woke up hours ago, feeling that I should pray hard, so I did. After a while, Dhia told me someone was coming and I needed to be ready. So I made some muffins and stoked the stove. Can I take a look?" she asked, stepping closer.

"Sure."

"Are you sure it was a something and not a someone?" she asked.

"I'm positive."

Shine slipped a little tube of salve out of the end table drawer. She opened it and a sharp pungent odor—like skunk, mint, and grapefruit—filled the air.

"Phew! It's strong, but it works really well on bruises. It's from Petra. There's a Blue that harvests it from the south side of a little island over the dragon bridge. Have you been to the dragon bridge yet?" she asked.

"No, but I heard you mention it before. Where did it get its name…? There aren't dragons near it, are there?" I asked, wondering if that was stupid question. The fumes from the liniment were strong enough to clear my sinuses. I dabbed at my eyes and nose with a tissue from a box near the couch.

"Oh no. No actual dragons. The bridge itself resembles a dragon. You'll understand once you've seen it."

Shine fell silent, daubing the liniment onto my shoulders and my swollen elbow, rubbing it in gently. My skin tingled and the bruises ached. She laid a layer of gauze over top of the liniment and then helped me slip on the borrowed T-shirt. It was light pink with small yellow flowers. It made me smile. The last time I'd worn pink I'd probably been five years old. The sweatpants were pink too. Between the outfit and the personal care, I felt like a small needy child.

"You need to learn to lean," came a small audible voice. I startled slightly.

I need to learn to lean? That was certainly not a concept I would have come up with on my own. Everything in my life up to that point had been urging me toward independence. Pulling myself up by my bootstraps. Getting things done. Making it happen. Not needing anyone or anything. My childhood motto was, *I do it myself!*

I understood the theory behind leaning on Dhia: trusting Him with my decisions. It wasn't nearly as easy to put into practice—I was working on that part. Leaning on people, however, was another matter entirely. Shine, as much as I liked her, was a flesh-and-blood person; and people are fallible. I strongly resisted the idea of leaning on any person, even one as nice as Shine.

My emotions were reaching the boiling point. Tears pricked at the corners of my eyes.

What in the world is my problem? I wondered.

"Take your time. You had a rough morning," Shine said, noticing my sinking emotional state. Her words cracked my dam, and emotion streamed down my face in the form of silent tears. I wasn't used to crying in front of people. My habit was to stuff and sanitize my feelings around fellow humans, then weep under the covers in the darkness when it just got to be too much. *Suck it up and handle it!* I told myself, but it didn't work. Too many feelings warred in my chest. Sadness, frustration, fear, desperation, mistrust...

Shine remained silent. Dim light started to filter in through the windows, but the raindrops were still coming down hard, falling fat and vertical. I moved from the floor to the couch where I wrapped up in an old quilt.

"Maybe I could get one of those muffins now?"

Shine had done spiritual battle and baked muffins on my behalf in the middle of the night. The least I could do was try her muffins.

"Absolutely!" Shine jumped to her feet, pleased that someone wanted the fruit of her labor. She hurried to the kitchen and returned with a surprisingly lovely, warm, cherry-studded muffin.

"No refined flours, and I used honey, not sugar. They're all natural." Shine proudly ticked off the muffin's attributes on her fingers as she spoke.

"And yet still surprisingly delicious," I answered. They actually were pretty good. Sometimes low expectations plus mediocre proceeds equals rave reviews.

The lights flickered.

"The power has been threatening to go out since last night. It seems like it's off more than on out here some days."

Shine filled refilled our teacups and set about arranging and fluffing the pillows and blankets around herself like a dog building a nap nest. Finally, she settled in, satisfied.

"Okay, now fill me in, if you are ready. What exactly happened?"

"Well, I was sleeping. At least, I think I was. I was having dark dreams… really dark. All I can remember is black and fear, despair. I woke up in my bed in a pool of sweat. I tried to sit up, but I couldn't. Something was pushing me down, hard. It felt like an elephant on my shoulders. I managed to get up on one elbow, just barely, and I could see something, like a dark mist moving by itself above me. I even saw the orange flashes from my dream."

I watched Shine's face. She looked serious but not surprised.

"Do you know what it was?" I asked.

"Well, evil spirits, demons, of course," she said, her tone was flat and even. "They make me so angry, the little pissants."

I almost laughed at that. It seemed a strange moniker for the swarming mass of fear that I had encountered.

"Have you been through something like that before?" I asked.

"Yes, something similar, though it wasn't that physical. Your bruises are awful! How did you manage flying?"

"Gritted my teeth."

"So when you realized this thing was on top of you, you prayed?" Shine prompted me to continue my story.

"Oh yes. I did. I wasn't sure what to pray. So I started with the Lord's prayer from the book of Matthew."

"And?"

"Well, that got things stirred up. The thing, whatever it was, started thrashing. But it was still on top of me. So I told it to leave by the blood and in the name of Jesus Christ—or something like that. And it left… all at once and in a hurry. It shattered my window on its way out."

"Really? It broke the window? It was strong then." Shine thought a moment. "Was there anything else strange?"

I replayed the events in my mind.

"Yes. The lights. I went to turn on the lights, but all the bulbs were burnt out."

"That's not unheard of. Whatever visited you was strong, really strong. It sounds like someone invited it."

"Not me, right?" I asked, hoping I hadn't done anything to bring that on myself.

"No, of course not. Remember the group I was telling you about? The people who oppose the Calling? I think they are getting more serious."

"I didn't know they were an organized group or that they could send something to attack us. How do they even know who we are?" I asked.

"I don't know for sure. I assume they've heard of the Calling, and they believe in it, but they serve darkness. I don't think they know what we do, exactly, but they know enough to pray against us."

"Pray against us? You mean they *pray* to the darkness?"

Shine nodded. "Sure."

"How do you know that?"

"Sometimes I sense warnings from God. Things to watch out for. This is one of those warnings."

"My great-aunt Nan warned me to keep quiet about the Calling. She says some people around here don't take kindly to it. Maybe this is what she means."

"Your aunt is a woman of prayer?" Shine asked.

I nodded.

"That's probably exactly who she means. It's a confirmation."

"A confirmation of what?"

"When I hear something in my prayers, something I can't directly confirm through the Bible, usually because it's so specific... I look for a confirmation of what I've heard. Sometimes from the Bible, a specific verse. Sometimes it's from another believer," Shine explained.

I remembered something the professor had said during my initial visit to Iona and asked, "Could they be druids? The ones who inhabited the island before the Christians got here?"

"I've thought of that. They certainly could be. The druids I've met seem, for the most part, pretty innocuous. They come to the island to soak in the history and the mysticism of it. They love nature, and they love the island. They search for peace. They want to belong to something, but rather than finding God, they accept a substitute. They don't seem to give the community any trouble. They are widely tolerant, and I think they like to see Iona taken care of. In the last few months, however, there have been three incidents of Blues having run-ins from some very hostile people."

"All women?" I asked.

Shine nodded. "They may have been druids originally, but they are something else now. Something a lot darker."

"Oh Lord, come and direct our conversation. Please protect this place, in the name of Jesus Christ, and by His blood," she said.

It took me a moment to realize Shine was speaking to Dhia, not me.

"How do you keep track, Shine? How do you know the difference between rumors and suspicions and truth?" I asked her.

Shine absently rubbed the space behind her ear with her thumb, a habit I'd seen her indulge before. "Well, that's where you listen. Carefully. You pay attention, and make no assumptions, but gather information. There have been enough warning signs to tell me something's definitely stirring. There have been other recent spiritual attacks—like what you experienced but less severe. That kind of evil really needs a catalyst, an invitation, to gain permission to mess with you. A few of us have had dreams and visions about an actual group that has it out for us. We just don't know who it is."

"I think I've met at least one person who is in the group," I said.

At that, Shine's head jerked up.

"You are kidding! Who?"

"The first time I came to Iona, the professor that gave the lectures and headed up the tour... she seemed nice enough, initially. She taught us about the island. She seemed excited about the history. At the end of the day, though, when I went to board the ferry, she and I were alone for just a minute. She spit on me."

"She did *what?*"

"I was the last person to get on the boat. She and I were standing on the dock, and she stepped out in front of me and told me I wasn't welcome here. Then she spit on my face. She looked almost surprised that she had done it."

"What else did she say?"

"Nothing. That was it. She turned around and walked away, back to the visitor's center."

"And her name? Where was she from?" Shine asked, leaning forward.

"I don't remember. She was a guest professor, visiting from a museum in England. I guess I could find out from the school, but what good would that do? Is there anything we can actually do about them?"

"Mostly we need to pray hard for protection. Prayer is the only way to fight spiritual battles."

"Does that really help?" I asked, feeling somewhat foolish that I didn't really understand exactly how spiritual things worked.

"Yes, it does. It's the only thing that helps. We have free choice, remember? People have given evil permission to destroy. We can also invite God back into the mix. When God's in the battle, evil loses. You said your great-aunt is a believer?"

"Yes."

"And she knows something about the Calling?"

"Yes. Her sister was Called."

"Then would she pray with us and for us, if you asked her?"

"I'm sure she would. I'm guessing she already does."

"Then ask her. We need as much help as we can get."

Doubt crept in and picked at a loose thread at the hem of my faith. The idea of fighting mostly invisible spiritual entities bent on my destruction and doing so through the prayers of a handful of women like my ancient great-aunt suddenly seemed ludicrous. It was easier to accept the reality of the attack, the pain in my shoulders, the desperation and fear I'd felt than it was to trust that prayer had the power to help. My doubt must have shown in my face.

"You did well, Kiah, for not having known what to do in a spiritual attack... especially one so physical. You did exactly what you needed to. You listen to God well. I'm sorry this happened to you, but the upside is that it's good practice for going to Kress... That's even harder."

She thought for a moment, then added, "Darkness and despair... they always feel similar. You have to learn how to press through. You are already doing that. The first battle, the first victory."

"Victory?" I asked. I was feeling decidedly "unvictorious."

"It isn't *your* victory, Kiah. It's God's. And you don't have to be strong on your own. You have to lean on His strength. It takes more strength than you might realize to fight panic, tune in, listen, and obey. Don't sell yourself short." Shine's voice was firm, her face sincere.

"Great... I'm adequate at taking a demonic beating. Maybe I can put that on my resume," I muttered. When I was at the end of my rope, sarcasm took over.

"What about right now, though, Shine? What about the next time? Will this thing, whatever it was, come back? Is it just going to keep coming after me, after us? Or was that the end of it?" I asked, knowing she couldn't give me good answers.

"I can't say for sure, but these things don't usually happen the same way twice. And we are in the fight now... Prayer warriors will be fighting on your behalf. The darkness cannot win." Shine unfolded herself and rose to stoke the fire. She was so calm, so sure of herself.

The rain continued, forceful, and heavy on the roof. The lights flickered, threatening to give up the fight with nature.

Worry, fear, and uncertainty amassed into a huge ugly lump in my throat. My flood of tears had ebbed, but that had apparently only been the first wave to break. Insecurity was the second.

"But what if it's just all too much for me, Shine? What if this whole idea was a mistake! Demons, people spitting at me, flying—did I tell you, I'm a bad flier! Really, I'm not that good at it!" I waved my arms in the air first in flying, then crashing motions to prove my point.

"And what if that's not all I suck at? I know God makes no mistakes, but *I* make mistakes. What if I fail? What if I don't do as well as you, or God or anyone else hopes that I will?"

Shine didn't seem interested in stopping my flow of words. I searched her face for disapproval or surprise but found neither.

"I didn't know what I was getting into when I said yes, Shine. I was just curious and discontent. I really had no clue what this was all about! I've been thinking... what if Mom was right, and I shouldn't be doing any of this? What if I was just looking for adventure because I was living in a small town and I saw an opportunity to get free? I feel like Alice in Wonderland, only I am not going to wake up from this, and there's no white rabbit to show me the way through. What if I'm... what if I'm just not enough?" My face was flushed, and my fists were balled.

"Is that all you got?" Shine asked. She sipped her tea and peered casually at me over the rim of her cup.

"What do you mean?" I was a little taken aback.

"I mean, is that all you got? Fear of not being enough? Feeling unprepared? A few early crash landings? Not knowing what you are getting yourself into? Is that it?"

"I guess that's it, yeah, besides being attacked by boiling black air while I'm *asleep*," I said, wondering where she was headed with her line of reasoning. I thought I'd made a pretty good case for my own inadequacy and right to fold.

"Well, if that's all you got, then you are in good company, because none of us feel prepared. That's because none of us *are* prepared. We are all flying by the seat of our pants... and that's metaphorical as well as literal. We all get scared. And none of us are enough. That's the point Kiah."

I was confused.

"So the point is to be scared and unprepared? The point is to be *not enough?*"

"Yes, that's exactly it! The point is to realize that about yourself, because that's true for *everyone*, not just you. Doing God's will isn't about you. It isn't about what you can do. It's about what He can do through you. Okay, let me explain it this way... You know what AA is, right? Alcoholics Anonymous?"

I nodded my head.

"Okay, well, what does every chapter of AA have in common? A belief in God, right? I mean, they call it a higher power, but that's semantics. Why do you think they all point people to God for healing?"

"Because they all failed on their own."

"Yeah, exactly. They all failed. And they all needed to realize their strength came from God and not from inside themselves. That's true for everyone. It's not just because they are alcoholics that they need Him. They needed Him all along, even before they tried to fill the void with alcohol. Just like you. Just like me."

"Well, yeah. I understand that. But this is different, isn't it? That's relationship difficulties and grief, loss of jobs... hard stuff, but normal. This is being attacked by demons and not knowing what's coming next and taking off into new territory every five minutes with no clue what we're getting ourselves into..."

"You just described the life of every person on this planet," Shine interrupted me. "Seriously. Do you think evil doesn't follow everyone... that demons aren't active everywhere? Seeing them only makes them easier to deal with! When you don't see them, they are harder to fight! They were there all along, Kiah, and they have picked fights with you before. You just didn't see them doing it. You didn't recognize them for what they were. This time, you did see them. Now you *know...* and that means you have the chance do something about it." Shine's eyes danced with fervor.

"So you aren't enough on your own. You aren't supposed to be. You weren't designed to be enough on your own. You can do all things through Christ, who strengthens you. Philippians 4:13. So you are afraid now? Well, God told you not to be, so don't stay afraid! Isaiah 41:10. 'Do not fear, for I am with you. Do not be discouraged, for I will strengthen you and help you.'" Shine cast the blanket off her lap and leaned forward to grasp my hands.

"And flying? You aren't even the one doing the flying, in case you hadn't noticed. They aren't even our wings. They are borrowed. Either that, or we are being carried. Why do you think that is? So that we *don't* get to feel comfortable with our own abilities, because they *aren't* ours and because it isn't our abilities God wants to use. It's *His* abilities we need to rely on. That's the *whole entire point.*"

The lights flickered and went out. It was morning, but the clouds were so heavy and the room dark enough that colors were barely distinguishable.

Shine released her grip on my hands and went to the beat-up little sideboard by the front door and pulled out half a dozen candles. She lined them up in the middle of the table and lit them. Then she lit the tapers on either side of the fireplace mantel and a few more tapers in holders that stuck out from the wood supports on the built-in bookshelves. The soft light brought color back to the room. The color was richer and warmer than it had been under the glow of the electric lights. I sat in silence, watching her, just letting her words soak in.

"God's solutions are always better than ours, Kiah. His strength is better than our own. If we rely on our own strength to get us through, we will fail. That's not just true for Blues. That's true any-where for anybody. It's true everywhere for everybody. And we will all fail, somehow, at some point, no matter how safe a life we try to live. You could go home right now, choose a less mysterious life, one that seems like a safer bet. No one would stop you. Do you really think you would stop feeling unprepared and start feeling stronger? Do you really think you would feel like enough?"

She had a point.

"No, I guess not. I never felt like enough *before* all this came up either... I just didn't feel like I was going to let anyone down before. If I failed, I would only disappoint myself. I feel like if I fail at this, I will have wasted people's time! Your time, Fa's, everyone's. I don't want to let anyone down."

Shine sat back down on the couch.

"There's risk in everything that's worth doing. If you and I hang out together long enough, I will disappoint you somehow, and you will disappoint me. That's just a given, because we are human. But that doesn't mean it isn't worth it. I can forgive, and so can you. Besides, I answer to God, not you, Kiah. If God asks me to spend time with you, then I've done His will. It doesn't matter what you do with the energy I put into our time together. I give it freely. You owe me nothing. It came from God, and it goes back to Him. I don't regret a moment spent serving. Look at it this way... If you had a patient, you worked all day saving his life, and then he died, would you regret spending your time on him?"

"No, of course not," my answer was firm. I didn't even have to consider it.

"Okay, what if he lived but turned out to be a complete jerk. Would you feel bad for having helped him survive?"

"No, of course not. It was still my duty to help him."

"Well, that's all there is to it." Shine nodded her head once, sharply to mark her point; then her expression softened a bit. "Except we aren't just each other's job. We are family—you, me, Fa, even the Blues you and I haven't met yet. We are there for each other. We are meant to hold each other up. You know that, right?"

Did I know that? Yes, I did.

Did I want that? I honestly didn't *want* to be close to anyone. I didn't want to lean on anyone. I didn't want to need anyone.

On the other hand, the sheer weight of conviction in my heart was undeniable. This was exactly what I was meant to do, no matter how hard it was. The doubt lifted.

I nodded my head. "I'm beginning to know it."

"I think it's best if you say it out loud. Get used to speaking your heart, speaking your convictions. The enemy doesn't read minds—

thank God for that. The enemy needs to hear your good intentions. There's power in the spoken word."

I found my voice. "I know I'm meant to be here."

Shine was right, declaring it aloud did carry power.

"Thanks for letting me babble," I said. Guilt was setting in over having been such a mess.

"It's nice to be able for me to be able to talk all this through too, you know. It gets lonely living two lives and not being able to talk much about the one that means the most to me."

"Yeah, I get that, for sure. I'm supposed to be thinking and talking about boys and homework, right? Like everyone else?"

"That's what we are supposed to talk about?" Shine grinned. "Okay, so have you met any boys yet?"

"No. Definitely not. I mean, there's only one boy in the nursing program. The odds aren't in my favor."

"What, they don't allowing interprogram dating?" She teased.

"I haven't really had time to find out yet. I'm not really looking. Besides, the only boy in our program is sort of dating a good friend."

"Stay away from that!"

"And he tends to drool," I added.

Shine made a face.

I went to the window. The rain was still coming down hard outside. The puddles in front of the cabin were growing larger and closer together. Soon they would be one large dark body of water.

"Do you know how long it's supposed to rain?" I asked.

Shine had already been rained out of her lawn grounds maintenance shift at the abbey.

"I've no idea," she responded. "What was the other normal thing we needed to talk about? Oh yeah, homework. How's that going?"

"The same as it was in high school, except it takes longer." I thought of the barely manageable nightmare that was my chemistry class and winced. I really needed to study before chemistry lab on Monday morning.

"Maybe once I get past the first year and the classes are more specific to my major, it will get better. I did start clinicals, though. We are working with patients at the nursing home. I was actually going to talk to you about that. I think that one of my patients could be a Blue."

"Really?" Shine rose to light a candle that had gone out.

"I'm not sure, of course. She's old... and yeah, all the residents there are old, but this lady is *really* old. I read her chart, and there's no year listed with her birthdate. It says 'age unknown.'"

"That's odd, but what makes you think she's a Blue?"

I returned to the couch.

"My mother gave me an old box this past summer. She said the stuff in it was for me, passed down from the Scottish side of the family. She won't talk with me about any of it. I get the feeling my mother was Called and said no, and she really doesn't want me involved with any of this. The box has journals, letters, a handwritten Bible, and some other stuff in it. The letters are old, written in Gaelic, from someone named Ailsa, to someone named Shae. They were obviously both Called. There are no dates on them, the letters, or the journals. I asked Fa about it, and she said that Ailsa was one of my relatives. She had heard of her. Apparently, Shae was a Blue as well. She stayed in the cottage next to Ailsa's. That's how they knew each other. But Fa doesn't know how long ago they lived. They were gone before she came to Petra. My great-aunt Nan knows about the Calling. She's actually the one who sent the box of books and letters to my Mom years ago. She hasn't ever heard of Ailsa or Shae either... I asked her."

"What does this have to do with the old lady at the nursing home?" Shine asked.

"I'm getting to that. Tsk-tsk, so impatient!" I teased.

I told Shine about Cumina, about her first short awakening, that she thought she recognized me and that I thought she'd called me Ellie but realized later that she might have been saying Aylie, short for Ailsa. I told her about the lack of history in her chart and her bill, which was prepaid in full.

"She asked why I called her Cumina and not by her nickname. I asked her what she wanted to be called instead, but she was fading by then. She slipped back into her normal unresponsive state pretty quickly. I looked up her full name in her chart. It's Cumina *Shae* Hedley."

"Wow." Shine picked contemplatively at a fraying hem along the bottom of her shirt.

The memory of my mother's voice echoed in my head. *"Don't pick at the loose stitches, Kiah, or you'll end up standing there naked with a ball of thread in your hand."* I resisted the urge to pass on the admonition to Shine.

"Cumina or Shae…" Shine was searching her memory for the names. "I've never heard of her, but that doesn't really mean anything. There's no real record of who was a Blue and when. And Blues don't tend to talk much about the past," Shine said.

"Yeah. I noticed that. Do you know why that is?"

Shine shook her head.

"I don't think they purposefully avoid talking about the past. It's more that they have their minds on the present. Women with the Calling are *called*, right? Handpicked? There are no walk-ons in the lineup, and God doesn't call people who are in it for the glory or people who want to make the history books. We just serve. We love. We want our time and effort to matter but not to be recorded. We don't look for any sort of recognition. Take me, for example… I love history, but I don't want my name in a book anywhere. I don't suppose you do either."

"That's true," I said. And it absolutely was.

"Can you talk to her again, the old woman?" Shine asked. The hem she had picked at was, indeed, unraveling. A few threads hung stuck out of the fabric, and a small piece of the raw edge of the fabric was showing. She didn't seem bothered by it.

"She's my patient again this Thursday. I thought maybe I would bring some of the things from the box to show her, to see if she recognizes them."

Shine got up and headed for the kitchen. "You ready for lunch?"

"Definitely."

The power to the little cabin remained stubbornly unavailable. Shine, just as stubbornly, insisted on having soup anyway. She heated homemade chicken rice stew in a pot on the woodstove and gave me the grand tour of the cabin. It took eleven minutes. We spent the remainder of the astonishingly normal afternoon chatting and playing cards. By 4:00 p.m., the rain had let up enough for us to don rain boots and slosh, slide, wade into the village. I was freshly slathered with pungent liniment and swaddled in borrowed clothing. It was time for me to go.

"There's one more thing I have to tell you before you go, Kiah. This group of unbelievers, the demons, even the slimy little visitors you had last night… they will never be your biggest enemy. You can learn their tells. You can learn to defend yourself."

"Who's my biggest enemy then?"

"Yourself," she said, and a chill ran up my spine. "The things you fear, the things you think, the things you decide. Knowing what *is* right from what *feels* right. It's not always the same thing. It's harder to see those things in yourself. It's why we are made to be the body of Christ: His hands, his feet, his spleen even. We work better together than alone. Do you understand?"

Did I?

"I think I understand. I will remember," I promised.

WHY

How often this question, high-centering and pointless, has no answer...

⁓Why didn't it go the way I planned it?
⁓Why didn't that person love me the way they should have?
⁓Why did this happen to me?
⁓Why did anyone have to die?

Why?
Drop the *y* and add a few letters...
If we ask *where* or *who* or *what* instead?

⁓What should I do now?
⁓Who can I turn to for help?
⁓Where is Dhia in all of this?

Bert was still sporting my broken window like a prominent black eye when I returned to the dorm that night. I found no questioning note under my door and no residual effects of the strange happenings of the night before, besides the shattered pane. The room felt warm, musty, and normal. I admit to spending some extra time on my knees, more out of nervousness than undefiled devotion, before going to bed that evening. The bruises had grown to amorphous shadows that crept down my back and up over my shoulders. I took the maximum dose allowable dose of ibuprofen to ease the pain of them and went to sleep.

The next morning, a scraping sound followed by a thud awakened me. I sat up quickly, still wary, and blinked at the light streaming in the window. A dark-haired young man on a ladder outside my window was picking at my makeshift window patch. I grabbed a sweatshirt from the floor beside my bed and pulled it on, grateful I had worn pajama pants to bed. Climbing onto the desk from the chair I joined the effort, shearing off the cardboard.

The young man's face appeared in the window hole, inches from mine.

"Thanks for the help," he said.

His scent hit me first... warm earth, physical effort, and soap. His eyes were deep gray but warm and friendly, the kind of eyes women get lost in. His proximity made my knees wobble. I was appalled at the fluttery rush that flooded my chest. It felt like weakness. So far, I had run far and fast from every boy who caused me to feel that way.

"Oh yeah... thank you for fixing the window," I mumbled, retreating hastily from the desktop back down to the floor. I wanted to ask him who had reported the broken window but didn't trust myself to form intelligible words. I had planned to get up, get dressed, and head to Nan's for a chat; but I couldn't dress with him hanging outside my window like a bat. Cold air was streaming through the hole, and the heater was soon clanking away desperately, trying to return the room to an acceptable temperature. I bundled up in a blanket, grabbed my chemistry notes, and read. Well, I pretended to read. I read the same phrase again and again, but the words didn't stick to my brain. I was sure my cheeks were pink, and I flushed darker at the very thought.

It took him only a few minutes to finish prepping the window and place the new glass. He climbed back down the ladder, peered briefly in the window, and waved good-bye. I waved back as nonchalantly as I could then waited until he and his ladder disappeared from view before scrambling across the floor on my knees to peer up over the edge and watch him walk down the path toward the center of campus. Just a few years before, I would scoff when I heard girls talk about guys.

"I don't know. He's just… so… *you* know…!" one girl would say.

And the other girls would bob their heads in agreement. Then someone would add, "Yeah, I know what you mean. I feel the same way about Jason…"

I would roll my eyes and wonder what they'd been smoking.

Look at me now, I thought, *blushing like an idiot and crawling across the floor to spy on the maintenance guy. Shake it off, Adenauer.*

I climbed off the floor and packed a few things into my backpack. I had less than an hour to hitch a ride into town if I wanted to catch the early train to Nan's. One of the perks of living in Europe was the ability to travel safely, cheaply, and easily. I made it to Nan's in a little under two hours. She and the family were out for the day. I let myself in with the key under the broken flowerpot. The house was silent, at least as silent as old houses could get. The floors creaked, and water dripped somewhere. The fire hadn't gone out on the heart; the family must have left recently. I climbed to the attic and spread the contents of Mom's box out across the attic floor. I ran my fingers over each item. The sense of mystery attached to the items hadn't evaporated. In fact, the book cover seemed more beautiful than ever in the wan light that filtered in through the dirty attic window and dust motes. I pressed my index finger into one of the indentations on the lower half of the cover and wondered what kind of jewel it had housed. Emerald maybe? Or sapphire? There was no way to know.

A Dhia, if there's something you want me to know something more about these items, please show me!

I picked up the handwritten Bible. The cover was plain, rough brown leather edged and bound with linen, adhesive and some sort of waxed string. It wasn't technically a full Bible. Rather, it was the New Testament with a few Old Testament books, psalms and proverbs, added in. It was still very large and heavy. The handwriting was small, delicate, and precise. I picked a passage from the book of Matthew and read it aloud.

"Ar N'Athair, at a air neamh…"

The words flowed easily. I was inordinately pleased with myself at how fluent my Gaelic had become. In the very next moment, I wondered if being pleased at my linguistic ability constituted an acceptable level of pride. What is the difference, really, between being proud of one's own accomplishments and being prideful, arrogant? It's a sliding scale, right? I forced my mind back to the task at hand. I could always do battle with my character later.

I began to read aloud again. A profound sense of urgency and passion welled up inside me that had little to do with the words themselves—as if I somehow sensed the excitement the scribe had felt while he or she penned it. I searched for a name, date, or a mark that might indicate who had scribed it but found nothing. The pages were faded with age but remarkably clean, as if it had always been treasured, never rifled through. I wrapped it in newspaper and replaced it in the chest along with the gold book cover but just couldn't handle the thought of leaving the Bible behind. It was the only connection I had with whoever had penned it, and I didn't want to let it go. I found a large sheet of stiff brown butcher paper on a desk in the attic and wrapped it, secured it with packing string, and stowed it in my backpack.

Next, I picked up a journal. Most of the pages were filled with descriptions of flowers, herbs, trees, and roots. Their medicinal and culinary uses were listed, though not in any sort of predictable order. Ailsa seemed to use the same sort of organizational system for her words that I did when I took notes, namely, "Just get the words on the page near some of the other words that apply to the same topic and hope you remember where you put them next time you need them." There was a wealth of knowledge in the pages, but it would take someone dedicated and task-oriented to sort it out. I skimmed the pages carefully, reading more thoroughly the passages that contained personal anecdotes. I was looking for clues to Ailsa's identity and references to anything else about the Calling. I started out on the attic floor, sorting and organizing, but the floorboards were too hard. I cleared a space on a small dusty settee, settling there for a while; that set me sneezing. Finally, I snagged a blanket from the living room and made a nest, Shine-like, on the floor then settled in to peruse one of the sets of letters. The letters were only slightly more personal than the journal had been with many references to herbal medicines, which were the most successful in fighting infections and natural sedatives that had proven themselves with few side effects. A capital *P* marked most of the remedies, indicating they were derived from plants on Petra rather than Earth. I found a few references to Kress territories, even individual Kress men who had given the Blues more trouble than usual. I marked the names of the cities on a notepad, wondering if the information could prove useful in the future.

The shadows in the room shifted as the day wore on, and I began to feel a little deflated. I had hoped for, although not outright expected, a flagrant discovery that explained why I had the letters, journals, Bible, artifacts, the book cover...*anything!*

My stomach growled loudly. I checked my watch. I had missed lunch, and it was almost dinnertime. I still needed to pack in some chemistry study time. It was going to be a late night.

School ground on. Ground? Yes, *grinding* is the right term. Little sleep, lots of paperwork, boring lectures... It was a Monday morning when the dean of Aodhagan's nursing school announced the clinical glimpse program, a new program designed to encourage nursing student retention. Apparently, many first-year nursing students had become disillusioned spending their time in nursing homes where the atmosphere wasn't particularly inspiring. Several students had already switched majors. The professorial staff came up with the idea of letting first-year students sign up for one clinical observation experience per month in other, more exciting settings— just to remind there was hope at the end of the tunnel. They posted a sign-up sheet. Trauma center, oncology, medical office, and surgical ward were the first four glimpses offered. By the time I reached the bulletin board, the sign-up sheet was dog-eared, and oncology was the only one option that remained.

I stepped from the elevator into the cancer care unit of the local hospital on Tuesday afternoon at 2:00 p.m. The Easter egg blue paint on the walls did nothing to dispel the air of quiet desperation that permeated the unit. I was slated to shadow Kelly, a veteran oncology nurse from South Africa, with a smile that radiated sunshine, something her patients definitely needed. Kelly and I were assigned three patients that evening. The first was a pleasant fifty-three-year-old breast cancer patient named Brigid. Her prognosis was good, and her daughters visited daily. Her disease was technically in remission. She was undergoing what everyone hoped would be her final round of chemotherapy.

Our second patient, a twenty-three-year-old leukemia patient, Keelan, was undergoing his second bone marrow transplant. He had lived at the hospital for the better portion of the previous three years. Despite every effort, his prognosis was not good; he was losing his battle with the disease. Keelan was the youngest child in a large supportive family; and several of his brothers, sisters, as well as his parents adamantly insisted on spending every night in the hospital with him. Officially, hospital policy forbade more than one overnight visitor per patient. In Keelan's case, a compromise was reached. An unused surgical waiting room one floor beneath the cancer unit stood empty while the hospital gathered the funds to turn it into a research lab. The nurses pulled a few strings and obtained keys, and Keelan's family moved into it. Once the administrators left for the day, the staff secretly opened up the on-call showers for the family's late-night use.

Our third patient, a seven-month-old infant girl with a new diagnosis of leukemia was due to arrive partway through the shift. She needed further testing to determine what type of leukemia she had and what treatment it would require. Normally, the type of testing she needed was done under sedation at an outpatient clinic. Catriona, however, was an orphan under the sole care of social services. Her temporary foster home was not vetted for children with medical needs, and her social worker wasn't able to secure placement for her in a medically certified foster home on such short notice, so Catriona was admitted to the hospital for her testing. The baby's social worker, Edina, arrived at the nurses' desk with the baby just after 5:00 p.m. Edina's face bore the wisdom and weariness of one who had seen too many hard things. It made her age impossible to guess.

I came out from behind the desk to introduce myself.

"I'm Kiah. I'm a nursing student working with Catriona's nurse tonight. I can take you to her room now. We have it ready," I offered.

"I'm Edina, pleased to meet you."

The baby was bundled, asleep in her arms. I led them to room 407, stopping to wash my hands at the door on the way in. Edina placed the still-sleeping child in the high-sided metal crib, and I raised the crib side panels for safety.

"She's taken her medicine… Thet's why she's sleepin' now," Edina explained. "They say it's a medicine for pain. Bone pain. Her foster mum says she was fussin' quite a bit, not settlin' well, so they took her to the doctor. They drew her blood and found this disease. There was a family interested in adopting her too. But now…" She shook her head sadly and sighed. "Well, I'm not so sure they'll maintain interest."

I peered through the crib bars at Catriona, and my heart sunk. I hadn't spent much time with babies, but she seemed underweight for her age. She looked so delicate, so fragile. She had no family and such an uncertain future; such a dangerous disease loomed overhead. Just thinking about her situation caused a small physical pain in my chest.

A Dhia, do you see her? Help her! my heart silently cried out.

"They told ye I willna be staying…?" Edina asked.

"No, I hadn't heard. No one will be staying with the child, then?"

Edina shook her head no again.

"I can bide fer a while, jest nae too long."

She wiped her forehead on her sleeve. I could tell she was exhausted.

"I'll go find her nurse, Kelly, and we will collect the information we need as soon as possible. We will take good care of her."

I put what I hoped was a reassuring hand on Edina's should for a moment, then exited the room and went in search of Kelly. We ran through the paperwork with Edina and left a reminder for tomorrow's nurse to touch base with her at a specified time. Edina left Kelly and I alone with Catriona. We stood in silence for a moment and watched her sleep. Anyone not looking for the earmarks of disease might have guessed her to be healthy. At first glance, she appeared to be sleeping peacefully, her bottom lip stuck out in a half-pout; but there were lavender patches under her eyes, and her cheeks had a sallow, yellowish cast. Her forehead, just between the wisps that were her eyebrows, was knotted into a worry line that looked very much like the one my mother bore. She was too young to be carrying such physical manifestation of the burden of pain.

"It's just sad," Kelly said, sighing.

I nodded my agreement. It was *so* sad that it was hard to know what to say.

Kelly brought down the crib rails on both sides of the bed, and we began to unwrap Catriona from her blankets and free her of her clothes. Kelly spoke in soothing tones as we worked, but she probably needn't have. Catriona barely roused. She squinted her eyes shut and tried to ignore us. Stripped of the normality of her clothing and clad in a hospital jumper with an identification bracelet around her wrist, she looked much more like the very ill little person that she was.

Kelly examined her from head to toe, explaining her thinking aloud as she went.

"Here, put your hand here," she said, guiding me to feel the soft spot at the back of the baby's skull. "It's sunken in a bit, can you tell?"

I could.

"That's a sure sign of dehydration. The social worker reported that she hasn't been eating well, and what she eats, she barely keeps down."

Kelly fetched a packet of IV needles, tubing and a small bag of saline from the medical cabinet beside the bed. My mind flashed back to a time not long before when I had watched another woman insert another IV on another patient—in a whole other world. A shiver went up my spine as my realities crashed into one another in my mind.

"You all right?" Kelly asked.

"Oh, yeah. Just cold," I answered.

I wasn't completely lying. The room was a bit chilly. I found the thermostat behind the crib and adjusted the temperature.

"Solid idea. We need to keep her warm, especially while IV fluids are running. They can cool a body quickly, especially a little body. We will put her next bag of fluids in the warmer before we hang it."

Catriona protested the insertion of the IV as vehemently as she could. She managed a few angry yelps, then settled quickly back into uneasy slumber.

"That's not a good sign." Kelly's mouth was a grim line. "She should have given us more trouble than that. She's weak. Hopefully the fluids help."

She hung the bag of sugared saline on a hook above the baby's crib and ran the tubing through a pump to regulate the flow of the fluids, then finished her exam and showed me how she charted her findings.

"I need to see my other patients, but I don't like how she looks." Kelly gestured toward Catriona. "Do you mind hanging out here while I work? I know you didn't come here to babysit, but she bears watching."

"I'd love to," I answered quickly.

Something absolute and fierce inside me wanted to protect the child.

"Good. I'll leave you to it then. Call me for anything." Kelly checked her watch and her paperwork and winced. One thing I already knew from my limited experience with nursing was that there was never, ever enough time to do everything that needed to be done. Nurses forever raced the clock and seldom experienced a sense of completion. They simply passed on tasks to the next nurse, and the next, and the next... Kelly hurried out the door.

I pulled up a chair next to the bed, but the bed was too tall and the chair too short. I abandoned the chair and took up a standing, leaning position at the edge of the crib instead, shifting from one foot to another from time to time to keep my legs from going numb.

Catriona's breathing was rapid and shallow. I checked her diaper—still dry. She hadn't peed since she arrived. Hopefully the fluids would fill her tank quickly. Her lips were cracked, and the bottom one had oozed a drop of blood. I caught the drip with a tissue, then opened a small foil tube of petroleum jelly and applied it to the crack.

Her eyes fluttered open, and she whimpered, mildly alarmed to find herself staring at a stranger. Too tired to truly react, her gaze clouded over, and she fell back to sleep.

I felt the desperate urge to do something for her. I felt like I was even *supposed* to be doing something for her. I just didn't know what it was.

"A Dhia, please help her," I pleaded in a whisper.

The urge to do something grew even stronger. I had felt the same way on my first visit to Petra when I saw the young man lying in his bed. I had known I needed to do something for him, that I needed to touch him.

"Is there something you want me to do here now?" I asked aloud.

There was no answer. The urge to help built to a throb in my chest, and tears were welling in the corners of my eyes.

"Tell me, Dhia. Tell me what to do."

I closed my eyes and waited, listening for a moment.

Use your hands, came the inaudible answer with startling clarity from deep inside me.

"How?" I breathed.

There was no answer. I stretched out my hands and let them hover a few inches over her small body, moving them back and forth the way I'd seen the Blues do at the valley. When I hovered over her chest, my fingers physically ached. I placed my hands lightly on her skin, and the aching ceased. My fingers tingled and hummed, and I sensed as much as saw a blue glow under my fingertips. I moved my hands down to her legs, knees, and feet, stroking softly as I went, then up to her arms and legs, over her face and head, then back to her chest. I lingered longer at the places that sent a twinge of pain through my fingers. When the twinge subsided, I moved on. After a few moments, the glow ebbed, and I could feel that the work was done. I wasn't sure *what* work had been done, but the urge to help that had been so strong before subsided completely. What I had initially thought was pure emotion had quite possibly been Dhia's method of encouraging me to action.

"How often have I misunderstood your messages?" I asked under my breath.

I felt a peal of laughter in my chest that was not my own. Dhia had a sense of humor—sarcasm even? I'd never thought of the possibility before, but I appreciated it.

Teach me, Dhia, teach me, I pleaded silently.

"I Am," came the answer. His voice was audible, loud enough to make me jump. I glanced reflexively around the room, even though I knew there would be no one to see. Another shiver ran up my spine, and Catriona giggled. I turned my full attention to her and realized she was wide awake and gazing with delight at the ceiling. I got the feeling she was seeing something I couldn't see, and I was a bit envious.

"What do you see, sweet girl? What do you see?" I smiled at her and clasped her hands in mine. She looked at me and cooed. Her eyes sparkled. Her cheeks had gained pink roses, and her lips were no longer dry. Even the bleeding crack was gone. I checked the soft spot on the top of her head—it was no longer sunken in. She kicked her legs and pulled my hands toward her mouth.

"Oh no, you don't want to suck on hospital hands," I chided her.

She blew a raspberry at me and cooed. I couldn't stop staring at her. She looked like an entirely different child from the one who had come to us that afternoon. There was a deep sense of satisfaction planted firmly in the center of my chest that I can only call pure joy. I couldn't stop looking at her, marveling at what Dhia had done. I knew that the child was no longer ill. She was still an orphan. There were still uncertainties in her future. She had already experienced more loss than I could imagine, but she wasn't walking alone. I knew that leukemia was no longer one of her obstacles. Dhia had done something in that room, and I was humbled and awed to have been a part of it.

"Thank you," I whispered, meaning what I said with every fiber of my being.

I changed Catriona's diaper and searched for a way to entertain her. She was bored and hungry. I selected a chain of enormous colored plastic pop beads from the bag of complimentary infant toys. She immediately shook them in the air, bopped me in the nose with them, then tried to jam them into her mouth. I began to wonder how to explain her sudden change in behavior and health status and settled on trying Fa's philosophy: "Say as little as possible." I passed the next few hours reading from the plastic storybook, reciting the colors of the pop beads and playing multiple rounds of peek-a-boo.

At length, Kelly popped her head into the room. "How is she?" she asked.

"Better."

"Better?" She approached the crib.

Catriona sat propped up in the crib, cooing and chewing on the pages of a plastic book designed precisely for that purpose.

"She looks fantastic." Kelly was surprised. "Maybe she was just severely dehydrated, and the fluids did the trick."

"Maybe."

"There's a nursing assistant on her way up. The cardiac unit has low census, so they floated her to us. She can take over your post. I'm sorry you had to just hang out tonight, but I'm glad you were here. We needed you. Maybe they will let you sign up for another shift since you didn't get to see much."

"It's no problem. I was happy to be needed. Nursing students spend a lot of time feeling in the way, so this was perfect," I assured her.

The nursing assistant arrived. She was a born baby entertainer—young, bubbly, and dressed entirely in pink. She scooped Catriona up, settled into the chair, and began to sing to her. I watched for a moment, wondering what would happen next for Catriona, then quickly made a decision to surrender my curiosity and be content with playing the small part that Dhia let me play. The rest was up to Him. I followed Kelly from the room and didn't look back. There was no need to look back.

As I left the unit that night, my insides bubbled with delight over what had happened. I passed the room of our third patient, Keelan. The door was open a crack, allowing me to see Keelan's mother as she sat at the edge of the bed, holding a washcloth to her son's forehead while he retched into a basin. As life flooded into one room, it drained steadily from another. My heart didn't know whether to stay high or sink low. Holding equal parts crazy joy and profound sadness, it felt as if it might burst.

THE DOORWAY

It was a Wednesday. Millie called from California, and we held a marathon phone chat that lasted late into the night. She had joined a competition debate team to meet a certain boy. She'd met him as she had planned, and they went out on a date during which she discovered he was the single most boring conversationalist she had ever met. Not only that but he *never stopped talking*. Actually, it got even worse than that: he liked her. He *really* liked her. She was seriously contemplating quitting the debate team and tossing around the idea of switching majors just to avoid seeing him again. We both knew she wouldn't actually do either. She just needed to vent. I tried to be sympathetic, but I felt a widening gap between us that wasn't a product of our physical distance. I was dealing with a whole different set of circumstances and emotions than she was, and mine… I couldn't share. I couldn't tell her how I felt watching the healing of a sick baby or describe my experience with the dark visitor. Leaving Millie out of the loop when it came to a large portion of my life wasn't exactly lying, but it felt like it. As I hung up from the call, I felt a pang of sadness—a sliver of loneliness, like a physical pain in my chest. I suddenly felt like a stranger who didn't belong on Earth but didn't belong on Petra either.

What does that leave me with, Dhia? Where do I belong? I asked Him.

You belong to me, came His answer.

There was a measure of reassurance in that, but I couldn't see Dhia, couldn't touch Him. I curled up on the bed in my dorm room and cried myself to sleep.

The rest of my week was fairly typical.

In chemistry class, I learned that I had scraped by with a B– on my most recent exam. I really needed to find a chemistry study group.

My introduction to nursing class had a guest lecturer scheduled for every class period *all week long*. Donal's assertion was that his goldfish would have done a more compelling job covering the subject matter, and I was inclined to agree with him.

The cafeteria decided to install a "healthy food choices" bar that was instantly popular. I wondered why they hadn't thought earlier of serving healthy food.

I will admit that I kept a keen eye on the campus maintenance people… half hoping and half hoping *not* to catch a glimpse of the sweet-smelling guy who had fixed my window. I saw a cranky older lady painting a gazebo by the sciences building and a pimple-faced short boy who barely seemed old enough to drive, let alone get a job, hiding out behind the rose bushes, smoking. A short waddling middle-aged man with dangerously droopy pants was changing light bulbs in our dorm. But there was no sign of my cute, young window-hero. I wasn't sure if I was disappointed or relieved. Maybe both.

I called my great-aunt Nan and told her I was experiencing some spiritual friction. I asked her if she would pray for me. She said she'd already felt it and was praying for my friends and me in earnest. She assured me she would continue to do so. Somehow, knowing she was praying for me restored some of the wind to my sails—wind that my conversation with Millie had stolen. At least one person on Earth had an inkling of what was truly going on with me.

On Friday, Cumina Shae Hedley died. Yeah, it surprised me a little too, even though she was old. On Thursday night, when her nurse readied her for bed, she roused and sang along with her favorite song. On Friday morning, they found her barely clinging to life, exhibiting telltale signs of a massive stroke—a bleed in her brain. I arrived at the nursing home that evening and learned that Shae was expected to go at any time. The staff nurses, sure a first-year nursing student, wouldn't want to be involved with the death process, offered me a new patient assignment, which I declined. I *did* want to care for Shae. I wasn't sure why Dhia had introduced me to her at the tail end of her life just in time to watch her die but felt the need to see it through.

Bonnie, the nurse assigned to Shae's hospice care, tried to prepare me mentally before we entered her room. She told me Ms. Hedley's heartbeat and breathing were already erratic and the sound of end-of-life breathing could be distressing. I stopped at the door. My breath caught in my throat. I had never witnessed a human death before and wasn't as sure of myself in the face of it as I thought or hoped I would be.

Pull it together, Adenauer! I told myself and stepped across the threshold.

The overhead lights were extinguished. Only a bedside lamp and the running lights along the floor that marked the way from the bed to the bathroom were lit. Two thoughts occurred to me as I hovered in the doorway. The first was that the running lights would never again fulfill their job for Shae. Her feet would never slip over the side of the bed, fumble into her bedroom slippers, and shuffle toward the bathroom door. The second was the strange but sure feeling that another door hung open in the room—a door I could not see. A mild breeze with no visible source brushed my cheek, carrying with it a sweet scent I didn't recognize before it disappeared.

The nurse beckoned me closer to the edge of the bed. The old woman lying still on the bed looked even smaller than the last time I'd seen her. A rolled towel had been propped under her neck to keep her head back and her airway clear. I could hear her ragged breaths, several short and shallow, in rapid succession, then a pause... then another breath, followed by a longer, deep, rasping breath that rose from the bottom of her lungs. The sound made me clear my own throat.

"Come, come," the nurse urged me closer again, her voice tender and steady. She seemed as comfortable with the dying as she was with the living, and her demeanor calmed my nerves. I borrowed her confidence and joined her at the bedside.

"Feel here, her cheek… note the temperature," she instructed. I pressed the back of my hand against her waxen cheek. It was papery and warm.

"Now feel here as well." The nurse moved her hand to her patient's upper arm, and I followed suit. The temperature of the skin on her arm echoed my own.

"Now run your hand down the arm slowly with the back of your hand."

I followed the nurse's instructions. The temperature of Shae's skin changed abruptly at her wrist. Her hands were gray and as cold as ice. "This is normal," she reassured me in a voice so low it was almost a whisper.

"As her time comes closer, her legs and arms will cool. It's one way to gauge how close your patient might be to passing. Of course, you listen to their breathing as well, and you can listen to their heart. Sometimes the heart slows steadily, sometimes it gallops, sometimes there are pauses. But the way I see it, there's no reason to bother your patient much with stethoscopes and probing at the end of their time with us." Her hands caressed Shae's as she talked to me.

"You just keep resting, Ms. Hedley. We are here with you," she said.

Shae, of course, did not register our presence.

"Can I talk to her for a while?" I asked the nurse.

She looked surprised but pleased.

"Of course, you sit right down on her bedside and speak to her. I have a few things to tend. Is it all right if I leave you to it? If you need anything, anything at all, you push the call button, and I'll come right back in."

I nodded, not absolutely comfortable there on my own but feeling unable to say what I needed to in the nurse's presence. The nurse patted my shoulder and left the two of us alone. I situated myself on the side of the bed and took hold of Shae's hand, then immediately dropped it again. The cold skin was a little unnerving. I placed my hand on the still warm skin of her forearm instead.

"Cumina, can you hear me?" I asked quietly in Gaelic, just in case anyone popped their head in and heard me talking. Not that I expected them to. The staff knew what was happening in the room and were bound to stay away.

Cumina, of course, didn't respond.

"I came tonight hoping to talk to you." I started in a low voice. "There were things I wanted to ask you. I'm not sure why Dhia introduced us, actually. I guess I thought, selfishly, that you could answer some of my questions. Now I wonder if maybe I'm just here for you, to be here with you as you leave, to say good-bye…" I trailed off, realizing I was talking more to myself than to her.

I was at a total loss for what to do. If my task was to simply hold her hand and chatter while she slipped away, then *why me?* Why couldn't the nurses do that just as well? There was that pesky pointless question again… *Why.* I changed it to "what." *What could I do for her now, at the very end of her life, that would mean something?*

The words of the old song that had roused her before popped into my head, and I began to sing them first under my breath, then a little louder. I watched her face closely but saw no flicker of recognition, no sign of awareness.

You aren't here for yourself. You are here for her. This isn't about you. I reminded myself and started into a second round of the short melody, trying to remember all the words correctly even though it really didn't matter all that much. I shifted my seat. I'd been sitting in the same awkward position on the edge of the thin mattress for quite a little while.

"I'm here, Shae. I'm here, and I won't leave this room until you do," I promised her. Out of the corner of my eye, I thought I saw her eyelids flutter, and my heart leapt. I studied her face closely, but she lay perfectly still, and I wondered if her movement had been my imagination.

"Shae? I'm here, right here. You can go now." I spoke softly to her.

At the sound of her name, her eyelids fluttered again, this time unmistakably; then both flew open at once. Her breathing instantly became regular. My heart rate doubled as her hand fluttered, grasping for mine. It was still ice cold, but I held onto it. Her clear gaze locked with mine. I held my breath.

"I knew you would come," she said in Gaelic, her words as surprisingly steady as her gaze.

"I need to tell you… and you need to listen close. Are you listening?" she asked.

I managed to nod, willing my heart to beat a little less loudly so I wouldn't miss whatever she had to say. My heart stubbornly refused to cooperate.

"There are three young men. They've fallen through to the Rock, and you need to go after them. Do you understand?" she asked.

"Oh no, I can't!" I said, immediately alarmed on a whole new level, for an all-new reason.

"I'm not Aylie, Shae. You have me confused with Aylie. I'm Kiah. I've never even been to Kress. I'm not who you think I am."

"I'm not confused, child," Shae intoned with absolute clarity, her eyes bright. I knew immediately that she was right; I was the confused one.

"Listen, child, carefully. I don't have much time, and you are needed."

Her hand was gripping mine tightly at that point, and adrenaline ran laps through my heart and up and down my limbs.

"Three young men fell through at the O Gate, and you are the lead. These men are at Sange's place. Remember that name."

"How will I know, Shae? How will I know how to get there?" I squeaked.

"Calm down, child. You will know. How did you know where and when to go before? You listen for God's leading, and you trust Him. Let Him quiet you. Just breathe and remember—O Gate and Sange. The rest will come to you. You won't go alone. There will be others."

Her hand caressed mine ever so lightly, as if she were trying to soothe me.

I took a deep breath.

"When do I go, Shae?" I asked quickly since I wasn't sure how long her lucidity would last.

"You will know. He will let you know. There's something else I need to tell you. Are you listening well?"

"I'm listening."

"You'll be asked to do things differently than the others. You need to know that. Don't fear it."

I waited for her to go on, but she just stared at me.

"I don't understand what you mean... Differently? You mean the Calling? I know about that..."

"No," she interrupted. "I mean differently from the other Blues. You were not made to live in their rut, child. There will be change with you."

I couldn't even fathom what she was referring to. *More* change? I was already living with more change than I could handle.

"Ailsa and I knew a change was coming. The Lord told us a long time ago. And we prayed for you. We loved you before you were born." She paused and chuckled, her eyes crinkling. "Of course, I never thought I'd actually *meet* you. I never planned to live this long. The Lord has a sense of humor and His own set of plans."

I opened my mouth to interrupt her, but she held up a crooked finger. "There's no time for questions. I don't know any more than what I've said. You will know more when you need to know it. Not before. That's the Lord's way. Just learn, serve, and listen. I know you will."

Shae's gaze dimmed and sputtered like a struggling candle flame, and her hand dropped, palm open to the surface of the bed.

"Oh, Shae, don't go yet. I have more to ask you," I begged her. My insides were churning. I felt desperate, watching her slip away from me like a quickly sinking ship.

"There's no more to say. I can see home now, child. It's lovely. It's everything..."

The flame of her gaze sputtered again and then went out completely. Her head sunk back into the pillow; and her breathing slowed and then rolled, deep and ragged for a few long breaths.

"Shae? Shae?" I asked quietly a few more times. I searched her face for the spark of recognition, but it was gone. I looked around the room, not quite sure of what I had just experienced. The heat clicked on, and I smelled the mild aroma of burnt dust, coupled with the faint, sour smell of death. The only movement in the room was the curtains swaying in the air from the vents. I intentionally slowed my breathing and prayed for Dhia to settle my nerves. I was grateful for the ensuing trickle of peace, however small, that wound through my center. I needed to focus, to store away every precious word that Shae had said. To stop thinking of other worlds and just be in the present one. Shae required a nurse at the moment, not a panicky child. I tried to focus on what I knew to do.

I felt Shae's hand with the back of my fingers. It was still ice-cold. I ran my fingers up her forearm; it was cold as well. The blood was circulating in smaller and smaller loops from her heart. Soon it would stop straying from the heart altogether and simply slosh back and forth ineffectively in the failing organ like wash water in a washing machine set to the gentle cycle. She was definitely leaving the world. I retrieved my stethoscope from its place around my neck, placed the earpieces in my ears and the bell over my patient's heart. I could barely hear the weak beats, first irregular and fast, then pausing. I counted one... two... three... four... five... six... seven seconds of pause before the rapid irregular rate returned. I curled the stethoscope back around my neck just as the nurse reentered the room.

"How is it in here?" she asked me.

"Oh, fine," I answered. "I'm just talking to her a little."

"That's good, very good." The nurse nodded approvingly.

She did a quick assessment. Shae's upper arms and legs were cold. Her face was slack. Her breath came in deep sporadic spasms that rocked her chest.

"Let it go now, sweet lady. You've done well, and we can take it from here," the nurse said, so quietly I had to lean in to hear her.

And then Cumina Shae Hedley was gone. I can't tell you how I knew the moment her spirit left the room, but I knew just as certainly as I know when a light is turned out. One moment she resided in her body, and the next moment she simply didn't. Her body even *looked* lighter than it had just a moment before. It lay there, a shell waiting to be returned to the dirt it originated from, since that its owner had no further use for it. The nurse placed her stethoscope over Shae's heart and listened for a full minute.

"She's gone now," she said simply, and I nodded in agreement.

I stood and stretched my arms. The unseen door had swung silently shut behind Shae as her soul departed. I waited for something like sadness or fear to descend upon me, but nothing did. I felt total peace.

Silently, I helped the nurse gather equipment, and we gave Shae's body a final careful cleansing, preparing it for the funeral home. When the bath was done, we gently rolled her body back and forth, positioned a cadaver bag under it and then slipped it over her shoulders and feet.

"Officially, we are supposed to tie the hands and the feet together." The nurse shook her head sadly at me.

"I don't do it, however, because I just don't want to. I don't think it's right. I know she's dead, and it doesn't matter anyway, but it doesn't seem dignified. With all the undignified things people go through in life by the time they die... and then all the undignified things their bodies will go through before they are placed in the ground, well... it's just one small thing I like to do for them," she said. A tear leaked from her left eye, and she caught it with her sleeve.

"And there, shedding a tear, that's the other thing I can do for them." She smiled at me, zipping the bag shut, peeled off her gloves, and dropped them into the trash can. "You will attend a lot of death, Kiah. It goes along with the job. It's a gift, I think, to be present when a human enters the world *and* to be there when they leave it. It's an important part of the job."

She stared off into the unseen distance for a moment, then lowered her voice. "We all handle it differently, of course. You will find your own little things to do, like everyone else... small rebellions against a harsh world. Small kindnesses that no one sees. No matter how unpredictable or tragic things get, those little things will provide some closure for you, and that's important. It will keep you grounded." She turned to the sink and washed her hands. I did likewise. I wondered if processing her feelings aloud and passing on her tidbits of advice was part of what helped her. I stayed silent, just listening.

"You did well tonight. Nursing is in your blood. You have the calling," she said. My ears pricked up a bit at her use of the word *calling*. I peered closely at her, but she took no notice and continued speaking. She seemed to be thinking of a different calling than the one I'd become used to thinking and speaking of.

"Someone told me once that nurses are born, not bred," she continued, tucking a stubborn piece of hair back under the elastic headband from which it had worked free.

"I didn't believe them at first. I had a firm belief that people could be anything they set their mind to be. But I've been around life and death long enough now to know different. Nurses are a different breed. I've met a few who tried hard but weren't born for it—Lord, help them. They didn't last. You, though… you have it in your blood. How are you feeling?"

How was I? I checked in with myself and realized I was doing surprisingly well.

I was feeling equal parts "stable" and "topsy-turvy." I had no urge to scream, faint, burst into tears, or curl into the fetal position despite the evening's events and the strange, weighty message Shae had just delivered. Thinking of her words made me sweat and my pulse quicken, however. I quickly brought my focus back to the task at hand.

"All right, I guess. I don't know if you can declare me a nursing success just yet. I didn't really do much nursing tonight. I just sat quietly and watched someone die."

"Well, watching someone slip away and just sitting by quietly when you know there's nothing you can do… that is one of the hardest parts of this job. Doing it with grace and infusing peace for your patient, that's even harder. It's not the technical tasks that take it out of you. It's the emotional parts that wear you down. You did well." She looked me square in the eyes to make sure I was listening.

I nodded my head to let her know that I heard her.

"Now for the paperwork and phone calls." She snapped back into action and headed for the door. The conversation was over, and it was time to get back to work. I followed her out of the room without looking back and pulled the door softly shut behind me.

I lay awake in my bed for a long time that night. I felt changed, somehow. Older, maybe? It was dawning on me that I had signed up for a lifetime of living extremely close to the line between life and death… and *that* was a hard fact to swallow. I'd given a lot of thought to helping with healing. I hadn't thought near as much about the inevitable losses. I had arrived home from the nursing home after midnight, exhausted. I was listening, consciously and subconsciously for Dhia to give me directions concerning the three men that Shae had spoken of. It was nerve-racking to know that it was coming, and soon, but there was nothing I could do to get ready.

"I understand now, Dhia, why you don't let me see too far around the bend," I whispered in the dark.

As for the rest of Shae's message, I wrote down every cryptic word she had uttered and surrendered it's meaning to Dhia. I turned out the light and climbed into bed, hoping to sleep, but my mind refused to cooperate with my plan. First, my feet were too hot, so I uncovered them. Then they were too cold. I covered them up with just a sheet, but the ends of the sheet were untucked and hung loose, which I found equally unsatisfactory. I tried lying flat on my back and staring out the window. The newly replaced windowpane was a deeper shade than all the older panes. When I tipped my head to the right and looked through the old pane, the moon appeared full and white. When I shifted slightly to the left, it changed to watery blue. I rolled my head back and forth. White moon, blue moon, white, blue, white, blue… Sleep was elusive. Shae's words kept forcing their way to the front of my brain.

She said I was the lead. The lead? The very idea of leading some sort of rescue mission made my lower gut twist uncomfortably.

There was no doubt in my mind that when I had arrived at the nursing home Shae had been completely unconscious and close to death. I'd seen the evidence of her stroke myself, as had the staff. Yet when she and I were alone, she had awoken suddenly and entirely and spoken very clearly. That constituted a miracle. Dhia's direct intervention was the only possible explanation. I wondered why He had chosen to deliver those messages to me in *that* way. He could have told me about the jaunt himself, in a dream, in prayer, even out loud for that matter.

I sat up in bed and replayed the scene in my memory. In my mind's eye, I saw Cumina Shae Hedley, her small light body barely making a dent in the flat mattress beneath her. Suddenly, her eyes flew open. Even the memory invoked a fresh wave of goose bumps. She said she knew I would come. She knew I wasn't Aylie. She called me "child," and Aylie wouldn't have been a child to her; Aylie was her peer, her friend.

That meant Shae knowingly related a message meant solely and clearly for *me*. My knot in my stomach doubled. She had said there were three young men who fell through O gate. They were at Sange's place, and I was supposed to lead. The very idea made my body begin to shake. I wrapped a quilt around my shoulders and slid onto the floor into what was becoming a familiar position—kneeling with my forehead against the edge of the bed.

"Lead what, Dhia? And how? When? Where? And what did she mean when she said I would be asked to do things differently?" I asked Him.

It occurred to me that I did more "saying" in my prayers than listening. So I waited, listened. I became more aware of my breath than I had ever been before. Short intakes, longer out... I deliberately slowed each breath. I was grateful for its strength and regularity. Even something as normal and forgettable as breathing seems notable and important once you've witnessed the lack of it. The wind picked up and began to move through the trees outside my window. The full moon arced slowly across the sky. My mind was a hamster climbing out of its spinning wheel to stand stock-still and stare through the glass wall of its cage.

I waited and listened for a long time until a note slipped underneath my door interrupted my reverie. I glanced at the clock. It was 2:41 a.m., and I'd been kneeling at the edge of the bed for hours. I pried myself off the floor. My legs, stiff and sore, barely held me. I hobbled to the door to retrieve the note. It was a dog-eared flyer printed on cheap yellow copy paper, advertising some sort of public gathering to be held outside the nearby village of Balqhidder. The date on the front of the dog-eared flyer read: August 24, 1989... three years before. I opened the door and glanced both ways down the hall, hoping for a glimpse of the delivery person. The hall was quiet and empty. I shut the door and turned on the desk lamp.

"Okay, Dhia, now what?" I asked.

I doubted He was planning to twist the fabric of time far enough for me to attend the actual event. On the back of the flyer were a short list of directions and a park site map. The park boundaries were marked by thick dotted lines. At the upper right edge of the map, someone had hand-drawn an extension of the park road with red pen and marked it with an asterisk next to a notation that said *7 meters*.

My heart jumped into my throat.

"Now?" I asked Dhia.

"Now," came the audible answer.

LOCH OCCASIONAL

It didn't take me long to pull on jeans and a sweater. I glanced at my reflection in the mirror. Aagh! My hair was as frazzled as I was. Is it even possible for a person to sprout new cowlicks in an established hairline once they've passed puberty? I tugged at it for a moment, then gave up and pulled a stocking cap over top of it. Socks, shoes, sweater, shirt, coat... I spun, fretting, in circles in the center of my room, unsure of what else to bring. Nothing seemed appropriate. I settled for two bottles of seltzer from the minifridge, which I stuffed into my backpack alongside an extra pair of socks. I had never felt so unprepared for anything in my entire life. I'd never *been* so unprepared for anything in my entire life. Locking my dorm room door, I snuck down the hall past Big Bert's door. Someone inside one of the rooms I passed muttered loudly in their sleep.

Sleeping normally at night... not being set upon by evil spirits or called out at midnight to unknown destination..., I thought, stopping for a moment to lean against the wall and just allow myself to feel jealous.

Am I really doing this? Really? I'm not cut out for this!

I waited for Dhia to argue with me or at the very least give me a supernatural confidence boost of some sort. He didn't. I urged my feet back into action and clicked the front door shut behind me. The wind, surprisingly warm, was still increasing in strength and speed. It had already torn a few of the weaker branches from the trees and flung them to the ground. I had no idea where I was going. I waited for the tingling sensation at the base of my neck but felt nothing. Apparently, I'd be walking, at least for the time being. Bracing myself against the wind, I headed straight down the main path. As I reached the circular drive on the center of campus, I noticed a lone car, engine running, parked in a "No Parking" zone. The driver stepped out of the car and motioned for me to join him. He shouted, but the wind carried his words away.

I hesitated. Mom's voice rang in my head, warning me never to approach a stranger. Especially a lone male stranger in the middle of the night.

I sent him, Dhia's voice reassured me. It wasn't audible, but it may as well have been. My concerns evaporated.

As I neared the curb, I realized the driver was not entirely a stranger. It was the young man who had fixed my window. My neck immediately flushed, making me appreciate the cover of darkness. The young man took my backpack from me. He engaged in momentary battle with the wind and the back door, finally managing to deposit the bag on the backseat. We climbed into the vehicle and wrestled the doors closed.

"Crazy wind."

"Yeah," I agreed. My heart pounded in my throat. I was painfully aware of the young man's proximity. I balled my hands into my lap and waited on pins and needles. He pulled the car slowly onto the road and pointed it toward the highway. The strong wind forced him to concentrate on keeping the car in the middle of the lane. He finally settled on a speed and technique that was satisfactory.

Am I supposed to speak or wait for him to speak? I wondered.

"You have the directions?" he asked.

"Me?" I asked, surprised. "What do you mean?"

"The directions," he reiterated.

"You don't know where we are going?" I asked.

"No, don't you?"

The speech center in my brain failed me. Why did he *smell* so good?

He glanced at me, realized I really didn't have a clue what he was talking about, and his expression softened.

"Sorry, maybe we should start with names. I'm Jack."

"Nice to meet you," I replied.

"And you are?" he prompted.

"Oh, sorry. I assumed you knew who I was since you knew to come pick me up. I don't really know how things work yet," I said, playing the part of Captain Obvious. Again. I played that part often.

He looked a little puzzled but smiled. "It's okay. Everyone starts somewhere."

"I'm Kiah."

"Nice to meet you. And the directions…?" he prompted.

"Oh, yeah, right." I flushed all over again.

What is he talking about? Get it together, Adenauer! My brain finally kicked into gear… the *flyer!* I had stuffed it into my pocket. I pulled it out and handed it to him.

"You might have to read it to me," he said, still fighting with the steering wheel to keep the car on the road.

Right. Of course. He couldn't drive and navigate at the same time.

"I assumed you were the one who delivered the flyer," I stammered, feeling flustered.

He shook his head.

"Then who did?"

He shook his head again and shrugged his shoulders, seeming as comfortable as Fa with not knowing the facts of his situation. "I'm just the driver."

I opened the paper and held it up to the moonlight. It was still too dark. I flipped open the visor, and the cosmetic mirror light winked on, providing just enough light for me to see the map. I read the directions to him and gave him the name of the park.

"Oh yeah, I know that place. Loch Occasional, right?"

It was my turn to shrug.

"There's a floodplain there. It's usually a dry wash, but when it rains, it fills up and makes a regular lake."

"Really?" I was intrigued. His description reminded me of the lake Fa and I had bathed in on Petra. That seemed like a lifetime ago.

"Have you seen it?"

"The lake? No, just heard about it. It's a pretty small park, though. I don't even think it's public."

An especially large gust of wind pulled the car to the left, and my hand shot out of its own accord, grazing Jack's arm.

"Sorry." I felt myself blushing again.

"Crazy wind," he repeated.

I contemplated asking Jack if he knew what I was supposed to do once we got to the park but decided speaking wasn't my current strong suit. We rode the rest of the way to the park in an amiable silence that seemed to work very well for the two of us. His presence was warm and reassuring, a welcome distraction from the impossible task ahead. And he smelled, well… he smelled great. (Did I mention that before?)

The wind waned a bit as we drove. Fat raindrops began to challenge the windshield wipers. We pulled into the park past a small sign that declared the area property private and warned trespassers to stay away. The gate stood unlocked and open just enough for the car to pull through. I peered through the wind and rain behind the car and saw a shadowy figure close and lock the gate behind us. Butterflies materialized in my stomach, and the muscles in my hands tensed involuntarily. I consulted the flyer again, and we followed what we hoped was the right road several miles through dense brush. The rain was coming down in torrents by that time, and the road ahead was barely visible through the windshield. Jack slowed the car to a crawl just as it widened and dead-ended in a small parking area.

"I guess this is it," Jack announced, making me jump. We had ridden in silence for so long that his voice sounded inordinately loud.

"I guess so. What next?" I asked without much hope that he would be able to answer.

"Out, maybe?"

We climbed out of the car into the downpour. I was immediately soaked through by the unseasonably warm rain. Jack trained the headlights onto the embankment in front of us, and we climbed the small bank and peered out across the valley that spread before us. Light was just beginning to sneak onto the horizon through a small break in the clouds, illuminating a rush of water that was quickly filling up the wash.

The light was slowly turning the water and the landscape from gray to gold.

"Now what," I prayed aloud, forgetting that Jack was still standing beside me.

"Are you talking to me?" Jack asked.

"No."

Just then, a small boat with a single occupant appeared, pulled our direction by the current.

"I think that's your ride," Jack said.

We scaled the small fence and met the boat as it arrived. The wind had built to a fervor again, rocking the vessel wildly from side to side. A tall dark feminine figure in the bow of the boat tossed us the loose end of a rope, and we nosed the front of the craft onto the shore.

I clambered quickly and gracelessly aboard. "You aren't coming?" I shouted to Jack over the roar of the wind.

"Oh no. I'm just the driver." He smiled and waved, tossing the rope back to us.

The boat immediately jerked away from the bank and bolted downstream.

I felt a small, surprising pang of loss as Jack disappeared from view. I turned my attention to the boat and its driver. She was tall and slender, with a strong nose and jet-black hair that whipped around the edges of her face. She was having considerably less trouble staying centered in the boat than I was. I sat quickly and took the paddle she offered, twisting around to see how she was handling her own oar. She demonstrated the technique, communicating in gestures, and soon we worked out a system that kept the boat from spinning; my paddle on one side of the boat, hers on the other. The roaring of the wind made speech impractical. The boat moved swiftly down the middle of the lake. The light in the sky changed again… gold to orange, orange to pink, pink to lavender. Watching the bank whiz by made me dizzy, so I kept my eyes trained straight ahead. Then the water beneath us was no longer gold-streaked gray. It deepened to periwinkle, reflecting the sky, confirming what I suspected. Loch Occasional was another gate.

The wind died down, and the waters widened out. The current slowed until we found ourselves almost static in the middle of a vast body of water much larger than the lake. Land was no longer visible. I glanced at my companion. She gestured, indicating we should veer left. The water was as still and clear as glass. A very large white form appeared, then disappeared now and again just in front of us but far below the surface of the water. It appeared to be some sort of animal. A whale, maybe? The current that accompanied it caught us, moving us swiftly forward. One moment, the lavender sky was just as cloudless and clear as the water, but close somehow, as if a giant bowl had closed down over the top of us. The effect was disorienting. The next moment, a heavy mist descended on the boat and obscured our vision. My companion remained unconcerned. There was no need to paddle any longer. The current was carrying us. We continued in silence for a while, just listening to the sounds of the water on the sides of the boat until a point of reference appeared out of the mist… a towering stone bridge.

I heard a woman's voice shout down from above and recognized it immediately as Fa's. The boat driver took hold of an iron handle that protruded from the bridge's footings and tied our rope to it. The boat jerked to an abrupt halt. We clamored over the side and started up the iron pegs that led to the bridge above. It was a long climb, and I tried not to think about what might happen if I lost my footing. We were both winded by the time we reached the top of the bridge. Fa's familiar, serious face materialized in front of me, and I hugged her impulsively.

"Good to see you. Come this way." She turned and began walking.

I followed quickly, not wanting to fall behind. The bridge rose sharply beneath us, taking us above the cloud layer. The view was breathtaking. The mist stretched out as far as we could see in every direction, but the bridge dipped and rose up and out of the fog repeatedly at somewhat regular intervals. It did, indeed, resemble an enormous dragon.

"How long is it?" I asked Fa.

"It's long. There are no signs to tell me exactly *how* long," Fa quipped.

"I have something I need to tell you, Fa. It's important." The message Shae had given me about the three young men weighed heavily on my mind.

"No, not now. Later," she insisted.

"But…"

Fa interrupted again, "There will be a time, but *later*, not now."

I gave up and glanced at the boat driver, who walked alongside me in silence.

"Fa, I don't think she and I speak the same language. Can you introduce us?"

"Her name is Rona. She knows your name. She doesn't speak, though."

"Ever?" I asked, surprised.

"Not everyone has to do the same thing, Kiah, live the same way," she chided me.

I was the second time Fa had chastised me in a few short minutes. I wondered if something was bothering her.

I turned to Rona. "Thank you."

She nodded and smiled back at me.

We continued along the back of the dragon, climbing repeatedly out of and then back into the mist. In the places where the bridge dipped the lowest, it almost touched the water. The mist made it impossible to tell how high exactly the high points were. After what seemed like hours and may actually have been… land appeared before us. The waves lapped the black sand of the shore.

"Is this an ocean? Or an enormous lake?" I asked Fa.

"No one has named it an ocean or a lake. You can call it whichever you like," Fa answered.

"What do you call it, then?" I pressed.

"Water."

The black sand stretched inland for a few hundred feet before tentacles of green grass and moss began to reach into it. The landscape was much wilder than the places on the Rock I'd previously visited. The scattered trees were enormous and twisted. Their branches arched from the trunk all the way to the ground where they anchored and started new, younger trees. We passed under some of their arches as we walked.

"They look like yews," I remarked.

Fa answered, "They are."

The air was warming, and I removed my coat and hat. We reached a road that split in two opposing directions. Rona took the right fork, not looking back, while Fa and I continued straight ahead. I was momentarily tempted to call out a "good-bye" to Rona, but it seemed almost rude to do so. Instead, I watched her disappear into the distance. It still seemed physically easier to move on Petra. My legs felt stronger, lighter. I hadn't slept the night before, however, and it had been many hours since I had eaten or even had anything to drink. My backpack with the seltzers in it was still in the backseat of Jack's car. I almost cried with relief when a small stone cabin came into view. We removed our shoes and entered. The interior was one large open space dominated by an enormous soft sisal rug. I wondered where the rug had come from. Petra? Or Earth? India maybe? I smiled at the mental image of a Blue trying to haul it the large unwieldy carpet through one of the gates.

"You sit. Rest," Fa instructed.

I didn't argue. I sank onto a cot inside the door and watched her move about the cabin. She pulled a jug of water from a rudimentary icebox that steamed when she opened it as if it were filled with dry ice. Perhaps it was. She handed me the bottle, then rolled the rug back, revealing a large door in the cabin floor. She tugged at the door. I rose to help, but she waved me away.

"You rest," she insisted, returning her attention to the trapdoor. She wrestled it open and descended a set of steep steps. I was too curious to stay put. I hauled myself to the edge of the black hole and peered into the darkness. A blue square brazier flared up and illuminated a well-stocked root cellar below. Fa gathered various foods from the shelves and came back up the stairs. She fixed a simple meal and brought it up to me. I was so tired that my vision began swam, and I snoozed even as I ate.

"Hey, eat first. Very important." Fa nudged me tenderly.

"I still have something I need to tell you. It's important, Fa…"

Fa held up a hand to interrupt me.

"Tomorrow. You tell me tomorrow," she said.

"But what if that's too late?" I asked.

"It's not too late, Kiah. I promise."

The word *trust* swam up from my center. I swung my feet up onto the cot, pulled a blanket up around my shoulders, and let sleep take me.

THE STRIPE

Something urgent and persistent knocked at my consciousness, and I came up out of sleep quickly. I wondered which world would flood my brain when I opened my eyes. I cracked one eye open to check. My pulse quickened, and I sat bolt upright in my cot in the little stone cabin. It was nighttime. Tangerine moons shone through two of the windows, giving everything in the room an odd, silvery orange hue. Orange? That was new. Our little group had apparently grown exponentially while I slept. I counted one, two, three, four, five, six sleeping bodies besides my own in the room. Some on mats on the floor, some on cots at the back of the room. Rona had evidently rejoined us at some point during the night as well. She sat at the table, staring either thoughtfully or prayerfully through the window; I couldn't tell which.

There was a bag open by my cot, a pair of jeans and a Benetton sweatshirt were hanging half in, half out of it. Obviously, some of the women who'd arrived during the night had come directly from Earth. There was a stack of clean jumpsuits folded on my bedside table, and I rummaged through them as quietly as possible until I found one that seemed my size. The dark blue fabric was silky to the touch and sturdy as canvas. It took a few moments to strap myself securely into the garment and latch the buckles and straps at the ankles, hips, waist, and across the chest. I wondered if I'd managed to don it properly but felt sure that someone would correct me if I hadn't.

There was a large open chest brimming with various boots and shoes in the center of the room. My own shoes were still soggy from the boat trip. I chose a pair that fit well and pulled boot covers over them, fastening them to the ankle of my jumpsuit the way I had seen the other Blues do. I felt more than a little like an imposter in the outfit. I wondered when Petra clothing would begin to feel natural.

Light was creeping into the sky, and Rona seemed content to sit and watch it. I, however, was having a hard time being still. My heart pounded so loudly with anticipation that it feared it might wake someone. I padded quietly to the door and out into the early morning light. Strong wind immediately tried to stuff my breath back into my throat. A fiery red sliver of sun, narrow as the edge of one sheet of paper, floated on the ocean horizon in the far distance. There were dark hills and groves of wildly swaying trees all around me. I could hear but not see rushing water like that of a fast-moving swollen creek. I scanned for the source of the sounds but saw none.

The cabin was nestled in the cleft of a tall narrow hill that climbed steep and fast to a rocky ledge high above. Wanting to gain a better vantage point, I sought a way to climb the hill. Much of the surface of the rock was covered in thick ropy vines that formed a gappy natural ladder. The hill itself sheltered me from most of the wind. I hefted myself up to the nearest section of vines and began to search for the next best step to take... and then the next, and the next... until I had crested the hill and climbed carefully into the center of the stone ledge at its top. The wind was strong. I chose to sit rather than stand. The ocean and the dragon bridge were clearly visible from my vantage point. Angry waves slammed repeatedly into the black sand beach, but that was not the source of the sound of the rushing water. The source, whatever it was, was much closer and remained hidden. The red sliver of sun had grown into a wedge. It didn't light up the sky nearly as much as it seemed it should. I wondered why. I would probably always have to wonder why. There were certainly no scientific experts on Petra to consult with. There were no books to read that could explain Petra's weather patterns. The urgent feeling that had awoken me was still with me... pushing, demanding attention. It had driven me out of the cabin and up the hill. I knew what the feeling was and acknowledged it reluctantly. It was fear, and it needed to be unloaded.

"A Dhia, today I'm scared," I whispered into the wind. I couldn't even hear my own words. I tried again, this time, shouting. The wind still drowned out the sound.

I felt a little sheepish. For months, I had been impatient. I wanted action. I wanted answers to all my questions about what was happening to me and what was coming next. I longed for opportunities and experiences to come faster, sooner. Now what I thought I wanted was happening, and all I really wanted was to curl up in the fetal position with my favorite blanket.

At age seven, I'd been enamored with horses. I dreamt about them, drew them, talked about them, and above all, begged to have one. My father finally took me to a neighbor's house to ride one. I took one look at that enormous perfect creature, the object of all my obsession and affection, and just about pooped myself. Fear flooded in and occupied my driver's seat. My father placed me in the saddle, and I clung to it, hands frozen to the saddle horn, smile frozen on my face while the placid animal plodded, half-asleep around the pasture after its owner. The fear that made me cling to the horn that day stayed with me. For years, my riding instructors repeated the phrase "Let go of the horn, Kiah. Let go of the horn," while I stubbornly gripped it tightly and entertained visions of being thrown far and landing hard. It wasn't until years later, when I dumped fear in the ditch and unclenched my hands, that I learned to balance and ride.

Let go of the horn, Kiah, I muttered to myself that morning. I lay on my back on the rock ledge and stared up into the wild, ruddy, stormy sky. I deliberately opened my hands and let them lie open skyward at my sides. I took a deep breath and made the choice.

"Okay, Dhia, I give you my fear… I'm letting go. I'm willing. I accept your timing. I accept your plan. I'll try to stop second-guessing and just trust you, but you have to help me do that. I need your help! What you are asking me to do…? I can't do any of this alone!"

I stared at my hands. I turned them over and over, examining them. The skin was white and smooth. The fragile veins visible at the wrists. My fingers were very long and straight, even my pinkies.

Mom had crooked pinkies, and they embarrassed her. It was something I had never understood. *You are what you are, right?* What was the point of wishing you had someone else's style of pinkies? A few days ago, my uber-normal hands had been part of something that was anything but normal. I had discounted the impossibly healed wounds under my hands on the man at the mountain as just the type of thing that happened on the Rock. But the strange sensation, the blue glow that only I seemed to see and the healing that happened at the hospital still had me unsettled. It was easier on my psyche when the Blue part of me stayed on Petra and my home life stayed normal. Nice neat boxes and clean lines—no confusion. Dhia, however, didn't seem to be staying inside the boxes and boundaries that made me comfortable... It didn't seem to be in His nature.

"What are you doing with me?" I asked aloud. "And why *me?*"

I heard no answer, but a stripe of what looked like red flame leapt from the sun on the horizon and blazed a wide red swath over my head all the way to the opposite horizon. I winced and twisted around to watch it. It faded slowly until it was no longer visible. I didn't know what it meant, but felt Dhia's calming presence.

The dawn light was spreading into the sky, and I was suddenly very aware of the women in the house below me.

How long have I been up here?

"Are we finished here?" I said aloud, half to Dhia, half to myself.

Fear no longer drove my heart rate and coated my palms with sweat. I still felt miserably unprepared but knew I was accompanied, empowered, and ready to try my hand at whatever came next. I scrambled back over the ledge and down the side of the hill to the cabin.

The energy inside the cabin had notched up considerably while I was gone. Rona was serving rice patties and fruit. A young blond woman I didn't recognize was repairing a jumpsuit. Another was donning her clothes, and Fa sat at the table with the remaining Blues, giving language instruction. Fa was vocalizing phrases, and the Blues were repeating them after her. The words were harsh and guttural. I sensed absolutely no color variation in the individual words. Every word was the same muddy brown. It had to be the language the Kress people spoke. My palms began to sweat again as I realized I'd likely be face-to-face with the Kress people in a few short hours.

Trust. Let go and trust, I reminded myself.

Rona handed me a cup of tea and a piece of fruit. I leaned against the wall behind the table, listening to Fa speak.

As I listened, I realized some of the words were familiar. German. The Kress language seemed to stem from the German language. I tuned in, trying to pick up as much as I could. The vowels were formed differently, originating more from the back of the mouth than German vowels. Many of the words were completely unrecognizable, but the similarities were unmistakable.

Silver-haired Gabije stood behind the table, repeating phrases along with the other listeners. I recognized her as the woman who had taught me how to stitch wounds. She caught my eye and smiled.

"I may never get the hang of this language," she clucked ruefully in Gaelic.

"Well, I haven't gotten the hang of flying yet either," I reassured her.

"We will both get some practice today." She patted my shoulder and grinned.

My stomach lurched.

"I should introduce you to everyone," Gabi added. "We don't all speak the same language, so that takes some getting used to... but it all works out somehow."

Gabi waved the other women over, and we all sat down at the table. There were seven of us.

Gabi introduced herself as a French and Gaelic-speaking physician. She lived and worked on the Rock.

Fa, of course, spoke not only English, Kress, and Chinese, but a few other languages as well. She drained her third cup of tea of the morning while Gabi introduced her. She always appeared calm, but I had witnessed how the pressure of an important pending task decreased her willingness to cope with extraneous questions and kicked up her thirst. Everyone had their own coping mechanisms.

Ess, a small, flinty dark-skinned woman with long stick-straight black hair was introduced as a skilled surgeon. She looked no less than forty years old and was fluent in Gaelic, Swahili, French, and English.

Rona stood like a statue behind Ess's chair, listening to the conversation. She apparently understood Chinese and presumably her native language as well, though no one seemed to know what that language was.

"Rona is the world's best observer and navigator. She has gotten us out of more sticky situations than I can count. She thinks three steps ahead—trust her," Gabi stressed.

I wondered if being free from the burden of speech allowed Rona to think faster and listen better than the rest of us.

"This is Lauren. She's a doctoral student from Canada." Gabi gestured in the direction of the very Swedish-looking blond woman I had seen sewing a jumpsuit earlier.

"How's it going?" Lauren greeted me informally, her hands shoved deep in the pockets of her robe. She had a casual air about her, as if we were preparing to tag team a craft project. She didn't look much older than myself. Lauren was a student of linguistics. She spoke English, French, German, Arabic, Kress, and was working on Hebrew as well.

Next came Mags, an older woman whose specialty was intimidating the Kress men in their own language. I could see why they found her formidable. She was tall and willowy but had the presence of a solid oak tree. She had rounded facial features and piercing green eyes. Her hair was a completely amorphous copper and steel mass on her head. That morning, it was unsuccessfully harnessed at the base of her neck by a strip of blue fabric that looked suspiciously like the jumpsuits we were wearing. Mags was an herbalist. She not only knew the location and purpose of every plant and herb on Earth. She knew her way around Petra's countryside as well. She spoke German, Gaelic, and Frotsi—whatever Frotsi was. I made a mental note to share Ailsa's journals and letters with her. If anyone could make heads or tails of them, it would probably be her.

Gaelic seemed to be a staple language among Blues. Gabi used it that morning, and those who didn't speak it were receiving translation from those around them. I wondered if Gaelic's prominence was related to the long history of Blues coming from Scotland and Ireland or if there were other factors.

Fa started in on her fourth cup of tea.

Cane rounded out the group. She hung at the edges of the milieu, her fingers in constant motion. She rubbed the tabletop as if doing so helped her keep her focus. Cane had incredibly short, plain brown hair—so short it was barely visible at the edges of her colorful homemade skullcap. Her eyes were vivid honey-colored pools. There was something wild about her.

"Cane speaks Gaelic, Kress, and, well…" Gabi hesitated, then decided not to say whatever she had been about to say.

Cane smiled a little.

"Cane works at the village. She was born on Petra," Gabi continued.

"Here?" I blurted.

"I was born not far from here, on the hill," Cane said. Her voice was smoky and a little rusty, as if it was rarely used.

Born on the Rock? There was a story there that begged to be told.

"She's a healer," Gabi clarified. "And she works with horses as well."

"Horses? There are horses here?" My ears pricked up.

"There are horses," Cane answered with a grin, her hands moving in small stroking motions.

"And this is Kiah." Gabi introduced me to the group. "Kiah is a nursing student from Scotland and the United States."

The room fell silent, and everyone stared at me.

"Are you waiting for me to speak?" I asked.

"You are the lead," Gabi said.

My heart leapt into my throat, and I swallowed hard, trying to force it back into its proper place.

"Okay, well, I guess I'll start with what I know, right? Three young men fell through at O Gate. They are at Sange's place."

We reached the dregs of my knowledge very quickly. Everyone continued staring expectantly. I floundered, trying to think of something spectacular to say. I felt my neck flush. My entire life my skin had been like a large video screen that broadcasted my emotions for all to see. I flushed, blushed, goose bumped, and broke out in hives at the drop of a hat, whenever things got real. It was somewhat humiliating. The Blues either didn't notice or didn't care, which I appreciated.

Rona unrolled a large hand-drawn map, spread it across the table, and secured the edges with rocks.

"O Gate?" Gabi asked.

"Yes, that's what she said."

"She?" Gabi started a little and tipped her head curiously at me. "Who is *she*? You didn't hear this from Dhia?"

"No… not directly. One of my patients told me, actually. This very old woman… she had a massive stroke. She was dying. She woke up suddenly and told me this just before she died."

Gabi pondered that for a moment. "He is new every morning. Dhia can and does do whatever he wants in whatever way He wants to. New *every* morning." A few of the other Blues nodded their agreement. She returned her attention to the map. It was incredibly detailed, with trees, bodies of waters, mountains, and valleys all marked with symbols. It was strange to see a map devoid of place names or words of any sort.

"Is it of Petra?" I asked.

Mags nodded.

Fa and Mags were discussing Sange. Kress was the only language the two of them had in common. Fa barked out a word I didn't recognize, and Mags made a phlegm-rattling sound followed by a grunt. The effect was almost amusing, as if they were of two different species and engaged in an argument.

Lauren sat down beside me and translated their conversation into English.

"The O Gate? That's on the north side right?" Fa pointed to the north side of the large gray area in the middle of the map that apparently represented Kress.

"I thought Sange ran brothels out of the southeast," Mags responded.

We are going after brothel slaves. I shuddered. I didn't even want to imagine it. Soon I wouldn't have to imagine it. I would see and experience it.

"He did, until Spe shut him down," Fa answered Mags.

"When was that?"

"Before the thirteenth stripe. It hasn't been that long," Fa answered.

"O Gate is in the middle of a swamp. The nearest town is Pak. Did he rebuild there?"

Fa consulted Rona in Chinese. Rona nodded.

"Then we go to Pak." Rona rolled and stowed her map. The buzz in the air climbed another notch in intensity.

Lauren rose from her chair, and I grabbed her elbow and whispered, "Have you gone on a jaunt before?"

"A few times."

"That explains why you are so calm," I muttered.

"Calm? Don't kid yourself. My insides are eating me just like everyone else's. This is hard, and it's scary... for everybody."

"They don't show it."

"They are choosing to trust. Thank God we aren't in charge, right? He is." She patted my shoulder reassuringly and left the table. I started to follow, but Fa's voice kept me back.

"Sit a minute," Fa instructed and I sat.

"Fa, does the Kress language stem from German? I recognize many of the words."

"Yes." She nodded. "A long time ago, the Kress people spoke German, but languages change over time, especially here. It's not the same now. You understood some, though?"

It was my turn to nod.

"Good. Keep listening. So for today you need to wear a jumpsuit and a robe. The robes intimidate the Kress. It's how they know who we are. We wear them always when we go into their territory."

"Okay, and what else?" I asked.

"What do you mean, 'what else'?"

"Well, when are you going to tell me what I'm supposed to be *doing*?"

"There is no more to tell. God will lead you, and you will lead us."

"Seriously? That's it?" I exclaimed a little too loudly.

Fa put her fingers to her lips. "Sshh, be calm!" she whispered. "Have you paid attention to his commands? If you had, your peace would have been like a river and your well-being like the waves of the sea."

I looked around the room, wondering if I'd missed something.

"What river? What sea, Fa? What do rivers and seas have to do with this?"

"It's from the Bible… Isaiah 58. Haven't you read it?"

"I guess not, because I'm not feeling very peaceful," I whispered, then sighed. "It's a big book, and I've been busy…"

"Maybe if you took time to read it, like I told you, this would be easier."

"You want me to read it now?" I asked.

"No, of course not. There's no time… but you will read more?"

"I will. I promise. But what about *now*?"

"Now you trust."

I gave Fa a look that communicated exactly how desperately fish out of water I felt.

She sighed. "Okay, I tell you one thing… even though you do not need to know but to *trust*. Just trust!"

"I will trust, I promise. Fa, just tell me as much as you can so I can stop freaking out long enough to figure out how to do that."

"You won't freak out. Once we get going, boldness will find you. You will see. You were made to do this. You are the *first* Blue to lead on her *first* jaunt. That means He has something special for you."

"The first?" My volume rose again, prompting another shushing from Fa. "You are kidding, right? I thought this was some sort of initiation everyone went through: make the new girl think she's in charge to test her mettle!"

Fa shook her head. "It's not a test. We don't deceive you. We tell you how things are, and you tell us how things are. Always. That is all. And, yes, you are the first Blue to lead on her first jaunt, as far as I know. You are a good apple, remember? You were picked."

I didn't know what being a good apple had to do with the task at hand. I was feeling more like a kumquat and didn't particularly want to be either one. There was, however, no use belaboring the point.

"Okay. Okay," I said, hoping and then choosing to trust... not only that everything she was saying was true but that fortitude would replace the butterflies in my stomach as soon as we were on our way.

"You did say you would tell me something, though, right? Something else I might need to know?"

Fa sighed. "Okay, I tell you this. Do you remember your first day in the valley? On the hill? When you saw the cloud? Do you remember how you felt?"

I remembered very well the cold sick feeling that had gripped me as I stared at the seething wall of darkness.

I nodded my head.

"And when something evil happens on Earth, when things are just not right... you know that feeling?"

I nodded again. I'd met evil up close recently; I remembered the feeling well.

"You will feel this same way today. Like ice water. And it will want to swallow you... to take you apart one thought and one feeling at a time. This is what being in Kress territory is like. The Kress people, they live with it. Evil is their cold comfort. They don't recognize it. For you, it will be a challenge. You must know that it is only a feeling. You have truth, and though darkness can taunt you, it cannot own you. You belong to God. You belong to your Dhia, right? He is your beloved, and you are his. You tell yourself this, again and again in your mind while we are there today. This is the truth. The blood of Christ—this is the power. It is all something to get used to, but you can do it. You are a good apple. God would not send you here if He didn't know you could do this, *with* His help."

Fa paused; then another thought struck her. "Also know this, Kiah... the Kress are afraid. They have reason to fear you. They live in fear. They will not even touch you. You, however, have *no* reason to fear them. And they know this too. They are not stupid, at least not most of them. You are new, and they might try to bully you. Don't let them do this. They need to know that you have truth and light."

Fa's words gave my flitting mind an anchor.

"Thank you," I said.

"Of course, now it's your turn. Who is it that will carry?" Fa asked.

"Carry what?"

"Carry the young men."

The memory of Gabije dropping into the room carrying the unconscious man sprang to mind.

"Oh, I don't know. Should I know? How do I know who to choose?"

"Before you say you don't know, you should check with yourself. Maybe you do already know. Maybe God has told you."

I thought pointedly about the rescue. I imagined our little group cruising purposefully toward the darkest place I'd ever gone. I closed my eyes and envisioned Gabi to my left, Cane at my right, and Lauren a little ways up ahead; and suddenly I knew.

"Lauren, Mags, and myself need to carry. I want to say you too... but there are only three men... so that makes no sense, right?"

"Stop trying to make numbers fit, and just listen to what God tells you," Fa said, handing me a robe.

"How? How does four carriers make sense?" I asked her.

"You will see,'" she quipped.

"Maybe I shouldn't carry. I'm not the best flier..."

"What did you see? What did God show you?" Fa interrupted.

"Lauren, Mags, you, and me. But I'm just thinking..." What I was thinking was that there were much better fliers than myself, and carrying an injured young man was best left up to them, but Fa interrupted me.

"Thinking is good. A very good thing. But God does thinking much better than you. This is the time to listen, not to talk yourself out of God's best. You do what He says when He says it. This will never be wrong."

"Okay. I get it." I had so much to learn.

"So do we go now?" Fa asked.

I checked in with my own heart before I answered this time.

"Time to go." I called out to everyone in the room. Everyone, regardless of the language they spoke, understood the sentiment, if not my words.

"Dhia, help me," I prayed aloud.

The other Blues murmured prayers as they gathered their belongings and checked their packs. The hum of devotion was electric, foreign, comforting. I added my own voice to the mix. The base of my neck began to buzz as I opened the door, and the red wind rushed into the room.

We passed several groups of large dark birds as we flew. They didn't seem bothered by either the strange color of the sky or our presence. They were thoroughly enjoying playing in the strong winds. My mind wandered badly as we flew, flitting back and forth between memories, questions and random thoughts. When geese fly south for the winter, everyone knows they fly in a *V* pattern, but do you know why one side of the *V* is usually longer than the other? Because there are more birds on that side. At least that's how the joke goes. I'm quite certain that the real reason they don't fly in an even *V* pattern is that they don't really care what they look like from the ground. They just fly in whatever formation works best for everyone… and when the wind whips up, they play in it…

Focus, Adenauer!

I was gliding through the sky with six other women, most of them virtual strangers. It felt so much like a dream.

Stay sharp. This is real, I reminded myself.

"Why is the sky staying so dark?" I shouted to Lauren to make myself heard over the roar of the wind.

"We call it a stripe. It's beautiful, isn't it?"

It was beautiful. Petra looked vastly different in red and gray than it did in its usual periwinkle and green state. A flock of white birds painted crimson by the sun fluttered up as we passed low over the trees they occupied. Millions of stars were still visible. The wind at our backs drove us forward.

"Is it seasonal?" I asked.

"No. It's one of the ways God communicates with us on the Rock. He's telling us how He feels."

"Will the sky get any lighter today?"

She shrugged. "We'll have to wait and see."

The sun was a burning red melon directly overhead, and we had left the wind behind by the time we stopped for lunch. The sky was still little more than twilight dark. We dropped into a grove of tall narrow trees not far from a small, perfectly circular lake. I hung to the back of the pack, watching the others' landing techniques, fervently hoping not to collide with anyone. I surprised myself by landing squarely on my feet beside Cane. A heavy mist lay thick under the canopy, and a smaller version of the canvas tent in the horseshoe valley stood barely visible in the fog up ahead. My skin tingled and vibrated all over from having been airborne so long. It reminded me of the way the bottoms of my feet buzzed after I climbed down from the rear seat my father's motorcycle after a long ride.

We reached the tent and filed inside. Cane lit the braziers. The space was laid out much like the one in the valley had been but held only six patient cots in the main room. The floor sparkled in the bluish light of the braziers just as I remembered. A heavy curtain at the back of the room separated it from the sleeping and eating quarters beyond. That room held as many or more cots as the front room but in a much smaller space. Fa and Lauren immediately took over the kitchen, and Rona donned rubber boots and a bucketful of tools and disappeared outside. The other Blues set about sweeping the floor in the main room, opening cupboards and arranging supplies. We weren't just there for lunch. We were prepping the space for use. The reality of our impending task fluttered in my chest again.

Not sure what needed to be done, I joined Ess at the supply cupboard in order to make myself plainly available.

She handed me a rather large bottle of oil, a few rags, and a small bucket.

"Clean everything," she instructed.

The pungent oil reminded me of the floor cleaner my mother used, piney and fresh. I set to work, and Gabi joined me. I wondered if the comfortable silence the Blues worked in was their regular habit or due to their particular personality mix. Or perhaps the upcoming jaunt was weighing on them. Maybe it was a little bit of all of the above.

Once the room was clean and Ess had organized the supplies to her satisfaction, we met in the back room for a meal of rice, veggies, and dried meat. The rice was an odd greenish color and slightly dry, but everyone had seconds. Rona had opened up the bath facilities in a separate hard-walled structure just outside off the kitchen. We each took turns in the shower. The water, housed in a large tank above the small wooden building, was lukewarm but welcome nonetheless.

The strange red daylight made the water that ran in rivulets down my legs appear amber red, like so much blood. The fear I'd woken with had hardened slowly into fortitude just as Fa predicted. I felt it, curled tight in my belly.

"A Dhia, help us," I said aloud for the millionth time. The water ran in my eyes and stung a little. It ran in my mouth and tasted sweet. I knew He would help us. He already was. My heart was beginning to understand that I still needed to ask; that's how it worked. Dhia liked to hear my voice, even when I repeated myself. It brought us closer. I felt Him when I whispered his name. That day, the need to pray was like the need to sneeze, to hiccup, or to breathe... impossible to ignore.

I finished showering and got dressed, joining the Blues in the tent. Lauren and Ess were circling the room praying over the instruments, the medicines, the cots, and everything else in the room. Fa knelt in the center of the room with Mags and Rona. I took up a post at the front door. Gabi did likewise at the back door. Cane sat cross-legged just outside on the ground, her hands still for the first time since I'd met her.

We prayed for the men we were going to bring there, for God's favor, His power, His will to be done. I felt His answering presence, powerful enough to be frightening, course through my veins. The light in the room changed quality, brightening as Dhia silently joined us, and time stood still... at least it seemed to. My feet were glued to the floor. My back felt melded to the door frame. I wanted to stay forever in that doorway, pouring out my heart to Dhia alongside these women, watching the azure light play across the floor of the tent like so many stars, the red light outside scatter like rubies across the lake. But I felt the irresistible urgency of need like a pent-up sob in the back of my throat. It was time to go. My shoulders buzzed as I lifted into the air, and the others followed.

KRESS

We flew for over an hour before we spotted the Kress border. The foliage along the ground thinned out considerably within the last mile or so of the dark cloud wall. We landed in a sea of tall grass that waved darkly in the wind. The cloud wall looked even taller and more intimidating from the ground than it had from the hills that surrounded the horseshoe valley. It looked solid and impenetrable like falling water in a glass column that hit the ground and rolled back upward with nowhere else to go.

I stepped forward and put my hand into the cloud. It swirled and parted as I touched it. I steeled myself for… whatever… and walked into the column. The others followed. There was zero visibility inside the wall. We walked a few feet straight forward in the cold thick fog, then out the other side into a large open area. I dropped to knees in the dirt and gasped, panicky, not sure if the air was breathable. I felt as I'd been plunged into a frozen lake, except that I wasn't exactly physically cold. Fear and evil clawed at my mind, and I dry-heaved, wondering if I might pass out. I wasn't the only one; Ess and Lauren knelt beside me struggling to acclimate to the sudden change. Lauren was retching as well and muttering under her breath.

"Breathe long and slow. Remember who you are. The nausea will pass. Some of us have a harder time in here than others, but it will pass. Take your time." Lauren spoke directly into my ear, "Remember, He is with us."

And He was. When I focused and closed my eyes, I grasped Dhia's presence. I opened my eyes and heaved again.

"Show me what to do, Dhia. What now?" I asked aloud.

The nausea finally subsided, and I felt able to open my eyes and get up. It was time to move on. The ground inside the wall was bare dirt with a few scrubby patches of grass here and there. The air was strangely still and smelled almost metallic, like old ice cubes left too long in the ice maker. The light that filtered down from above was still reddish but darker, as if a film covered the sky inside the cloud boundary. The stars were no longer visible. The outline of buildings rose in the distance on the far side of the open field ahead of us. I felt the urge to run, so I ran. We all ran. Our feet pounded the dirt so fast and hard that I wondered if they might lift us into the air. We ran for quite a while before we reached a row of dwellings and slowed to a walk. There were row upon row of small cement huts with fires burning in each yard. Fa pulled her hood up over her head, and we all followed suit, walking in a tight group. There were people about, barely visible on the meager light, but they disappeared as we passed before I caught a glimpse of any of their faces. Sadness and fear clung to the people disappearing around corners and into the huts as we passed. I could feel it trailing from them like jet streams as they fled. News of our presence seemed to move faster than we did. Soon, the yards we passed were completely empty before we reached them.

The rows of houses ended, and we crossed another field—one which I suppose one might call "planned greenspace," although there was absolutely nothing green about the space. Grid rows of dark purple beans erupted from mounds of gray grass. We stepped over and around the mounds. Tall cement buildings rose on the far side of the open space to our left, and shorter cement buildings spread out to our right. I felt the urge to turn toward the northeast and gestured in that direction, looking to Fa for confirmation. She nodded and I headed northeast into a dirty city block of small squat buildings. It appeared to be a business district. Simple signs hung outside most of the doorways. Most bore inverted triangles and varying series of numbers. There were no lights on inside or anywhere near.

"Brothels. Not open until nighttime," Lauren whispered.

I shivered though I still wasn't cold.

I heard the commotion up ahead before I saw its source. We passed a final row of nondescript buildings and found ourselves in a large circular lot with a wooden dais at its center. A large group of Kress, probably a few hundred men in total, faced the dais. The sheer number of them was intimidating. I reminded myself of who I was and who Dhia was and that He was with me. The men wore various types of clothing: pants, tunics, shirts, mostly plain and simple but surprisingly modern in style. I somehow expected people totally given over to evil to appear slovenly and caveman-ish, but that didn't seem to be the case for Kress. A few of the men turned as we approached, and I noticed an obvious difference between Kress men and every other man I'd ever met. There were large jagged black stains that extended down their faces from brow or hairline to chin or neckline. Each stain was a slightly different shape, and I wondered if the marks were a naturally occurring consequence or tattoos. Either way, I felt in my bones that they were marked by their own choice to utterly reject Dhia. Seething hate for us shone in their eyes, and their fear of us was palpable. I didn't find myself hating them back. Instead, I felt a sense of despair and sadness.

The event being held was a slave auction. Nine men stood on the dais, stripped naked, bound at the wrists with their hands chained together above their heads to a bar running a few feet above their heads. Three well-dressed Kress men stood on the dais, apparently pointing out the attributes of the individuals up for sale. Horror bloomed in my gut and pulled at my heart and my eyelids. I wanted desperately to shut my eyes and run. I had expected to struggle with the ugliness I knew I would see, but there was no way to prepare for the way I felt.

Help, I begged silently.

I closed my eyes and took a deep breath, feeling Dhia shore me up again from the inside.

The crowd parted as we approached the dais. Our presence was disrupting the proceedings. My heart pounded in my throat, but I felt the need to meet each glance head on, unblinking. It worked. Each Kress shrank back or slunk away when I looked at him. I approached the dais and looked closely at the slaves hanging by their wrists from the bar.

There are nine men here… not three… so which are we supposed to take? I asked Dhia silently.

Look, came the answer.

I looked. The first man on the podium had a facial stain as did the second, the third, the fifth, the sixth, the eighth, and the ninth. The two remaining men—one dark-haired and one blond—did not. They were fully human, not Kress. They were certainly two of our targets. *But where was the third?*

I glanced up and down the line again. He wasn't there.

"So?" Fa whispered.

"There are only two," I answered in a low voice.

"Which two?" she asked, and I realized she couldn't see their facial markings.

"The fourth and the seventh from the left."

"And the other?" she asked.

"I don't know. Give me a minute," I whispered. Panic began to creep up my backbone. *What was I missing?*

"We don't have a minute," Fa whispered back, propelling me up onto the dais with her firm hand at the small of my back. "It's best to keep moving."

Of the three Kress officials on the podium, one seemed to be an auctioneer; one looked like hired muscle; and the third was a mani-cured, paunchy, bearded man who sat on an expensive-looking chair in the center of the podium looking very much in charge. Fa steered me toward that man. Mags followed close behind.

"Sange," Mags said.

Sange seemed to recognize Fa. He spit on the ground in front of us and said something venomous. The word *hexen* jumped out at me from his slew of words. I recognized it as the German word for *witch*.

Mags leaned toward the man and whispered something to him. Fear glinted in his eyes. Fa had been right. They were afraid of us.

"Don't come near me," he said, half demanding, half plead-ing. I understood his words clearly though he spoke Kress. I glanced around, surprised I'd understood. Apparently, Dhia saw fit to translate directly for me. I began to feel as if I were watching a foreign movie with Dhia-supplied supernatural subtitles.

"We need all three," Fa said. "Now."

"You have claim to only two of these men. You may take them and go before you make me sick." Sange pointed to the slave lineup. Mags approached number four. His hands were tied too high in the air for her to reach, and she flew up to the bar to untie him. The men in the crowd murmured and stepped back away from all the Blues. A few muttered *hexen* at her under their breath. I could still feel their hate, but their fear outweighed it. I shuddered at the thought of what might happen if the scales tipped, and the hate took over.

A Dhia, be with us, I pleaded silently.

Mags looked at me, waiting for my direction on what to do next.

"Lauren," I said. Lauren joined Mags on the dais. Together, they brought the young man to the ground. Lauren stayed with him, and Mags moved on to number seven, glancing back at me again.

"You," I said, indicating that number seven was her charge. Mags released him. Four and seven lay motionless on the floor of the platform, and the Blues gathered around to prepare them to be airlifted. I wasn't sure if the men were conscious. For their sakes, I hoped not. Blood quickly pooled under number seven and ran in rivulets down the crooked planks of the dais. I didn't allow my thoughts to dwell long on what the experience might be like for them. I didn't have the bandwidth to feel and think at the same time.

"Where's the third?" Fa asked Sange.

"There is no third," he answered with a smirk.

But there was a third, and I realized quite suddenly that we didn't need Sange's cooperation in order to find him. I knew exactly where he was.

"I already know," I told Fa.

"She doesn't even speak correctly?" Sange said in a cocky tone, noting that I spoke in English rather than Kress. "She must be new?" He stood and faced me. Anger flared in my chest, and a set of words came unbidden to my mind, forcing their way onto my tongue. I centered myself in front of the large man on and spoke them, not even knowing myself what they meant. I saw a blue flash of light, and the crowd gasped, retreating a bit more. Sange sat back down.

I turned to face Fa.

"I know where to go. I know where the third target is. The others need to take these men back to the camp. We will meet them," I said.

"You are sure we should split up?" Fa asked. TThe question in her eyes told me it wasn't the way things were normally done, but I was one hundred percent sure of what Dhia was asking me to do.

I nodded.

I quickly informed the other Blues of the plan and Fa, and I started down the platform steps. For the first time, the buzzing in my shoulders was a sweet, welcome sensation. We lifted off and flew low over the buildings toward the East. Kress scattered under us, screaming and pointing as we passed. I saw the long, low barracks-style building on the edge of the town and knew it was our destination. Inside, we would find our third target. We landed on the roof.

"Have you been here before?" I asked Fa.

She shook her head. No.

I was sure we were at the right place but had no sense for how to enter. We crept along the roof, scouting for a way in and found a manhole with a metal door. We hauled it open and dropped through into the building. The smell inside was sour and fetid, like dead mouse, unwashed skin, and burning chemicals. There was a heavy perfume in the air as well that did nothing to mask the overwhelming odor. I gagged, and my eyes streamed.

"You okay?" Fa whispered.

"Yes," I said, wondering how she could stand the odor. "What is that smell?"

"What smell?" She sniffed the air and looked at me quizzically.

Apparently, Fa neither saw the stains on the Kress's faces nor smelled the horrible odors that were assaulting my senses.

Lucky me.

"Never mind," I told her.

We had dropped into a corridor that extended several hundred feet in either direction. Wall torches, about one-third of which were lit, ran the length of one side of the hall, interspersed with small oblong boxes. The boxes were locked, slotted along the top, and etched with the word *Zahlung*—German, and apparently also Kress, for "payment." The other side of the hall was lined with heavy curtains of the type you might find in cinemas or auditoriums. I pulled back the nearest curtain to reveal a room with a table, chair, and a large low bed-like platform in the center of the room. A naked man lounged on the bed. He winked at me, gesturing provocatively as I pulled back the curtain, then jumped off the bed and scurried into the back corner of the room when he realized I was a woman. He was not our target.

Every cell in my body screamed at me to leave that place. I didn't want to walk that hall, smell that odor… I certainly didn't want to see behind another curtain. What I wanted, however, was not important. What mattered was what I chose to do. We hurried along the hall, pulling back curtains, looking for our third target.

Where is he? Please show me! I begged Dhia, feeling almost angry that He was having me look into every cell rather than just telling me directly where to go. Cell after cell contained Kress men, most young and brazen with dull, sullen gazes. I was at least relieved that it was midday. Several hours remained before the brothel would be open to customers. A Kress man in a long formal-looking tunic appeared in the hallway and began to approach us, then recognized us and quickly reversed his direction and ducked around a corner.

We were reaching the end of the main hallway, and I was beginning to feel desperate.

Where is he?

I lifted the last curtain and found a set of locked double doors.

"Just a minute," Fa said, her finger in the air.

She disappeared down the hall and returned shortly with the staff member we had just seen. He jogged toward me, wide-eyed, staying just out of Fa's reach as she barked orders at him from behind. She seemed to be threatening to touch him if he didn't do as he was told. I wasn't sure exactly what she was saying… Dhia had ceased translating for me. The staff member had his keys out and ready. He opened the doors quickly for us. It was dark inside the room, and Fa pointed to a torch in the hallway, motioning for the Kress to retrieve it. He did so, placing it on a stand inside the room, then tried to back into the hall. Fa stepped behind him and urged him into the room with us. He was too afraid to refuse. Perhaps it was his first experience with a Blue. The look on his face made me wonder what rumors circulated about us.

The room we entered was larger and more ornate than the other cells we had seen. Curtains lined the walls, and the tables were carved with shapes and swirls. Chained to the wall in the back of the room was our third target. He lay naked in the fetal position and turned away from the light as we entered. Fa and I reached him quickly, and he shrank from us, covering his head in his hands.

Fa convinced the Kress to unlock the man's hands while I grabbed a blanket from the bed and wrapped it around him. I crouched beside him, speaking softly. "Don't be afraid. We aren't here to hurt you. Here, it's just a blanket, see? We are here to help you. Look at me. Look at me."

I touched his chin, and he turned his head toward me. His dark blond hair was shaggy but clean. He seemed slightly older than myself. There was very little understanding in his eyes. I'd seen that look before on the face of the boy in the valley. It was the look of someone traumatized past the point of reason to the very edge of sanity. There was a series of straight, even cuts along his left cheekbone and across his forehead. The right side was still seeping blood, which ran into his eye. I cringed inwardly but tried to maintain a comforting facial expression.

"Look at me. We are here to help you," I repeated.

My words finally reached him. Recognition flashed across his face.

"Do you understand me?" I asked.

He nodded.

"What's your name?"

He didn't respond at first. He searched his mind for a moment, then said, "Aaron."

"Aaron, I'm Kiah, We're here to help you."

That was enough for him. He threw himself into my arms. Caught off guard, I almost toppled. Fa stabilized us from behind to keep us from falling over. He clung to me, trembling violently. I caught a strong sudden glimpse of what it must be like to be a mother, cradling a frightened child. I felt an overwhelming surge of empathy but just as quickly pushed the feeling aside. I struggled to my feet, with Fa's help, hauling the man with me. I wanted to get out of there, fast. We wrapped him completely in the blanket, and Fa set about strapping him to my chest.

How in the world *am I going to fly this way?* I wondered, then realized the answer lie in the question. I wasn't *in* the world… not the one I was used to anyway. I was relying entirely on Dhia for my strength and direction. I wasn't responsible for reasoning my way through the situation or for making anything happen. I just needed to listen well, heed directions, and be ready to step off whichever cliff Dhia pointed me toward.

The Kress staff member grabbed his chance while we were busy to escape into the hall. Fa set to work, strapping the man into my jumpsuit. Luckily, he was strong enough to help hold his own weight in a standing position. I spoke quietly in his ear as Fa worked as quickly as she could. She wrapped a second blanket around the man and secured my chest strap around his back, then a waist strap, hip strap, thigh strap and finally the ankle straps. I widened my stance as much as I could but still had to rely on Fa to hold us steady. I felt the familiar tingling along my shoulder blades and glanced at the ceiling. It seemed low. I held my breath, waiting for the tug. When it came, the man startled, letting out a grunt of surprise.

"Hang onto me. Don't let go," I told him, though I doubted I needed to remind him. He was clinging tight already, whimpering wetly in my neck. Fa opened the double doors, and we dipped through the doorway, then turned down the hall in the direction we had come. Fa joined me in the air, and we rose to the vaulted ceiling. The Kressman whom Fa had intimidated into unlocking the door for us was apparently a tattletale. Several other Kress were now gathered with him in the hall below us, pointing, shouting, and ducking as we passed. Fa sped past me and to the double doors at the far end of the hall and held them open for us as we exited.

Freedom… sort of. A large group of Kress had gathered outside to gawk. The air there was notably clear of the stuffiness and rank odor of the brothel but still felt oppressive and close. I felt sadness and fear tear at me as we rose quickly up and over the slave market, clearing the tall buildings in the business district.

I had reached the end of my intuitive direction at that point and was simply following Fa. The man gripped me tighter as we took to the air, burying his face in my neck. I was sure his fingers were bruising me. I could feel his entire body shaking. I realized that flying probably wasn't something he was expecting. I wrapped my arms around him and spoke in his ear.

"You won't fall, even if you let go. I've got you. You are strapped in, remember? Just take it easy. You are safe."

The word *safe* seemed to have a positive effect. He loosened his grip a little, so I repeated it. "You are safe now. You are safe."

We were far enough above the ground that I could see the layout of the city. It was arranged in the shape of a large circular target with the business district as the bull's-eye. The next ring was greenspace, followed by a circle of smaller buildings and more greenspace. The housing units formed the outermost ring.

Fa broke hard right, away from the cloud wall as we breached the final ring. I wondered where she was taking us. We were coming up on yet another set of concentric rings. Food growing circles interspersed with dwelling circles comprised of small tents and huts. Fires burned here and there, and figures moved in and among the dwellings.

"Women's camp," Fa explained. We weren't extremely close to the camp but close enough to be seen. One woman shouted and threw something at us, another outright hissed at us. A child growled loudly at us and threw a rock, which narrowly missed Fa's head. I had seen enough. We rose sharply and headed for the cloud wall. Fa burst through first, and I followed close on her heels. A surge of relief flooded my being as we broke free, and tears sprang unbidden to my eyes. I let them come. The wind was strong, and my charge reacted to the change by tightening his grip again. In my relief at reaching the free space, I had almost forgotten him for a moment. Aaron. He had said his name was Aaron.

"You are safe, Aaron," I reminded him. "It's just wind. I've got you. I'm going to let go a little, but the straps have you, okay? Just relax. Can you hear me?" I felt him nod.

"Good, just a little longer... then we will land and get you taken care of."

My arms were aching. I kept hold of his head with my left hand and stretched my right arm. I found that by switching arms every few minutes, I could keep his head supported and keep my arms from going numb at the same time.

"Doing okay?" Fa asked me.

Aaron startled. He had obviously not realized that someone, Fa, was flying with us.

I nodded. I was definitely tiring, but it wasn't dire at that point. It occurred to me that the increased ease of movement I experienced on Petra probably helped to make flying with added weight possible.

Fa rolled upside down underneath us, where I couldn't see her. I wondered what she was up to. She stretched her arms all the way around to my back, holding Aaron solidly between us. The weight on my neck back and hips decreased immediately.

"Better?" Fa said from somewhere below me.

"Yes," I confirmed. It was much better.

EMPATHY

We flew all the way back to camp that way, like a bizarre flying sandwich complete with plastic wrap wings. The crimson sun was sinking toward the horizon as we landed. Aaron had either passed out or fallen asleep. The lake and the tent slid into view below us. The ceiling of the tent was rolled back, and the braziers were lit. The other men were already settled into cots and being tended. Fa let loose of us, and I dropped in through the ceiling eager to deposit my charge. Cane and Mags were waiting on either side of an empty cot. Fa joined them, and the three of them quickly set to work on the straps as we hovered just the surface of the cot. I expected it to be a cumbersome process, but the other Blues were experienced. They worked quickly and efficiently. The movement and the light awakened Aaron, and he clung tighter to my neck.

"We're here, Aaron. You're safe. You can let go now. You are on the ground. These women are here to help you."

Aaron glanced around but didn't let go.

"Don't go," he pleaded.

I wasn't sure who he was talking to.

"I'm not going anywhere. I'll stay right here, but you have to let go." I pried his fingers from around my neck and rolled to the side. My feet touched ground. Finally! My back was stiff and sore, and my limbs felt rubbery, but there was no dome to rest. Aaron lifted his head off the pillow, wild-eyed, taking in everything going on around him. I took both his hands in mine and leaned in close.

"Look at me… Look at me, Aaron." He glanced at me, wild-eyed, but I could tell he barely saw or heard me through his panic.

"Where am I? Where did they go?" he asked hoarsely. His accent was decidedly American. I assumed the "they" he referred to were the Kress.

"Don't worry about them right now. You will never see them again. You are safe here. See these women?" I indicated the other Blues, and Aaron nodded.

"They are here to help you. Let us help you. Can you do that?"

He nodded again, indicating that he would try, but didn't relax. Ess appeared at my shoulder. She hung a pink glass bottle of IV fluids from a hook above Aaron's head and ran the medicine through the tubing.

"What is that?" Aaron demanded.

"It's medicine. It's okay. You are safe here," I repeated. He clearly didn't feel safe, no matter what I said. He sat bolt upright in bed and dove into my arms the way he had in the brothel. With his head tucked tight in my neck, he began to rock slightly back and forth, moaning. I looked to Ess for direction. She drew up another medication and added it to the pink bottle then readied an IV setup. I surveyed the room as best I could. The tent hummed with activity. Rona was struggling to close the roof flaps. Cane was meticulously stitching the bloody flayed back of her blissfully unconscious patient. Lauren was speaking French to our third patient, trying to soothe him as Gabi washed, and inspected his wounds. Fa seemed to be running point—shuttling supplies, hot water, and medicines back and forth about the room.

Ess caught my attention. She was ready to place IV access.

"The doctor needs your arm, Aaron. You know what an IV is, right? We need to place an IV… to give you medicine." His grip tightened, indicating he heard me speaking, but he said nothing.

Ess whispered something to Fa. Fa disappeared into the back room and returned quickly with a long-needled syringe designed for deep muscular injections. Aaron was no longer able to cooperate. It was simply too much for him to handle. Ess pulled the loose end of the blanket away from his lower back and, with one quick movement, expertly speared his right butt cheek with the needle. He barely flinched.

"You are going to feel sleepy, Aaron. You're okay. Just sleep. We won't leave you." I stroked his hair and whispered into his ear as one would a small frightened child. The medicine worked within a few minutes. His rocking slowed to a stop, and his grip on my arms relaxed. I was able to lean him back onto his pillow and slip off the cot. He slept.

"You should change clothes and shower," Fa immediately suggested. "We will take care of things here."

I looked down at my jumpsuit. She was right. My left shoulder and neckline were soaked with what I assumed was a mixture of blood, saliva, and tears. Blood and mud smears dotted my legs. Ess swiftly placed the IV and started fluids. Aaron was out cold. There wouldn't be a better time for me to clean up.

I hurried to the back room, located a fresh set of scrubs, and headed to the bathhouse for a quick shower. My skin and hair felt greasy, and I couldn't shake the odor of the brothel. I peeled off the jumpsuit and discovered the source of at least part of the odor. My left pant leg was soaked with urine that wasn't mine. You know it's a rough day when someone pees on you, and you are too busy to notice. Suddenly, full realization of the horror of what I'd just seen hit me square in the gut like a bag of rocks. I climbed into the cold shower and scrubbed my skin hard with the little pat of travel soap but couldn't get rid of the greasy, violated feeling that filled my chest. I could have scrubbed until my skin bled and not gotten rid of it. A hundred horrible moments from the day, moments that I had brushed aside at the time, jostled into line, and marched through my mind. I let them come for a moment. My throat made an awful tearing sound that I didn't recognize, and tears streamed down my face. There was so much I didn't understand and couldn't process. There was so much sin, so much hate, so much despair, so much pain. I leaned my forehead against the shower wall and let the cold water course down my body for a few minutes, but it was too cold to stay for long. I couldn't afford the luxury of hiding out. I forced myself to dry, dress, and headed back to the tent, stopping to vomit in the bushes on the way.

"You too?" a voice asked from out of the darkness, startling me. In the dim light, I could barely make out Lauren's form under the tree by the front door of the tent.

"You aren't alone. I throw up every time," she said drily.

"Really? It doesn't get any better then?"

"Not for me. Happens every time."

"Great, then. Something to look forward too."

"Everybody processes trauma differently. Some Blues get a little more used to it. They don't experience things as deeply."

I wasn't so sure what I'd experienced was something I wanted to get used to, even if I could.

"How do you do this then, Lauren? What do you do? If it sucks this much every time?"

"Well, for starters, I throw up."

"Check."

"Then I cry… a lot for a while afterward—usually cry and pray simultaneously. I let God know exactly how I feel about it. Sometimes I cuss."

"Does that help?"

"No. It never helps. I just wanted to be hundred-percent honest with you. Sometimes I even punch a wall and scream at God. Then I let Him hold me for a while… and eventually He heals up the torn parts of my heart until there's just a scar left. I know the general process now. I know how I tend to handle it. I just let it come and deal with things the way I know I need to. It's harder for me than it is for some. I was gifted with an extra dose of empathy. Sometimes… most of the time actually, it doesn't feel like a gift. Being extraordinarily empathetic means I process some of our targets' pain directly. Not always… only when God chooses for me to feel it. Sometimes I relive their memories in visions and in dreams. It mostly happens afterward… not during the jaunt itself. I'm not trying to scare you. I just want you to know that if it happens to you, you should tell one of us. We can help you. Don't try to handle it alone."

"You relive their pain *directly?*" I sought clarification. "Why? Why would Dhia allow you to experience that? What is the point?"

"Well, sometimes when I feel their pain, some of it transfers to me. It's like carrying someone's burden. It can make it easier for them—sort of like swallowing a portion of someone's lethal dose of poison so they don't die. It makes you sick, but you hope that at least it saves their life."

"It actually works that way?"

"Yeah. It actually does. Not every time of course but sometimes, when God allows it to."

Knowing my pain could relieve someone else's; that I could actually ease their burden was the only comforting part of the whole terrifying concept.

"Other times, the empathy just gives you a glimpse of what's going on with them, so you can know how to help them better. Have you ever felt someone else's pain, really felt it deep inside yourself?" Lauren asked.

I remembered the boy in the horseshoe valley, feeling first his pain and fear and then the relief when the medications hit his bloodstream.

I nodded. "Yeah, I think so."

"I thought maybe you had. I saw it on your face when we crossed the Kress boundary today. Just don't keep it to yourself if it gets worse."

Lauren leaned her back against the tree. She looked worn out.

"Is it always worth it? This job, I mean... all of it? Seeing these things? Taking on people's pain?" I hoped I was asking an acceptable question.

Lauren bit her bottom lip and considered my question carefully before she spoke.

"Yes, it's always worth it, though it doesn't always feel that way in the moment. Sometimes I have to step back and remember whom I work for and that He sees what I don't see. He doesn't do things the same way I do. God is faithful to heal the rescued, and he is faithful to heal the rescuers. He has a plan, and He's written me a part in that plan... I choose not to miss out on that, no matter how hard it is."

Lauren placed her fist over her heart as she spoke, as I'd seen Fa do when she was choosing to trust God with something ugly or difficult that she didn't understand. Then she placed her hands on my shoulders and looked directly into my eyes. "You weren't made to wrestle with the fallout of these people's trauma on your own. If you do, it will eat you alive. Understand? We were made to do this together."

Her tone was forceful and absolute, almost scolding, but I understood what she meant. My normal coping mechanisms, which were barely adequate for dealing with my own problems, weren't going to be able to touch these issues. I needed to learn to lean. I just wasn't sure how.

"Point taken," I responded.

"Promise?"

"I promise."

Lauren seemed satisfied with my response.

"See you back inside," she said, then left me alone.

I felt completely wrung out. My back ached, and my hands shook. I was still nauseous, either from lack of sustenance or the emotional toll of the day's events. Probably both.

My passion for helping people warred with my revulsion at having peeked into the depths of man's inhumanity to man. When I thought of what my future as a Blue might hold in light of what I'd already seen, my courage faltered. A long, horrifyingly sad road seemed to stretch out before me. The human part of me knew that what I had experienced paired with what was to come could tear me to pieces—that it had already started to. I could not rid myself of the memory of the sound and sensation of the man's terrified cries. Utter agony had literally breathed down my neck, and I felt like a piece of it had entered me and was now stuck, bitter and awful in my heart. I dropped to the ground at the foot of the tree.

What if I can't do this?

But you can, came Dhia's silent answer. *You can if I say you can… And I say you can.*

"Then how, how do I do this?" I asked Him aloud.

Let go, Dhia's voice echoed in the little valley, and a strong gust of wind ruffled the treetops far above my head.

"What does that mean?" I shouted into the sky.

Had I been in a better frame of mind, I probably would have thought twice before yelling at Dhia. A red flare streaked across the sky, just like I'd seen that morning. This time I didn't duck.

"What do you mean? What do you want from me?" I shouted again. "Let go of *what?*"

There was no answer except for the wind, but I didn't need one. I already knew the answer. Lauren's words came back to me. She had *chosen* the part God had written for her no matter how hard it would be to handle. And she'd told me in order to accomplish the tasks set before me I'd need to learn to lean. I needed to let go of control.

"But *how?*" I asked. Every instinct told me to run far and fast, to shield myself from what I'd already seen and whatever was still to come.

It was something I couldn't figure out on my own... something I wouldn't be able to conquer in a day.

Did it really work that well anyway, Kiah... avoiding hardship and muddling through on your own? I wasn't sure whether the question came from Dhia or myself, but either way, it was a valid point.

Life is hard anyway, no matter which road you choose. Doing hard things with lots of help, and Dhia's guidance was bound to be much better than doing hard things alone. I looked down at my hands again. They were clenched tight. I held my hands up in front of me, palms up, and forced them open, breathing deeply. I felt some of the weight inside me rise and leave through my fingertips. I stayed that way for a long time, choosing to let go, second by second, letting Dhia fill me with his strength and peace. At length, my insides steadied. I didn't feel rejuvenated and refreshed by any means, but I was ready to walk back into the tent, which was all that was required.

While I had showered and had my minibreakdown, Fa and Ess had tended Aaron. They took the opportunity afforded by his heavy sedation to pull a curtain around his bed, wash his wounds, tape his broken ribs, and clean and stitch the worst of his wounds... those caused by repeated rape. The familiar skunky strong smell of cosh, the antibiotic purple mash I'd seen Fa mixing at the mountain, hung heavy in the air. They were stitching his facial wounds when

I returned and waved me away to find food, rest, and hydration. It was decided that Mags, Lauren, and I would be on night duty: Mags, because she knew herbs better than anyone, and our patients were battling infections and needing their immune systems and nutrition boosted; me, because Aaron had identified me as a safe person, and they wanted me at his bedside during the night in case he roused; Lauren, because she spoke French and had been communicating with our conscious French patient, Henri.

I retreated to the back room as directed and found Lauren, face-down and snoring on a cot in the corner. Mags was dishing up food for herself. I joined her at the small table. Over a plate of cooked grains, roots, and bizarre veggies, Mags filled me in on what they'd learned from Henri. Henri and Adrien worked for a large finance company in Paris. They didn't know each other well but shared a common interest in hiking. In early October, they had set out for a three-day hiking/camping trip in the French Alps. Sometime during their second day, they'd mistakenly fallen through to the Rock, smack-dab in the middle of Kress territory. They didn't comprehend, of course, the sudden change in terrain. They wandered from the open area where they landed into a Kress town where they were taken and sold as slaves. They were forced first into hard labor where they worked as hard as they could to avoid being beaten. Eventually, they were sold to Sange for work in the brothels. Henri told Lauren that Adrien fought every Kress who approached him, even under threat of death and repeated beatings. Henri eventually stopped fighting just to save his own life.

"Adrien may pay for his resistance with his life. He hasn't regained consciousness," Mags said.

Mags looked exhausted. Her hair was even wirier and more unruly than it had been that morning. She was switching back and forth from German to Gaelic in a near-drunk manner, spouting words in whichever language came to her first. "I don't know. There are things we can try. We are giving some medicines now that may help. We will just have to wait and see. Henri says he was unconscious for many days before the slave auction." She rose and poured us both large mugs of fermented tea. It was hot and black, and smelled of ginger and mushrooms.

"And Aaron? Where did they meet him?" I asked.

She shook her head. "They don't know him. They've never met him. They didn't even know he was at Sange's place."

"So he wasn't with them when they went through…" It wasn't a question. I was thinking out loud.

Then where had he come from?

Mags shook her head. "He's younger than the other two. The Kress value that. They kept him separate."

That explained the fancier room and the locks on the doors. I shuddered and tried to dismiss the memory. I wondered why Dhia hadn't sent us sooner. Why would He allow these things to happen in the first place? They were unanswerable questions. I put my fist over my heart as I'd seen Fa and Lauren do and glanced up at Mags. She had her fist over her heart as well.

"Get some rest. You'll need it for tonight," Mags instructed.

I wondered how it would be possible to fall asleep with the events of the day swirling in my head. I pulled my feet up on to the cot and drew a blanket around my shoulders. Surprisingly, was asleep in minutes. I awoke to Rona shaking my shoulders. The soft light shining in the doorway from the main room made her look like a shadow. I followed her into the main room, where all the braziers except those around Adrien's cot were lit. Mags, Fa, Ess, and Lauren were clustered around the bed. Cane knelt on the cot between Adrien's feet, holding his ankles. A faint blue glow emanated from her fingertips.

Gabi, her long silver hair mussed and unbound, looked as if she'd just been awakened as well. She was standing at the head of the cot. Her fingers, glowing cobalt, were laced through the hair on Adrien's head. Adrien appeared to be dead. Thankfully, the curtains were pulled tight shut around the other two patient cots.

I whispered to Fa, "What should I do?"

She didn't answer but lifted my hands to hover a few inches above the man's chest.

"Feel anything?" she asked me.

I felt nothing but cold. I moved my hands toward his neck and felt a faint amount of warmth and a small vibration. I touched his neck, and my hands glowed blue, but the vibrating sensation evaporated. I moved my hands up to his head and traded places with Gabi. I held my palms out flat over the crown of his head. A strong electric current of confusion and anger shot through my hands, shoving me backward, squarely onto Fa's toe.

"Sorry," I told her. My hands shook, and my insides quivered.

"Is okay. What did you feel?" Fa asked.

"Faint vibration over his neck, cold over his chest, confusion and anger in his mind... Shall I try again?"

I was relieved when Fa shook her head. "No. He is going. His heart is failing. The lights in his mind are going out. He has given up."

Fa pulled a wooden folding chair over from nearby, and it reached the space behind my knees just in time. My head spun, my heart pounded, my vision clouded, my knees buckled, and I sank into the chair.

"Head forward," Fa said, kneeling in front of me and supporting my head as I folded in half. "Just breathe. It will pass. It's just a feeling. You are not in danger."

Fa put her hands on my either side of my head, rubbing my temples lightly with her fingers. She was praying for me. I breathed deeply and felt the coldness, confusion, and anger that I seemed to have borrowed from Adrien dissipate.

I sat up slowly. "What was that exactly?" I asked.

It was Lauren who answered. "It was that gift we were talking about earlier. Remember...? Empathy. Congratulations. Looks like you've got it." I couldn't tell whether she was more sarcastic than truly congratulatory, or vice versa.

"Is there a return policy? Gift receipt, maybe?" I asked ruefully. Of all the oddities I was discovering about myself, this one frightened me the most. It *always* had.

"Nope. There's no exchange policy either. It's valuable, though. You will come to appreciate it. I promise." Lauren smiled at me and rubbed my shoulders.

"How am I supposed to help if I'm always passing out?"

"You won't always pass out. You will learn how to respond. You'll only feel their pain when it truly serves a purpose."

"Tha e marbh," Cane announced, letting loose of the pulse points in Adrien's feet. The Gaelic word for *dead* shot through me.

He is dead.

Ess listened for a heartbeat with her stethoscope and confirmed Cane's assessment with a nod. I'd just witnessed a second death in the span of a week.

A Dhia, help me, I prayed reflexively, silently.

A small, ironic flame of hope rose to life in my heart. It was a hope that had absolutely no basis in my circumstances. It was a hope related solely to the goodness of the women I was with and the goodness of Dhia Himself. I clung to it.

TIME TO MOVE ON

I spent most of that night at Aaron's bedside as he slept. I monitored the medications and fluids and protected his airway just as Ess taught me to do. When Aaron's chin drifted down and his breathing became sonorous, I readjusted the towel roll behind his head so he could breathe easier. I counted the drips in the drip chamber of the IV tubing, adjusting his arm position when the flow slowed or stopped. At some point in the middle of the night, the weather they called the "Stripe" lifted rather suddenly. New silvery moonlight replaced the red. It filtered through the windows, reflecting off the flecks in the floor. The room—so full of energy, sound, and light just a few hours before—had turned quiet and peaceful. Aaron was beginning to rustle in his bed on his own. His breathing was easier, and his jaw was no longer slack. Eventually, he awoke but settled easily back into sleep when I spoke to him and held his hand. The medications quelled his anxiety.

Lauren had pulled a shorter-legged, narrower cot out from under Henri's and sat on it, reading, as Henri slept. Mags had a regular production line going. She was mixing crushing potent herbs and decanting fluids to make decoctions. She filled bottles and bags, stowing them in sealed tins in the cupboards. I wondered shortly what they had done with Adrien's body, but I only half wanted the answer. The task of dealing with his body hadn't been assigned to me, and I was having enough trouble dealing with the tasks that I *had* been assigned. I was beginning to understand why the Blues only dealt with what was just in front of them—Dhia usually gave them the strength for only that and nothing more. Not having to worry about what all the other Blues or even Dhia Himself were doing conserved energy and emotional bandwidth.

Morning finally dawned, bright and clear. The aroma of cooking sausages melded with that of Mag's herbal efforts and waking noises began to emanate from the back room. Rona bustled through the front doors of the tent. She looked less regal and mysterious than usual in an old pair of gray overalls. Her hair was arranged, birdlike, into a large black messy bun on top of her head. It was the first time I'd seen her out of uniform. She wrinkled her nose at the strong odors in the room and opened the roof flaps. Light streamed in, and the early morning periwinkle sky seemed incredibly vivid and bright after the stark red light of the past twenty-four hours.

Okay, Dhia, what will today bring? Whatever it was, I was sure it wouldn't be what I would expect even if I bothered to form expectations. I stretched my arms over my head and winced. My back was knotted in a million places.

Gabi materialized from the back room, stretching and blinking, to stand behind me. Fa joined us, followed shortly by Ess, Lauren, and Cane, then Mags and Rona. Cane and Rona were both in overalls with dirt-stained knees. They grouped around the cot, and each placed their hands on Aaron's arms and legs as he snoozed. Fa motioned me toward the head of the bed, and I cradled the back of Aaron's head in my hands. I had to convince my fingers to touch Aaron's head. Fresh on my mind was the memory of the night before—touching Adrien's head and ending up crouched with my head between my knees. My fingers made contact with his scalp. Nothing surged through me. I let out a deep sigh of relief and relaxed. Aaron stirred but stayed asleep. The other Blues began to pray in audible whispers in various languages. The tingling feeling that often ran up and down my spine, an indicator of Dhia's presence, was strong and fast like a string of moving twinkle lights that ran in a continuous circuit.

I was coming into a new understanding of prayer. Prayer wasn't like waiting in line at a government office: "Fill out these request forms in triplicate, young lady. You can expect an answer within six months *if* you are lucky, *and* you are extremely good…" (Read in nasal tone by an angel with glasses perched precariously at the end of his nose.)

To pray is to commune with *Dhia Himself.* To experience the brush with the divine is the highest privilege, and in prayer, you can experience that *anytime!* Prayer holds aspects of art, beauty, form, and desire. I began to yearn for prayer for its own sake. It soothed my soul and filled up my empty spaces. I longed for it. I also found myself praying in new ways. Some situations seemed to call for distinct languages, just as some words called for certain colors. We clustered around Aaron's bed that morning, inviting Dhia to fill the room and have His way. I felt the need to pray in German, though I still cannot tell you why. I folded my voice into the other voices around mine, and despite the sad circumstances, my heart vibrated with hope.

That was the first of many prayer gatherings I attended around patient beds in the healing rooms of Petra. There was often a concerted prayer effort in the morning and then again in the evening and any other time that it seemed needed. There was no formula for the prayers offered, but most of the women seemed to begin in praise and worship then move into asking for wisdom, direction, and healing. On that particular morning, Cane stood just to my left. She ran her hands lightly over Aaron's chest, and the blue glow played under her fingers. Her fingers lingered intermittently from time to time as she listened to silent directions from Dhia that none of the rest of us could hear. I caught glimpses of words and images in my own mind as I prayed, moving my hands tenderly over his skull. I made sure to cover every inch. If I saw the word *pain*, I prayed for an easing of it. If I saw the word *confusion* or *clarity*, I prayed for clarity and understanding. I saw the word *brokenness* and begged Dhia to provide wholeness.

As we prayed, the room brightened. A few twists of hot pink lightning and accompanying thunder shot across the hole in the ceiling. Aaron jumped a little and began to rouse at a few of the louder peals but quieted quickly when I spoke into his ear, telling him it was safe to stay asleep. As we prayed, his rumpled brow seemed to relax. His cheeks pinked noticeably—whether from a supernatural increase in his health or the physical heat of the Blues' healing hands on his skin, I wasn't sure. Everyone eventually fell quiet, and the session drew to a close. He was sleeping peacefully, so we left the curtain and moved on the Henri's bed. Henri was still painful and exhausted despite a full night's sleep. I wondered how long it had actually been since he'd gotten a good night's rest. He'd probably racked up an enormous sleep debt. Lauren spoke to him in French. She asked permission to pray for him and explained what we would do. He seemed dubious but nodded his head and smiled weakly in our direction. Lauren took up position at the head of the bed. Cane and I stood opposite each other at his shoulders, and the other Blues filled in around the cot, encircling him. Cane and I began to move our hands above his chest. Just over his liver, I felt a sudden surge of cold shoot through my hand. I jumped a little, and Ess shot me a questioning look.

"Cold," I whispered.

She furrowed her brow a bit, considering, then nodded.

I wasn't sure exactly what a cold liver indicated, so I concentrated my prayer there and continued to pray. The cold began to numb my fingers but didn't let up. It was quite obvious that it was affecting me more than I was affecting it.

"What now, Dhia?" I asked.

Take note and move on, came the silent reply.

I complied.

Henri's wariness changed quickly to peaceful rest as he realized we didn't have major medical intrusions in mind. The session wound down, and we all gathered across the room near Mag's herb table. We pulled a few short cots out from under the empty beds and gathered in a circle.

"Henri," Fa said, starting our little discussion in her typical minimalist form.

Lauren filled everyone in on the night—how Henri had slept, his pain level, his mental and emotional status, the condition of his wounds, what medicines he had used and how well they seemed to be working. He had been taking liquids only, and not keeping them down well; but as his emotional distress eased a bit, his vomiting had quelled. It was decided that he would receive healing stomach herbs in the form of tea and decoctions and then progress to solid food as tolerated. He was painfully thin and in desperate need of calories. Cane shared that he had reacted painfully even to light pressure on the bruised area over his right kidney, and she had sensed of torn tissues there when she had laid hands on him. The blood in his urine confirmed a kidney problem. I shared the coldness I had experienced over his liver.

"Coldness can be an indicator of disease," Ess explained. "Mags and I will give some liver medicinals. Will you check it again throughout the day? Not everyone senses things in the same way. If you have sensed this at this time, then you are the best judge of any change that might occur."

I nodded, impressed once again at the way the Blues worked together. They relied on each other. Dhia could have gifted each of us to do every part of the job, but He didn't. He qualified each of us uniquely to work together, depending on each other. The phrase "so that no one may boast," a quote from the biblical book of James, came to mind.

We finished reporting on Henri and moved on to Aaron. I took a page out of Lauren's playbook and reported on how his night had gone. His wounds seemed less extensive than Henri's, but he was much more emotionally friable. It was decided that I would stick close and remain available as they lightened his sedation. Fa and I would take turns delivering his care to limit the number of new faces he needed to deal with. If all went well, we would get him up and dangle his feet over the edge of the bed at some point before nightfall. He had a whole slew of natural and medicinal preparations that were urgently required. Ess and Mags would hash out the specifics as soon as the meeting broke up.

"Now the three of you who worked all night… go out of here. Food is on the stove. Eat and rest," Fa commanded. I'd never wanted anything more.

I stumbled to the back room and lifted the lid off the still-warm pan I found on the little stovetop. Sausages. I didn't know what kind of meat they were made from, and I didn't care. As I searched the cupboards for plates and silverware, Rona entered the room and gestured for me to go to my cot. I wasn't sure what her plan was but knew questioning a woman who never spoke was pointless. I sat on the edge of the cot and watched her. She poured a concoction of hot water and oil over a washcloth and handed it to me, indicating I should wash my face. Even the skin on my face was sore. Next, she poured a basin of hot water and put it at my feet, handing me a towel. She gestured for me to put my feet in the basin, and I obeyed. The water was warm and scented with something woody. By the time she had served me a plate of sausage, fruit, and rolls, I was in tears. I wanted to protest. I was supposed to be the caregiver, not the receiver, right? I felt wholly undeserving.

"Be still and receive." Dhia's audible voice made me jump. I glanced at Rona, but she didn't react. She hadn't heard it.

"Thank you," I told Rona through my tears, and she smiled and kissed me on the forehead. I finished my food and leaned back against the pillows as Mags and Lauren entered the room. Lauren appeared freshly showered. Rona poured another two more basins of hot water and repeated her ministrations with Mags and Lauren. The word *goodness* flashed across my vision for a moment, followed by the word *beauty*... I made the difficult choice to relax and receive. The warm water drained the tension from my body. Rona brought me a fresh shirt, large and linen, and a pair of soft pants. I climbed into them, barely able to stay awake. She passed out mugs of grassy tea; and we all drank, dried our feet, and laid down. Rona, having effectually tucked the three of us in, left us to rest.

We didn't remain much longer at the lake. Fa had originally chosen the location because of its proximity to Pak, the part of the Kress territory we had visited; but the tent was large, and the weather was cooling. It was difficult to keep both the large healing room and the smaller sleeping room warm. Henri developed a yellowish cast to his skin, which further indicated the possibility of liver problems. Ess and Lauren agreed that he needed to be moved to a medical facility that could address it. Dhia hadn't healed him through prayer alone, and his dysfunction was something that herbs and our limited medications would not help. He needed to be returned to the city nearest the gate he fell through. I couldn't help but wonder what he would remember of the Rock, of Kress… What would he tell people at home?

Fa had said that Dhia helped obscure their memories and protect the secret of their time on the Rock. I couldn't help but wonder how exactly that played out. How many people walked around Earth with limited amnesia and strange scars they couldn't explain because of their time here in this bizarre place? Did it play out in their dreams? If so, I hoped they would remember the love and care they received rather than the horror of their captivity. I had so many questions but knew better than to let them spill forth aloud.

All in good time. My grandmother's voice echoed in my head.

We decided that Gabi, Lauren, Mags, and Rona would accompany Henri safely home. I use the term *we* lightly. I mostly blinked and stared and nodded my head sleepily while Fa, Gabi, and Mags made the decision. At that time, my leadership abilities were restricted to the times when Dhia was directly steering my ship and directing my feet, which was fine by me. I didn't know enough about the options to even think of making suggestions. Once the decision was made, Henri and his entourage cleared out quickly, leaving me with a cold vacant feeling that I wasn't sure was purely physical. I was getting used to the other Blues, and their departure left me with a tangible ache inside. It also left us with the question of what to do with Aaron. Physically, he was healing, with no signs of infection; but a flood of fear, trauma, and anxiety raged behind the wobbly seawall of his restraint. One moment he was a fearful child in the grip of a nightmare that he couldn't shake. The next moment, he was himself: an adult man in his early twenties, appalled that he had soaked his pillow in tears and his sheets in urine. We began by moving him into the sleeping room with us. The other Blues and I arranged our cots around the edges of the room, stacked the rest of the cots, and placed Aaron's bed in the center of the room.

"We are doing for him what he needs. It's still early, and he has much pent-up emotion to spill. He will improve over time," Ess told me when I asked her what else we could do for him.

"Why doesn't he remember who he is, or where he is from? Will that memory return?" I asked her.

She shrugged. "There's no way to know."

Aaron's functional memory was limited to his own first name and his experiences in the Kress territory. He didn't know his age, his hometown, or how he came to the Rock. We decreased his sedation as much as we could for as long as we could to allow him to converse and take walks, eat, and visit the showers. He exhausted quickly and slept only when heavily sedated. Even then he woke up regularly with nightmares. Sometimes he required physical restraint.

Three days stretched into four, and I began to wonder how long I had before the skewed Petra time exceeded my earthly time limits.

"You have time, Kiah. We won't let you miss your classes. You will know when it is time to go," Fa chided me when I questioned her on the topic. I knew that's what she would say. I just needed to hear her say it.

Those of us who remained fell into a working rhythm of sorts. I learned to sleep hard and fast in a utilitarian manner whenever it was my turn to rest. We shared the chores: filling the water tanks, cooking, baking, restocking the fuel for the stove. We cleaned Aaron's wounds, monitored his mental status and his meds, and helped him build his strength, taking him for walks by the lake. He remained despondent and fearful, as if something inside him had broken... something that resisted mending. He was becoming a little more restful, a little more engaged, but the progress was painfully slow.

We spent a lot of our quiet time praying and reading. Cane read to us in a language I'd never heard. No one understood her words, but everyone understood the heart behind them. Ess sang, sometimes to herself, sometimes we joined in. On the sixth day after half the Blues had left with Henri, I awoke with a new urgency. It was time to go, but where?

"Dhia, where are we going?" I asked quietly, several times. There was no answer. Everyone else was still asleep, so I headed outside to walk and clear my head. I rounded the corner of the tent and ran straight into a horse. The horse seemed less surprised at my unannounced presence than I was at his. He stopped grazing and stared at me with large liquid gray eyes. I glanced around, wondering where he had come from. He didn't have a saddle or a bridle. He didn't even wear shoes. I approached him slowly, and he allowed it. There was something strange about him. It wasn't as if he had something *more* than any other horse I'd met. It was as if he had *less*—as if something was missing… Fear. Fear was missing. My uncle had always told me that horses are only afraid of two things: everything that moves, and everything that doesn't. That horse, however, had no discernible trace of fear in his being. He didn't even seem naturally cautious. I stopped a few feet away from him and fluttered my arms in the air like a giant bird. He didn't spook, bolt, or even flinch as a horse should but stared at me as if trying to figure out just what sort of idiot I was. Just then Hedi, one of the first Blues I'd met in the valley on my first visit to the Rock, exited the bathrooms and joined us.

"Hallo!" she called to me in German. "I brought you some supplies, food. How is it going?"

"Oh, fine. It's good. Is he with you?" I asked, pointing to the horse.

"Oh yes, He brought me here. Isn't he beautiful?"

I nodded my head. He was beautiful—a solidly built, marbled steel gray and caramel buckskin.

"He's not tied. Won't he leave?" I asked.

"Oh no. The horses here don't need saddles, bridles, fences… They listen to Gott… better than people do most of the time. They work with us."

I was intrigued. The five-year-old inside me suddenly wanted nothing more than to mount up and ride, tack-free and fear-free into the sunset. I settled for stroking his powerful neck.

"Want to help me?" she asked, heading for a pile of freshly cut wood behind the tent. It looked like she had been busy. I followed her reluctantly. She whistled loudly, and three more horses trotted toward us from a nearby group of trees. They wore bulky packs. We unloaded the supplies and wrestled them inside.

Fa met us at the front door of the tent and took a bag from me.

"Well?" she said.

"Well, what?"

"You were up early, and you know something. I see this on your face. So?"

"Well, we need to go—today I think—to the village, if that makes any sense."

"I agree. I feel the same. Aaron will stay there with the other men that didn't go back to Earth—those who have nowhere else to go. It is a safe place for them to wait."

"To wait for what?" I asked.

Fa shrugged. "To wait for God to say that their waiting is over."

"How many men are there?" I asked.

"I'm not sure," she said, not even bothering to estimate an answer for me.

-----------The Big House-----------

Heidi and I returned, arms full of supplies, to the tent. Aaron startled noticeably as we entered the room, then stayed wary at the sight of Hedi's unfamiliar face. His hands shook. I sighed. The conversation would be harder than I thought. Aaron still trusted me more than the other Blues. He relied on my presence. I didn't relish the thought of telling him I'd soon be leaving him behind on a foreign planet with total strangers.

Dhia, give me the words! I pleaded silently.

"Aaron, this is Hedi. She's with us, okay? She's with us." I took his hand in mine, and he nodded.

"Let's go for a walk, out at the lake," I suggested.

He nodded again and followed me outside. The sweat suit that he wore was one of those that the Blues kept on hand. A few sizes too large, it made him appear even more gaunt and thin than he was. He looked so tired.

"We are leaving today, right?" Aaron immediately asked.

"Yes," I said, surprised and relieved that I didn't have to say it myself.

"So where am I?" He had asked us that question countless times, and we had stalled, telling him just to focus on resting and healing.

"I don't know who I am, I don't know where I am, and now I'm leaving. I don't even know where I'm going. Are you still going to tell me just to wait?" His voice had a sharp edge to it. It was the first sign of anything beyond defeat that I'd heard from him. It was good to hear.

"No, Aaron. I'm going to try to answer your questions today."

I led the way to the edge of the lake, and we sat on the ground.

"I can't tell you who you are, because we don't know who you are. I wish we did. That's the truth. If you remember, then we will do our best to get you home again." I looked at him, gauging his response, but he was just staring out over the water.

"I can't tell you where you are from because we don't know where you are from." I hesitated, but he didn't respond.

"You hear me, Aaron?" I asked him, brushing his hand lightly with my fingers.

"Yeah, I hear you. That's the part you don't know, so what *do* you know?"

"Well, that part's harder to explain, so I'll just tell you straight out, and you can ask me questions. Just wait until I'm finished. Deal?"

"Deal," he agreed, finally turning to face me.

"This isn't Earth. You fell through a gate, of sorts, into a place called Kress. The Kress keep slaves... you know that part. I'm not sure how long you were there. Do you have any idea?"

Aaron shrugged. "Not really, no. A few months maybe? I don't know."

He was starting to tremble. I grasped his hand firmly.

"Look me in the eye, Aaron. You don't have to know. You don't have to figure it out. You won't go back there, ever. I can promise you that."

"Not Earth?" he asked, as if that part of what I had said was just starting to sink in.

"It's hard to grasp, I know. It's new to me too. I'm still getting used to the idea myself. Just let it settle."

"So why are you here? You are American, right?" he asked.

"Yeah, I am. There are a handful of women who do... this." I gestured toward the tent, not sure how to describe our work. "They, that is... we... are called Blues."

"You work for the government?" he asked.

I laughed. "Oh no! Of course not. Good grief. No. Nothing like that."

"Then who do you work for?"

"God," I said.

It was his turn to laugh, but he didn't. He just blinked, thinking.

"That makes sense," he stated flatly, as if he had suspected that all along. "So you are angels then… That's what I thought you were."

"Angels?" I snorted. "Oh no. Nothing like that either. The flying is what you are referring to, right? That's just transportation. It's not our wings, not our power. We are just women. I promise."

He didn't look hundred-percent convinced, but didn't argue. I noticed he wasn't trembling any longer.

"So where are we going, then?" he prompted me to continue.

"It's a village. There are more Blues there, women who live and work there. They can keep helping you heal, work on getting your memory back. There are a few other men staying there who were rescued from Kress as well."

"Others?" he asked, a little uneasy at the thought.

"Unfortunately, yes. Most go back home, but some need longer times here before they return."

"Why?"

"I don't know. I haven't met them. This is my first jaunt… my first time going into Kress territory."

"You don't live here?"

"No."

"Where do you live, then?" he asked.

I hesitated, not sure I should say more, then hedged, "Scotland, for now."

"When do you go back, then?"

"Soon."

His body tensed.

"You will leave me, then—with the new people?"

"I think so. They are good people, though, Aaron. They are Blues, just like us. You will be safe there. They are far more experienced than me. They'll know how to help you." I tried to sound reassuring.

"It's silly, isn't it... being so freaked out all the time, scared of everything, not even remembering who I am." He balled his hands into fists, his knuckles blanched white. He looked like a frightened child. I took his hand in mine again and lifted his face to look in his eyes.

"No, it's not silly! You need to know that. It's stress and shock—a totally normal reaction to unthinkable trauma. You are basically the only normal part of this whole situation. You've touched true evil through no fault of your own and are lucky to be alive. Now you have time to heal. The Blues will take good care of you. You can trust them."

"Then what?" he asked. His eyes were large and round, and the pain in them tore at my soul.

"I don't know," I answered truthfully, "but God is good, Aaron. That I *do* know. I wouldn't be here right now if that weren't true." I subconsciously slipped my closed fist over my own chest. A few tears escaped down my cheeks. I didn't try to hold them back; there was no reason to. Aaron leaned his head forward onto my shoulder, as he'd done the day we took him from the brothel, and I stroked the back of his head for a few moments.

How do moms do it? I wondered. *How do they pour their heart, soul, and energy into other people every day?*

Just like this, came the reply from deep inside my chest.

"Ready to go?" Cane called from the direction of the tent.

Aaron sat up and nodded at me. His face was cleared, and he smiled a little. Perhaps having a few answers had lifted his spirits.

We rejoined the others and began to pack the few supplies we would take with us. Hedi would travel on horseback; the rest of us would be flying. We donned our jumpsuits.

"Faceup, or facedown?" I asked Aaron.

He looked puzzled.

"I can strap you in face up, the way you rode before, or facedown, so you can see below us."

"Seriously? Facedown. Absolutely," she answered, looking almost excited.

My neck and shoulders buzzed, sending butterflies through my chest and stomach once again. Fa secured Aaron to the front of my suit, and we shot into the air like a pair of reverse parachutists. Ess, Fa, and Cane joined us in the air, and we headed westward toward the village, flying close enough to clearly see the trees and fields and rivers as we passed them. The sky was layered with thin, quivery lavender clouds. The midday air was warm. Aaron held tight to my hands at first, perhaps not as sure of his choice to fly facedown as he thought he'd be. Soon, however, I felt him relax. He pointed at a flock of white birds below us.

"Beautiful, isn't it?" I asked.

"Yes."

A Dhia, let even this be healing for him, I asked silently. I didn't have to hear an answer to know that it was.

We reached the village in a few short hours. Fa and Cane descended with us, steadying Aaron and I so we could land on our feet. We landed in an open field in front of a large three-story stone lodge. I was surprised. It was by far the most elaborate building I'd seen on Petra outside the cities of Kress. I looked east down the little road that ran in front of the lodge, recognizing the line of cottages that dead-ended at mine. It was still incredible to think that I actually had claim to anything in this strange place.

The road ran west a few hundred feet, then bent south. A large stone structure stood, partially visible, at the bend in the road.

"What's down there?" I asked Fa.

"The main part of the village."

I was curious, but there wasn't time to ask more about it or explore it. Aaron, still weak, sank exhausted to the ground. After a few restful minutes, Cane and Ess helped him back to his feet, and we all climbed the steps into the building.

It smelled wonderful inside. Dinner, I hoped. A dark-skinned woman with perfectly straight white teeth met us at the door.

"I'm Cora," she said, bowing slightly. I almost returned the bow but caught myself. I was relieved that someone there spoke English. That would make the transition easier for Aaron.

"Come in. Come in… this way." Just off the main hall to the right, a set of double doors opened into a combined dining and living room where two women I didn't know were setting a large table. There was a young man in a chair in front of the fire. He rose to greet us as we entered.

"Willkommen," he said, extending his hand. I shook it.

"Nice to meet you. Do you speak English?" I asked him.

"A little. I'm Stefan."

"This is Aaron," Fa said.

Aaron had retreated behind Fa a bit. Stefan respected his space. "It's nice to meet you," he said, returning to his chair.

"You too," Aaron murmured.

"I'll take you to your room," Cora volunteered. We followed her down the hall toward the back of the building. There were two small healing rooms there, with patient cots separate from Blues' quarters by curtains.

"You'll stay here, Aaron. You have no roommate, for now."

Aaron sat on the cot, his expression drawn and tight once again. Fa, Ess, and Cora slipped from the room. I helped him lay back on the cot and pulled a blanket over his shoulders. Fear seemed to come and go like a recurring flash flood.

"I'll stay here with him, at least until he's used to the new Blues." Cane spoke up, in Gaelic. She was at my side, running her hands unconsciously along the edge of the cot in her usual habit. Aaron, of course, didn't understand her words.

"You can do that?" I asked, relieved.

"Of course." She nodded, her large, round eyes taking in Aaron's distress.

"Cane will stay here with you, Aaron… when I go. You know her. You won't be with strangers." Aaron didn't speak but grabbed for her hand and mine. His shoulders were hunched, and his eyes were wild again.

Ess poked her head back into the room just then, took one look at Aaron, and headed to the medicine cabinet. She returned with a syringe full of sedative and administered it. Within minutes, he was asleep. Fa delivered us a curry-type vegetable soup, rolls, and tea. Cane and I ate picnic style, lounging on the floor while Aaron slept.

I hadn't had much time to talk to Cane alone, and a few questions burned at me as we ate.

"So you were born here?" I asked, again in Gaelic, the only language we shared.

"Yes, on the hill," she answered, as if I should know what or where the hill was. I waited for her to elaborate. She didn't.

"And you live in one of the cottages?" I asked.

"No." She shook her head vigorously.

"Here, at the Big House, then?"

She shook her head again, then thought about it. "Sometimes."

I felt like I knew less at that point in the conversation than when we started talking.

"I live where He sends me," she explained. "It's different every day. If I had to pick a place, I'd say I'm happiest with the horses."

"Where do they live?" I asked.

"Wherever He sends *them*." She smiled. "You ladies... from Earth... you are so funny. You need addresses, names, titles, directions. Do they really help you feel better about yourselves?" I looked at her, wondering if she was teasing or chastising me, but she wasn't doing either. Her question and her expression were completely guileless.

I thought hard about her question. It was something I'd never thought about before. Titles, addresses, names... they *did* provide a form of security. They signified belonging, and even status; but it was false security.

'No, I guess they don't."

It was her turn to look puzzled. "Then why are they so important to you?"

"I'm not sure. Maybe because people want to know they belong somewhere, and when they don't rely on Dhia for that sense of belonging, they have to find it in their job, their associations with other people, even their address."

I watched her weigh my words, face turned to the ceiling, running her hands along the edges of the blanket in her lap.

"That's sad," she finally said.

"I agree."

"I didn't know my mother. She died when I was born," she stated in a matter-of-factly tone. "There was a very old Blue. She lived on the hill, alone, waiting. She raised me."

"Waiting?" I asked. Fa had mentioned once that some of the Blues were simply tasked to "wait" for something. I wondered if it was the same waiting that Cane was referring to.

"Just waiting on Him," she said again, as if I should know exactly what she meant. She went back to sipping her soup.

Talking to Cane took even more "getting used to" than talking to Fa. She said what she meant, meant what she said, and didn't care for, or even seem to know any, social conventions. It was freeing.

"You take the big cot tonight," she said, pointing at the second patient cot. "You are bigger, and I don't need the room. I'll pull in a mat from the other room. I like them better anyway."

I started to protest but stopped, realizing that she said only what she meant. If she said she preferred sleeping on a mat, then she truly did.

"Sounds good," I said, instead.

She grinned and bounded silently out of the room in search of bedding.

HERE AND THERE

It was a quiet night, but I barely slept. I knew the next time I slept, it would be under a different sky, with the hum of electricity and the clanking of pipes to lull me to sleep. Sometime in the middle of the night, I gave up even trying and got up. Cane was asleep, flat on her back on her mat on the floor. Her arms and legs lay at awkward angles, making her look as if she had been dropped there from a great height. She looked like a small child in her knit skull-cap and oversized scrubs. I stepped over her and heard her murmur something unintelligible in her sleep. I snuck down the hall and out onto the porch, grabbing a blanket from the settee in the front room on my way by. It was a clear night. The lavender moon, seeming close enough to touch, loomed much larger than the silver ones. I ventured down the little road until my little stone cottage came into view. A shiver ran up my spine again. I'd been there only once, but something in me had known this place my whole life. I recognized details from my dreams: trees, rocks, the color of the dirt, the stone cottages.

When I was thirteen, I dreamt I attended a bonfire with a small group of people in a circular amphitheater. I'd awoken from the dream with the smell of smoke in my nose and the laughter of the people whose faces I didn't recognize and couldn't remember ringing in my ears. That same amphitheater lay hewn into the ground just beyond Shae's cottage. I proceeded past that and stopped in front of my own little stone house, lit up in the lavender moonlight.

I remembered, at the age of seven, asking Mom if we could make gray icing so the gingerbread house would look more like the real one. She told me there was no such thing as gray gingerbread houses, so we made brown. But I still painted little icing windows in all the right places, to match this stone cottage in my dreams. When I was nine, my family moved to a new town, and I was angry. My new teacher asked me to draw a picture of my house, and I defiantly drew the stone cottage from my dreams instead. No one protested. My teacher had no way of knowing what my new house actually looked like.

The stone cottage had been a regular, albeit random, fixture in my childhood dreams. Running through fields filled with thousands of multicolored windmills, I would find the cottage incongruously dropped into the center, smoke rising from the chimney. Chasing a moving train, lungs bursting, desperately trying to climb aboard before it was too late, I'd glance to the side and see the stone cottage on a platform where the train station should be. Crossing a steaming lake at nighttime in a rowboat, the cottage would float by on a raft. I never entered the cabin in my dreams. It remained forever just out of reach, evaporating as I reached for the porch or the knob on the front door. Still, my dream self always identified it as home.

Standing before it in the dark, I was fully aware that I could reach out, turn the knob, and enter. I could make a fire in the fireplace, light the braziers, and make a cup of tea, but I didn't. It didn't seem like the right time. Instead, I retraced my steps to the lodge and crawled quietly into my cot, finally able to fall asleep.

In the morning, Aaron felt hungry and well rested enough to have breakfast with everyone else in the main room. There were plenty of eggs, large fried purple tomatoes, brown rolls, and tea to go around several times. The early morning sun pinked the edges of everything in the room, putting it into soft focus. I knew today was the day I needed to leave, but I really didn't want to. This odd group was becoming my family. Silent tears slid down my cheeks, *again* as I listened to the warm, albeit fractured, conversation being translated and relayed into multiple languages around the table.

"Leaving today?" Fa whispered in my ear.

"Yes."

"You'll be missed," she promised.

It was a comforting thought.

After breakfast, I caught Ess and Cane in the hall and quietly announced my upcoming departure.

"I'm leaving today as well," Ess said. I noted the purple pouches under her eyes. "It's time to go home and get back to work, so I can get a rest." She stretched, popping her back.

"What is your job at home, exactly?" I asked.

"Trauma surgeon," she said.

It didn't exactly sound relaxing.

"You haven't done this part before… leaving the Rock after your first jaunt. It's hard. Let it be as hard as it is. Just don't let the sadness eat you. You must take it to God." Her gaze was direct, her words more of a command than a suggestion.

"I will," I promised.

"I'll take good care of the boy," Cane said. It took me a moment to realize that she meant Aaron. It seemed odd that she would call a man twice her size a "boy."

"You won't forget your first jaunt. It holds a place here." She pointed directly at my heart.

I gave them each a hug and followed Cane back into the healing room.

I sat on the edge of the bed and woke Aaron gently.

"You are leaving?" he said quietly, even before his eyes opened.

"Yes," I answered. He sat up, and I hugged him tight to my chest for a long time.

"Will I see you again?" he asked.

"I'm not sure, but I think so," I answered truthfully.

"Thank you."

"Of course. You get well," I mumbled. I sucked at good-byes.

"I will." He smiled a small smile, and I knew suddenly that he *would get* well.

I kissed him on the forehead, promised to pray for him, and left the room without looking back. He was in the right place. He wasn't my charge any longer.

Fa met me in the hall.

"Ready to go?" she asked.

"Yep."

I followed her out the front door, anticipating the buzzing at the small of my neck, but felt nothing. Fa set off through a grove of trees behind the lodge, and we crossed the small field beyond it as quickly as we could. It was raining steadily. We climbed the hill at the far side of the field, slipping a little in the mud. On the other side of the hill, the rain was quickly filling a small valley. Within moments, it was a lake.

"Boat?" I shouted to Fa above the roar of the water. I didn't see one.

"Not this time," she said, jumping in.

I had no choice but to follow, and quickly. I pushed out into the water and let the current take me to the center of the lake. I let my legs float up behind me, flattening as much as possible. The current propelled us forward, faster and faster, until the sides of the lake were nothing but a blur. Panic tried to grip me. There seemed to be nothing to keep me from drowning. *Nothing except Dhia.* I kept my gaze trained on the back of Fa's head as a point of reference. The sky darkened, and it was soon no longer morning, but night. Fa slowed and clasped my hand, signaling that we needed to dive down. I nodded, took a deep breath, and she pulled me under. A few feet below, the current released us, and we veered hard left and popped back up out of the water in the center of Loch Occasional. We swam in the dark for a few minutes before the bank came familiar. The beam of a flashlight, accompanied by a hand, appeared out of the darkness.

It was Jack. He hauled first me, then Fa to shore. The sight of him and the feel of his warm hand on mine sent a warm buzz through my core. I was suddenly, stupidly, self-conscious. *What do I look like?* I wondered. *Drowned rat, probably.* At least it was dark. He handed me a towel.

"I'm sorry, I only brought one," he said.

"No problem. I'm going back in," Fa told him. "Good-bye, Kiah."

"Good-bye," I said, reaching to give her a quick hug. She hopped back into the water and disappeared.

"Is she going to be okay in there?" Jack asked, clearly concerned.

"Oh yeah, she's fine. I promise." I was beginning to shiver.

"I assumed you would be in a boat. I didn't bring any clothes for you," he said. "I carry an overnight bag in the trunk… for my work. You want to see if anything of mine will fit?"

"That might be a good idea." My teeth were beginning to chatter.

He retrieved the bag, and we rummaged through it. I chose a T-shirt, sweatshirt, and a pair of plaid drawstring pajama pants. Jack politely retreated into the woods for a few moments while I struggled out of my wet clothes and into the dry ones. By the time he returned, the rain had slowed to a light drizzle. I climbed into the passenger seat and blotted my hair with the towel.

Jack started the car and pointed the heat vents in my direction.

"Back to the college, right?"

"Yes."

He turned the blower to high heat, and we rode in silence for a while before he spoke up.

"I prayed for you, this weekend. I don't know where you went, what you were doing, but since God had me take you there and then woke me up to come get you and bring you home… well, whatever you were doing must have been important. So I prayed for you."

"Thank you. I needed it," I answered quietly. "I still do."

Many thoughts and emotions tumbled through my head, not the least of which was how wonderful it felt to be wearing Jack's clothes and riding in his car. My neck and ears flushed hot and red once again. I didn't trust myself to speak.

"Then I'll keep praying for you," he said. After a while, he added, "I think maybe I missed you too."

My heart thumped wildly, and I blurted out, "Why?"

"I'm not sure. I just did. Is that okay?"

"Yeah, of course. It's fine…," I said, feeling weak and awkward.

We rounded the last sharp corner onto the campus drive, and I instinctively shot my left hand out to steady myself on the bench seat between us to keep from sliding into him.

"Where's your residence?" Jack asked.

I gave him directions to Bert, and he pulled up right in front of the dorm. I retrieved the bag of soggy clothing from the backseat.

"What time is it, anyway?" I asked as he opened the car door.

"1:00 a.m."

"And what day is it?" I winced, knowing it was an odd question.

"Uh, Saturday. Well, early Sunday morning I guess."

He didn't ask why I didn't even know what day it was. That was good.

The awkward moment arrived. I liked him, and realized that maybe he liked me too. It was the first of such moments for me. Neither of us knew how to say goodbye.

"So maybe I'll see you sometime. You work on the campus grounds then, right?" My mouth felt dry. I didn't make eye contact.

"No. I work in town."

My head snapped up. "Then why were you fixing my window the other day?"

"Well, sometimes I just get the feeling I need to do something specific, something *really* specific. God asks me to do it. You know… like take a sandwich to a homeless person on a specific street corner. That sort of thing. I thought it was a little weird to fix a window at the college. Then coming here to drive you wherever you needed to go? It's definitely not the kind of thing I'm used to doing. I'm actually not really sure what all this means."

"That makes two of us," I answered. I had assumed Jack knew more than I did about the Calling, or the jaunt. I was surprised to hear he knew even less. He may not have been a Blue, but he certainly seemed to listen to God well. We were both standing in the rain on the sidewalk. Someone had to move.

"I should go," I said, gesturing toward the dorm.

"Oh, yeah. Of course. Good-bye."

Jack turned back to his car, and I hurried inside, plopped the bag of clothes on the floor, and crawled directly into bed.

Banging and shouting awakened me. The banging was definitely knuckles on wood. It wasn't immediately clear whether the shouting was angry, alarmed, or just annoying. As consciousness found me, I realized I'd been listening to the assaultive noise for more than a few moments. I rolled off the bed and was headed toward the door when it burst open. Aggie stood in the doorway with Big Bert's large square face visible just over her shoulder.

Aggie sized me up. Satisfied that I wasn't dead, she turned to dismiss the nosy resident assistant.

"All right, she's fine. You can go now," Aggie told her, shooing her away. "Thanks for unlocking the door."

"We've been knockin' for a hoor! What's wrong wi' ye?" Big Bert exclaimed.

"Nothing's wrong with me. I'm fine," I told her, opening my eyes wide and adjusting my shirt in an attempt to look as presentable and "just fine" as I possibly could.

"See, she's fine. Thank you for your help!" Aggie said, edging Big Bert out of the doorway and closing the door on her curious face as gently but firmly as she could.

"Okay, she's right. What's wrong with you? You look awful, and it's 2:00 in the afternoon! Why are you still sleeping? You stood me up... the concert, remember? What happened to you?" Aggie plucked a leaf out of my hair and held it out to me, as if to prove my delinquency.

"And what's with all the leaves and men's clothing?"

I was drawing a total blank. I had no idea what concert she was talking about. I took the diamond-shaped leaf from her. I could think of no good answers for her questions, so I stayed silent. Aggie's bare feet found the damp spot on the carpet around my bag of wet clothing. She opened the bag, wrinkling her nose at the stale odor.

"Any chance you went swimming in your bathrobe... and a weird set of scrubs?" she asked.

I needed to say something. *What would make sense?*

"Those are pajamas actually. My pajamas. And, yeah, my bathrobe," I answered lamely.

"And you swam in them, then changed into some guy's pajamas and wore them home to sleep in? What's he wearing?" She cocked one eyebrow at me.

"I have no idea what he's wearing. I mean, there is no *he*. The pajamas... they are mine... from my aunt. She has sort of weird taste. And I didn't plan to go swimming. I fell in… to the lake, I mean. It wasn't really a planned thing."

"You were wearing weird pajamas at a lake last night, just for fun, and fell in?"

I recognized her tone and expression. It was the same as my mother's had been when the six-year-old version of me had tried to convince her that the family dog had etched a butterfly into the windowsill with one of her straight pins.

I nodded. I wasn't completely lying. I just wasn't telling the whole truth.

"And who gave you the clothes you are wearing? Are you going to tell me they belong to your uncle?"

I shook my head. No.

I had no clue what to say. I didn't have much practice at outright lying. Nothing I could say would make sense. The situation seemed suddenly hopelessly funny. I started to giggle. The giggle grew into a laugh, and as sometimes happens with me, mirth completely took over. I rolled back onto the bed and held my sides, gulping and snorting until my eyes ran and my sides and belly hurt. Aggie simply stared.

"It's a boy, right? This has to do with a boy… and that fact has driven you utterly insane," she concluded. She seemed proud of herself for having figured out my secret.

"Well, I guess it would be accurate to say that there *was* a boy involved, but I'm sure it's nothing like what you imagine," I assured her.

"You have no idea what I can imagine."

I was pretty sure she couldn't imagine *this*.

"You have mud on your face," she said.

I ran my hands over my face and found a dried mud crust that extended from my upper lip to my ear. When I went to the wall mirror for closer inspection, every one of my muscles screamed at me. My shoulders and neck were the worst, and my left calf had developed a charley horse. I did my best not to limp.

I looked pretty bad.

"Maybe I should take a shower," I said, plucking more debris from my hair.

"I'd say so. What do you want me to do with these?" Aggie asked, holding my scrubs aloft from her fingertips.

"Oh, nothing. Really, I'll wash them later," I assured her.

"They are soaking the floor, and they smell musty. If you wait any longer, you might have to move."

"Oh, okay… I guess you can wash them if you want to." I struggled to accept help. I never knew what to say. "Thank you," I added. Somehow the phrase always seemed trite and inadequate.

"And your sheets?" she queried.

There was a large discolored swath in the center of the bed just where I'd slept.

"That might be a good idea," I said.

"So no concert tonight, right?" Aggie said it as more of a statement than a question. "That's all right. Donal is being an *hímszamár*. He can go alone."

I wasn't sure I wanted to know what a *hímszamár* was, but it didn't sound good. I imagined it had something to do with Donal's stubborn streak, which was quite long, almost as long as Aggie's. I didn't ask her to elaborate.

"You don't have to stay home because of me. I promise, no more midnight bathrobe diving. You go ahead and go. I'll just hole up and read, or study," I protested.

Aggie eyed me and shook her head. She had made up her mind. There was no point in arguing.

"You, shower. Now. When did you last eat?"

I shrugged and tried to remember. Aggie looked seriously concerned about my well-being, and I wished I had more assurances to offer her. I was simply too tired and overwhelmed to think of any.

"Yeah, okay… I'll start the laundry and get food. You wash up," she directed.

I started to protest again, but she pointed at the door. "You smell like the basement of the admin building. Go now."

The showers were in use, but the small tub room was vacant. It had a shower head as well. I entered the little room and set my towel and clean clothing on the cracked plastic stool. I turned on the water, letting it run until it was hot… too warm for a standing shower but just right for sitting under. The memory of another shower, colder and redder, sprang full force to mind; and an unexpected surge of sadness and desperation rushed so suddenly into my chest that it frightened me. The light seemed too harsh and unbearably bright. I turned on the fan to cover the sounds of my sadness and flipped off the light. I adjusted the water to near scalding and climbed in. I curled up, crying, in the bottom of the tub and let the water wash over me.

I'm not sure I can explain, even now, all the reasons I cried. It was for Aaron, for Henri, for Adrien, and for myself. I cried at the unfairness of what they went through and for how I felt about it, but it was more than that. I'd seen evil. It was something I could never "un-see." There was a well of sadness, deep enough to scare me, in the center of my chest.

The word *kakopathia* swam back and forth in my mind. *Kakopathia* means the experience of evil—the suffering and the disease that result from evil. I didn't even have to experience what those three men had to recognize it. I'd caught a glimpse of it in their eyes and through my hands when I laid them on Adrien. Just remembering it took my breath away. I squeezed my eyes shut tight, but the memories didn't lessen. It had changed me. I couldn't go back to not knowing.

Is there healing for things like that? I wondered.

I knew the answer must be yes; otherwise, what was the point? I just couldn't imagine it.

You don't have to imagine it. Just trust it. It comes from me, came Dhia's voice.

In my sadness, I'd actually almost forgotten about Dhia.

How could you allow this, Dhia. How? My soul begged the question for me. I was beyond forming words. I let the water run over me but didn't feel comforted.

What were Fa's words? I tried to think. *Beauty, goodness,* and *truth.* I remembered them and knew vaguely that I'd been awash in them in the past few days, but I couldn't grasp their meaning or remember how they felt. The sadness was so much stronger. I wanted to go back in time and "un-know," un-see, but there was no going back. There was only forward.

Slowly, I became aware of Dhia's presence. I felt, first, a warm pressure in the back of my throat. The warmth spread down through my chest, occupying the space of my sadness. He was grieving with me.

Misery really does love company.

After a while, the sadness ebbed. It changed from an untenable, surging force into a point of awareness. Then peace joined it, and my breathing slowed. I felt like I could move again. I climbed from the tub, feeling my way through the darkness to the light switch. Squinting in the light, I donned my clothes and headed back to the room.

Aggie had made popcorn, scrounged up some cookies, and opened a tin of canned pineapple. She wasn't exactly a gourmet chef, but I appreciated her efforts.

"You sure you are okay?" she asked, handing me a cookie.

I wondered how bad I looked despite the shower. Grief is ugly. It leaves marks.

"Something happened, didn't it?" she asked.

I nodded in confirmation.

"Something you can't talk about?"

I nodded again.

"Okay," she said, patting the bed. I sat. She didn't ask me any more questions that afternoon. I saw a side of her I'd never have guessed she had… The need to be there for me trumped her need to know. Apparently, you never know who your friends are until you scare them a little, dissolve into hysterics, and need them to do your laundry.

Food improved my mood considerably. I hadn't realized how hungry I was. The videotaped reruns of a TV show that billed itself as "a show about nothing" made me feel even better. I wasn't in the frame of mind for anything deeper. Sometime during the second episode, I fell asleep and dreamt of a woman who didn't move her arms when she walked.

On Petra, the Kress territories were spiritually dark, all the time. It was more than a negative aura. It was a pervasive, seething presence of invited evil. It felt different than the evil I'd witnessed on Earth. Earth's evil was dressed to disarm and distract. It was darkness dressed up, for the most part, in attractive colors. Kress had a bare naked, aggressive version of evil wholly welcomed by the Kress people. Every person in the community had said yes to darkness, and the darkness didn't have to masquerade as light. Outside the Kress boundaries, in every other inch of space on Petra, was light: a freedom from evil and an access to Dhia that was easy to become accustomed to. Demons weren't allowed to roam freely there as they did on Earth. Darkness wasn't allowed wander past the Kress boundaries into the light territories. Earth felt like a confusing mixture of Kress and Petra: a spiritual gray space where dark masqueraded as light, and light was obscured by darkness. The worst part of it was that not many people on Earth even knew to seek the light. They stumbled around in the spiritual twilight wearing their rose-colored lenses, declaring themselves content with spiritual slurry.

The first week back at school after my first jaunt was hard. Really hard. Imagine the worst case of jet lag ever, and add a hefty hangover; then add chemistry class… You get the picture, right? I wondered how much of my malaise was physical (the air on Earth *was* a little heavier than on the Rock) and how much of it was spiritual. My head ached constantly; not even ibuprofen helped.

Dhia was heightening my awareness of certain things. I began to sense the burden of darkness that people carried more clearly than I wanted to. It was a Wednesday afternoon, and the rain fell in a constant draining drizzle as I walked through the park at the center of campus. I'd been back less than a week. I felt soul-weary. I stumbled over nothing several times and finally stopped at a bench to sit down. I was haunted by the pain I'd seen on the faces of the men we rescued. I couldn't shake it. To some extent, carrying other people's pain was something I'd been doing my whole life. I witnessed people's pain, their confusion, and their callousness, and took it on, as if I adding rocks to an invisible pack on my back. Before the jaunt, the weight had been bearable, but it was suddenly much too much to bear. I couldn't carry it any longer.

What do I do with this, Dhia? How do I live with knowing all these things I don't want to know? I asked silently, staring up into an angry gray sky.

It's not your burden to carry. It's mine, He answered clearly and firmly.

"I know that's true. I *know* it, but how? How do I let you carry it? How do I let go when I feel their pain so strongly? Why do You show me these things? Please take them from me!"

I didn't give them to you. I never wanted you to carry them. Just let go. Dhia's voice rang in my chest.

"I don't know how!" Desperation welled up inside me.

Just let go, He repeated.

"Show me. Show me how!" I insisted.

Let go, He said again in a clear quiet voice.

I was shaking by then. I'd passed the point of caring whether or not someone saw me curled up on the bench in the rain. My legs were leaden. My arms had gone completely rubbery. I couldn't have moved even if I needed to. I managed to inch my hands open, palms skyward. I made the mental choice, once again, to let go.

"I'm letting go," I whispered. "I'm letting go."

I wasn't a quick learner. I'd been in a similar position before on the Rock—holding tightly to something I had no business carrying. Sadness, grief, confusion… whether it was mine or someone else's, I just needed to let go. I can't say why some lessons are learned in an instant, and some take a lifetime. I guess that's just how it is.

I lay in the rain letting Dhia help me sift through my memories and find the heaviest, hardest ones. I surrendered the image of Aaron curled on the concrete floor of the brothel. I surrendered the image of Adrien dead on the cot in the healing room. I even surrendered the memory of the sad lady in the pink suit that I'd seen at the grocery store many years before.

I took deep breaths, holding my hands open, palms up, choosing to give up the weight I could no longer stand to carry. I don't know how long I stayed on that bench, waiting and letting go, but eventually, the weight lifted. I still knew that confusion, pain, and darkness were out there all around me; but it no longer pulled and clawed at me. It no longer owned me. The pervasive headache eased, and the planet seemed to level out as my dizziness disappeared. At length, I felt strength seep back into my arms and legs. I got up and returned to my dorm.

WINTER BREAK

It was the week before winter break, and the first finals week of my college career. Anyone who has been to college knows what *that* means. Tensions ran high, rest was almost nonexistent, caffeine abounded. Aggie and Donal seemed to be getting along again. Perhaps they were too busy and sleep-deprived to argue. Distraction made cramming for exams harder on me than it should have been. I packed as much information into my brain as possible, but the details sifted through like sand in a sieve. I didn't have my usual "nailed it" feeling after exams. Instead, I had a solid B vibe. College classes had lost their top-priority status.

Most of Aodhagan's students split as soon as their exams were over. By Friday evening, Bert was already eerily quiet. The dorm was slated to close down over the holidays, but a handful of freshmen had not managed to find a place to spend their Christmas break. One boy, Sandeep, didn't plan to return home to India to visit his family at any point during his college career. His parents worked multiple jobs as it was just to keep him there. He was a permanent Bert fixture. The school gathered the stragglers and sent them all to one of the newer dorms for the duration of the break, where they could be adequately supervised by two staff members who were similarly disposed. Saturday morning, I slept in late, then packed my bags with clothes and souvenirs. I tucked in some kitschy local items I'd picked up for Millie and Nate. I wasn't flying home right away. I had scheduled a few days at Nan's house first, ostensibly, to unwind… actually, to have some quiet time to dig into items I'd stashed in Nan's attic.

My cousin Elsie agreed to give me a lift. She was late, and I was feeling generally irritable and impatient. Alone in the empty dorm, I felt like the last cow left in a field nibbled bare and then deserted by the herds. They had moved on to something lush and green, and I stood alone in the dust. When I couldn't stand it any longer, I turned my thermostat down to sixteen degrees Celsius as instructed and left my room, locking the door behind me. I lugged my bags to the entry porch at the front of the building and plunked myself down on the top step to wait for my ride. It was cold out, but being outdoors helped me feel like I was at least *on my way.*

I watched the driveway for Elsie but secretly wished Jack's little silver car would appear instead. Thinking of Jack made my chin feel numb. I seemed to be emotionally capable of caring for grown men in crisis on the Rock and yet dissolved into a complete puddle whenever I saw, or even thought of Jack. I wasn't sure if that was normal or a serious character flaw. Maybe it was both. *Would that make it a seriously normal character flaw?* It was, at the very least, a tad pathetic. I hadn't seen Jack since the night of my swim in Loch Occasional. I'd told Shine and Fa that I found it easier to accept the reality of the rock than the reality of Jack… and that was true. I'd had crushes on boys before, but this felt different. Maybe because he was less like a boy and more like a man. *What did that make me?*

It was Elsie's little orange road cone of a car, not Jack's, that careened around the corner of the drive and rescued me from my thoughts. The last bit of my irritability at being left behind melted away with Elsie's appearance.

"Sorry, I'm late!" Elsie shouted out the window at me as she pulled to the curb.

"No problem," I shouted back.

We hadn't seen each other in a few months. Elsie hugged the stuffing out of me and then shook my shoulders in false anger.

"You haven't called, haven't written, and haven't come to see us on the weekends the way you promised to. Are you too good for us? Or did you find a man? Or wait… are you flunking school?"

I had tried to mentally prepare myself for Elsie's inevitable rapid-fire barrage of questions; but it still took me a minute to collect her questions and respond. I was used to spending time with the quiet contemplative Blues, so Elsie's questions felt almost abrasive.

"Uh... no, no, and no. In that order—or any order, actually. No boys. I'm not flunking. And I'm absolutely not too good for you. It's quite the opposite. I'm probably not nearly good enough." Elsie didn't respond. I wasn't sure she'd even heard me. She leapt on to the next topic of conversation, which was herself. We stuffed my luggage into the car and set out for Nan's.

Elsie had met someone. A man. He was a professor, easily half again her age, though she didn't know for sure because he wouldn't tell her what year he was born. *That is a sign of something, right... something that isn't good?* While we drove, she yammered on and on about his car, his talent, his penchant for antique musical instruments.

"I told Mum and Da all about him this week," she said. "They aren't pleased, and that's an understatement. You should be glad you are staying with Aunt Moira and not at my house this week. Da's even quieter than usual."

"Is that possible?" I asked.

"The air around him...? It's *cold*!" She lowered her voice and mouthed the word 'cold.'

Considering what I knew of Uncle Kade, I could imagine it. Sometimes, what my own father *didn't* say when he was upset carried more weight than what he did say.

"I think I'm in love, Kiah," Elsie bubbled.

"How do you know?"

That question caught her off guard, as if she hadn't yet asked it of herself.

"Well, I'd rather be with him than without him. That's love, isn't it?"

"Or loneliness."

"You feeling all right?" she asked.

Was I? No, I wasn't feeling quite right. I just wasn't sure why.

"I think I'm just tired. Cold. Why? Do I look bad?" I flipped down the visor and peered into the lighted mirror.

Elsie ignored my self-consciousness and continued, "At least Aunt Moira lives alone now. You won't have kids constantly underfoot. You can get some rest."

"She's living alone? What happened to Evan and his kids?"

Elsie explained that things had become a little tense between Nan and Evan's wife, Kate. That… I could imagine as well. Nan was sweet but opinionated and somewhat demanding. Apparently, the house next door to Nan's had come available for lease. Evan snatched it up and moved his family into it. The new arrangement gave Nan, as well as Evan's family, some breathing room from each other. Evan continued to run Aunt Moira's little farm from next door. We pulled into Nan's drive. There was smoke in the chimney, and firewood stacked from the ground to the eaves to the left of the little front door. I climbed out of the car. My feet felt heavy, and my shoulder joints ached the way they did when I was coming down with a virus of some sort. *Great.* I did not want to get Nan sick.

Nan met us at the door, and I wrestled my bags into the house.

"I might be getting sick, Nan. Hug at your own risk," I warned her.

"I'll risk it," she said firmly and hugged me firmly.

Elsie was impatient to get somewhere. She stayed on the front porch.

"I've got to go, Aunt Moira," she informed Nan, kissing her on the cheek. "I've got a date tonight."

Nan eyed Elsie sternly.

"Ye be good. And dinna do anythin' I wouldna do," she cautioned Elsie.

It occurred to me that Nan was the type of woman who did anything she pleased, as was Elsie.

"I'll be good," Elsie reassured her, backing off the porch.

"Call me!" she shouted to me.

I waved and shouted my thanks to her as she drove away.

Nan took one look at me shook her head.

"Ye look beaten and ancient. If I didn't know ye better, I'd say ye were sixty years auld." She clucked her tongue and waggled her head, disapprovingly.

"That's not much of a compliment."

"It wasna meant to be a compliment but a statement of fact. Ye'll go to the settin' room, and I'll fetch ye tea and soup," she demanded.

She chased me to a big overstuffed chair and pushed me into it and pulled a blanket over me. It was before noon, but I felt sleepy. I amended my plan from spending the day in the drafty attic translating old documents to something that consisted of tea, crackling fire, and Nan's companionship. Nan delivered black tea, chicken stock soup, and crackers, then settled herself into her favorite chair. My eyes were already half-mast, and my face was beginning to feel hot.

"It isna jest a braw, is it?" Nan stated, more than asked, meaning it was more than a virus that had me worn out.

"I honestly don't know. There's been a lot of change. Maybe it's that." I rubbed my hot, prickly eyes.

"I can see thet. And I've been praying fer ye. Have ye been servin' then?"

"Yes."

"And yet, yer here. Ya havena disappeared…"

She seemed curious as to how things worked—how it was possible that her sister's Calling had taken here away from them, yet I remained.

"No, I haven't disappeared. Not permanently, anyway," I murmured.

"Maybe we can speak more once yer feeling better."

"I'd like that," I said and meant it.

I drifted off to sleep, awakening intermittently to change positions. At some point, though I don't remember actually doing it, I moved to the fainting couch at the back of the room. With no responsibilities or schedules to tend, my body gave itself over to being sick. When fever sent me into shivers and then rigors, Nan added more blankets and brought me a cool wet washcloth for my forehead. The room swam when my eyes were open, so I kept them shut. The memory of washing the face of the injured boy in the valley on the Rock drifted through my mind. My illness lasted for two days, and I slept most of that time, rising only to change positions or visit the bathroom. I had fragmented dreams wherein Petra and Earth took turns dancing and clashing with one another. Pieces of multiple conversations skittered through my head—all too quickly for me to make sense of them. At one point, I dreamt I was in a close dark-blue space, like a giant clamshell, with trickling warm water under me and warm wind blowing over me. It was a strangely familiar place. I occasionally pried my eyes open to see Nan stoking the fire or knitting in her Damask rose-covered chair.

I awoke in earnest early Monday and checked my watch, the silver watch my father had given me.

"It's the kind that nurses use," Dad had assured me, pointing out the handy red second hand. He'd given it to me at the airport as I'd left for college. I suddenly missed him and was glad I'd see him again soon.

It was 3:18 a.m., and I was wide awake for the first time in days. Whatever sickness had gripped me had finally passed. My mouth felt lined with cotton, and I was thirsty. Nan wasn't in the room. I hoped she was tucked, asleep, into her bed at the far end of the house. I stoked the fire on the hearth, which was low and threatening to go out, then snuck into the kitchen and drank a large mason jar of warm water. I sported the sour funk of an ill person who has sweated but not showered in a few days. I located my clothing and showered before I headed to the attic.

I pulled down the retractable steps in the hall as quietly as possible. A rush of cold air flooded the hallway. I fumbled around in the dark for the light switch. It was the old-fashioned type with two buttons. I pushed the top button, and the bottom button popped out. The light came on. The attic was full of crates, broken furniture, and old lamps. Everything was dusty but well organized, as if the items there were stored but not forgotten. Aunt Moira had lived through some very lean times. She knew the value of things.

The arm of a couch peeked out from under a large pile of boxes. I moved Nan's containers to the floor, taking care to keep them in order, and found the remainder of the couch underneath. While in serious need of cosmetic repair, it was, at least, sit-able. I dragged the trunk that held my items over to it and sat down. I removed everything from the box and laid it all on the floor. Most of the letters were still bound in bunches with ribbon. The few I'd already opened were secured with parcel twine. I pulled the tarnished little cross out of the box and set it on top of the lid, inscription side up. There were Ailsa's three leather journals and the gold book cover, which I unwrapped and set to the side. I carefully added the Gaelic New Testament, then stood back and surveyed the entire contents of the box.

Dhia, what am I missing? Where do I start? Is there anything here You want to show me?

I didn't sense a response. At a glance, everything looked just as it had the first and the last times I'd perused it. I sighed, feeling a little impatient. I leafed through the journals and found sketches and descriptions of herbs, trees, and herbal remedy recipes. Only the third journal was different. It contained sketches as well but not of plants and herbs. Words were scribbled here and there, arrows pointed to different parts of the sketches. Houses, landscapes, maps, roads, faces—all drawn haphazardly, as if the writer were jotting them down quickly before they escaped her. My heart raced. There was something familiar about the pages. They could easily have been pages from my own journals at home—except that, of course, they weren't. It was Ailsa's dream journal.

I checked the flyleaf, without much hope, for the year it was penned. No luck. I started on the first page and worked my way slowly through the book. On the second page, the image of the stone cottage on Petra jumped out at me. I wondered if Ailsa had drawn it from memory, having known the place, or if it predated her introduction to Petra. There were no notations on the page to answer my question. I moved on. Many of the pages, just like the scribbles in my own dream journals, would be incomprehensible to anyone but the scribe. One page, for instance, showed what looked like a hastily drawn aerial map, with a squiggle through its center that could have been a river. Groups of carrot marks here and there seemed to indicate treed areas. On the edge of the page was a small cluster of question marks circled six times and a larger question mark underneath the circles that was underlined twice. There were no identifying marks. It could have been a map of anywhere. I read the Gaelic text on the page that followed. It read, *"I'll try again, Dhia. I feel you sending me, but I can't seem to make it there. I've gotten lost each time. Help me, Dhia. Guide me. Direct me. I'm willing. Send me."*

The steps behind me squeaked as Nan ascended. She took her time. Finally, her white head appeared in the stairway. Engrossed in the words and pictures that had emerged from Ailsa's mind, I'd totally lost track of time.

"I thought I might find ye here," she said.

"I woke up early, so I thought I'd look through this stuff again."

"Did ye find what ye were looking fer?"

"I honestly don't know what I'm looking for… or even if there is anything to find."

"If there is something there for ye, ye'll find it… in the Lord's time… I've nae doubt of thet," she assured me. "Come down now and eat. Ye've been unconscious for days. Ye'll be needin' scran."

Scran meant food. I'd learned the term from Elsie. Elsie also taught me it was best not to argue with Nan. Under Nan's watchful eye, I gathered the items together and placed them back in the box. Then I thought twice and took the letters and the journals back out of the box.

"Takin' those with ye?" Nan observed.

"Yes. I'll have time on the plane to look at them more."

I clicked off the light and followed Nan down the stairs to breakfast. My legs felt a tad more wobbly than they had when I'd awoken a few hours before, and I was lightheaded. Nan had called it… My body did need fuel. Luckily, Nan was a fan of serving hearty breakfasts. Fried eggs, little square breakfast sausages, beans, broiled tomatoes, and bread waited for us in the kitchen.

"I don't think I can eat all this," I protested.

"Ye ne'er ken until ye try."

A SERIES OF STORMS

I flew home to Washington State that day. To say that the plane ride was bumpy would be the worst kind of understatement. The captain announced the possibility of turbulence as we taxied away from the hangars, and he wasn't kidding. I soon learned the true meaning of the word *turbulence*. From the moment we left the ground, the aircraft vibrated, rattled, and hummed at five times the normal intensity. We pitched sharply left, right, up, and down at irregular intervals—as if something large and angry was trying to shake the Boeing 747 out of the sky. The flight attendants even looked worried, buckling themselves into their little seats in the kitchenette and just outside the cockpit door. They sported wide-eyed, frozen expressions and braced their arms against the walls. *So much for looking to the experts for reassurance.*

My plan for the trip home had been to peruse the journals, maybe read a book or two, and think over what to tell my friends and family about how I'd been spending my time. I actually did none of that. Rather, I gripped the seat; braced my legs against the bulkhead; and, with my eyes shut tight, contemplated the short fragile nature of life.

The middle-aged primped and curled, overly perfumed woman in the seat beside me turned out to be a squealer, and a vomiter—an obnoxious combination. Perhaps I should have had compassion for her and offered trite reassurances, but I couldn't make myself feel anything but annoyed by her utterances. I shut my eyes and focused on breathing instead. There were few other viable options. After what seemed like eons, but was closer to an hour and a half, the turbulence eased. Everyone in the cabin breathed a sigh of relief, and most began to queue up for the restrooms. The flight attendants regained color in their faces, collected the used airsick bags, handed out fresh ones, and prepared to serve drinks. They stashed filter bags of freeze-dried coffee here and there throughout the cabin. It was a good idea. The smell of stale puke and fresh coffee grounds was a half step more tolerable than that of stale puke alone.

My seatmate immediately set to harassing the flight attendants, demanding a seat for herself in first class. She "couldn't possibly handle another minute in the tail of this steel beast." We were actually seated a little over halfway back, near the wings, but no one chose to argue that point with her. She promised to pay for the seat change, no matter what the cost.

"Even if I have to sell my children into slavery to cover it," she declared.

I believed her.

There was apparently room in first class, and while I pitied the people who would be gaining her company, I was hugely relieved on my own behalf. The flight attendants barely managed to serve a meal and retrieve the trays before another storm hit... then another and another. Each time, I clutched the arms of my seat and closed my eyes again, trying to find a zone of peace or at least tolerance. Somewhere over the middle of a big blue ocean, I began to wonder if my presence in that series of storms was mere coincidence. Is there really such a thing as coincidence? I'd certainly grown up thinking so. I had cynically believed that things simply happened the way they did for no reason and with no purpose whatsoever. I'd seen people as an enormous gaggle of accidental Earth tourists—each bound to have occasional uncanny experiences owing to the sheer number of people on earth and limited number of actual available experiences. The more dramatic a person was prone to being, the more poignant they would find those coincidences. Accident after accident, coincidence after coincidence, disappointing lack of significance after disappointing lack of significance… and all that added up to life. *Yeah, uplifting—I know.*

I was beginning to see holes in my previous theory. If Dhia was real, which I *knew* Him to be, then I wasn't meant to simply endure whatever happened in my life as coincidence. Whether it was good, bad, or just plain confusing, I was meant to learn from it. He had a reason for allowing anything He allowed. I thought of the Blues, with their fists of faith placed over their heart. Taking by faith what I didn't understand was a tall order, but I could start by noting the coincidences and lifting them up for Dhia to examine and explain if He so chose.

But what could I possibly learn from being tossed and shaken like a rag doll in a large metal object, hurtling through electrical storm after electrical storm? My head and heart pounded as the plane made a particularly precipitous drop and shuddered violently side to side.

What's the lesson in this? I asked Dhia, silently. There was no response. I snuck my eyes open and saw lightning dance wildly in the clouds in the distance. It was frighteningly beautiful. I felt very small.

Everyone on the plane—including, it seemed, the very jet itself—breathed a collective sigh of relief when the wheels touched squealing down, bounced, and then finally stayed fast to the tarmac at Seatac International Airport. It took every bit of concentration and effort I had to summon my wobbly, useless legs back into service. I used the seat back to pull myself upright and hold myself there. I noticed the flight attendants clutching the seat backs and fumbling, shakily, with the overhead bin clasps. That, selfishly, made me feel a little better. The impatient tangle of arms, legs, voices, and baleful glares between passengers customary at deplaning didn't occur. It wasn't that people were being gracious; they just didn't have the energy to squabble or "take cuts" in front of each other in line. People were just grateful to be getting off with their limbs intact. Perhaps that was the lesson: don't take exiting storms in one piece for granted. Point taken.

I climbed the walkway from the plane on my newborn colt legs at exactly the same speed as the elderly man beside me. He caught my eye and said, "I've flown planes for sixty years. I've never experienced anything like that before. Some of these people will never get back on another plane after that."

I nodded. "I imagine that's true."

The passage narrowed, and he dropped behind me, still talking to me, as we entered the terminal.

"You aren't one of those people, though. You are not that kind of girl. You keep climbing back on the next flight, ya hear? There will be more for you like this one. Don't fear them."

I turned to ask him why he would say such a thing but came face-to-face with a disheveled waxy-faced mother with a wide-eyed toddler glued to her chest and a young boy clinging tightly, silently, to her hand.

"Excuse me," I said, feeling bad for almost mowing her over. I glanced over her shoulder to catch sight of the old man. He was nowhere to be seen.

"It's okay," the young mother said. She didn't sound okay; but the plane trip, not my clumsiness, might have been the source of her distress.

The terminal, glaringly bright, exuded an unsympathetic amount of energy. The world didn't know we'd just spent the last eleven hours in fear for our lives. Life marched right on. I scanned the crowd for a familiar face and spotted my father near a newsstand. I made my way toward him, smack dab into the center of another storm.

My mother was gone. Gone, with a capital *G*. I can't remember what words my father used to tell deliver the news to me. Frank, bald ones, I imagine... but I honestly can't remember. I only remember feeling suddenly very, very cold. My fingers went icy, and my toes curled. My stomach dropped. I shivered and stared at my father, waiting for an explanation that made sense to my brain. We sat on an empty vinyl bench, and my father told me what he knew.

I'd never seen my father look older or more childishly vulnerable. His face was drawn, and his eyes were tired. I'd never before seen him at a loss for what to do. He'd always held a firm belief that if you just reason things out and put one foot in front of another the path will eventually show itself. My mother's disappearance had rendered that belief unreliable. There was no path, and nothing seemed to make sense. Two days before, my mother had risen early, showered, dressed, posted a note on the fridge that gave reheating instructions for the stroganoff she'd prepared for dinner, and announced her intention never to return, asking that no one attempt to contact or come after her. Then she left. She never arrived at work.

The police were immediately called to the house even though technically she hadn't been missing long enough to be reported missing. Dad answered every question the officers had, to the best of his ability. *No*, this was absolutely not normal for her. She was usually quite predictable and punctual. *No*, she'd never disappeared before. She was not generally given to irrational, emotional acts or whimsy. *Yes*, there had been some marital difficulties, but no more than normal. After years of existing as barely more than roommates, there was a degree of emotional distance. *Wasn't that normal with marriages?* (The cops said they didn't know about any of that. They probably weren't the best people to give unbiased opinions on what was normal, since abnormal was their job.) They left Dad with more questions than he'd had when they arrived. They said they'd be "doing all they could to find her," whatever that meant. They also left him with some assignments, which was a relief to him. It gave him something do, something to concentrate on. He'd spent the last two days combing the financials for inconsistencies, withdrawals, obscure accounts, anything that might indicate what Mom had been planning or where she had gone.

Somehow, my father and I managed to collect my luggage from baggage claim, find the car, and point it toward home.

"I didn't call you and tell you this before you left, Kiah, because I didn't want you to worry. I hoped by the time you got here I'd have something I could tell you. I was sure I would... but there's nothing. I thought maybe she would reconsider, or at least call. I was sure by now we would know something..."

We had reached the first of two mountain passes between Seattle and home, and it was beginning to snow.

Dhia, help me! My father is supposed to know what to do. He's sup-posed to tell me what to do, how to handle this! Please help us!

I felt warmth on my right shoulder, like a hand resting lightly there. I turned instinctively toward it but saw nothing.

"It's okay, Dad, that you didn't tell me. You did the right thing," I tried to reassure him.

His face relaxed just a little.

"Where could she be? Where could she have gone? Do you have any idea?" he asked. He glanced in my direction, actually seeming to hope I might have a guess.

I shook my head. "I don't know. Did you find anything? In the money? The finances? Did she take any money with her?" I asked.

"I talked to Peggy, the woman at the bank, the one who gives out the suckers?" I nodded, indicating I knew who she was, and he continued, "She helped me go through the accounts and make sure nothing was missing. Everything looks fine. But there's another account listed under your mother's maiden name. Peggy says Liz opened it last year and closed it last month. I need permission to access the account information, though. My name's not on it. Maybe if she doesn't come back, the cops can look at it? I don't know. Maybe they can't, if it looks like she's left of her own accord. The account is closed now, anyway, so I don't know how much help that will be."

"At least that means she isn't dead, though, right?" I thought out loud.

Dad startled, and his eyes widened. He seemed as surprised as I was that I'd said that out loud.

"If she really did plan to leave, which I think she did, then yes... I'm sure she's alive. I can't imagine she would ever want to harm herself."

I couldn't imagine her harming herself either.

"So that's good, then," I asserted, grabbing for the silver lining.

"Yeah, that's good."

Our family didn't usually touch much, but since the bottom had fallen out of our "usual"... I squeezed my dad's hand lightly as it rested on the gear shift. We dropped into silence, each in our own thoughts. I had a thousand questions: *Where had she gone? Why? Had life simply gotten too hard? Was her marriage to my dad just too much to handle? Maybe the silence of aloneness was preferable to the silence of closed hearts, clustered intolerably close, that defined our home? Maybe my choice to answer Dhia's call had been more than she could bear?* They were questions that neither I nor my father could answer, so I kept them to myself.

The long snowy drive was a familiar one. I'd made it many times before. Even in the dark, I recognized the turnout that led to the small deep lake where my first friends-only campout had occurred—three girls and a cooler of hotdogs and root beer in the back of a truck camper for two gloriously adult-free nights. We'd felt so grown up and adventurous when the trip started. Bright and early on the third morning, we had dragged our cranky, malodorous selves home rather than sticking out the rest of the day as originally planned. We each chose to wholeheartedly accept each other's pitiful excuses for our early departure. It seemed so long ago.

We also passed the exit that led to my mother's favorite cross-country skiing trail, and I felt an unexpected twinge of loss so sharp that physical pain radiated through my shoulder. I trained my eyes onto the dark sky outside the car window. *Where did she go?* The snow clouds had cleared, and the stars were visible far in the distance. The sky seemed somehow deeper and emptier than usual. I felt momentarily as if I might fall off the Earth, straight up, and tumble into the sky. It was disorienting. I held tight to the seat belt and a song that my mother had sung to me when I was very young ran through my head.

If I needed you, would you come to me? Would you come to me, to ease my pain? If you needed me, I would come to you. I would swim the seas to ease your pain... It had been comforting then; now it raised a poignant question. Would she come if I needed her? I was pretty sure she wouldn't. Maybe that's why she left... because she just *didn't* feel needed anymore. Maybe frosting cakes and ordering decorative baskets had kept her with us. Maybe my needs pinned her to the floor, and when I left, she floated away. Or maybe it wasn't about me. A clear picture of my mother sprang to mind: donning her jacket, watering the plants, writing a note about stroganoff, striding out the front door where she added her briefcase to a prepacked suitcase already stashed in the backseat of her little car.

"Hey, Dad, did you check to see if any of her clothes are missing?" I asked suddenly.

Dad shrugged, clueless. "I don't even know what clothes she owns."

That was true. He barely knew what clothes *he* owned.

"How about her favorite suitcase, the red one? With the leather straps and the butterfly clasps? Is it there?"

He shrugged again.

It was well past midnight when we pulled through the center of Kenoa. The streets were icy and empty, and cold wind blew in off the dark river. Dad slalomed a few downed trees, and we passed a small huddle of men in the contemplative phase of repairing a sparking, severed power line. More storms, more wind, more electricity. We reached our driveway and pulled up to the front of the house. I noticed that the little lights weren't twinkling under eaves; turning them on was Mom's job. Now that it was up to Dad, they might never be utilized again. At least Dad had forgotten to turn off the front porch light when he'd left to pick me up that morning. We could see our way clearly up the front steps. We braced against the cold wind and wrestled my luggage into the house. Chump came unglued when I opened the door, hurtling his furry body into my arms. He danced and yelped and wiggled everywhere; and I hugged him hard, my head buried in his fur, letting his exuberance disguise my emotion. Dad deposited my bags on the kitchen floor and stood still, trying to decide what to do next. Going to bed seemed most reasonable, but I sensed that neither one of us were up for that right away.

"Tea?" I suggested.

He looked at me quizzically for a moment, as if trying to remember whether or not he liked tea, then accepted the suggestion. He began to rummage through the wrong cupboard for the tea bags.

"You get the water going. I'll get the tea," I suggested.

He was amenable.

Chump danced endless circles around our feet as we assembled a cheese and cracker snack to go with our tea and moved to the living room. Dad lit a fire in the fireplace, and I settled into the corner of the couch. Chump vaulted unexpectedly into my lap. He had learned as a pup never to climb onto the couch, but that evening he sensed that all bets were off. I let him stay. He laid his large tortilla-chip-smelling head on my lap and begged silently for a cracker.

Dad sat in the rocker, staring into his tea cup.

"Did you call Nana? Uncle G.? Or Grandma and Grandpa? What did they say?" I asked Dad.

"No," he answered.

"No? You didn't call them?" I was a little surprised.

"Well, yes, I mean, I called your Oma and asked how she was… and if she had heard from Liz. She said no, of course not. She asked me why I was asking. I didn't want her to worry, so I changed the subject."

"And Grandma Margaret?"

Dad didn't answer.

"Has she or Grandpa K. heard from Mom?" I pressed.

"I didn't call them, Kiah… They are on a cruise that won't dock for a few days. The Bahamas, remember?"

I shook my head. I didn't know. Mom didn't tell me much of anything, especially about her side of the family. A cruise did sound like something they would do. They took full advantage of every age-specific discount that came along. They'd made their first warm-weather excursion to some place south of the equator ten years before and had, unfortunately, been wearing Hawaiian garb, ever since, regardless of the season. They lived lives straight out of a Price is Right showcase: vacations, cruises, RVs… I once asked my mother, if she was sure she was even related to her parents. "Unfortunately, Kiah, I'm quite certain of it," she'd answered through clenched teeth.

Dad ran his hair through his hands and continued, "There's no sense in calling them while they aren't even on this continent. Besides, I thought maybe she'd show up again, and then we wouldn't have to worry anyone. Maybe it's time now, though… to at least tell my family."

"Maybe tomorrow," I thought out loud.

He nodded in agreement.

"I'll help with that if you want me to, Dad."

He didn't respond. He wasn't really listening to me.

"I'm glad you are here, Kiah," he said. I could tell he meant it.

"Me too. I'm really sorry about... all of this." Tears threatened at the corner of my eyes again, and a tinge of fear flitted through my chest, though I'm not sure what I was afraid of.

"So am I," he said, placing his uneaten crackers and tea on the coffee table and rising to his feet.

"Where could she be?" he asked no one in particular. His tone was equally sad and angry.

I wanted to ask Dad if her leaving surprised him. I wanted to ask, looking back now, if he'd seen any signs that this was coming. I just couldn't bring myself to say the words out loud.

"Time for bed, I think," Dad said abruptly.

He squeezed my shoulder and headed for the guest room rather than the bedroom he shared with his wife. I could understand that. It was probably hard to sleep in a room meant for the both of them. It had always been more of her room anyway. I climbed the stairs to my room and stood in the doorway, just looking. I'd made the bed before leaving for college, and Mom had remade it. She always tucked the comforter under the pillows in a way I never did. I sniffed the comforter: strong fresh fabric softener scent—the kind that came in the big blue bottles with the pink lids. It was the kind she only bought occasionally because the dryer sheets were more cost-effective and easier on the septic system. It was the kind she bought when she knew I needed a pick-me-up. I conjured up an image of her buying the fabric softener, washing the bedding, smoothing the comforter, tucking it in just so, believing that I'd find great comfort in it. The mere thought sent a fresh wave of gooseflesh across my back, and anger arrived. How could she? What could she have been thinking?

I'll just make sure the beds are made, and scented, properly before I devastate my family by vanishing...

I didn't know what to think, how to feel… but knew I wasn't going to crawl in that bed and fall fast asleep between my favorite sheets.

"No!" I murmured defiantly under my breath. Sleeping in that room just didn't seem right, or even possible. I wasn't sure if it would ever feel right again.

I picked up my still-packed bags and went back downstairs without looking back.

They say hindsight is 20/20, right? That if you knew then what you know now, then you would have done things differently? If I had accepted my mother's softly scented, hospital-cornered, perfectly smoothed and tucked, useless provision for me… if I had flipped back the comforter and found her carefully penned note on the pillow—would that have changed the course of what followed…? *Pure conjecture. Moot point. There's no way to know. Don't go there. Stick to the facts.*

OFFICIALLY MISSING

The next morning, the sun pierced through the clouds at a wintry angle to find my left eye. I was squinting and trying to reorient myself when the fact that something was terribly wrong slammed down in the middle of my chest. *Mom is gone*, I remembered. My heart raced. I sat upright and took a few deliberate deep breaths. My trips to the Rock had given me some practice at settling into disturbingly new realities. I wished, desperately, that I was back on the Rock but had to set that reality aside. One thing at a time.

I had sacked out for the night on the living room couch with a few blankets snagged from the linen closet. I fished under the coffee table for my watch and found it: 10:52 a.m. Seriously? I sat up, still in my clothes from the day before, and noted the double film of fear grease and air-travel grease that coated my skin. The scent of coffee grounds and faint puke lingered in my nose. Gross! Must shower! *Is this what adults do—spend most of their time stinking for one reason or another?*

I could hear Dad talking on the phone on the other side of his closed office door. I cracked the door and peeked in. He had visibly regained his sense of purpose and, with it, his skin color. He sat tall in his chair, rapping his pen against the desk with his "my brother is so bullheaded" expression on his face. Relief swept over me. Score one for the Adenauers! We were down, but not out.

"There isn't any more to say, Gary," I heard him tell his twin brother. "We don't know anything. It looks like she left of her own accord. There's certainly no reason to panic… No, for goodness' sake… *don't* say anything to Ma. No. I'll call her… There's no sense in you coming here either. I'll make the calls and then let you know. Maybe you could go be with Ma once I've talked to her. That's something you could do… sure. That'd be good, but wait for my call, all right?"

I caught his eye and pointed to my hair, mouthing the word, "Shower?" at him. He nodded and waved me away. I turned to run to the shower and promptly tripped over Chump, who was patiently, quietly waiting near the front door for his morning toilette. I sprawled face-first on the tile floor of the entry.

"It can only get better from here, right, Chump?" I mumbled to the dog. Chump cocked one ear and looked confused. He understood seven words total, and I'd only used one of those: his name. He blinked anxiously and tap-danced toward the front door, indicating that his need was still pressing. I climbed off the floor and let him out.

"You okay?" Dad appeared in the front hallway with a concerned look on his face. The thump must have been louder than I realized.

"Oh yeah… I'm fine. I just forgot how to walk in a house with a dog in it," I explained, feigning a casual attitude.

"Your face is bleeding." He smirked. "Maybe I'll wait for the dog to finish his business, and you can head for the shower while the coast is clear."

"Maybe that's a good idea."

Falling down as a small child is just a forgettable part of every day. You brush off and rush on, pell-mell. Falling down when you weigh over a hundred pounds and have lived over almost two decades is a tad more jolting. I limped in the direction of the bathroom. The incident let Dad smile and broke some of the tension, though. That was good. And life goes on in so many ordinary ways, even when something momentous happens, something that rocks your world.

Mom is gone. I shivered as the thought struck me again.

I peered out the small bathroom window down the canyon and pressed a wet washcloth to my rapidly swelling cheekbone. The washcloth was pinkish when I held it away to look at it, not profusely red. That was good too. It seemed I wouldn't bleed out or require stitches. The road that led away from our house seemed longer than it used to. The sky seemed farther away and empty, as if it had grown since yesterday, and I had shrunk. There were millions, billions of people out there, and my mother was one of them. My hands broke out in a cold sweat.

Where is she? I wondered.

The events of the next few days tumbled by me in a real-time blur broken up by fragments of singular crystallized moments. Uncle Gary talked to Oma came against Dad's wishes. He camped out in the living room for almost an hour before realizing his presence really was unnecessary. Dad thanked him for coming, and Gary headed for Oma's house to give the short pointless update: *we still know nothing.*

Millie arrived around noon. I think Dad must have called her. She hugged me for a long time, though I didn't really feel it. It wasn't comforting. We camped out in front of one movie, then another. We ate mostly chips and ice cream that day—straight from the bag and the carton, respectively—and drank tea. Soon there was only chip dust in the bags and empty wax paper linings in the little tea boxes. Someone had to go to the store. It wouldn't be Dad. Dad had to stay by the phone in case the police called. Ugh... phone. My mother's disappearance taught me to hate the phone. It rang incessantly. Everyone we knew, and everyone we didn't really know but seemed to know of us called us. It wore on our nerves, but it had to be answered every time. "In case there was news" or "in case it was *her.*"

So the task of grocery shopping fell to Millie and me. The problem was, I wasn't sure what to buy. Chips? Ice cream? What else? *What else do people even eat?* I couldn't remember. Nonetheless, Millie and I donned our boots and coats and grabbed the car keys. We were headed for the door when we heard a quiet knock. Millie's mother and Nate's mother were huddled together in the cold on the front step with bags of groceries. We stood and stared at them for a moment.

Do these two women actually even know each other? I wondered silently.

"Well, there's more in the car, girls, go on and get it. Bring it in!" Nate's mother urged, breaking the silence. We scrambled to do as we were told, scooting past them and out to Mrs. Gorse's station wagon. I was halfway to the car when the unbidden wall of emotion hit. Nervous Judy Gorse and overemotional Claire Mancini were in my kitchen, cooking for me and my dad because my mother was not. It meant two things: first, that something was really wrong; and second, that they cared. The combination of those two facts hit me right in the gut.

"Thank you, Dhia," I said aloud, just before my knees crumpled, and I squatted in the middle of the drive.

"Um, Kiah? You okay? You aren't speaking English..." Millie squatted beside me, concern written all over her face.

"Oh yeah, I'm okay. Just give me a minute," I responded, mopping my nose with my sleeve like a kindergartner. Apparently, I'd slipped unconsciously into another language. I wasn't sure which one. "I keep thinking she will be back any minute, you know? Like maybe she will realize that she made a mistake and just come back? But then I know she won't... and your mom is here, making food in my kitchen... and Mrs. Mancini, for goodness' sake! And somehow, I think that means this is real. She's gone. Really gone."

"Do you think maybe something happened to her? Like kidnapping or something? Maybe she didn't mean to go?" Millie asked, almost hopefully.

I thought about that for a moment but shook my head. I knew at a place deep inside myself that her leaving was her choice.

"No, she's gone because she means to be gone... That's the kind of person she is. Once she makes a choice, that's *it*... even if she realizes later that it was the wrong one. I don't think she's coming back." It was scary to voice my darkest fears, out loud, to inspect them as they hung in the air. But once I'd said them out loud, I felt better somehow, as if putting them out there stole some of their power to make me afraid.

Millie didn't respond. She just waited with me. I felt a warmth on my shoulder and looked up, expecting to see Millie's hand there, but saw nothing. I wondered if Dhia Himself was touching my shoulder or an angel. Either way, I wasn't alone. A small burst of energy propelled me to my feet, and I headed for the station wagon, where Millie and I collected the last of the groceries, then headed back indoors.

Prior to Nate's departure for college, everything his mother, Claire, cooked came—frozen, plastic-wrapped and boxed—from the freezer. As soon as he'd left, however, she had taken up Cooking, with a capital *C*. "To keep my mind occupied," she explained, unwrapping delicate handmade rolls of fragile dough layered with parchment paper. In the last few months, she had learned to broil, braise, sauté, bake, and work culinary magic with a crockpot. She was beyond thrilled to share her newfound culinary expertise with us.

"We plan to cook, clean, and stay out of your way, Marshall," she was promising my father as we entered the kitchen with the last of the groceries. He was standing, stunned, in the doorway of the kitchen.

"That's so kind of you, Mrs. Mancini. You really don't have to bother, though. I'm sure we will be just fine...," he started.

Claire cut him off. "Nonsense. You have much more important things to do than figure out how to cook. Judy and I are happy to be here. We wouldn't rather be anywhere else." She patted Dad on the back. Dad raised an eyebrow, but Claire didn't notice. Nobody ever pats my dad on the back.

"Your daughter has been a delight to us for years. It's time we repaid the favor," Claire continued.

She smiled at me and winked, as if I was a five-year-old girl with pigtails. I may as well have been... The warmth of her words made tears brought tears to my eyes again. I blinked them back.

"She's right, Marshall. You need to be able to concentrate on... well... whatever else you need to concentrate on right now. I'm pretty good with cleaning supplies and comfortable with the phone. I'd be happy to field phone calls for you, if you like," Judy added.

I could substantiate her comfort level with the phone. Her home phone was basically an extension of her arm or her ear, however that worked. That won Dad over. He was as tired of answering the phone as I was.

"Sold," he said. He briefed Judy on what to say and which phone calls to pass on to him, and she took over the giving the useless information-free updates: "No, we don't know anything. Yes, it's very sad. No, no one saw this coming. How could they? Yes, we will get the word out if and when she returns. Thank you for calling."

By the time Judy and Claire left for their own homes that evening, the house was clean, and the fridge was full of simple ready-to-cook meals. The phone even fell quiet. They promised to be back the next day. The next few days were repeats of the day before. Judy and Claire would let themselves in, then wash, bake, answer the phone, launder, repeat throughout the day. Millie and I watched movies and helped in the kitchen. We attempted, time and again, to talk about normal things: school, boys, the future... but Mom's disappearance robbed us of the ability to carry such conversations with conviction.

"Maybe we could go to your room and hang for a while, Kiah," Millie suggested at a particularly spectacularly boring moment.

"I don't think so," I said quickly—coldly too, I imagine. I averted my eyes and didn't expound. Millie took the hint and didn't push the matter. I liked that about Millie.

Dad, as usual, spent most of his day in his home office. I think he was trying to work, but I'm not sure how much he actually got done. Every hour or so, he wandered through the house, checking on me as if I too might disappear if not closely watched. I know now what people mean when they say that trauma brings people closer together. Even though we didn't talk much, I'd never felt so close to him before. She hadn't just left him or me; she had left *us*. I wasn't sure how I would be able to leave him when it was time to return to college.

The police scheduled a visit and arrived at the house late in the week. They were ushered into the living room where they sat daintily on the edges of the furniture, not wanting to give the impression that they were staying for any real length of time. Dad, Millie, and I sat on the couch and waited for them to speak. Judy and Claire stayed in the kitchen, politely pretending not to listen.

They had no leads and no news. Everything seemed to point to Lisette Bonner leaving her life behind completely of her own free will. "There's nothing more we can do for now, I'm afraid," the sergeant said. "She had her own bank account, cleaned it out, and then closed it properly. She hasn't broken any laws by leaving. We've put her picture out on the wire, so she's still officially missing, but there's not much more we can do at this time. You are certainly free to put the word out there… post flyers, things of that nature… talk to some of the TV stations, do some interviews. Maybe someone will recognize her and give you a call. As far as we are concerned, however, there's been no crime here. There's nothing else we can do."

"Yeah, you said that part before," Dad said, running his hands over his face and hair, making it stand on end.

"We are very sorry, sir. We know this is hard." The second police officer delivered his message with a vocal squeak and a high degree of awkwardness. It sounded very much like a phrase he had gleaned from a section of the police training manual entitled "The Type of Things to Say When There's Nothing Else to Say but You Have to Say Something in Hopes that the Devastated, Disappointed People Don't Yell at You for Being Utterly Useless."

I had an odd impulse to comfort the fidgety young man. He was approximately my age and obviously new to the job. I wanted to tell him that he had done enough for us, although he really hadn't done much for us at all. Maybe that was the kind of training he needed and obtained by working on my mother's case: to learn how to handle it when loss or death won. I wanted to tell him that loss would get easier to deal with, that he should shrug us off and move on, because there *would* be something active he could do, somewhere, for someone else. I wanted to say those things, but I didn't. I stayed silent.

The police officers rose to their feet, indicating that the short meeting was over. They reminded us to call if we heard anything from Mom. Dad walked them to the door and thanked them for their time. They looked relieved and grateful that he dealt with them so congenially, without harsh words or crying jags. Then they were gone.

"You want to do what they suggested, Dad? You want to do TV interviews, pass out flyers? Should we do that?" I asked Dad when he returned.

He didn't answer for a long time but stood staring at the carpet, deep in thought. Millie and the moms peered from the kitchen doorway like a trio of wide-eyed owls watching Dad and I tiptoe our way across a rickety bridge over a great crevasse.

"Somehow, that seems disrespectful." Dad spoke quietly to me, as if he and I were alone. "When Lisette does things, she does them deliberately. She usually means what she says, and she always means what she does. She's made a decision. It's something she thought out. Something she wanted. It's not what I want, and I don't agree with it, but I don't want to disrespect her." He sighed and then continued in a louder, more decisive voice. "I won't make her into a front-page spectacle. That's not what she wants... and it wouldn't help, Kiah. You know that, right? She wouldn't come back just because we asked or commanded her to... or she'd never have left in the first place. She thought this through."

The owls shifted their gaze to me, waiting for me to respond.

I thought about Dad's words and knew what he was saying was true. "Yes, I know that, Dad." My chin irritated me by quivering.

"Okay, then. We take it one day at a time from here."

"Okay," I agreed, relieved that he ignored my tears.

And not pursuing my mother did feel strangely okay. I knew if she didn't want to be found, we wouldn't find her. Even if we did find her, what then? She didn't want us anymore. I felt very cold. I cast a glance around, looking for a blanket to pull around my shoulders, and saw none. I'd been cold for days. It wasn't the kind of cold you feel when you are too tired or the kind of cold you feel when the temperature outside drops a few points and you feel the need to add a layer of clothing until you get used to the change. This was a bone chill that I just couldn't shake—a spiritual thing that had leaked into my physical being. My mother and I weren't involved in each other's daily lives, and we had never delved into each other's hearts and souls, but she'd always been *there*... across the house, across the room, across the pond. She'd always been a force to be counted on and reckoned with. If my heart were a house, then her absence tore a hole in the attic or the outside wall or the garage... The damage was done somewhere that I couldn't see but could absolutely feel. Cold drafts of air whistled in from the unseen rift, rendering my insulation ineffective. I just couldn't get warm.

"Well, Claire, you promised to teach me how to cook. Now's as good a time as any to get started," Dad announced suddenly, clapping his hands together as a signal that it was time to move on. He successfully broke the mood. A smile broke across Claire's face; her expertise was needed. Dad followed her into the kitchen.

DRESDEN

December 24, Christmas Eve. Dad insisted it was a day to celebrate what we had, not obsess over what we had lost. He appointed it a turning point of sorts. He insisted I go for a horseback ride. I woke up extremely early, before the light snuck into the sky, and headed to Mary's place. The owls weren't joining our household that day. While I enjoyed their company and their help, I was somewhat relieved. I felt a little guilty that I hadn't seen Dresden since I'd come home. I'd planned to spend a large portion of my break at Mary's barn, petting, riding, and treating him; but my mother had changed all that. The sky was crystal clear. The icy roads required precise, steady movements. By the time I reached Mary's barn, light had begun to filter into the sky. Dresden looked startled, then ecstatic, in a dance-y, horse-ish way, to see me. He nuzzled my neck for kicks and then my pockets for treats. The latter action let me know he definitely remembered me. Whenever I'd been away for too long or missed a feeding time, I tended to stash a treat away in my pocket for him to find. I know… it's a bad habit! It teaches the horse to expect favor *and* to nibble. I did it anyway. He nuzzled my left coat pocket, and I produced a carrot. My long absence was immediately forgiven. Wouldn't it be amazing if human-to-human relationships were that simple?

I tacked up the horse and rode out into the low mountains behind Mary's ranch. The mountains were bare and mostly white, with jagged brown gashes where deer or cougar had bedded down or pieces of rock or earth had given way and tumbled down the hill.

The ground gave a little with each step Dresden took, making for reasonable footing. I mostly let the horse pick the pace, enjoying his whims. He moved out quickly at first, then slowed to a meander as the terrain grew steeper. We reached a ridge and watched the dregs of the sunrise, crossed a creek and wound round behind a small lake. The sulfury-smelling mist rose from the water told me that a natural hot spring fed into it somewhere. I doubted the water was actually warm, but it was at least a bit warmer than the air.

I halfway hoped that Dresden would take me somewhere inspired and mysterious that morning, as he had once before. I wished that Dhia would direct him, perhaps to someone who could explain what my mother was thinking, explain what she was doing, reassure me that everything would be okay. I didn't really expect it, though, as nice as it sounded. I hadn't known Dhia to work that way... making things easier for me in *my* way and for *my* selfish benefit. He seemed to have a bigger plan, one I didn't understand. I just needed to keep choosing to trust Him.

The landscape and the lack of humans to interact with encouraged my mind my wander. I still couldn't put my finger on exactly how I felt about Mom. One moment angry, the next sad, then the next hollowed out and empty. My only sense of security and hope lay in the one thing I knew for sure; Dhia *did* know. He *did* know what I should do, and he *did* know where my mother was. He even knew my innermost feelings when I didn't know them myself. So I made the choice to trust.

"I trust you!" I called out to Dhia, across the lake. Dresden startled at the sound of my voice and shifted uneasily.

Speaking to Dhia aloud was becoming my way of playing Marco Polo with the divine. Sometimes, I longed for a visible sign of his presence, like what I experienced on Petra. Earth was a spiritual gray space, compared to the black-and-white nature of Petra. Dhia's presence was visible and tangible in the healing rooms on the Rock. His absence was stark and obvious in Kress territory. Earth, comparatively, was a disorienting mishmash of good and bad, right and wrong, which obscured my perception of His presence. To be on Earth was to constantly cast about in spiritual fog. Faith and trust were necessary to keep moving toward Him. I waited, listening, and watching, for any sign or word from Dhia but saw and heard nothing.

Mom is gone. The panicky, short of breath, sweaty-handed, heart-pounding feelings I'd experiences the day I'd learned of her disappearance had given way to disconcerting numbness. It was as if my foot had fallen off somewhere, leaving me with a short stumpy leg that impaired my walking ability but registered no pain... Just a strange chill, an awareness of loss with no true emotion attached to it. I felt cold, but not alone. I *knew* Dhia was with me, even though I couldn't see, hear, or feel Him. His presence registered in a place not even the cold could reach.

"I trust you," I repeated a few more times, reaffirming my choice. Three words sprang to mind. *Truth, goodness, beauty*—the virtues Fa had spoken of. "I can't feel them right now, but I'm willing to try. I'm willing to look," I whispered.

Where was *Truth* in my current situation? The truth was that Mom had left us—of her own accord. There wasn't much hope in that. There must be a deeper truth, Dhia's truth.

"So what is it?" I asked Him.

"I will never leave you," came the answer... not from myself and so loud in my head that I jumped, startling Dresden who had been snoozing underneath me while I stared out over the lake. That truth brought with it a bit of warmth.

Next... *Goodness.* That was a tough one.

"Dhia, where is your goodness in this?" I asked quietly. A bitter taste filled my mouth as I waited for an answer.

A Bible verse from the book of Psalms came to mind. *Taste and see that the Lord is good. Blessed is the man who puts his trust in Him.*

Dhia is always good. *Always.* I knew it, but I could barely feel it.

"I trust you," I repeated. Saying it aloud helped me feel it a little more strongly.

And there was *Beauty.* Ha! Nothing seemed beautiful at the moment. I glanced around at the terrain again... white and brown with bare trees. Bleak. The lake steamed like a bowl of unappetizing soup. I didn't see or feel anything beautiful around me except

Dresden. Dresden. Dresden was beautiful. I lay across his neck and breathed in his smell. Dresden was getting restless.

I returned to Mary's where I untacked and brushed the horse. I thanked him for the ride with another carrot and returned home. It was midmorning, and my time with Dhia had shored up my emotions a little. Both Chump and the smell of hot breakfast rushed out to greet me when I opened the front door.

"Eggs," Dad explained as I entered the kitchen. "Years ago, I was an egg expert. Want some?" He was smiling and wearing a ridiculous Christmas elf shirt that Mom had bought for him years ago, atop an old pair of baggy pj's and his holy sneakers.

"You look homeless," I informed him, trying to keep the dog from knocking me over.

"Is that a no to the eggs, then?"

"I'll take an egg. Is that sausage I smell?"

"Microwave sausage. It was one of Claire's beginner courses," he explained. "Actually, I was a short order cook for a while in school. I was quite good at frying sausage and eggs to order. I kind of liked the cooking part. I just didn't really like taking orders."

"Really?" I was surprised. "If you liked it, then why haven't I ever seen you cook?"

"Once we were married, your mom thought she should do the cooking. It made her feel good. I didn't want to take that away from her."

I wondered how many other things he'd enjoyed but given up in order to bolster Mom's confidence. I didn't know what to say about that, so I said nothing.

"Your mom was a sad person when I married her, not sure of herself. I thought I could help. I liked to make her laugh," he continued, sharing with me something else I hadn't known.

"If you know how to cook, then why are you taking lessons from Claire?" I asked.

Dad laughed a short, ironic little laugh. "For the same reason, I guess, that I left the cooking to Liz a long time ago. It makes Claire feel useful, and she needs to feel useful. Everyone does, Kiah." He patted one of my shoulders.

Uncle Gary and Oma arrived shortly before dinnertime. Oma stood five foot three inches tall. She led the charge into the house, her coarse gray hair pulled cinnamon-bun style to the top of her head. Her mouth formed a straight line, even when she smiled wide. Just then, it was turned down at the edges, and her brow broadcasted determination. She marched straight up to Dad and took him by the shoulders. "It's not your fault, Marshall. It's not right, and it's not your fault that she's gone!"

"I know, Ma. I hear you. I heard you the last time," he said.

"Well, some things bear repeating!"

She turned to me next, grasping my shoulders in a similar fashion.

"It's not your fault either. Do you hear what I'm saying? Each of us makes our own choices. You don't get to carry other people's burdens, because it's not fair to *them*."

"You mean it's not fair to me?" I asked.

"No, I said exactly what I meant… it's not fair to *them*. It's not fair to your mother if you carry her burdens for her!"

I could tell she had a very specific point, which I was missing.

"How's that, Oma? I mean, how is it unfair to *them*?"

Dad gave me a look that said, *Please don't encourage this conversation to last any longer than it absolutely has to.* I pretended not to notice.

"People can't address their own burdens if they aren't carrying the full weight of them. You can't address the burdens that aren't yours. Let your mother carry her own burdens. They are between her and God." Oma's finger was pointed directly (or at least as directly as it could be, considering it was a very crooked finger) at my nose. She kept her eyes fastened on me, waiting for an answer or at least a sign that I understood.

I understood her point. Sort of.

"I hear you Oma. I'll try," I promised.

"Just trying isn't good enough, Kiah. You might as well just quit now, as 'try.' You must make the decision that it *will* happen, and then you *make* it happen. You find a way," she said, jabbing me in the sternum to punctuate her words. My eyes widened. I was used to Oma being forceful, but not quite that forceful.

"I will, Oma, I'll let my mother carry her own burdens," I promised, fighting the urge to back away to avoid being poked again.

"We hear you, Ma. Why don't you come sit down?" Dad gestured toward the couch.

"I think I'll get some tea first, if that's all right by you." Oma stuck her chin into the air and strode into the kitchen.

We don't have a lot of easily swayed, directable personalities in our family.

Uncle Gary followed Oma into the kitchen, an apology for delivering Oma implicit in his facial expression. "Merry Christmas," he said. I fought the urge to remind him not to carry the burden of Oma's decisions.

It was tradition in our family to open presents on Christmas Eve. First, there were chili, cheese and crackers for dinner. (Don't ask me how that tradition got started.) Then we would gather around the Christmas tree and trade gifts. Oma wouldn't have stood for having it any other way. The four of us made a pitifully small group: Gary on the couch, Oma perched on the edge of the love seat, Dad in the rocker, me on the floor beside Chump, ready to "play Santa." That honor was reserved for the youngest person present who possessed the skills to do the job—those with the ability to read the tags and the self-control not to rip open the paper and chew the gifts inside. The job fell to me since Chump had no thumbs.

Most of the gifts under the tree had been chosen and wrapped by my mother weeks before. I suddenly wished Aunt Barbara and Uncle Craig had joined us, along with their four noisy, moist young children. They hadn't been able to come, however; flights from Boston were too expensive around the holidays.

That was the first year I'd purchased presents for any of my extended relatives. I didn't know what the protocol was exactly... When does a teen whose parents have always done all the Christmas shopping turn into a young adult, expected to buy for others outside the immediate family? I'd dipped my toe into adult waters by buying a few small things for those slated to be at our house during the holidays: Uncle Gary, Oma, Mom, and Dad. I'd done all my Christmas shopping at one time, in the same place during one of the first social excursions with Aggie and Donal. The concert we'd purchased tickets for was held in the basement of a retired monastery. The venue had been drafty, dank, and poorly lit. The music was horrible as well; all of us agreed on that point... too many guitars in one place, and we weren't convinced they were all playing the same song. We'd arrived a few hours before the start of the musical disaster and ducked into a shop housed on the upper floor of the defunct monastery. It touted the selling of only handmade European items and had a fair collection of interesting knickknacks. I'd salvaged the otherwise useless trip by doing all my Christmas shopping in one fell swoop. For Uncle Gary, there was a stag horn knife. For Dad, a set of carved wooden refillable pens. For mother, a red-and-gray plaid wool blanket. A small intricately carved German cuckoo clock for Oma, large enough that she could see the numbers, small enough to be hand carried on the plane. I'd also picked up a piece of local jewelry for Millie, which I'd already given her.

My Christmas purchases huddled together under the perfectly trimmed tree, each wrapped in butcher block paper and tied with red string. In contrast, Mom's gift contributions were shiny and bursting with bows and curling ribbon. The larger ones bore sprigs of plastic holly and red bead berries. Oma had wrapped her gifts in solid, sturdy, flat red paper. She'd used the same paper for every gift I'd ever seen her give, for as long as I could remember. I wondered if she had an endless roll of it stashed somewhere, perhaps under her bed, or if she'd simply found a reliable supplier she could go to whenever she ran out. In a world where everything seemed to be changing, the solid predictable nature of the familiar red paper brought actual tears to my eyes.

"You feeling okay?" Uncle Gary asked, a little gruffly.

"Absolutely," I lied, not wanting to explain that I was crying over Oma's choice of wrapping paper.

Everyone except Oma looked relieved and pretended to be reassured. Oma's eyes glittered, and she wore a dubious expression.

I turned purposefully away from her and handed out all the gifts except those marked for my mother.

"So what do you plan to do with her gifts, Marshall?" Oma asked abruptly, voicing the elephant-shaped question hanging in the room.

Dad looked relieved. "I think I'll store them, maybe in the garage. They'll be there for her if she ever wants them."

I knew exactly the space that waited in the garage: the one recently vacated by the box of family items, a box also intended for but rejected by my mother. I didn't know if there was irony or symmetry in that, but it was certainly a pattern. We took turns opening gifts at a leisurely pace, exclaiming mildly over what we received, until everyone had finished; and there was a sizable mound of crumpled paper and ribbons on the floor.

"It was a good haul," Uncle Gary declared, stroking the tiny salt-and-pepper soul patch he was endeavoring to grow.

All of us nodded in agreement. There seemed to be nothing else to say. My mind flitted to Petra, and I allowed myself to wonder for just a moment whether Christmas was celebrated on Petra. The time difference would cause a problem… How would anyone know when to celebrate? It was too difficult to think simultaneously of Petra and Christmas at home without my mother. My head began to ache. I tried to lock Petra back into the vault at the back of my mind. At 8:57, Oma got up, gathered her handbag and her coat, and headed for the door. It was time to go.

You remember what I said. You let your mother carry her own burdens," she said once more before she left.

"I'll remember, Oma."

The house felt large that night. I wrapped up in a quilt and fell asleep on the bathroom floor, listening to the low hiss of warm air escaping the register.

MOVING ON?

Christmas Day was quiet. Oma stayed home, citing as her reason her "bad circulation," which the doctors called rheumatism. Being out in the cold made the pain in her joints flare up. Old age was turning her into a homebody. Since Opa had died, she'd worn a path in the carpet that ran from her sitting chair near the front window, to the tea kettle, and then to the bathroom and back.

"Is Uncle Gary coming?" I asked Dad, settling in on a barstool to watch him fry eggs.

"Nope. He's spending the day with a woman." He expertly flipped and caught one egg after another with his spatula.

"Is it like a date?" I asked Dad.

"Yeah, I guess so—a pretty serious one, I'd say. It's Christmas with her parents," he answered, turning the sausage.

We ate breakfast at the breakfast bar again. I wondered, idly, how long we would each avoid sitting at the dining room table and sleeping in our own beds. I was sure some sort of therapist who dealt with loss could give us an estimate on that sort of behavior, if we were interested in such a thing or if it really mattered.

"How long has he been dating? Did he tell you when he met her?" I asked.

Dad gave me a blank look. "I know he dates every once in a while. I'm not sure if he told me about this lady or not... First time I realized it was serious was a few weeks ago, when he told he planned to spend Christmas with her."

Obviously, Gary's love life didn't occupy much space in Dad's head.

"Well, good for him," I said, suddenly liking the idea that my uncle might find someone special.

"Yeah, I hope it's a good match, *this* time," Dad said.

This time? Uncle Gary had never, to my knowledge, been married or even seriously involved with a woman before. I decided to leave that stone unturned.

Claire had left us a heat-and-serve baked ham meal with mashed potatoes and the kind of green bean casserole with the crunchy onions on top. We heated and nibbled at the edges of the meal. There was enough food left over to feed us for a week or more. Chump enjoyed more than his fair share. After dinner, we retreated to the living room, each with a new book we'd received at Christmas, with the intention of spending a lazy afternoon reading. It would normally have been my idea of a perfect afternoon, but the rift torn by Mom's absence disrupted it. I pushed Play on the stereo, hoping music would improve things, and Nina Simone's throaty voice filled the room. It was the music Mom tended to play when a case at work was particularly troubling.

I reached for the stereo again, planning to find something more neutral to listen to, but Dad stopped me. "No, leave it," he said. He had his book in hand but wasn't reading it. Instead, he stared out the window down the canyon.

The music pushed me over the edge. There were things that needed to be said, and neither of us was saying them.

"Okay, so what do you want me to do about school? I mean, should I stay here for a while?" I blurted.

Dad gave me another blank look, and I wondered if the number of blank looks he gave had increased or if I'd just been privy to more of them since my mother's absence.

"You? Stay here? Why?" he asked, nonplussed.

"Well, I don't know... because Mom's vanished, and I don't know what's going to happen with... all of that. You will be here alone. And what if she comes back? Or what if she doesn't? Or... I don't know, just..." I was totally flustered. Hot, unexpected tears materialized. Talking with my father about serious things had a way of unraveling me that I had never understood. I hated feeling overwhelmed and unintelligible.

"Kiah, there's nothing you can do here. Absolutely nothing... do you understand me? There's no reason for you to be here. I'll go to work, like I always do. You will go back to school, just as you should. And we will deal with this, like, well... like people do. I don't know how that is exactly, but we'll figure it out. Your mother doesn't want your life to go on hold because of her. She would never want that. Neither do I."

Something hot and angry burst in my chest. "How do you know? It doesn't seem like she was thinking of me or you, at all!"

Dad didn't respond.

"What I mean is... are you sure? You don't want me to stay here, even for the next semester?"

"Why? So you could sit at home and worry about me while I worry about how this is ruining your college career and your life? Does that sound like a good plan?" Dad wasn't a yeller, but the pitch and intensity of his voice was rising. He took a deliberate deep breath and ran his hands through his hair.

"No, I guess that wouldn't help," I admitted.

I watched a thought dawn on him, and he cocked his head slightly to one side. "You don't feel like you need to stay home for a while, for yourself, I mean... do you? Are you too worried to do school right now?"

"Oh no. I'm fine. I mean, fine enough to go to school. I don't need to stay for me," I assured him. It was the honest truth. Being at school sounded a lot less stressful than being at home.

Dad looked relieved. "Good. I knew you were strong enough to handle this." He had abandoned his book to the floor.

"That's what Mom said, before she sent me off to school, you know. She told me how strong I was and that I could handle anything. I thought she was giving me the 'college jitters' pep talk. Maybe she was trying to get me ready for... this," I said, throwing my hands in the air.

"What else did she say?" Dad asked, his curiosity piqued.

"Well, she said I was strong and getting stronger. She said she hadn't given me as much as I deserved, and she shouldn't have hidden God from me or something like that." I glanced in Dad's direction, trying to gauge his response.

"Oh yeah?" His eyebrows went up, and he leaned forward a little. I had his full attention at that point which was rare. "God, huh? She doesn't talk about God often."

"No, she doesn't. She's weird about it. Why is that?"

"I don't know, for sure, Kiah. I really only heard your mother talk about God one time. It was when I first began to date her... She had these sad bouts, like I said before. Really sad. At first I thought maybe a man had left her, and she was having trouble getting over it. She refused to talk about it, though. She got really quiet whenever I asked her about it, so I stopped asking. Then it was on Christmas Day actually, come to think of it... I was supposed to take her to meet my parents. I went to her apartment to pick her up. All the doors and windows were open, and it was freezing. I thought maybe something bad had happened to her. I ran inside and looked through the apartment for her. I found her on the floor in her closet in her pajamas, holding an old box with her name on it. She was just sitting there, teeth chattering, and crying. I asked her if she was okay, and what was going on."

"Did she tell you?" I asked; my heart thumped wildly. I was pretty sure I knew exactly what box she had been holding.

"She didn't really answer... just looked past me, out the window. So I asked her if it was about a man, maybe a man that left her, and she looked right at me and said no. She said she was the one that did the leaving. She said she had made the choice to leave him. I asked her who he was... whom she had left..., and she said the strangest thing. She said, 'It wasn't a man I left, Marshall. It was God. I left God.' I had no idea what to say. I'd never heard her talk about God before. I still don't understand what she meant. She left *God...*? And she didn't say it in the way people usually say those sorts of things... as if they don't believe in their religion anymore. She really seemed heartbroken, as if she had left a lover."

She had, I thought. I bit my tongue.

A piece of the puzzle that was my mother fell into place for me. Dad was right. She was heartbroken. She loved Dhia, and He loved her. Dad couldn't possibly understand. To him, God was an ethereal concept he didn't put much stock in. To Mom, Dhia had probably held her heart, and yet she chose to leave Him. *Why?*

"What did you do?" I asked.

"I took the box from her. I had to pry it out of her hands and put it on the shelf. I picked her up off the floor, and I hugged her, tried to warm her up. She was ice-cold. I told her it was okay, that I loved her, and that she didn't have to worry about any of it anymore. And after a while, I thought it really *was* okay. I mean, eventually, she snapped back to herself. She got her clothes on, we closed the doors and windows, and I took her to my parents' house for Christmas dinner like we planned. She seemed fine after that. A few months later, I asked her to marry me. I thought I could make her happy. I didn't want her to ever feel like she did that day on her closet floor. I thought I could do that for her."

Dad looked sad and tired.

"It wasn't your job, you know, Dad. To make her happy."

"Yeah, maybe. It felt like it was, though. I obviously failed at it."

"If you failed, then I failed. She left us both," I reminded him.

Dad didn't respond to that. I don't think he really heard me. He returned to staring out the window.

"I never understood her. Your mother was always a mystery to me. She still is," he finally said.

I wondered how my father would feel if he knew his daughter was developing the same kind of feelings for the divine that he had tried to rescue his wife from. I decided to save the introduction of my own belief in Dhia for a better time.

"Dad, the day she talked to me about God, she told me something else too. She said she wasn't as strong as I thought she was and that I wasn't a child anymore—that I would be seeing the world through different eyes. Maybe it was her way of saying everything that needed to be said. Maybe it was her way of telling me good-bye."

"Maybe." He ran his hands through his hair so that it stood on end once again.

"Net-net?" he asked, signaling he'd reached about all the talking he could take. *Net-net* had always been his way of wrapping up a conversation, weighing the pros and cons and deciding on a course of action.

"Net-net? Mom's gone no matter what. So I go to school, you go back to work, and we see what happens from there," I said.

"It's a plan, then," he agreed.

The ringing of the telephone awakened me the next morning. I had been sleeping on the couch just outside my father's open office door when I heard my father answer the call. The local newspaper had caught wind of our family crisis. Dad gave them the bare facts and declined any further interviews, in person or over the phone. He promised to phone them in the event of her return. I think his fingers might have been crossed. He didn't plan to withhold the basic facts from the media, but he certainly didn't plan to play the media game or ride any of the media circus rides.

I noted the clear blue sky outside and felt the ache of the empty pasture outside the window. It would have been a perfect morning for a ride. Dresden, however, was miles away. Lucky him—he would undoubtedly be sleeping in. Chump was doing the potty dance at my feet. I pulled on a pair of sweats and took him outside. He liked morning walks and eagerly led the way down the long drive toward the mailbox, lifting his leg at random intervals up and down both sides of the driveway to mark the property as his own. I popped open the mailbox to find bills, grocery store flyer, more bills, and credit card offers, and then froze. Postcard. A printed sketch of potted violets on the front of the card and a simple message on the back.

"I'm doing well. Don't worry. I wish you the best."

It was signed, simply, *Lisette.*

A surge of anger welled up inside me. *Wow, Mom, really? You couldn't even fill up the entire postcard?* My fingers clutching the card were sweaty, and my heart thudded at my ribcage. The card was postmarked a few days before Christmas in Seattle.

I ran back to the house and showed the card to Dad, who took it, tight-lipped, and read it thoroughly before speaking.

"That was warm and newsy," he said dryly. Somehow, the fact that we had both responded with sarcasm was a comfort.

"It doesn't really change much, does it?"

"No, it more confirms what we are doing is the right course of action, I'd say," he replied, tucking the postcard into the top drawer of his desk.

"She left a long time ago, right, Dad? I mean, in her heart?"

"A long time ago... if her heart was ever really here at all," he confirmed.

Not long after, the owls arrived. Once I'd given them that name in my mind, it stuck; I only hoped not to slip up at some point and call them that aloud. Judy and Claire set about scrubbing toilets and organizing leftovers. Millie and I made popcorn and box brownies and settled ourselves on the couch. We talked about cute boys, creepy boys, tough classes, egotistical professors, crazy roommates. It still took a great deal of effort for me to stay focused on her words, and I didn't have many anecdotes to contribute. I sensed an ever-widening gap between us. The percentage of things going through my head that I felt I could actually share with her was so small.

"I'm sorry, Millie. I guess I'm just not much fun right now," I said, after the third time in an hour that I had to ask her to repeat her question.

"Well, your mother made casserole, left a sticky note, then skipped the country. I think that entitles you to be a little out to lunch," Millie responded.

"So I'm out to lunch, huh? It's that bad?"

"Yeah, it's pretty much like hanging out with a cheese grater. Do you want to talk about her—your mother? Maybe talk about how you feel about her leaving?" she suggested.

"Sure, I'd love to. *If* I knew how I felt. I just sort of feel... nothing. Not really mad, not sad, not happy, obviously... I'm just sort of blah. Cold. I've felt really cold ever since I got home. A lot colder than usual. That doesn't make any sense, though, does it?"

"No. None whatsoever," Millie agreed.

"Well, that's all I've got."

"Did you ask God about it—about your mom? I mean, you're a Christian now, right? God's supposed to be good at helping people handle stuff like this."

"So I hear. I've talked to God a little, I guess. Not enough. I'm not sure what to ask Him. I'm not even sure I want to ask for her to come back."

"Seriously?" Millie looked surprised.

"It's not that I don't want her here. It's just that I'm starting to wonder… what if she was able to be happy somewhere else, in a way she wasn't able to be happy here? What if she sort of needs a new start? What if she really can't love us right now? Not that she doesn't want to, but maybe she just *can't*. Maybe she needs something she can handle better… a place where she's not a lawyer or a mother or a wife."

"Well, maybe. But the least she could do is be decent about it. Get a divorce like normal people do. Pack up. Move to the beach in Italy and send postcards every few months. People do that all the time." Millie wasn't sympathetic.

"Then she would have to deal with the scrutiny of others. That's not something she's cut out for," I said.

"But she's strong, right? She's a lawyer, so she has to be."

"You might think so. I don't think it works that way, though. Before I left for school, she told me that she wasn't as strong as I thought she was. She told me I was stronger and that she was proud of me. I thought she was just being sentimental. I guess she was really saying good-bye."

Millie thought about that for a while, then sighed. "Okay, so let's get real… Why won't you sleep in your room anymore? I keep seeing your blankets and clothes behind the couch. Is it because you miss her?"

"No! I wish." I snorted. "That would be more classy. I think I'm being a rebel actually. She bought my favorite fabric softener, washed my bedding with it, and made up my bed. As if she was doing me a favor, you know? Like she was taking care of me? I kind of felt like, if I accepted that as enough… it would be a lie. It gives me the creeps, thinking of sleeping in that bed. It feels like it's not my room anymore, like she stole it from me. Besides, I'm giving up fabric softener for good. It's just chemicals. Did you know that most of the world doesn't even dry their laundry in machines?"

"Wow. That's deep." Millie nibbled the last hard edge of a brownie and refused to follow me down my bunny trail. "So you aren't going to sleep up there *ever* again?"

I shrugged. "I don't know. I guess if I feel differently about it someday, then I will."

"I leave for school tomorrow," Millie announced. "The flights this week were cheaper than next week. When do you leave?"

"Three days."

"You ready?"

Was I? "Yeah, I guess. There's nothing else I can do here. I'm not really excited about going back to classes, though. I'll have to find my brain somewhere for that."

Not to mention the Rock, I added silently. Just thinking about Petra made my eyes cross.

I watched Millie pick popcorn kernels out of her gumline and insert another video. I felt guilty for wondering when she would stop babysitting me and my crisis and go home. The movie ended, and there was nothing more to do or so, so she left. We both promised to write more often than we had during the first half of the year, though we both knew we wouldn't. Our friendship had been based on hanging together and discussing life as a theory. That connection was broken; I felt it. I wasn't even sure it was my mother's fault. Millie and I were growing apart. Another loss.

I changed into my pajamas, said good night to Dad, rolled into my favorite quilt on the couch, and drifted into the strangest dream I'd ever had.

THE DEVICE

It was nighttime in the dream. An enormous building, windows darkened, loomed large ahead of us. It looked almost abandoned from the outside, except that the spongy grass was evenly clipped and the walkways were clear and clean. My companion strode past the locked front doors and hurried around the corner of the building. I jogged a little just to keep up with her. *How does she walk so fast when her legs are shorter than mine?* We passed a second door, rounded another corner, then a third, then a fourth, *how large is this place?*—before we arrived at what seemed like a service entrance. My companion pressed a small button to the left of the door, and although I heard no bell or buzzer, a man answered. He wore a solid gray uniform with a white patch on one should that bore three solid purple bars. The uniform's formality, or lack thereof, landed it somewhere between "surgical scrubs" and "military officer's uniform."

His eyes widened in recognition when he saw my companion. *Was it respect that registered on his face?* Uncertainty, definitely. Maybe even a touch of fear. *Was my companion scary?* I looked at her again. No—a touch severe maybe, but not scary. Her face was set, calm but determined. If she recognized the doorman, it didn't show. The man stepped backward quickly to let us pass, then pulled the door shut securely behind us. I could see the outline of large overhead lights lining the ceiling above us, but none were lit. Sections of dim rope lights lit as we passed, lighting our path as we walked, then winked out behind us—*economical.*

The hallways were sterile and white. We passed multiple closed doors, some with windows, some without. I was curious as to what was inside the rooms, but there wasn't time to snoop. My companion, seemingly sure of her destination, was rushing headlong into the bowels of the building. We reached a T at the end of an interminable hallway and turned left. My companion picked up the pace even more. I followed, and we hit the set of double doors almost at a run. We stood blinking for a moment in the bright light, waiting for our pupils to adjust. We were in a medical unit of some sort. The upper half of each wall was glass, and glass doors led to rooms on our right and left. The front rooms were empty. Several medical personnel ran past toward the sounds of someone in a great deal of pain and distress. My pulse quickened. We followed into the hotbed of commotion: a large glass room, with a solitary hospital bed in its center. No less than ten people, all in gray uniforms identical to that of the doorkeeper, occupied the room. The man on the bed writhed and screamed. He was young, perhaps in his twenties, his dark hair plastered to his forehead. Bluish veins popped up in ropes along his forearms. No one, absolutely no one, was touching or trying to help the man. They all looked helpless, clueless, almost afraid. My companion pushed through a few bystanders and approached the young man.

"Kiah, come over here. Stand on the opposite side of the bed from me," my companion commanded. Apparently, she knew my name. I stepped forward and joined her at the bedside. She took hold of the man's hand and brought her face close to his, speaking to him in a language I didn't recognize. I took hold of his other hand, and he gripped my fingers tightly. He may have been in pain, but his strength seemed to be holding up just fine. My fingers immediately began to purple.

One of the gray-uniformed men stepped forward in an authoritarian manner. He was tall and angular, with a tense jaw. "Who are these people?" he said, pointing at my companion and me. They can't just walk in here and take over? They have no idea what we are dealing with here!"

"And you do?" my companion interrupted him, then returned her attention to the patient. He was still yelling, panting, and writhing, but was paying attention to her voice. His intensity and volume had decreased a few notches.

"He could be contagious!" the man continued. "Or incendiary!"

"Leave her alone, Mark. She has privileges," a woman's voice said from the back of the room.

"What kind of privileges? She's not even wearing the uniform!"

"She's not military," the woman's voice continued. "She has color clearance."

"And what color is that?"

"Black," she answered.

Mark closed his mouth and took a step back. He searched the room for the woman attached to the voice and found her.

"Really?"

The woman, a middle-aged woman with a steel-gray bob, confirmed with a nod. "I need everyone to clear this room except for Shannon and myself," she demanded.

I glanced around, trying to figure out who Shannon was, but not everyone headed for the door as directed. A few, obviously ruffled and unsure what was going on, remained stubbornly motionless.

"He *is* incendiary, if that helps you decide," my companion informed the stragglers. That did it. They cleared the room quickly, leaving the woman with the gray bob, and a mousy man crouched behind her, whom I assumed to be Shannon.

The woman approached my companion.

"What do you need, Chelsea?" she whispered, as if whatever was incendiary in or about the patient might be voice activated. I'd been hoping that my companion, apparently named Chelsea, had been exaggerating about the "incendiary" part; but Gray Bob seemed to believe her.

"Five milligrams Prev. to start. I want to take the edge off but not snow him... in case we need to ask him some questions. I have no idea why he's so far from the device base and still alive. Usually these devices trigger within twenty-five miles. I'm guessing, by his level of pain, that it has, at the very least, begun to deteriorate."

370

Gray Bob nodded and gestured to Shannon, who had heard the request.

"Have the team put up the drapes as well," she added. Shannon scurried out the door.

"And you are?" Grey Bob asked. She was speaking to me.

"Kiah," I answered.

"Phyllis," she said.

"She's an empath," Chelsea added.

"You sensing anything, then?" Phyllis asked me.

"No, not yet."

The only thing I sensed was the numbness in my rapidly cooling, purple fingers and the sweat at the base of my spine. The man on the bed hadn't lessened his grip on my hand. I forced my mind past my fears over the word *incendiary*, mentally screening out the large dark fire-resistant drapes that the other uniformed staff members were hanging all around the outside of our room. I refocused my attention on the patient. Shannon returned with a few vials of medication, and a large bore intramuscular needle.

"He has a device implanted. It's designed to deteriorate or detonate as he moves away from the base, the home device it's paired with. It's supposed to keep slaves from running away," Chelsea explained. "Help me roll him."

I wriggled my hand out of his, with some difficulty, and grasped his opposite arm, rolling him toward me, as Chelsea helped from her side of the bed. His rigid body was rather easy to move, but he screamed louder with motion. His head pressed up against my shoulder. I held his back firmly as Shannon delivered the medicine into his thigh. I listened to his breathing and watched him for signs that his pain was easing.

After a few minutes with no change, Chelsea nodded to Shannon again. "Ten more please."

Shannon drew up another dose and delivered it. This time, his yelps grew quieter; and his arm muscles, under my hand, relaxed a little. I nodded at Shannon, and we rolled him back onto his back. He tensed and hissed but didn't scream as he had before. Progress. Chelsea remained calm, but I saw a few beads of sweat on her temple that mirrored the beads of sweat on her patient's face. She began to speak to him in the strange language again. He answered through his teeth. I desperately wished I could understand what they were saying.

"It's a J7," Chelsea said as if that should mean something to me, "meaning surgery is the best option. The device can be safely removed, but it has to be done in this room. It's not safe to move him. The move would be too risky. The magnetics in the building could trigger it… Hey, how did he get here?" Chelsea interrupted herself.

"Walked in," Phyllis said.

"Walked?" Chelsea asked incredulously. "How did he manage that? How did he get to this building?"

Phyllis shrugged. "You now know everything we know. I hoped maybe you would be able to tell us how he got here."

"Wow, okay. Do you have a surgeon who can do this? Now? Before further deterioration damages his organs?" Chelsea continued.

"General surgeon?" Phyllis drummed the fingers of her left hand on her right arm. It was an odd habit. It made me wonder if she was left-handed.

"Yes."

"Yes. His name is Mark Meade. You met him a few moments ago…" Phyllis pointed toward the hallway.

"Mr. Bedside Manner?" she muttered.

"I'll get him," Shannon volunteered. He fled the room, not waiting for permission.

"Will he live?" Phyllis asked Chelsea quietly.

"I don't know," Chelsea responded. Her facial expression was neither hopeful nor despondent. She began to speak to him again in hushed tones, and his eyes flew open and darted back and forth in fear. He grabbed my hand and hers and asked her a question that I didn't understand. She answered it with a single foreign word, and tears leaked from the corners of his eyes.

Just then, Mark Meade reentered the room.

"We don't do surgery in patient rooms." He addressed Chelsea in a condescending tone, as if she were a child.

"You do today," Chelsea responded.

"It's against policy." Meade rolled his eyes and flexed his jaw muscles again.

"You'll remove this device now while I'm still here, or it will deteriorate to the point that it *will* explode on its own, inside this man's rotting corpse. You can't take him out of here, dead or alive, without risking that. So today you *will* do surgery, here. I will assist you, and then you will never ever speak of this to anyone, ever again. Is that clear?" Chelsea's eyes flashed, and I felt the urge to blurt, "Yes, ma'am," but caught myself.

"Yes, ma'am." Meade echoed my thoughts aloud.

In rather short order, the room was transformed into a surgical suite. Pale yellow drapes went up just inside the solid black fire-resistant curtains, dampening the sounds and voices—giving the room a soft Easter-like medical danger zone ambiance. Phyllis started two IV lines: one in the man's left hand, the other in his right forearm, holding tension on the ropy veins to keep them from rolling as she penetrated them with the needles. Shannon set up IV pumps and tubing, then started a sedative drip. The patient was beginning to stir but stilled as the medicine began to flow, his eyes became glassy. Chelsea kept talking to him, stroking his arm, until he stilled completely and lost consciousness. Then everyone seemed to move at once. A breathing tube was quickly inserted. Shannon handed me a pair of scissors, and we cut every stitch of clothing from the patient's body. It was loose, ragged, dirty clothing that didn't look modern or familiar. Someone carted it away in a large burn bag. Chelsea set up a basin with hot water and strong-smelling antiseptic soap, and we scrubbed the man from head to toe. He had accumulated what looked like dirt and sweat from several hard, shower-free days, but he wasn't filthy. His nails were clipped short; his hair was relatively healthy. We worked to retrieve a few pieces of glass we found imbedded in his neck, shoulder, and scalp, scrubbing the ragged skin and quickly applying bandages. If we were going to open him up in a nonsterile environment, the least we could do was get him as clean as possible first. Some of the wounds were large enough to warrant a few stitches, but that would have to wait for later.

Chelsea briefed Dr. Meade in the corner of the room while we worked. Meade had calmed down a bit and was begrudgingly accepting Chelsea's authority. A tall Chinese woman arrived with a push cart of anesthesia medications and equipment. She took her place at the head of the bed. Chelsea passed me a few small vials of oil and sticks of the familiar antibacterial incense.

"In a bit, you can go out and get the incense going just outside the door... Don't ask permission. Just do it," she advised.

"Where should we apply the oil?"

"Every inch of him, even if it takes the whole bottle—and don't breathe deeply."

I donned a mask, grabbed a vial of oil, and set to work. Shannon and the surgical techs who had joined the party wore questioning expressions, and Dr. Meade began to bluster once again. I could feel the tension in the room rise. Oiling surgical patients was almost more than they could take.

Phyllis addressed Dr. Meade. "Don't question it, Mark. Just go with it."

He glowered at Chelsea, who offered no explanation. She pulled a set of instruments from her backpack and began arranging them on a rolling tray, then ducked under the drapes into the corner of the room near the sink. She held the drapes up and waited for someone to join her. "Perhaps your assistants can help me scrub in, Dr. Meade?"

Meade nodded at his surgical techs, and they scurried under the drape, gladly drawing as far away from the overpowering oil fumes as possible. Pine notes that leant strongly toward turpentine, mixed with the unmistakable smell of the purple cosh fruit. My eyes watered as I rubbed the oil into the patient's skin, making sure to apply extra over his abdomen. My fingers tingled to the point of pain as I neared his abdomen. I was pretty sure I could precisely pinpoint the location of the implant by sensation.

"I need a Sharpie," I called out. The nurse nearest me jumped a bit, but no one moved. "Sharpie, you know... permanent marker? Someone has one, right?" I repeated, a little louder and more insistent this time. My abrasiveness was effective.

"Of course, yes, of course," said the woman nearest me. She hurried off and returned in short order with a permanent marker. I wiped the oil from the patient's abdomen with a sterile cloth as best I could and ran my fingers over his skin, relieved that only I could see the blue glow. The implant was too deep to palpate, but I could sense the edges of it by the pain and tingling in my fingers. I marked the edges of what I sensed on his skin, then went back to the center of my oddly shaped sketch. There was one particular spot that sent waves of dizziness and nausea straight up through my fingers into my gut and head. I gasped involuntarily and didn't linger there. I drew a careful circle around that point and one other particularly trouble-some spot near the lower margin of the shape. It looked much like a child's first submarine sketch.

Chelsea returned in her surgical gown, resembling a five-year-old playing dress-up. Her surgical gown, much too large for her small frame, was wrapped twice and secured tight around her waist. She examined my drawing. "Yep, that's what they look like. Good work. You sure there's two hot spots, not just one?" she asked.

"Definitely two, but this one's much stronger," I said, pointing to the slightly larger circle.

"That makes perfect sense."

I was glad it made sense to someone.

"This will make it much easier and safer to remove. Get dressed and light the incense…It's a screen for the rest of building. Then hurry back. I need you in here," she commanded.

A screen? Against what? I wondered.

I did my best to look confident and not confused.

"You know my skill set, right?" I didn't want to loudly announce my shortcomings, but surgery was something I knew next to nothing about.

"Yes, I do," she confirmed, catching my eye, acknowledging my unspoken concern.

It would obviously be another high-stakes situation where I knew very little and would need to fly by the seat of my pants… this time, with multiple sets of eyes scrutinizing my every move. My gut rebelled, and I took a few deep breaths, trying to dispel the cramps.

Phyllis gestured at me to follow her, which I did, out into the hall. A table just outside the door was set up with a small marble slab and a clamp.

"For the sticks. Will it work?" Phyllis asked me.

"Yes."

I set up the incense and lit it. We ducked into a small room across the way. She handed me an old gray uniform with the triple-barred white-and-purple patch barely hanging on to the left shoulder. I dressed silently and quickly, then scrubbed in, scouring my skin until the entire area from hand to forearm was the appropriate shade of red. Phyllis helped me into to a surgical gown, then cleared the way back across the hall so I could stay sterile. Some of the smoke had found its way through the vents into the room. It followed the air currents across the ceiling like a wispy, opaque river.

Chelsea had a bowl of oil set up on the table beside her instruments and three sets of Petra gloves, the thin translucent ones that seemed almost invisible. "Glove up and dip in," she ordered.

I applied the gloves, keenly aware of the eight sets of eyes that followed my every move. I dipped my hands into the oil, coating the gloves. The gloves were so thin that I could feel the feel the warming effect of the liquid as if it were directly on my skin.

"You too, Dr. Meade," Chelsea directed.

"I think I'll stick to conventional methods," Dr. Meade barked, still searching for somewhere, anywhere, to put his foot down.

Idiot, I thought. *When would he learn?*

"Suit yourself." Chelsea's voice was even and calm but with a slight edge to it that warned that her patience was wearing thin. Something told me I didn't want to be around if it wore all the way through. "I must tell you, though, that the material in *your* gloves will interact with the chemicals in the device inside this man, melt the material into your skin, and put you at high risk of disease transmission. There are biological components of this device mediated directly by the properties of the oil I've provided, as well as the incense burning near the vent system in the hall. If you choose to use your own gloves and methods, I can guarantee second-, if not third-, degree burns; and we would need to immediately isolate you for a period of not less than three months to insure the safety of the others on your team and in your community. Are you still intent on employing conventional methods?" she asked. Her eyebrows rose, disappearing under the elastic edge of her surgical cap.

"No. Considering the information you've provided, I think your methods might be best. Perhaps you could be more forthcoming with your rationale, in the future?" A mottled flush rose from Meade's collar up toward his taut jawline. I wondered if his teeth might someday crack under the constant pressure of his jaw muscles.

"If I take the time to explain everything you don't currently know about this patient, this device, and my methods... the patient will expire in the interim. You'll need to trust me and follow my lead, or we will lose this patient and endanger your staff. I've been incredibly patient with you thus far, but we have very little wiggle room once we begin the procedure. I need to know now if you are willing to work with me or if you insist on continuing to work against me—in which case, we need to call in another surgeon immediately."

The room stood still. Meade's flush shot to his hairline. He looked very much like a walking beet, a character from that popular children's show in which vegetables walk, talk, and wear clothes.

"I understand you fully, ma'am. It's not necessary to call someone else in. I'm prepared to proceed." Meade climbed decisively aboard Chelsea's boat and under her authority.

"Good," she said, pointing to the gloves. He donned the gloves and dipped them into the oil. He cast a glance her direction, startled at the sensation of the oil through the gloves.

"You can trust me, sir," Chelsea said without looking at him.

"No one leaves this room, from this point on, until we are finished. If you want to go, go now."

Everyone looked at each other, their looks communicating silently... *You going to go? No? Me neither. I'm good.* I don't know if fear of looking like a coward or pure unadulterated curiosity kept their feet planted. Maybe both.

Fourteen minutes. It had taken only fourteen minutes to prep the room and the patient for surgery. It was time to begin.

Chelsea directed. I palpated. Meade cut. Layer after layer of skin and then tissue were carefully dissected. Chelsea stressed to Dr. Meade that we couldn't afford to nick the device. Chelsea asked me after each subsequent cut to confirm the precise location of the "hot spots" to see if the device had moved. "They are generally stationary, but every once in a while, they flip," she explained.

The device was housed in the peritoneal cavity, outside the intestines, fortunately. Dr. Meade teased away the last layer of fatty tissue, exposing the device, and everyone leaned in to take a peek. It wasn't what I expected. It looked rather like a lopsided lavender egg with its shell worn thin in several places.

"That's just the capsule," Chelsea explained. "We need to keep it as intact as possible. Kiah? We need your fingers again."

My poor fingers were aching. They wanted nothing to do with the lavender egg, but I overruled their protests and ran them over the smooth surface. It was a thinner covering than I expected. I could feel the angles and edges of the device itself underneath.

"Here," I said.

The pulse through my left hand was strong enough to make me jump. Chelsea marked the spot with a black dot. I found, and Chelsea marked, the second hot spot as well. It was toward the lower margin of the egg, exactly where it had been on my initial drawing. I took a small amount of satisfaction at that.

Chelsea reached in and gently lifted the egg out of the patient and deposited it in a large silver basin the tech's had prepared. There was one hole in the device cover from, which a silvery fluid was leaking. Chelsea wasn't pleased at that.

"It explains the pain," she said, pouring oil over the device and into the patient's open abdominal cavity. Dr. Meade began to speak, either to protest, or to ask a question, but thought better of it. "He will most likely have pain in his belly for some time, from the leakage. There doesn't seem to be any permanent damage, however."

"Do you feel anything else, Kiah?" Chelsea asked, pointed to the patient's open belly.

I inserted my hands gingerly, "looking" for trouble areas with my fingers. "Here, it's very cold," I said. Chelsea dabbed oil there, and I moved on. Some of the tissues made my fingers cold; some made them tingle as the device itself had. By the time I'd located the last of the trouble areas, the smell of oil and surgery in the room was almost unbearable. I had seen several people excuse themselves, ducking under the curtain into the corner to escape the fumes, only to be drawn back moments later by curiosity.

"Okay, Dr. Meade, go ahead and close," Chelsea directed. "Kiah, join me." She rolled the cart that held the tub and the device away from the bed and stabilized it against the wall.

"Grab my instruments," she said. I realized then that Chelsea hadn't yet used her own instruments. I rolled her tray to her. Several medical staff members not assisting Dr. Meade with the patient edged close, trying to catch a glimpse of the device. Apparently, it was of more interest to them than the patient. They'd seen patients before.

Chelsea took a pair of scissors, blunt edged on the bottom but extremely sharp, and cut through the lavender skin of the egg. She carefully avoided the hot spots. The covering peeled away easily. The appearance of the device itself was rather anticlimactic. It very much resembled an old car part but made of a metal I'd never seen before. It was steel blue with coppery orange areas that looked like engine oil spills in parking lot puddles.

"These, here… are the capsules that house the biological material." She pointed to the "hot spots." The capsules resembled large brown antibiotic capsules. Even looking at them made me horrified and nauseous for reasons I didn't understand.

"Can you feel them?" she asked.

"What do you mean?"

"I mean, you seem to sense something about them. Is it just the coldness you mentioned?"

"No, they don't feel cold. They make my fingers tingle, make me a little dizzy, and nauseous. They turn my stomach actually," I said under my breath, not wanting to announce and then explain the sensations to anyone else.

"Lucky you," Chelsea said, though not in the sarcastic voice I expected. Her voice dropped to barely audible as well, and I leaned in to hear her. "It would make this job a lot easier if I could sense them.

So, for future reference, don't cut into the capsules. Ever. You are a Blue, so it might not kill you, but would most likely kill everyone else in the nearby vicinity. I wasn't kidding Meade about that part."

I hadn't thought she *was* kidding. She didn't seem like much of a joker.

"Future reference?" I asked, drawing her back to her earlier statement. "Should I expect to be dealing with these in the future?"

"I imagine you will," Chelsea said. "The Kress from section 14B implanted them. Write that down, section 14B. You need to remember it."

I gestured upward with my empty hands. I had nothing to write with, or on.

She threw me the Sharpie. "Write it on your arm."

I dutifully scribbled 14B on the inside of my wrist.

"Section 14B is a large city. Massive really. I'm not sure what the Kress even call it. It's basically the Hong Kong of the Kress world. Fewer people, obviously, but relatively speaking... Anyway, we've run into a few of these devices now, and I expect there will be more. They are very effective."

She furrowed her brow, perhaps shutting out memories regarding the destructive capacity of the device before us. "This man is lucky. I have no idea why the device didn't detonate when he left base range. By the way, the smoke from the incense combats the bacteria inside the capsules in the device but also makes it less likely to explode."

"Explode?" I asked, drawing back a little. Chelsea grabbed my shoulder and brought me back into range of her whisper.

"Well, yes. If they explode when they are inside someone, there's usually not a fire. Usually. But if they explode in the open air, they create quite the fireball."

"How do we keep that from happening here, today?" I asked. My own stomach had dropped through the floor, and I was impressed that Chelsea was still speaking as casually as she was.

"Glad you asked. Here," she said, pointing to small hole in the top of the egg.

"It's a lock. Here's the key." She handed me a long handled metal object with three protruding, distinctly shaped prongs. "You just insert and turn."

"It's that easy?" I asked, hesitant to touch the device.

"It's that easy. The Kress don't want to make it any harder on themselves than they have to. They have to dismantle them once their slaves die."

Of course, I thought and shuddered.

I inserted the key and turned it. I heard a small click; and chamber at the base of the device emptied black fluid into the basin, which hissed and flared slightly when it hit the oil.

"So that's it. Now they just need to bury it."

"Dr. Meade!" Chelsea called out too close to my ear, leaving it ringing.

Meade had finished closing the wound. He hurried over to Chelsea.

"This needs to be buried. Deep. I'll deal with the bacterial capsules myself. But the device is harmless now."

Meade eyed it, as if he wasn't so sure.

"Got it?" Chelsea prompted him.

"Oh yeah, of course. I'll have someone deal with that right away," he responded.

Chelsea retrieved a small rubbery pouch from her instrument kit and slipped the biological capsules out of their nests in the device and into the pouch.

"Each of these capsules contains a different biohazard. Bacteria, most likely, but it could be viral." She sealed the edges of the pouch with fluid from what looked like an eye drop container, and the seam in the pouch effectively disappeared.

"Why aren't Blues affected by the contents?" I asked.

Chelsea shrugged. "Beats me. His protection, I guess. I'll take the capsules back to Petra with me. There's a depository for them at the village."

"What do we do about him?" I asked, pointing at our patient. I wasn't sure if we were supposed to stay with him, take him somewhere, or leave him here for someone else to sort out.

"I was sort of hoping you would know," Chelsea said, chewing her lower lip.

"Me? How would I know? I don't even have a clue where we are!" I exclaimed too loudly. The medical staff, busily dismantling the makeshift surgery suite, stopped to stare at me.

"Ssshh!" Chelsea said. "It's not always prudent to announce your knowledge gaps." She grabbed my sleeve and helped me out of my surgical gown. I returned the favor, helping her out of hers as well. We de-gloved and washed our hands, applying another layer of the stinky oil for good measure.

"Besides, what makes you think I know where we are?" she whispered.

"You don't? Well, you marched right in here like you owned the place!"

"I was listening to the Lord, and he said, 'Hurry, go this way,' so I did. But he seems to have stopped giving obvious directions at this point. I don't know if you've noticed, but He's prone to doing that from time to time."

I had noticed.

"How did you know my skill set? Or that I was supposed to come with you?" I asked.

She pointed upward.

"How did you know to come with me?" she asked.

"Same," I answered.

"Well, I'm getting nothing at this point," she said, chewing her lip again.

"I'm not getting anything either." I had drawn a measure of comfort out of my supposition that Chelsea knew exactly what was going on and what we were supposed to do next. Now I realized it was false security. No... not false. Misplaced. Dhia knew what was going on, and we were listening to Him. So really, nothing had changed except for the fact that He'd gone radio silence. I had no doubt that He would produce an answer in *His* time. I just wasn't currently comfortable with His timeline.

"Well, I guess we better start praying a little harder then," I asserted.

"Yeah," she agreed. With her hands on her hips, she started toward the still intubated, unconscious patient.

I tried to walk forward, to follow her, but my feet were stuck fast to the floor. I tried to stick my hands out for balance, but they wouldn't move. I felt myself falling but couldn't make a sound. My mouth was glued shut. I fell slowly to the left, mentally bracing myself for the moment my head hit the concrete, but that moment never came. I tumbled straight through the concrete as if it were a shadow, headfirst, twisting, turning, past several more floors of the building. I felt nothing but saw everything: flashes of sunrise in the window, then close-ups of flooring and subflooring materials, carpet, desks, beds, cupboards... on and on for several floors until I landed facedown in the darkness.

TO WAIT, TO SEE

To crest, to warp, to slide, to dive,
eyes wide, ears pricked
Breathe on me, and I will see
How many more colors are there,
coasting far and fast, that I have missed?

        —Show me

You're taller, further, wider, lighter,
and I've fallen back

        —Lift me, throw me, push me
        Knead me, and I will bend
        Feed me, I will trust

Back and forth, many times, yet still listening
Forsaken rocks torn
Beauty melted in the suns
Indeed seen, and fully known
Broken? No, bent—to fit 1,000 reasons

    —There's no one known deeper, farther, wider

Bread cast on the water…

Cast and see, seek not
If it feeds 1,000 fish and doesn't return, it means the same
Needs: sucking, pulling, sour!
The Earth pulls, spoilt, rancid, at the feet,
Draining

 —Look up

Fallacious need! See, know…
Blow away the shell and say aloud its name!
Answers sought

 —To understand, or to hear?
   —To speak… no, to hear
  To hear, then to speak

With no guide, falling, yearning
Pieces on the ground glittering, scattered…
Usable. True purpose revealed
—Cast and seek not, there's no truth in it
Wait…
For here is wisdom, solace, grounding
For immer, always, there is a hope
It floats, it is not eaten, murky, lost, bereft, void
Hope rises…
watch, and so, see
Goodness, fresh with tantalizing beauty waits
Truth laughs a clean, calm, real foothold into view
Rise, see, taste, sniff, touch
Have you forgotten?

 —I see you
  —And I you

We
 Thank you

See
    You're all I need
Remember
    Remind me
I Am
    I know
     Hand in hand?
Heart in heart
    Float with me
Always
    Every good and perfect thing… I remember
Just wait
    I am weak

I am strong, I see

To go, just go, farther
To live long, long, long, at lovely feet
To taste true hope: beautiful seeds, fuchsia, melon-sweet, and precious
To linger there, to savor, not to fear
—To remember truth

    Don't leave, stay with me
    Closer, deeper
    Stay solid, tarry
    Breathe on me

ONE FOOT IN FRONT
OF ANOTHER

I awoke to a mild suffocating sensation. I was facedown on the living room couch and freezing. All my blankets were in a tousled pile on the floor beside the couch. I picked my head up, then sat up. Chelsea and the hospital, the patient with the purple egg inside him… had obviously all been part of one of my vivid dreams. I breathed deeply, waiting for the strong scent of oil, incense, and burning tissue to clear my nasal passages. No such luck… *and* there was fuzz on my tongue. I hate that. I tried rolling it from my tongue and spitting it out but was unsuccessful. I decided instead to chase it with a drink of water. My legs felt sore and stiff, and my fingers were very tender. I hoped the lingering effects of the dream would evaporate quickly. *It felt so real.*

I made it to the kitchen by feel and turned on the lamp near the toaster, thrusting my hands under the light in an attempt to figure out why they hurt. A few of the nails on my right hand as well as one on my left were purpling, as if I'd hit them with a hammer. I turned them over. My fingertips were bruised. The skin was sensitive and tingly all the way to my wrists. I lifted my hands to my nose. The scent of the oil was so sharp that it made my eyes water. I cried out in astonishment, then winced, covering my mouth with my forearm, hoping I hadn't woken Dad. My lips tingled where my hands touched them. I listened a moment but heard him snoring. He was still asleep. Chump heard me and hauled himself into the kitchen. He sniffed me, then backed away, offended at the oil scent. He took up his regular kitchen post, staring at the fridge, waiting for snacks to make their appearance.

I headed to the bathroom in fear of what the mirror would tell me. I flicked on the lights and stood for a moment or two with my eyes closed, steeling my nerves. Finally, I opened my eyes. Relief washed over me. No gray uniform. I was wearing the ancient red plaid PJs I'd dug out of my bottom drawer for couch sleeping. I sniffed my hand again, hoping the odor had dissipated. It hadn't. It was still strong enough to sting my eyes and the lining of my nose. I examined my bruised fingers, turning my hands over and over, searching for clues as to how I could have inflicted so much damage to them while asleep in my living room. My heart fluttered when I noticed *14B* scrawled on my wrist in permanent ink. *How had a dream managed to leave me highly scented and physically marked?* It occurred to me that it was possible no one else would be able to smell the strong oil. Perhaps the scent was stubbornly attached to my memory rather than my skin. Chump, however, seemed to notice it. I didn't want to take any chances. I slipped out of my clothes and into the shower where I vigorously scoured my skin with Summer Rose Explosion exfoliating body scrub. It was the most obnoxiously highly perfumed product I could find under the sink. I had hoped it would remove the turpentine scent; instead, it left me smelling like a tarry burnt rose garden.

I checked the clock and returned to the couch. It was 4:00 a.m., but there was no way I would be falling back to sleep. I folded the blankets, sniffing them suspiciously. No new information obtained. My nose was officially overwhelmed. As I combed through the couch cushions, looking for my socks, something "un-socklike" dropped to the floor. I picked it up. It felt like a patch.

You have got *to be kidding me!* My stomach dropped, and I dashed to the bathroom to inspect it in the light. It was indeed a white patch with three solid purple bars. I immediately felt light headed.

Locked knees and narrow stance make a bad combination. I spread my feet apart and bent my knees slightly to combat the wooziness.

"That is expressly against the rules," I gasped, addressing Dhia. I bent at the waist and waited for the stars to clear from my vision.

"Whose rules?" came the quiet but absolutely audible answer.

I jumped, as always.

"Well, your rules… right? Okay, obviously not. You don't break your own rules. So maybe… the Blues' rules, at least? I mean, I didn't even *go anywhere*, Dhia. I was *sleeping*. I understand the dreams… I understand you speak through them. I've gotten used to that… sort of. But actually *going* somewhere in a dream? Is that what I did? Or is this just a gift? Did someone just drop this off and spritz me with stink spray? What in the world does this all mean?" I was trying to yell in a whisper voice so as not to wake Dad. It came out as more of a squeak.

I heard a quiet laugh. Apparently, I was amusing Him. I guess I understood that. I was standing in my bathroom in the middle of the night, squeak-whisper-yelling at my mirror.

The Called, the Blues… always did things the same way though, *right?* Weren't there certain rules? Certain ways of doing things? Things that usually happened in usual order? As bizarre as it got, there were still *some* laws, *right?* It seemed that way anyway. Suddenly I remembered what the old woman, Shae, had said.

"You'll be asked to do things differently than the others. You need to know that. Don't fear it."

Different—*this* was certainly different.

"Okay, Dhia, You are going to tell me what this all means, right?"

There was no answer.

As if your personal time line or opinion makes any sort of difference to the Guy who runs the universe, Adenauer, I chided myself, then added aloud, "In your time, of course, Dhia. In your time."

With shaky hands and sore fingers, I slipped the patch into my pocket.

Now what? I scribbled the highlights of my dream in my journal. Chelsea, Dr. Meade, Three purple bars, 14B… then forced my mind back on track. It was a Thursday morning. An unusually solid bank of fog outside the living room windows gave me the sensation that our house was drifting in desperate need of mooring. I was more than ready to dock and head back to school. Luckily, that was set to happen in just a few days. I didn't know whether I should call the crazy night experience a dream or an excursion. My brain searched wildly for a category and settled on the word *event*. The Triple Purple Bar Event.

Before the event, I'd been emotionally off-kilter, adrift in the fog of my mother's bizarre departure. My brain knew that my purpose hadn't vanished along with my mother, but my heart wasn't convinced. It couldn't see past the loss to what might come next. I'd felt aimless, as if my mother had taken with her my compass, and thus my ability to know true north. I'd always lived in the moment, so when the moment was dark and difficult, it was easy to give in to hopelessness. I had the tendency to suck so completely into my current surroundings that everything and everyone not in attendance slipped away. My parents sent me to summer camp when I was ten years old, and I virtually forgot I had parents while I was there. I remember being greeted by my dog at the front door when I returned, tired and dirty, from several weeks of horses and outdoor crafts. "Oh, yeah! I have a dog! And I like him!" It was a joyful rediscovery.

That crazy dream, that event, lit up the purpose on the horizon beyond the unanswered questions my mother had left with us. Maybe it was the *14B* scrawled on my wrist that had stubbornly survived the Summer Rose Explosion onslaught. Maybe it was the pain in my bruised fingers, especially under my nails. All of it came together to scream: *Move on! There's more ahead! This is only one moment. Don't linger in it!* I pressed my ring finger, which was especially tender, and winced.

"*Your place isn't here. It's time to look forward. It's time to move on.*" It was Dhia's voice, reverberating up, quiet and solid, from deep within my core. The voice of truth echoed my own thoughts, and it was unmistakable. I couldn't help Mom. She had wandered outside my sphere of influence. And... she wasn't my job.

Let your mother carry her own burdens, Oma's voice echoed in my memory.

I couldn't help Dad… That wasn't my job either. I made the decision to get moving again. I didn't plan to stay frozen to the spot where my mother dropped me.

Dad was meeting with a prospective client in town that day. I needed to pack for the trip back to school. My bag had torn on the flight over in the severe turbulence. The airline had taped it shut with bright orange duct tape. I headed for Mom and Dad's room to seek a replacement. Somehow it seemed easier to enter Mom's room than my own. There was an air of submission in sleeping in my own bed, the one my mother had carefully prepared for me. I wasn't willing to submit. But there was an air of rebellion in rifling through *her* closet. *That*, I was willing to take on. Childish? Maybe… but she had abandoned the contents of that room. That made it fair game.

I boldly pushed the door open and entered the room. The bed was perfectly made, the way she'd left it. There was a light accumulation of dust over everything. The clean towels in my parents' bathroom were hung, perfectly even, from their rods. It looked like a hotel room. I mussed one of the towels just for sport. I spotted a small unopened bottle of my mother's favorite facial lotion and opened it, sniffing the milky pink liquid. The smell triggered the memory of my mother's room in a different house, when I was five years old. I remembered standing, mesmerized at her side, watching her remove the black cap from the little bottle. She had poured a small amount into her cupped hand and smoothed the pink privilege over my cheeks with her fingers, avoiding my eyes.

I recapped the bottle, pocketed it, then entered the small walk-in closet. It had been years since I'd actually stood amongst her clothes, but my fingers remembered where the light switch was—on the right hand side, halfway back between the door and the sidewall, behind Mom's lounging cardigans. In the past, Mom's clothing had dominated Dad's in a 4:1 ratio. Sometime in the past few years, my father had moved all vestiges of himself from the space, probably to the closet in the study. Perhaps when I'd left for Scotland? Maybe before? It didn't really matter.

I began to pull items off the top shelf. Boxes of summer clothes, old hats, wrapping paper, summer shoes, boxes of photos… They all hit the floor with a satisfying thump. Scarves, books, trinkets, suitcases, makeup bags… *how many makeup bags does one person need anyway? They must be the type that came free with purchase from the department store makeup counter.* Too soon, all the shelves were disappointingly empty, and I had made a decent-sized pile of flotsam and jetsam in the middle of the closet floor. I found only two suitcases large enough to pack my clothes for the trip back to college: a blue hard-sided case left over from the 1960s and my mother's favorite suitcase—the red one with the butterfly closures… the one I'd been looking for. I dredged it out of the pile and clamored back over the junk and out of the closet. Switching off the light on the way out of the room, I returned to the living room.

While moving my belongings from the battered gray suitcase into my mother's classy red one, I came across Ailsa's journal. Funny how plans changed. I'd hoped to spend my winter break combing the pages for clues to who Ailsa was, or at least clues as to what being Called meant to her. As it turned out, I'd all but forgotten about the journal amidst the turmoil of Mom's abrupt departure.

I was suddenly no longer in the mood to pack.

THE RED DOOR

I abandoned my unfinished packing project on the living room floor, patted the dog, grabbed my car keys from the kitchen counter, and left the house. Halfway into town, my little car and I dropped out of the fog and into the cold clamshell of the valley. It was cold. Really, really cold. I pulled onto Kahn Street, home of the shabby business strip and the little stone church. Red door. Good incense. Thick carpeting. Everything felt the same as it had the last time I'd been there. It had only been a few months, so logic said, "*Of course* it's the same," but *I* felt so different, and my realities had changed enough that the sameness was extremely comforting.

I found Sam in the same place I'd found him on my first visit, sitting still in the pews, lost in either thought or prayer. His countenance seemed a little rumpled… like a damp towel pulled from the dryer too early. Sadness? Fatigue? I couldn't put my finger on it.

He turned and smiled when I entered the room.

"Hey, it's nice to see you."

That was enough for me. I crumpled—not physically, thankfully, but internally. Tears streamed down my face, and not in the beautiful, crystalline, single-drop sort of fashion that you see in the movies.

"Let's go into the office," Sam suggested, his face blurring into a warbly blob. He steered me by the elbow into his office where I did crumple onto the floor. He moved to his desk chair and sat quietly for a long time. Finally, I'm not sure how much later, I came up for air and found a box of facial tissue waiting on the carpeting beside me.

"Sorry, I was overdue for that, I guess," I managed, weakly.

"Want to tell me about it?"

"I would if I knew exactly what it was all about... I guess, first of all, there's my mom. She's gone. I'm not sure that's all it is, though... I don't know."

I wasn't making much sense, and I knew it. My thoughts and emotions weren't even making sense inside my own head.

"Gone? Gone where?" Sam asked.

"I have no idea. She cleaned the house, made the beds, cooked a meal, left a note on the fridge... one of those little square notes with the sticky strip on the back, you know? Anyway... then she left."

Sam sought clarification. "So she left for where? Permanently? Or for a bit of a break?"

"I don't think she means to come back. Ever. I'm pretty sure of that actually. I feel it inside," I said, placing my hand over my heart to indicate where the feeling originated from. "And she said so. I believe her."

"Wow. Well, I know you well enough to trust your instincts."

The small compliment, especially because it was stated as fact and not meant just as a compliment, boosted my spirits.

"You won't try to reassure me that she will come back soon, and I shouldn't worry, right? I haven't talked to many people about it yet, but no one seems to know exactly what to say. It's like you can peruse the greetings cards for tips on what to say when someone dies, but there's no cheat sheet for what to say when someone's spouse or parent takes off one day with no forwarding address and no explanation. 'Well, I'm *sure* she'll come to her senses and come back soon,'" I mimicked the awkward well-wishers in a sweet, nasal tone.

"I don't plan on saying anything like that," Sam reassured me.

"Good."

"Are you worried, though? You mentioned being worried."

Was I? I wasn't worried for *me*. I had a sense of direction and a team, however scary and new, that included Dhia. I wasn't worried for Dad, either, at least not much. *Was I worried for Mom?*

"No, I don't think so," I answered, after a long pause.

"I get the feeling that Mom is going to be fine, as fine as she gets, anyway... like maybe she's better off somewhere else. Like maybe she never wanted us or needed us in the first place. Maybe there's something she needs that she won't find here, with us." I rose from the floor and settled onto a folding chair, nestling the box of tissues into my lap, in case I sprung another sudden leak. "Maybe being away from us is what she needs."

"What makes you say that?" Sam face drew into a question mark.

I made the snap decision to tell Sam about my father finding my mother in her freezing apartment, rescuing her from her grief. As I finished the story, understanding began to dawn in Sam's face.

"So she left God," he said, "and it broke her."

I nodded. "Broke her... I think so. I think maybe she sees things, hear things... visions and dreams, that sort of thing. Like I do. At least, I think she used to. I don't know about now. It sort of runs in the family," I finished lamely.

Runs in the family... it sounded ridiculous, even to my own ears. There was *so much more* to it than that, but I wasn't willing to go into details.

"I've never really heard of such things running in families," Sam pondered. "You're sure?"

I nodded again. "Pretty sure."

"So she left God," Sam said again, visibly computing. "And then she never talked about God with you... for pretty much your whole life?"

"Never. Well, until I left for school this past September. I told her that Dhia, I mean God, spoke to me sometimes and that He was going to be part of my life. She didn't like it. She said she'd been afraid of what would happen if she taught me about God, so she never had. She said I had the right to choose for myself. She actually seemed really afraid… which I thought was weird. She said believing in God was *different* for me. That it would be different and that she wanted to protect me from it. I told her I'd already chosen. I told her I'd said yes. I think maybe she couldn't handle watching that. I think that might be why she left."

I waited for Sam to contradict me, but he didn't.

"You might be right. She might be leaving because of whatever she fears or she might not. But it's not your fault either way."

"I guess so," I said.

"It's pretty normal to blame yourself when things like this happen. It's normal to think of all the what-ifs and wonder if you could have stopped it—but you couldn't. Your mother made her own choice."

I pulled a few tissues out of the box and staunched the renewed flow of my own tears.

"Still hard, isn't it?" Sam asked.

I nodded.

"You've grown up in the last few months," Sam said. "You've had a lot of new experiences?"

I nodded again.

"Were any of them the unusual kind?"

"I don't even know what usual or normal is anymore. Is there such a thing?" I asked.

Sam smiled. "I guess that changes for each person. So have you had any experiences that were unusual, for *you*?"

I gave him my best you-don't-want-to-know look.

He didn't ask for clarification.

So what has He been teaching you—God, that is?"

"Teaching me?" I blinked and tried to figure out how to sum up what Dhia had been teaching me. I wasn't sure where to start, so I said the first thing that popped into my mind.

"Beauty… I think I'm learning what beauty is." I was surprised at my own answer.

"You've seen some beautiful things, then?"

"And some ugly ones. I think that seeing what was truly ugly made me notice what was beautiful, you know?"

I was thinking of the healing rooms.

"He's teaching me patience too. I'm only sort of getting that." I rolled my eyes, and Sam smiled.

"That lesson takes a lifetime," he said.

"Yeah, well... I guess listening too. He's teaching me to listen. He doesn't always speak and answer the same way every time. Sometimes He doesn't seem to answer at all. I guess that means He just hasn't answered *yet*, right?"

"Or sometimes His answer is no. God doesn't usually feel the need to explain His reasoning when He says no."

"I've noticed...," I said, "thus, the impatience."

"So now what? You are going back to school soon, I suppose?"

"Saturday. I thought about staying here with Dad for the rest of the year since Mom's gone, but he doesn't want that. He would just worry about me, and I would have nothing to do. Besides, Dhia sort of told me last night that He has things for me to do elsewhere."

"How did he do that?" Sam asked.

I curled my discolored fingers under my palms.

"That's sort of a long story. Basically, He reminded me who I am, who He made me to be."

"That's good then," Sam said, not pressing for details.

"Yeah, it's good," I agreed.

"Oh, I almost forgot." Sam disappeared behind his desk, rummaging in the bottom drawer for something. "I took my mother on one of her estate sale extravaganzas the other day. She loves estate sales. I found something that made me think of you. I bought it, in case I saw you again some time." His voice was muffled by the desk between us.

He emerged, successful, and handed me a silver medallion with a flying eagle engraved on its face. It was larger and much more intricate than a coin, with open spaces in the sky and pinholes in the Celtic knots that encircled the piece. A Celtic cross was visible behind the eagle, its edges dissolving into the knots. My pulse quickened as I noted the word *Iona* twisted into the knots at the lower edge of the cross on the medallion's face. I thought instantly of the cross with the same inscription that sat in the dusty trunk in Nan's attic. I flipped the medallion over and found the following scripture engraved in Gaelic, words so small they were barely visible, on the back of the piece.

Do you not know?
Have you not heard?
The Lord is the everlasting God,
the Creator of the ends of the Earth.
He will not grow tired or weary,
and his understanding no one can fathom.
He gives strength to the weary
and increases the power of the weak.
Even youths grow tired and weary,
and young men stumble and fall;
but those who wait upon the Lord
will renew their strength.
They will soar on wings like eagles;
they will run and not grow weary,
they will walk and not be faint.
Isaiah 40:28–31 (Translated)

"What is it exactly?" I asked, hoping he knew more about it.

"I'm not sure. I thought it was interesting, though… the Celtic artwork, the bird… I don't know what it says exactly, but it seemed to suit you," he said.

"It's Isaiah 40:28–31. Where did you find it?"

"Seattle. That's where my mother lives. I found it in a box with paper clips and pencil stubs."

"Pencil stubs?"

"Yeah, pencil stubs. Pencils used until they were this big." He held out his finger and indicated a length running from his fingertip to his second knuckle.

More questions, the type that Sam couldn't answer, niggled at my brain. Sam looked extremely pleased with his purchase. Perhaps he enjoyed the thrill of a good secondhand find more than he wanted to let on.

"It was an old woman who'd died. Her son was running the estate sale. I asked him about the piece, but he said he'd never seen it before. His mother was Irish, though. He thought it must have been from her side of the family."

It was time to go. I thanked Sam for everything, and he walked me to the door. The fog had cleared. I drove home.

That night I dreamt of a sandy lake beach. The trees around the lake were wind-whipped reddish sticks with sparse greenery. The wind plucked at a faded beach towel that hung from the back of a wooden beach chair. On the shore stood one of those tall outdoor heaters that pumped out wavy lines of heat. A crisp paperback whose title I couldn't quite make out sat on the seat of the chair. The sky was low and gray; the sun dipped toward the horizon. Looking down, I saw bare feet—not mine but my mother's, extending from the hem of a pair of ragged palazzo pants. It was as if I were her or she were me. A scratchy gray cardigan hung past our knees. We stood behind the chair for a long time just staring out over the ripples on the water.

I woke from the dream feeling neither happy nor sad… just thinking of my mother. *Was* she on a beach somewhere… trying to decide whether or not there was enough light left in the sky to read by? Or was the dream just my brain's way of bringing a little bit of her back to me? There was no answer.

Lemon yellow pieces,
Broken, shriveled,
Lost and valued,
Soft edged outside,
Shining on the inside in a dark and forgotten place.
Old today,
Young tomorrow,
Gone with the rain or borne away on dusty feet
Glistening still, even unseen.

Seeds, really…
Of beauty,
Truth,
Goodness,
Peace, and
Hope Rising.

—The words came to me all at once the next morning, as they often did, and I scribbled them in my journal before they could escape me.

MIDNIGHT SHINE

The last day of holiday break, the phone was silent. No relatives, no newspaper reporters, no nosy neighbors called. Somehow, as obnoxious the constant ringing of the phone had been, its silence was even more disconcerting. It seemed like when a whole person disappeared the world ought to sit up, wring its hands, and fuss for a while. It didn't. Instead, it went about its business, and I was expected to go about mine. I wondered how Dad would handle the emptiness in the house once I was gone. Maybe it would just take getting used to. Or maybe things had been hard enough between them that her absence would provide a sense of relief. Or maybe he liked being alone. The sky that morning was gray, and the clouds drizzled sympathetically. Chump, sensing my impending departure, spent the morning with his tail tucked between his legs. He jumped into the trunk as I loaded my luggage into the back of my father's vintage BMW and refused to get out. He looked pathetic, sitting in the trunk between my bags. Rain puddled on the smooth little dished-out area above his nose just below his large sad eyes. Dad lifted him out with some degree of difficulty, promising to give him extra goodies while I was away. The trip to the airport was subdued. There wasn't much left to say. Dad parked the car in the airport parking lot and packed my luggage onto the cart, taking no notice of my possession of my mother's distinctive red butterfly suitcase.

When it was time to say good-bye, we hugged, and Dad said, "I'll call you if I hear anything from her."

"So will I. I love you."

"I love you. Keep in touch… I mean that," he said. I could tell he did.

A profound sense of isolation accompanied me to the airport that day. It separated me from everyone. It muffled other people's conversations and made it hard to concentrate. I felt almost as if I were encased in glass. Even the ticket agent at the reservations counter had to repeat herself a few times to get her questions through to me. Luckily, no one on the plane required my interaction. The airplane cabin hummed and whirred as it always did; and everyone pretended, as they were expected to, that they weren't in awkward prolonged physical contact with total strangers. I waited in a line of three outside the tiny airplane bathroom when a series of loud unmistakably fart noises emanated from the other side of the flimsy folding door. Everyone ignored the occurrence, as was prudent… everyone except for the little boy just ahead me in line who was holding fast to his mother's hand. He began wondering in that slightly-below-shout-level whisper than little boys have, whether the person's food was in jeopardy of falling out of his bottom. His innocent questions were more than the passengers in the immediate area could handle. A smattering of junior high–like giggle fits broke out. Thankfully, the second bathroom opened up just then, and the little boy and his beet red mother were quickly ushered into it. By the time the noise perpetrator vacated his stall, blissfully unaware of his indiscretion, most of the laughter was under control. The levity of the situation broke the invisible wall that separated me from everyone else. It reminded me that life, complicated or not, really does *always* go on… You hurt, you cry, you vomit, you fart, you laugh; and if none of that kills you, then you move on.

Aodhagan looked the same and felt the same, but I felt different. I wasn't sure exactly what to say to people about my mother's disappearance, so I said nothing at all. There seemed to be no upside to telling them, since nothing anyone said or did would make any difference anyhow. Inviting awkward conversation and stares wasn't high on my priority list. I mapped out the route between my classes, noting how long it would take me to get from place to place and purchased a second pair of wellies, aka rubber boots, for the daily trek. My new boots were vivid blue and printed with multiple red birds in flight. They reminded me of Petra. The second half of the school year was somewhat easier on me than the first, though the classes themselves were just as rigorous. First of all, I knew what to expect. That was always good. Second, my study skills had improved somewhat. One of the drawbacks to being smart enough to breeze through much of high school is the steep study habit learning curve at the college level. *You aren't* that *smart, Adenauer!* Learning to truly study had been a bit of an uphill climb, but thankfully it was beginning to click.

Aggie, Donal, and I had signed up for microbiology that semester—the big bad wolf of the nursing program science courses. I earmarked two blank notebooks and packed several sharpened pencils, along with my big-girl panties, for the first day of the class. The professor was a stocky scowling man with a gleam in his eye that was not quite mean but definitely unsettling. He made it clear within the first five minutes of class that there would be no room for drama or excuses on his watch, *or humor, apparently.* We toured the lab where he introduced us to the innocuous fridge-looking device that warmed the petri dishes. The smell that wafted from the warmer full of active cultures when the door was opened was indescribable. Honestly, there were no words. Only one girl actually vomited; the rest of us just gagged politely and held our noses. I wondered immediately if Scottish drug stores stocked those little blue pots of mentholatum—a nostril full of that would come in handy for micro lab time. It turned out that they do.

At lunchtime, Aggie, Donal and I slogged through the rain to the cafeteria, which was housed in the great hall of Aodhagan castle. There was something about dining on jackknife-style laminate cafeteria tables in the great hall of a bona fide period castle that seemed just plain *wrong.* Even the chandeliers did little to ameliorate the damage that the seating options inflicted on the room's ambiance. I wasn't the only one who felt that way; letters and articles demanding respect for the Great Hall in the form of period-appropriate tables and chairs appeared in the school newspaper on a semiregular basis.

There was always something, however, that took financial precedence over the aesthetics of the cafeteria tables… leaky plumbing in the administration building, inadequate chemistry lab equipment, out-of-date computer equipment. So the tacky cafeteria tables lived on, leaving us each with the choice of whether or not to be offended by them.

It was Campus Club Recruitment Day. Booths advertising various student groups and clubs of all kinds were set up all along the west wall of the enormous room. We collected our food and settled near a few nursing cohorts at a table near the Scottish Women's History Club booth. As soon as we sat, we realized we'd made a mistake. A short, roundish, spectacled girl at the women's history booth spotted us and, gathering her clipboard, made a beeline for the empty seat beside Aggie.

"I'm Jen. I'm representing the Scottish Women's Club, or SuCH for short."

"Somehow I thought you'd have to be Scottish for that," Aggie said. Her disdain at being solicited during mealtime showed in her voice.

"Och, nae, ye can hail from anywhere." Jen affected a Scottish accent, then dropped her voice and leaned in as if she were about to impart to us an enormous life-changing secret. I'm actually Scottish, though—quarter, at least. And you?"

"Hungarian," Aggie declared.

"Well, luckily, you don't have to be Scottish to join. You just have to care." Jen picked up her clipboard and her pen and gave Aggie a hopeful look.

Aggie's look clearly communicated that she did *not* care.

"I care," Donal said. "Can I join?"

Jen startled a bit, as if she'd only just realized the tall lanky Irish boy sitting across from her, chewing his drinking straw.

"Uhhhh… I don't think we have a lot of men in the club… or any men actually. I'd have to check on that."

Aggie kicked Donal under the table.

"Ow! What was that for?" Donal rubbed his shin and glowered mildly back at her, then admitted, "All right, I don't care either."

Jen looked relieved and turned to me.

"Can I tell you a little about our organization?" she pleaded.

"Absolutely," I said without conviction. The history of women in Scotland was something I actually had interest in, even if I'd rather dip my head in boiling oil than join a campus club.

Jen dove in.

"Well, our organization has been around as long as the college has. We were practically the first organization on campus. Our goal is to honor the place Celtic women have had in history, which predates even the country of Scotland itself. Are you aware that before Romans occupied this area, Celtic women often occupied places of authority? They were warriors, leaders in government, spiritual leaders. When Roman influence trickled in, with its male-dominated ideals, that changed." Jen shook her head, sadly.

"You are talking about the druids right?" Aggie asked. "I thought the druids were mostly men."

"Oh no!" Jen looked aghast. "In the seventeenth and eighteenth century, it may have been mostly druid men in power, but before that time, many women held places of power, authority, and influence. We have no written history of the time, because the druids and druidesses kept everything up here"—Jen pointed to her temple—"rather than writing it down on paper. We want to honor their history and see women in Scotland recognized for who they are and always have been. The SuCH club exists to honor the legacy of women in this part of the world."

There was a delight, a fervency, in Jen's eyes that exceeded what I'd expect out of a history club member.

"So you are druids, then?" I asked her.

The question caught her off guard.

"Ah, no. I... well, no. We are a club, that's all. We aren't religious. It's more like a sorority, really, except we don't live together. It's a sisterhood."

"Do you pledge?"

"What do you mean?"

"You said you were like a sorority, so do you pledge? Swear in? Take vows? That sort of thing?"

Jen cast a nervous glance toward her booth where her SuCH sisters were all busy talking to new recruits.

"I'm really just here to get people interested in signing up for a new member's meeting. I don't know much past that," she admitted.

"Then you haven't sworn in yet, yourself?"

Aggie and Donal were wide-eyed, watching me grill Jen, wondering what I was up to.

"Well, no," Jen answered.

"But you've been to the meetings?"

"Some of them."

"You don't have to attend all the meetings as a member?"

"Some of the meetings are open to new members... that's me. Some of them are open to senior members only." Jen's voice dropped to a whisper then; a flush of secrecy crept up her neck.

"The meetings aren't open to all students? I thought all student group meetings were supposed to be open to all students and attended by a faculty member," Donal said, his curiosity piqued.

"Well, they are—all the regular meetings are open, of course," Jen stammered. "And we have a faculty advisor, Professor Mac—from the history department."

"But the nonregular meetings? The confirmed member meetings? Those are closed?" I asked.

"You know what... actually, those meetings aren't even on the club schedule. I'm not sure I was supposed to mention them. Maybe they aren't really official, maybe... I don't know. Do you mind not mentioning I told you? I don't really know the rules yet."

The poor girl seemed close to tears.

"We won't say a thing," I promised, patting her hand to reassure her. I wondered why she had come so unglued.

"Wouldn't want yer to miss oyt on earning your plaid patch," Donal muttered under his breath. That earned him another, slightly more vicious kick in the shins from Aggie. Jen was too preoccupied with her fear of failure to notice the exchange.

A middle-aged woman at the SuCH booth scanned the room with her eyes, found Jen, and strode purposefully in our direction.

"Yer ma is coming," Donal warned.

Jen looked. "Oh, that's our advisor... the one I was telling you about. She's a wonderful professor. All the students like her. I'm sure you've heard of her."

"Actually, I haven't," I said.

"So have you signed up some new recruits?" the professor asked Jen, flashing us a wide plastic smile as she reached our table.

"I'm not sure. I was just going over some of what we were about, and they were asking questions," Jen mumbled nervously.

"Well, we really need to get the word out, and we don't have a lot of time... We can answer more questions at the new member's meeting," she prompted.

"Of course. Maybe I'll see you there?" Jen fumbled with her clipboard, freed a flier, and offered it to me.

"Maybe so," I said politely, reaching for the pamphlet.

Professor Mac's gaze met my own, and her expression froze for a millisecond. I recognized the coldness in her eyes and braced subconsciously for what might come next. *Spit, maybe?* My palms broke out in a cold sweat. Professor Mac's hand shot out, and she intercepted the flier, tucking it into the front of her own clipboard.

"I don't think we need to waste any more of their time, Jen. Let's move along," she said briskly, standing back to let Jen out of her seat.

"Uh, okay, shouldn't I at least..." Jen began to reach for another pamphlet to replace the one the professor had taken.

"No, that's enough." The professor's brusque response left no room for argument. She nodded her head in curt dismissal of us.

Jen, befuddled, got up from the table and followed the professor back to the SuCH booth, mouthing the word *sorry* to us as they hurried away.

The three of us stared after them.

"What in the world was that about?" Aggie wondered aloud.

"I've no idea," I said. Only that wasn't the whole truth. I *did* have a pretty good idea what it was about. The professor's obvious dislike of me was more than reminiscent of that of the guest professor on Iona. There were too many alarm bells going off in my head for everything I'd just heard about and witnessed to be a coincidence.

"Well, I'm hooked," Donal declared. "I've never been so excited about anythin' as I am aboot this opportunity."

"Shut it," Aggie said. She and Donal had left the stage of gleefully finishing each other's sentences. They'd landed squarely in the crotchety-old-couple phase… a phase that I earnestly hoped was a fleeting, transitional one.

"I think it's more than a history club. I think maybe they actually are druids. Some of them anyway," I said.

"Druids? I thought you were joking with her about that. I thought druids were a thing of the past. Maybe any leftover were just old ladies who liked nature." Aggie cocked her head and looked at me questioningly.

"Oh, there are druids," Donal said. "I do know that much."

"And how do you know that?"

"My auntie's one," he answered, "and she's serious aboot it."

"Really?" It was my turn to be surprised.

He shrugged his shoulders, indicating that we'd reached the end of his knowledge on the subject. "I don't know her. She's my ma's sister, and she lives in Creeslough, far away enoof that my ma can pretend she doesn't exist. I've never met her. Da says we don't consort with witches."

"Druids and witches aren't the same thing," Aggie said, "are they?"

Neither of us answered her, because frankly, neither of us knew.

"I have a friend who knows some druids." I was thinking of Shine. "She says most of them are relatively nice and do lots of things to conserve nature, preserve history, that sort of thing. I think it includes white magic. Even white magic with benign intent is more dangerous than some of them really know."

"So they aren't really witches, then? That's just an old wives' tale?" Aggie asked hopefully.

"I don't know," I answered honestly. I really wasn't sure. I had the feeling, however, that it was something I should look into.

"So how did that professor know you, and what did you do to make her hate you?" Aggie asked.

"I've never met her before," I answered.

"Seriously?"

"Seriously."

"Wow. Not a very nice lady then."

"Maybe it's not her. Maybe it's me. I just have that effect on some people." I gave Aggie my most charming smile.

As we bussed our tables, sorting trash from recycling, from washable dishes (years before America caught on to the eco-conscious trend), my mind wandered to Shine. I had the feeling she'd be very interested in knowing what I'd just experienced. On the way out of the cafeteria, I snagged an abandoned flyer off the floor. It detailed the upcoming SuCH Club informational meeting.

As it turned out, I didn't need the flyer. Thursday of the next week, just before 10:00 p.m., I heard a soft knock at my door. I had just climbed into bed, stiff-necked and scratchy-eyed from hours spent cuddling my microbiology book. I ignored the knock, hoping the knocker would take the hint and flee the scene. No such luck. Another knock sounded, louder, and I climbed out of bed and opened the door. It was Shine, dressed warmly, head to toe in shades of gray.

"So? Where to?" she asked.

"Where to? Bed! At least that's what I had planned. Maybe not, though?" I rubbed my eyes and tried to mentally prepare myself for an alternative course of action.

"You didn't get the call?" she asked.

"Phone call or call call?"

"Call call, of course." Shine's voice was annoyingly energetic.

"No, I didn't hear anything. Probably too tired." I didn't even try to stifle an ear-popping yawn. "I'm sorry. I'll get it together. Come on in." I dressed as quickly as I could, praying silently as I did so.

Dhia, it's the middle of the night, and I'm so tired. Honestly (as if dishonesty is even a viable option with you), I'm in a horrible mood. I want nothing more than sleep. I'm not feeling up for a midnight trip to anywhere. But I'm willing. Help me. Help me be more willing than I am.

"Hard week?" Shine asked.

"Yeah, you could say that. Or, no… Actually, it started before that. My mom left."

"Left? Left here?"

"Ah, no. Left home. Left us. She wrote a good-bye note and left town with no forwarding address, no sentiment. She just left."

Hot tears began to brew behind my eyes; they surprised and angered me. I hadn't planned on an emotional meltdown. I busied myself with my shoes. I hadn't been allowing myself to think about Mom for more than a few seconds at a time since I'd gotten back to school. Somehow, talking about her out loud was more than I could handle. Feelings I didn't understand had begun to bubble to the surface when I least expected them to. Shine didn't say anything until my shoes were tied, then sat down beside me on the rug and wrapped me in a big hug. She didn't offer any words and didn't ask any questions. She just held me until my tears stopped. After a few minutes, they did stop. Peace flooded into the raw spaces in my chest, and I was ready to go.

"Thanks, I needed that more than I thought I did," I said.

"I lost someone once, and that's what I needed… a big hug," Shine said, blinking back tears of her own. I couldn't tell if she was crying for me or for herself. Maybe it was both.

I grabbed my coat, and we left the dorm.

DRUIDS?

A blanket of fog hung thick across the campus. The mist swirled as we walked, soaking our clothing. A familiar car, engine running, appeared ahead of us. My heart pounded.

"I think that's our ride," I informed Shine.

"You sure?"

"Pretty sure."

We drew near to the car and saw Jack standing at the curb, rubbing his hands together and bouncing up and down a little to keep warm.

"Are there two of you this time?" he asked.

"It seems so. Jack—Shine. Shine—Jack."

They greeted each other appropriately.

"Let's get in before we freeze," Jack suggested.

Shine bundled into the backseat of Jack's little silver car, and I took the front, on account of the length of my legs.

"Where's your coat?" I asked him.

"That's a long story. I haven't been home since this morning and wasn't expecting to come here. You know how that is… I was sort of hoping I could stop by my apartment and grab it, if that's okay with you, before we get going."

Shine and I looked at each other. Neither of us could think of a reason not to, especially since none of us knew where we were going anyway.

"Sure, no problem." Shine nodded her assent, and we were on our way.

Jack's apartment was a small cubby above the glass shop where he worked in the center of town. Shine and I waited in the car with the motor running while he booked up the stairs to grab his coat and a pair of boots.

"So you know him?" Shine asked as soon as Jack exited the vehicle.

"Yes… well, no, not really. Sort of. Dhia sent him to fix my window the morning after that demon broke it. Then Dhia sent him again on the night I went to Loch Occasional."

"So he's a divinely appointed chauffeur? He just shows up to drive you places?"

I nodded. "Not just for me, though. He says he goes wherever God asks him to, whenever He asks him to. He's kind of like a Blue, and yet… not."

"Kind of like we should *all* be… I mean, *all* those who follow Christ."

"I guess that's true," I agreed.

A hole appeared in the fog, and the moon shone through, full and bright enough to make me squint.

"And you like him… a lot?" she continued.

"Why do you say that?" I blurted a little too loudly.

"I can just tell," she said, playfully punching me in the arm.

"Great. I hope *he* can't tell."

"You are probably in luck on that account. Guys aren't great at picking up on that sort of thing—even guys who listen to God," she assured me.

Jack returned to the car. "Okay, ladies, it's about an hour's drive," he said, pulling the door shut quickly to preserve the warmth inside the car.

"I'm glad someone knows where we are going," I said. I was in yet another situation that hinged directly on the whim of a supernatural someone, *The* Supernatural Someone. The realization made me shiver… I sort of hoped it always would.

During the drive, I filled Shine's ear with what I'd learned about the SuCH club at the college. She knew more about the druids than I did.

"They believe nature is sacred. They have a lot in common with Wiccans, actually… though some actually believe in one god or goddess. Some believe in many gods, some in no god at all," Shine informed us. "Druids are into their ancestry as part of their spirituality as well. They often believe in reincarnation. And they practice magic, the divination of spirits."

"So some of them actually believe in God?" Jack asked.

"Well, they believe in *a* god, but it isn't actually God Himself, which means it's a false god," she explained. "They do actually talk to spirits—spirits of darkness that masquerade as light."

I shivered through another outbreak of goose bumps and prayed silently for discernment and wisdom to know dark from light and good from bad.

"I wonder how much this group actually knows about us…," I pondered aloud.

"And how much of the hatred some of them have shown toward us is just the demons riling them up and pointing them in our direction?" Shine finished my thought for me.

I nodded my head.

"I'm curious about that too," she said.

"You said you wondered how much they know about *us*. Who is *us*?" Jack inserted his question gingerly. Shine and I had gotten so carried away with our conversation that we'd all but forgotten Jack was there.

"Well, we're believers. Christians," Shine explained.

"I gathered that much. But are you in an organization of some sort?" he asked.

"We aren't that organized," I muttered, chuckling a little.

"Not an organization really. Just people interested in doing the will of God. That isn't always popular these days," Shine added.

The road began to bend upward and wind into the forest hills north of town. We crested a steep hill and peeked out above the cloud layer into the brilliant light of the moon. The road dead-ended in an untended gravel lot occupied by half a dozen cars.

"This is it?" Shine asked.

"I think so," Jack said, donning a scarf and crawling out of the car.

Shine and I followed, our breath silvering in the frigid air. It was *cold!*

"So now what?" I said.

Something about the place made me instantly ill at ease. I took a long look around, trying to gauge the direction from which the uneasiness was coming. As a general rule, I loved being outdoors at night— but that place, that night, was an exception to the rule. Something was very wrong. I scanned the parking lot in every direction, and my gaze landed on the cars. I had a suspicion that whoever owned them would not be thrilled to meet up with us.

Is that you talking, Dhia, or my paranoia? I asked silently.

I received confirmation in the form of cold sweat that broke out at the base of my spine.

"I'm not so sure we should be seen tonight," Shine said, eyeing the cars warily.

"I second that," I said, relieved to hear her agree.

"You coming with us?" I asked Jack.

"Yes," he answered quickly and absolutely, "I'm not sending you into the woods alone, not when you two have the heebie-jeebies."

"The heebie-jeebies? Did your grandma teach you that term?" I asked.

Shine took off, quickly and quietly, past the other cars and up the trail. Jack and I followed. The moon lit the way well enough, as the trees were rather sparse and bare. Jack and Shine's feet made almost no noise whatsoever on the moss-carpeted first floor. I tried to follow suit, avoiding twigs and branches that would roll or snap. We walked for fifteen minutes or so. Our breaths came quicker and hotter as we climbed until we heard the quiet hum of many distant voices. We stepped off the trail and grouped behind a clump of trees.

"Anyone know what's up there?" I whispered.

"I think there's a henge out here somewhere… a small one," Jack said.

"Have you been here before?"

He shook his head. No.

We followed the sound of the voices, then, rather than the trail, through the trees and further up a steep hill where the light of a bonfire flickered. Women gathered in small groups around the fire in the center of a smallish, roughly circular henge. Their boisterous chatter covered the sound of our approach, making it easy for us to draw close, unnoticed. We hung back from the circle and planted ourselves in a small copse of trees outside the reach of the light, close enough to hear their words and observe their activity. Some of the large rock slabs that formed the henge stood erect. Some had toppled. One hung awkwardly to the side, as if it had begun to fall years ago, and the moss and brush had caught and held it partway through its descent, freezing it into place. I had to pee… Ever since I was a little girl any form of hiding, even the game of hide-and-seek, had kicked my kidney function into high gear. I ignored my excitable bladder and trained my focus on the activity inside the circle.

There were around twenty women, most of them young, in the circle. I recognized a few as students from the college. One woman stood out from the others. She was dressed in a long lavender robe, much like a formal choir gown, with multiple pleats and deep pockets. She stepped up onto a mound of dirt at the base of the precariously sideways rock slab and waved and whistled for everyone's attention. As she turned her face toward us, I recognized her as Professor Mac, the SuCH club advisor I'd met in the cafeteria. An eager chorus of shushing broke out, and the group grew quiet. The professor thanked everyone for coming and asked the current members to step forward and identify themselves. More than half the group did, and someone passed out lavender gowns which the current members pulled on over their coats and sweatshirts. They resembled a raft of lavender penguins blinking expectedly at the professor. The newly robed crew began a low-humming chant, and Professor Mac raised her volume to be clearly heard above the noise.

"These are your senior members, girls. Like you, they have completed at least a year of SuCH membership. But they have chosen, like many others before them, to take a further step in the time-honored and proud tradition of Celtic women. Each of you here was recommended by one of the senior members. Each of you will be invited to don this robe and begin a journey of partnership with the Earth, with the trees…"

The professor's voice droned on, but I had heard enough. My skin was crawling, and I caught a whiff of sickly sweet burning and sulfur that didn't come from the fire but from the air above the professor's head. Something there began to move and vibrate as she spoke, then streaked in our direction. A streak of orange flashed at the corner of my vision, and something bumped my shoulder hard, pushing me backward onto the ground. Jack hauled me to my feet.

"You okay?" Shine asked.

"Yes, but we need to get away from here! Whatever that was, it meant harm," I whispered as loudly as I dared. I was shaking but no longer cold. Adrenaline flooded my system, sending a rush of blood to my legs, and I wanted nothing more than to sprint for the car, but that didn't seem prudent.

"What the *hell* was that?" Jack asked.

"Exactly," Shine answered him. "I agree with Kiah. Let's go."

We backed away as quickly and silently as we could down the trail, and hurried to the car. We didn't speak until we were safely inside with the doors shut.

"That's them," Shine stated in a matter-of-factly tone as Jack backed the car out and headed for the main road.

"Are you okay?" Shine asked, leaning into the front seat to ask the question.

"Yeah, I just got bumped." My heart was still racing in my throat, but my hands had stopped shaking.

"All they can do is bump you. They don't have permission to do much of anything else."

"Who? Who doesn't have permission…? What are you talking about?" Jack asked, bewildered.

"Spiritual warfare. There were demons there," Shine answered.

"And you *saw* them?" Jack's voice cracked a bit.

"Yes. Well, sort of. It's not like seeing an animal. They aren't exactly solid figures."

"It's more like the air is darker where they are and moves in ways it shouldn't. And sometimes there are orange flashes. They stink too," I added.

"Really? You smell them?" Shine asked.

"Yes. Don't you?"

"I've never noticed. I have allergies, though. My sense of smell isn't the greatest."

"Well, don't sweat it. You aren't missing much." I wrinkled my nose at the memory of the burning stench.

"I guess I haven't given much thought to evil spirits. I certainly didn't know people could see or smell them... or that they could knock a person over." Jack swallowed, eyes wide, struggling to process what we had experienced.

"It's not typical. That's for sure. Staying hidden, deceiving people, calling good bad and bad good... that's what they usually do, because it serves them best. Once you cut through their pretty little lies and call them out, they can get a little more cantankerous. They don't have any real power against believers, though. The shed blood of Jesus Christ ends their options, and they know it. They can't do a thing about it. All they can do is poke at us after that," Shine said.

I was tired of getting poked at.

Then Shine began to pray, asking Dhia for wisdom and discernment, thanking Him for his protection. She had a habit of breaking off from conversation with people and into prayer without pretense or warning. It took a few moments for me to realize she was talking to God, and not to Jack and me.

"So was that the professor you met this week?" Shine asked.

"You talking to me? Oh yes... that's her. Her name is Mac. She's the club advisor."

"And did you recognize any students?"

"A few, but none I know well."

We had come out of the hills and onto the flat by that time.

"This next road is my stop," Shine announced suddenly.

"Here?" Jack asked, incredulously, taking his foot off the gas and letting the car slow. We were still in the country. Only a few scattered farmhouses were visible.

"Yes, here," Shine assured him.

He pulled the car to the shoulder at the next road—a dirt road that wound into the trees.

"Jack, it was nice to meet you. I can see why He picked you," she said, squeezing his shoulder as she climbed from the car.

She kissed me on the forehead. "I'll be talking to you soon."

"I have no doubt. Thank you," I said.

"Of course," she said. "It does get better with time, if you let it."

I was almost certain she was referring to the loss of my mother. I wondered what she meant by that… *if I let it*? She darted out of the car and down the dirt road, disappearing around the bend. I fought the urge to scan the skies for her.

"I've tried not to ask—really I have, because I get the feeling I'm not supposed to. But… disappearing down dirt roads and into lakes in the middle of the night? And demons? Seeing and smelling actual demons? I have so many questions," Jack said.

"So do I." I sighed, "You aren't the only one."

He looked at me, then trying to ascertain whether I was hedging or telling the truth. His eyes were deep pools in the darkness, and I was mortified to find that they melted me a little inside.

"You know more than me," he said, directing the car back onto the road.

"About what?"

"About who you girls are and what you do. Take her, for instance." He jerked his thumb in the general direction of the road where Shine had disappeared. "And the lady on the boat… and the one who swam into the lake and disappeared?"

"I guess I know a little more," I admitted.

"Anything you can tell me?" he asked.

I studied his face. His jaw was tight, and his brow was furrowed.

"What's wrong? You seemed okay with having questions before… You didn't ask me anything about the window or the lake. Why now?"

I asked.

He didn't answer.

"Jack? Are you okay? You seem spooked."

"Yeah, I'm spooked! Before, I was just going where God asked me to and doing what He said to. It seemed natural to do. There were things I didn't understand—especially the lady that dove into the water and disappeared... What was that about? But that was okay with me. I was just being faithful, but now..."

"Now?" I prompted.

"Well, now, I kind of *know* you. And tonight in the woods when that spirit, or whatever it was, attacked you... it scared me. I didn't see it, but I felt it, and I wanted to protect you. You aren't a stranger to me anymore. This isn't just one of God's little test projects. I don't know what you do, but if it's fighting demons... I guess I don't really like thinking of you doing that..."

"It didn't really attack me. It just brushed me. I'm okay," I tried to reassure him.

I thought of the demon that had tried to squash me in my bed and wondered what he would think of *that*. I certainly didn't plan to tell him about it.

"You didn't really answer my question about what you do. Are you some sort of... demon fighter? Or what exactly?"

"No, definitely not a demon fighter," I said. Then I thought about it for a moment and amended my statement. "Not any more of a demon fighter than any other Christian, at least. I'm almost as new to these kinds of things as you are. There's not a whole lot more I can tell you, though... about what we do. It *is* kind of a secret. The other ladies and I, we just serve Dhia... God, that is. That's all."

"Like missionaries?" he asked.

"Yeah, I guess you could call it that. God tells *you* where to go and what to do... and then you do it, right? Do you think of yourself as a missionary?" I asked.

"No, I never have before, anyway."

"Well, it's like that. We just do what He asks us."

"It's not the Calling, then?" Jack asked, glancing at me.

That startled me. "Uh… yeah, actually—it is. It's exactly like that. What do you know about the Calling?"

"I don't know much. I heard some stories from my great-aunt. She's Scottish. She said that there was something called the Calling, and some of the women in my family line had it. My parents said it was just an old wives' tale, and my great-aunt was crazy. Actually, I think she *is* crazy… She insists on wearing the same pair of socks every single day—blue with purple stripes on one foot, yellow with red dots on the other. They have to wash her socks secretly while she sleeps. And she eats a teaspoon full of garden clay every morning. "For my constitution"—Jack mimicked an old-lady voice—"I found her stories interesting anyway, though. I used to listen to her for hours."

"She lives here in Scotland?" I asked.

"Oh no." Jack shook his head. "She grew up here. She moved to the USA when she was seventeen years old."

"What else did she say?"

"Just that God calls hearts of men and women from all over the world, for His purposes. And that in Scotland, there was a special group of women who had 'the Calling.' She said they were set aside for a special purpose, but she had no clue what the purpose was because it wasn't her that He called to it. I didn't believe a word of it at the time, but I found her stories interesting. So she was right?"

"Yeah, she's right, except that it's not just women from Scotland."

"And you have the Calling?"

"Yeah, I do." My heart pounded as I said the words aloud. "Although I don't think it's a matter of *having it*… it's not a disease… as much as I have been Called, and have said yes."

Jack slowed the car and turned onto the Aodhagan campus drive, then parked.

"My great-aunt told me she was fifteen when her own aunt was Called and then disappeared soon after without a trace." He swallowed hard and stared out the driver's side window. "That's why her family moved away from Scotland."

"They thought they could avoid God by leaving Scotland?" I asked.

"Yeah, well… people don't always think rationally when they are afraid of something."

I thought of my mother then. That was true.

"Is that what bothers you? Are you afraid I might disappear?" I asked.

He didn't turn to face me. I laid my hand over top of his clenched fist.

"Jack, look at me. I won't disappear. I know what you mean by disappearing… I've heard the stories too. But I won't disappear. It's not like that for me… It really means that much to you?"

He nodded almost imperceptibly, sending a hot jolt of unfamiliar emotions through my core. The dome light blinked off automatically, and Jack switched it back on.

"I promise, if I had to go away for some reason… I would tell you. Okay? I promise. I don't think it's likely. It's, well, it's… it's different for some who are Called. Some stay here. Shine and I… we live here. Then there are others, like the ladies you saw at the lake. They travel more, from place to place. They stay away more. But that's not me, okay? That's not what I've been asked to do."

"Are you sure? Are you sure He won't ask you to go away?" Jack asked.

His question hit a raw nerve. There was no way to be absolutely sure.

"Not one hundred percent sure, I guess, but what about you? If He asked you to go away, somewhere, wouldn't you go?"

"Yeah, of course," he said without hesitation, then paused. "I guess I see your point."

"It's no different for me. I promise. I'm here now. He led me here. I plan to graduate from nursing school here and get a nursing job just like anyone else. Just like you, right? You plan to stay in your job until He tells you otherwise?"

"Yes," he said, beginning to relax a bit.

"I'm a little afraid to ask, Jack. I don't understand why this matters so much to you. You barely know me. Is it a protective thing? You aren't responsible for my safety, you know…"

He interrupted me. "I don't know why, for sure. I thought I was just doing what He asked me, fixing your window, giving you a ride somewhere. Tonight, though, when that thing knocked you over in the woods… I was afraid. I was afraid you were hurt. I was afraid, for just a moment, that I'd lose you." His voice was barely audible.

"I don't know what that means, Jack. How could you lose something you don't have? I mean, we've only met a few times… We're almost strangers. Not strangers, exactly, that's not what I meant to say…"

"I don't feel like we are strangers. I just feel like there's something *more…* maybe something more than friends…If you don't feel the same way, that's okay. I don't expect you to." He sighed and tightened his grip on my hand, awakening me to the fact that we'd been holding hands for several minutes. "I don't know what I mean. I'm just trying to be honest with you. I think I care more about you than I thought I would… in a different way than I expected to. I didn't mean to say any of this… and I'm sorry I'm not saying it well…"

I put my finger up to his lips to shush him. "It's okay that you say what you mean. It's refreshing. Let's promise to say what we mean to each other, okay? Always?"

"Okay," he agreed. "Your turn."

Eek! I didn't mean right now! I thought. My brain scrambled for footing. *How do I feel?*

"I don't know how I feel, honestly. I haven't even considered that you would ever care to do more than give me a lift because He asked you to. So I'm confused too. I know what feelings you mean. I mean, I think you smell good…"

"I *smell* good?"

Oh. My. Word! Did I say that aloud??

"What I mean to say is, I feel something else too. You aren't alone in that. I have some feelings too. I just don't know what they mean, exactly…" Words failed me then.

"I should really go inside. I have class in the morning. Early," I finally managed.

Jack nodded, staring at the seat between us, but didn't let go of my hand.

Impulsively, I leaned forward until my cheek touched his and my head rested on his collarbone. We stayed that way for a few moments, saying nothing.

"Maybe we should get together sometime. Coffee or something... Do you like coffee?" he asked in my ear.

"Tea, I like tea more. But coffee's okay too."

"Tea, then. Saturday, maybe?"

"Eleven o'clock on Saturday?" I asked, not wanting to break contact, *ever*.

"Eleven it is."

I straightened reluctantly. Letting Go of Jack's hand, I opened the car door.

"Thanks for the ride," I said as brightly as I could.

"Anytime."

I bolted for the dorm and didn't look back.

I didn't sleep much that night. I brushed my teeth, first thoroughly without toothpaste, then, realizing my mistake, applied toothpaste and repeated the process. I prepared a cup of chamomile tea and sipped it, hoping it would calm *something*... my racing mind, my pounding heart... but it didn't, a*nd* it tasted like toothpaste. I'd never felt for anyone what I'd felt that night for Jack. It was even more amazing to me that those feelings seemed to be reciprocated. I'd had crushes before and knew instinctively that this was *not* just a crush. I just didn't understand what it *was*. I barely knew Jack, but his eyes and his entire essence reached into me and triggered something wild and frightening—some part of me that I didn't know I had and certainly did not understand. Perhaps it wasn't something I was meant to understand, but to discover. Dhia had brought Jack to my doorstep; Dhia was the One I needed to ask.

"A Dhia! Help me! I don't understand this... this thing with Jack and me. I mean, what *was* that? It certainly isn't what I expected. It isn't what I was looking for. It scares me!" I prayed aloud.

It scares most people, came His familiar voice from somewhere inside me.

"Really?" I hadn't thought of that. Maybe it did scare most people, but they were just more willing to risk that kind of rejection than

I was. Another wave of realization swept over me: Dhia and I were talking about *love*... and not the motherly kind that nurses are supposed to have for their patients. It was the passionate kind that sparks between a man and a woman—the kind my mom and dad thought they had, at least I assumed they thought they had, at some point. That realization set my heart back to flop-and-race mode once again. Love was something I felt far from ready for. I had never before considered that anyone could have feelings for me of *that* kind. I'd always imagined myself as a solitary, lonely sort of person—working my way through adulthood, eating through book after book in my free time. I had never once pictured my life complicated by romance.

"It's just one guy, and it's just one shared moment of feelings. Get a hold of yourself, Adenauer," I told myself sternly. But there was a stubborn part of me that wasn't listening to reason. It felt like something more than just a passing fancy. Dhia had sent Jack to me, after all. He even knew about the Calling. He loved Dhia as much as I did, maybe more... and he probably knew more about Him, at least in the conventional sense.

"Okay, Dhia... what do I do? Tell me what to do!" I whispered into the darkness.

Go to tea with him on Saturday, came the answer. The simplest answer is often the right one.

FIRST DATE

I winked out of consciousness at approximately 5:00 a.m., and my alarm clock rang at 6:15. I was not just tired. I was utterly fatigued to the point of nausea. I sat up, grabbed the wastebasket just in case my heaving stomach planned to follow through on its threat, and fumbled for the switch on my reading lamp. The bulb was burnt out. It was then, sitting in the dark on my bed, wondering if my first-period professor would really sweat my absence all that much, that I remembered *why* I was so tired. SuCH, bonfire, woods, Shine, Jack… aaaaggghhh! Jack!

The memory of his body heat radiating off his collarbone through my forehead and into my brain (probably causing permanent thought impairment) rushed back to me, and I did it… I threw up a little.

"Good grief, Adenauer, you handled *that* well," I said aloud.

I sat still and just breathed until I felt awake enough to stumble across the room and flip the overhead light switch. It was burnt out as well. The little hairs at the base of my neck stood on end. I couldn't help but wonder if one of the little beasties had followed me home from the henge. I pulled the chain on the desk lamp and was relieved when the light came on. I took stock of the atmosphere in the room anyway, sniffing the air. I seemed to be alone.

I barely made it through my classes that morning. My ability to shelve the past and future in order to focus on the present utterly failed me. A thought train labeled, *Oh my* word, *a guy* likes *me!* screamed through my head at random intervals, blowing through almost every task I put my mind to;—the roar of it drowned my rational thoughts.

Aggie plunked herself down in the chair beside me at the micro-biology lab. I didn't have to see her expression to know she was out of sorts. Her angry plunk was always louder than I imagined someone of her slight stature could muster.

"Grumpy or angry?" I asked her.

"There. Are. No. Words!" she responded.

I decided not to dig further.

She looked at me and her expression changed.

"What about you? Are you sick, or dying?"

"Sheesh! Do I look that bad…?"

"Wait a minute. Don't tell me, I want to guess…" She squinted at me, searching my face for answers.

"Midnight bathrobe diving again?"

"Um… Go Fish," I said unconvincingly. I poked my head into my bag and pretended to look for a pencil.

"Go Fish?" she asked.

"It's a card game in which you say what kind of card you need and if the other person doesn't have it…"—her childhood in Hungary must not have included Go Fish—"never mind. What I mean is no, I didn't go midnight bathrobe diving. Not this time…"

"You stayed up all night with that guy again, though, didn't you?" she accused in an overly loud voice. Several students stopped working and stared at us.

"Thet sounds like a conversation for yer personal time, burds," the professor scolded.

"Of course, sir. Sorry." I glowered at Aggie and began to prep the culture sets we were supposed to work on.

Aggie lowered her voice a few notches.

"Thanks a lot!" I hissed at her, acutely aware of my prickling, pinking cheeks.

"So, tell me, it *is* a guy, right? The same guy?"

I scowled at her again, not sure how to respond.

"Ha! I guessed it. So your place or his?"

"Neither! Good grief! You know me better than that. I know you'll be disappointed, but I was *not* alone with a guy all night. I was with a group." It wasn't a big group, but I didn't plan to explain that.

"He was there, though, right? You have a man in your life, and you just don't want to say anything to me about it. Why? I'm trustworthy."

"Ha!" I snorted.

"What does that mean?" Aggie feigned offense.

"It means ha! You are being so nosy..."

"Well, I'm just concerned, that's all. Usually people meet, they have a date, maybe hang out for a while. Utter secrecy, cold lakes, and clothing exchanges are not normally immediately involved."

"Okay, I see your point. But just because nighttime was involved, doesn't mean I'm sleeping with anyone."

I must have said the last part too loudly, because a guy at the table in front of us snorted.

That's what you were concerned about, right? Or at least what you want to know? It's not like that *at all*. I went hiking with a small group, and we sort of got lost," I whispered.

"Hiking. At night. With some mysterious friends I don't know and you won't talk about? Winter diving and midnight hikes... that's what you expect me to believe?" Aggie's hands were planted firmly on her hips.

"Yes. I do. Because I'm your friend, and I've never lied to you before..." I stopped abruptly and thought about whether that was actually a true statement. *Had I actually lied to her before, in the course of protecting my secret from her?* I hated lying. I hated keeping secrets.

"Okay, then are these friends of yours from the school?" Aggie persisted.

"No. They aren't... Look, I can tell you a little about the guy. Would that make you happy?" I asked.

"It's a start," she said, smearing culture B onto what I hoped was petri dish B.

"He's really nice," I said.

"And?"

"And what? He's nice."

Aggie waited for me to continue.

"And he actually seems to like me, which is weird, right?"

"Why would that be weird?"

"I don't know. It *feels* weird."

"You mean it feels good?" Aggie elbowed me.

"Yeah, I guess so…," I admitted, "and weird. I'm going to see him on Saturday."

"Oooh, daylight hours, right?"

"Yes, brat. Daylight hours. It really *isn't* what you think."

"Then tell me… what is it?" she asked.

I thought about that for a minute, then answered, "Honestly, I don't even know. Hey, what about you, Miss Grumpy-pants? Is Donal the reason for your mood?" I asked.

She shot daggers at me with her eyes.

"That bad?" I asked.

Aggie didn't answer. Instead, she stomped across the lab to the warmer with our petri dishes. Even the professor stepped warily out of her path. Apparently, it *was* precisely that bad.

Just after lunch came Mandarin Chinese Language class. It was oral chapter review day, but the Chinese professor may as well have been speaking Greek for all the sense his words made to my numb mind. Luckily, Friday afternoon nursing clinicals were cancelled due to instructor illness. I immediately slammed Nap Time into the open slot in my schedule. I showered, dressed in my comfies, hung blankets over the window to block out the light, adjusted the temperature, placed my pillows in the perfect positions, turned on a fan for white noise, and crawled between the covers to wait for sleep. Sleep didn't come. Instead, my vision began to sparkle in bursts of color, which intensified and spun at the periphery. It had been a while since I'd had a full-blown vision.

I waited quietly for the visual sparkles to clear, noting the scent of coffee beans, florals, and fresh ground mustard. The coffee scent was the strongest. The sparkles turned to smudges, then sharpened slowly into stalks of French lavender tied in large bunches. Stems chopped flat, they stood on end like bundles of asparagus. The bundles were arranged neatly down the center of a long table, alongside multiple small vials of oil, flat dishes of whole coffee beans, and long handled swabs. I looked down at my hands. They were not my hands, but my mother's. Shorter, wider, and thinner skinned than my own, with slightly twisted pinkies and perfectly applied pink-tinged polish on each nail. I was a watcher through my mother's eyes. There was a dish of fresh ground mustard in her hand, which she set down on the table. She wore a long eyelet dress, a kind I'd never seen her wear, and moved efficiently but deliberately. She walked the length of the table, clipboard in hand, methodically checking and arranging the vials and decorations on the table. She made notes in French, which I, of course, could not read. There was no sound in the vision—only color, scent, and form. It lasted only moments before the colors spun together and faded out, leaving me in the dark to ponder, what I'd seen and why. I wasn't sure if there was something in the glimpses I was supposed to note, something I was meant to understand. I turned on the bedside lamp and scribbled the details in my journal. I made a quick sketch of everything I could remember, then fell fast asleep and slept straight through to the next morning.

I awoke to light streaming through the window. The sky was clear, and the sun was alarmingly high. The clock informed me that I'd seriously overslept. Ten forty-two Saturday morning. I had less than twenty minutes before I was supposed to meet Jack. My very next thought was that I had no idea where to meet him. We hadn't established a meeting place. Precise planning hadn't mattered up to that point, where Jack was concerned. It probably wouldn't stand in the way of *this* particular meeting either. As quickly as possible, I coached my pillow-dried hair into presentability at the sink and threw on jeans and a sweater. Almost late, I almost bowled over a slow-moving student in a towel on my sprint down the hall. I slowed when I hit the front doors, attempting to make my exit appear casual.

First date ever! My brain screamed at me, which sent my heart scrambling sideways in my chest. I checked my watch, 10:02, and headed for the spot at the center of campus where Jack had dropped me off a few nights before. The sky was completely cloudless, and the air was frigid. It felt odd to be meeting Jack for no urgent Dhia-arranged reason. His silver car idled in the loading zone with its tailpipe puffing smoke like a cigar. Jack jumped out and opened the door for me as I approached.

"I hoped this was where we were meeting," he said, climbing into the driver's seat and pulling the car away from the curb.

"I hoped so too… the only place that made sense, really…" My voice squeaked.

"Maybe we should exchange phone numbers at some point so we can be sure?"

"Yeah, that might be a good idea."

I could think of absolutely nothing else to say.

What if I can't think of a single, solitary thing to say to him all day long? I worried. *Or what if, under normal circumstances, he finds out that I am the most boring individual he's ever met and we part awkwardly with him, secretly hoping Dhia never asks him to chauffeur me again?* Having thought it, the stubbornly cynical part of me just *knew* that's exactly how it would be. I tried to brush my paranoid thoughts aside. They couldn't possibly help.

"Tea house isn't far, maybe twenty minutes or so," he said.

"Okay."

We both fell silent. I listened to the hum of the motor and the thrum of the tires on the road.

"I'm seriously nervous," Jack finally confessed.

"Oh, good," I said, relieved.

"Good?"

"Not that I'm happy for you, I'm not, I mean… I'm just nervous too. I'm glad I'm not the only one. I mean—I've never been on a date before," I blurted, immediately wondering if I'd actually said those words out loud. "Not that this is a date, or anything, really… I don't mean to put expectations on it…" I stumbled over my words, feeling the familiar hot flush of embarrassment creep up my neck.

"It's not a date?" he asked.

"Well, I don't know, is it?"

"Yeah, I thought so. You didn't?" He looked confused.

"Well, yeah. I did. I guess… yeah. I thought it was a date—sort of, at least. It's kind of strange to think of it as being a first date when my friends already wonder what's up because they found me sleeping in your clothes… Oh. My. Word! I will just shut up now because *nothing I'm saying is coming out right!*" I clapped my hand over my mouth, and noted Jack's grin.

"I guess I can see that being kind of suspicious," he said. "So this is your first date in… ever? Or just for a long time?"

"Ever," I admitted.

"Wow, how did you manage that?"

"I don't wear trendy clothes, I keep my nose in my books, and I tend to say what I think too often. That might have something to do with it. Also, I've always said *no* to every date every time I was ever asked by anyone."

"Every time?"

"Yep, every time. It's not like I got asked a lot…"

"I guess that makes me special."

How about you? Do you date a lot?" I asked him, wanting to redirect the spotlight to any place else but me.

Jack shook his head. "Just once."

"Oh yeah? One date… ever?"

"No, one girl." His eyes clouded a little.

"Oh… and what happened?"

"You do cut right to the chase with the hard questions, don't you?" Jack glanced in my direction and tried to smile.

"I'm sorry, that was a little blunt. You are by no means obligated to answer."

He ran his hands through his dark shaggy hair just as my father did when he was stressed. "No, it's okay. I want to answer it. I dated one girl, for a couple of years. I thought we'd maybe be together forever. We were tight. Then she died."

"Oh my gosh, I'm so sorry!"

"It's okay, I mean, it is how it is, right? God has other plans for me." Jack's voice was a little rough and deeper than usual. "She died a few years ago, before I moved here."

"Is that why you moved here?" I asked.

"In part, I guess. My parents split the same year she died. She was hit by a car. My parents—they are technically married, but don't speak to each other anymore. They don't live together. I had baseball scholarships… but I just couldn't imagine going to college and play-ing ball after that. It stopped being fun. Everything stopped being fun."

"So what did you do?"

"Sort of ran away, I guess. I cashed out my college account, bought a ticket to Scotland. I knew my uncle lived here, so I showed up on his doorstep."

"So that's not really running away, right…? If you went to see your uncle?"

"It's a long story, but my uncle didn't know even I existed until I showed up on his front porch. I'd never met him before. Luckily, he let me in. Then he introduced me to God, just about right away. He runs the shop I work in… my uncle, that is, not God. My uncle and God are pretty close, though… so I guess you could say God runs the shop." Jack's voice was fuller again and less husky. We pulled into a parking spot under a tree across from an old mixed-use building. He killed the engine, and neither of us moved.

"You didn't know God before you came here?" I asked.

"Nope. Actually, Stacey was a Christian… my girlfriend. She was always talking to me about God. I just wasn't interested at the time. I kind of thought the whole concept was kind of like 'the Force' from *Star Wars*."

"And you didn't buy it, right…? Does that make you Han Solo?"

He snorted. "Hardly. A week or so before she died, she talked to me about God again. She said she needed to know I would at least look into it."

Look into what?"

"She wanted me to try church."

"Did you?"

"I attended a service with her."

"And?"

"And… nothing. It was boring. There were lots of old people and coffee stains on the carpet. I don't remember a single word the preacher said."

"So you were really open-minded, then…," I teased.

"Ha, very funny. How about you… I suppose you love church, right?"

"Uh, actually I don't really go to church either," I admitted.

"Really? Even now?"

"Even now. I guess maybe I could find a church to go to now. Maybe someone could explain some of the Bible to me. I read it. I just don't always know what everything means. So much of church isn't about God, though. It's hard to want to be there. I haven't been a Christian for very long, and my family didn't go to church. Well, a few times, for funerals and weddings… you know, the usual."

"So how did you know you were Called?"

"I think we are in the middle of *your* story right now. You were at the coffee-stained church with the boring preacher…," I prompted him.

"Right. I went to her church with her… with Stacey. I didn't care much for it. We had a fight, one of the biggest ones we'd ever had. She wasn't sure she wanted to be with someone who was so cynical about her faith. We didn't talk much for a few days; then her family was in a car accident. Drunk driver. She died at the scene. I was at home when I got the call. I went to tell my parents, but Dad was drunk, and Mom wasn't home. I packed my bags, and the next morning, cleared out my savings account and headed for the airport."

"You had a passport?"

"Yes. I'd wanted to travel ever since I was little. I got my passport before I got my driver's license. I just hadn't ever used it. I was at the airport, looking at flight prices, and found a discount price for flights to Scotland—one way, for three hundred forty-nine dollars. I took it as a sign even though I didn't believe in signs and boarded the plane. I haven't been back since."

"So you came to Scotland to see your uncle, even though he didn't know you existed?"

"Well, he's technically my uncle once removed. My great-aunt told me about him. I think I mentioned my great-aunt before?"

I nodded. He had. She was the one who had told him about the Calling.

I showed up on his doorstep, explained who I was, and he invited me in. He told me about God over dinner that night, and I just knew he was telling the truth, that Stacey had been telling the truth too. I just hadn't seen it before. Then suddenly I did see it. I don't know how else to explain it."

"You recognized truth," I said.

"Yes, exactly. I recognized truth. I think God let me see it or maybe I let myself see it... I'm not sure which. Anyway, I made a promise to Him, to God, not my uncle... that I would do anything He said from there on out."

"You weren't mad at God for letting Stacey die?"

"No." Jack looked surprised. "I never thought of being mad at God actually. He didn't kill her. Someone's stupid choices killed her. I don't think God had it in for her. We live in a hard world where people make crappy choices and sad things happen. Something else happened that first night at my uncle's house... God spoke to me. Out loud. He told me I was exactly where I needed to be, and I believed Him. I decided to work in my uncle's shop until I figured out my next move, and I've been there ever since. God hasn't told me to leave yet."

"And your parents? Do they know where you are?"

"Oh yeah. I called them. They don't much care, though... They are so wrapped up in being angry at each other they don't have time to fuss over me. I think they were relieved to have me gone."

Wow," I said.

"Wow—what?"

"I don't know, just... wow. All of that. I'm not sure what to say."

"You don't need to say anything," Jack said. "Nothing anyone says makes any difference anyway."

"That's a lot of loss."

"Yeah, I guess it is. Life's like that... either you grow old and you lose people, or they grow old and they lose you. It's loss either way."

"Aren't you kind of young for that kind of cynicism?" I asked.

"Is it cynical? I don't feel bitter about it. I think its truth. Does being young mean we should disregard the truth?"

"I guess not. I know a little bit about loss too. My mother is gone."

"Gone where?" Jack asked.

"That's what everyone asks. I don't know where she went. She left us. She just posted a note for my dad on the fridge that said she was leaving, and she never came back. That was it. She just left."

"Wow. When did that happen?"

"Over Christmas break."

"Seriously? *This* Christmas break?" He sat up straight in his seat, and his voice gained volume. "Just a few weeks ago?"

"Yep."

"And you don't know where she is?"

"No clue."

"Wow," he said, running his hands through his hair again, standing a strip of it on end like a Mohawk.

"Why didn't you say anything before? How are you so sane about it?"

"Who says I am sane? Actually, I think Dhia's holding me together. What would be the point of freaking out anyway? It wouldn't make any difference. She's gone. Somewhere else… doing something I'm not a part of, and she doesn't want to be found."

We sat in silence for a moment.

"Nice look," I finally said, pointing to his hair.

He flipped his visor down and attempted to fix his hairstyle. My flippancy worked. The solemn mood broke.

"Should we go in?" he asked.

"Absolutely."

The tea shop wasn't what I'd expected. I'd expected a dark corner cafe that smelled like must and dust and boasted Ceylon, English Breakfast, and Darjeeling… maybe the proprietors would be an older couple dressed in plaid with delightful, unintelligible accents. Or maybe it would be staffed by trendy young women with multiple tats and piercings. Instead, the tea shop was housed in a sun-filled, plant-strewn atrium on the roof of the old building. The back wall of the atrium and part of the ceiling were solid wood. The remaining three walls and portion of the ceiling were greenhouse glass. It was an Asian teahouse. The owners, elderly and standoffish, spoke rudimentary English only. I tried out a few of my newly acquired Chinese phrases on them as we ordered and watched their scowls morph into wide smiles. They took great joy in pointing out the errors in my pronunciation and declaring I would never be able to master such a difficult language, though they encouraged me to keep trying. They promised to give us "the best tea, the kind we save away for only *best* customers." *Wink, wink.*

"You are taking Chinese, huh? Brave woman. I tried to learn another language once. The words just wouldn't stick to my brain," Jack said ruefully.

"You haven't picked up any Gaelic since you got here, then?"

"No. My uncle and his friends speak it all the time, but I don't understand one word. You?"

"I speak it actually. I'm kind of a word buff. I always say the only thing I'm good at is spelling," I said sheepishly.

"Which is untrue, of course…"

"Not really. I'm not good at the things that most people value."

"Like what?"

"Like… for instance… walking in a straight line," I said.

"Seriously?"

"Yes! Seriously! I'm a total klutz. I fall down all the time."

"Okay, well, no one wins awards for straight line walking anyway. So what else do you suck at?" Jack leaned back in his chair, and I realized it was the first time I'd seen him truly relaxed. His eyes crinkled at the corner when he smiled, as if he were much older than he really was. He was close enough that I could smell his warm, piney scent.

"Hello? You there?" he asked.

"Oh yeah. Sorry. I guess I drifted. What I suck at… that was the question, right? Well, I suck at math. Numbers fly right out of my head. My brain is math Teflon."

"Oh, come on, everyone sucks at math. You have to do better than that," he chided.

"No, actually, some people are *very good* at math. Successful people—it's true! I've met some of them."

"So do you want to be good at math?"

"No, actually. Then I'd have no excuse to hate it."

"Well, there you go then. Math is highly overrated." He grinned, and my heart fluttered. The realization that I would do almost anything to see him smile again scared me.

"Small talk. I suck at small talk. You can't tell me that people don't value cushy, pointless small talk. Like… 'How are you?' or 'What a cute baby!' or "It's such bad weather. When do you think the sun will return?' All those things that other people say are *painful* to me. I never think of them at the right times. My inability to engage in small talk has successfully ended many conversations almost before they even start." I rolled my eyes, remembering a few of those stunted discourses.

"You are right on that point. Most people highly value conversation that, if properly dried out, would fertilize the lawn," he admitted.

I had been taken a sip of my roasted green tea and promptly snort-laughed a swig of it up into the back of my nose when he said that. I grabbed a napkin, trying to avoid shooting tea out of my nostrils at him.

That's excellent first date etiquette! I thought wryly.

"Are you okay? You should try drinking, laughing and breathing at *separate* times, not all at once. Haven't they taught you that in nursing school yet?" he asked, donating his napkin to my cause.

"Not yet. Good tip, though, I'll keep that in mind." I dabbed at my streaming nose and eyes.

"She's fine. Seriously, fine. Just got something down the wrong tube," Jack explained to the female shop owner who rushed over to check on my health. Her face resembled a dried golden apple.

"Tube?" she asked, hoping for clarification. She probably also hoped I wouldn't choke to death in her establishment.

"I'm fine. Really. Fine," I assured her.

"She caught Jack's eye and gestured at me, as if instructing him to keep an eye on me, and he gave her a thumbs-up. That satisfied her, and she returned to the kitchen, clucking and muttering, 'Xiao xin,' meaning 'Be careful' as she went."

"So you like words, though not false or pointless ones." Jack recaptured the point.

"Yeah, I never thought about it quite like that before—but yes. That's exactly true."

"And you speak some Chinese…"

"Well, I've only started Chinese recently. I speak German and Gaelic, though… better than I speak Chinese. And English, of course."

"I guessed as much," Jack replied.

"Sorry, my friends call me Captain Obvious."

"They do?" he asked.

"No, actually they don't. But they probably should. I call myself that. I'm better with words on paper than in person. I don't always put them together well when I'm talking. Open mouth, insert foot…"

"Well, I'm impressed, at the languages part, anyway…"

"Oh, *please* don't be impressed. It's a hobby. What are you good at…? Baseball, I imagine?"

"Yeah, pretty good, but not great, and that's not false modesty—it's just fact. I could hold my own, but even before Stacey died, I started getting bored and restless. I wanted to do something more important than run in circles and swing a bat. I just didn't know what it was."

"Do you know now?" I asked carefully.

"No. Not really. But I'm not restless anymore. At least, not since…" He paused for a moment.

"Since when?"

"Well, since I met you, I guess. I mean, I didn't really know what I wanted to do at college anyway, so college was no big loss. It was actually a relief to kiss that idea good-bye. My uncle taught me how to listen better to God's voice, and that was great, *really* great. But I felt like I was supposed to be looking for something, you know? Like God had something he wanted me to do, like something was coming… I just needed to keep waiting and watching for it. So I did. I did whatever He told me to, and I kept looking. I still am, I guess." He took a sip of his tea before he continued. "Then He had me drive you to the lake that night, and it was like a puzzle piece that fit. I stayed awake for a few nights, wondering *how* it fit. I haven't figured that part out yet."

"That's kind of how Dhia works," I said.

"Dhia?"

"Yeah, *Dhia* is the Gaelic word for *God*. It's what I call Him," I explained.

"Dhia…" Jack mulled the name over in his head. "I like that. What I *do* know, is that you are a part of whatever Dhia wants for me. Not that I assume anything about you and me. I'm just saying that I think maybe what He has for me and what He has planned for you… maybe there's something in common there. That day at the lake I felt like He was finally showing me a little glimpse of what He's been prepping me for. I'd never been involved with anything so… so… strange, so obviously of Him. The lake, the lady on the boat, the fact that we were out there at night with mysteriously appearing road maps and no one but God to actually set up the meeting… Have you ever been involved in anything like that before?" he asked.

"Uh, no. Not quite like that," I admitted.

I've been involved in stranger things, though, I thought. I didn't say that part out loud.

"I'm sorry about your mom," he said suddenly.

"I'm sorry about Stacey and your parents," I replied.

Jack reached across the table and took my hands in his. They were rough from manual labor, and the warmth of them sent a shiver up my spine.

"I didn't plan to date, ever again, after Stacey died. I thought maybe that was my one chance, and it was a short-lived one. I don't really feel that way anymore. I want to see you again, if you want to, if that's okay,"

"So you want to see me again because Dhia told you to?" I asked.

"No. He told me to pick you up and drive you places in my car in the middle of the night and fix your window. He didn't tell me to date you. He also didn't tell me *not* to date you. I want to see you again because there's something special about you. I *chose* to ask you here today."

I took a deep breath and tried to accept his words. *Special...
I want to see you again... I chose to ask you.* It was *so* hard for me to
believe those words had just been directed at me.

"I'm not sure what to say to that," I finally said.

"Because you don't think you are special?" he blurted.

"Wow, okay... now who is being blunt and bold?"

"Turnabout is fair play," he said, his charcoal-gray eyes boring
holes in my faces. It took everything in me to hold his gaze. *Most
people don't have gray eyes. Or do they...? Adenauer, snap out of it! You
can think about eye color later!*

"Sorry, what was the question, again?" I asked.

You have a hard time accepting compliments, don't you?"

"Definitely. I always have. But my grandma tells me it's much
less awkward for other people if you accept a compliment than if you
reject it. So I'm working on it."

"She's a wise woman. Compliments do more *for* you when you
accept them too. Did you ever notice how the bad words seem to
stick with you, and the good words tend to bounce off and roll into
the gutter?"

"I've noticed."

"I don't think that's the way God meant it to be. So I'll try
again. I think you are special, and I'd like to see you again," he nodded at me, urging me to respond.

"Thank you. I think you are special too. And I'd like to see you
again as well," I said carefully.

"That was pretty good... I'm not sure I really believe you. You
should work on the warmth of your delivery." He smiled.

I punched him gently on the arm.

"Ow!"

"That didn't hurt... Besides, you deserved it."

"Touché. Want to tell me anymore about your Calling?" he
asked.

"No. Not yet. I mean, I would, but I don't know much myself.
I don't know what to say and what *not* to say."

"There are rules about that?" he asked.

"I don't know. Nothing written, if that's what you mean, but I don't know. I mean we just do what Dhia asks us to do. No different than you, really…"

"Except that mysteriously appearing and disappearing women and lakes are involved."

"Well, yeah… except for that."

"I get it. No pressure. I'm just curious," he assured me.

"I know. Me too."

We switched to safer topics after that. We chatted a while longer, downing enough tea to inordinately please the shop owners and send each of us on multiple trips to the bathroom, where the oval toilet was topped by an ill-fitting circular toilet seat. I filled Jack in on the college classes I was taking and what my hometown was like. He told me about his American and Scottish family members, and the grudges they held against each other—enduring, painful grudges that forever split the family. He talked about his job. After a while, it felt like time to go. We paid the check, promised the little old Chinese couple we would be back so they could pick apart my grammar again and drove back to the college. Jack dropped me off at the now familiar spot at the curb. We remembered to exchange phone numbers. I wrote his number on a note in my purse; the note was pink, and my purse was brown. He wrote my number on his hand.

"I think it's unhealthy to write on your skin. The ink can soak into your bloodstream," I told him.

"I'll keep that in mind," he answered in a way that made me think he probably wouldn't.

He laid his hand against my cheek and said good-bye. I let my cheek rest against his palm for a moment. It wasn't time for a kiss, and we both seemed to know it. I walked slowly back to the dorm, letting the beautiful clear sun and sky fill up my soul. I whispered, "Thank you," as I walked, and I felt Dhia smile at me. A small bubble of joy flared in my chest.

STILLNESS

That was the first of twenty-nine days of atypical sun at Aodhagan. A local weather person dubbed the time "the Snap" at some point during the dry stretch, and the term stuck. I personally thought the word *stretch* was more appropriate for it than the word *snap*, but no one asked me. It wasn't just rare to have such a string of dry days in January and February… It was extraordinary. The twenty-nine days passed without a cloud in the sky or a whisper of wind. Everyone marveled and a few of the braver students, (or stupider, depending on how you look at it… it was sunny. Not warm,) even donned shorts to celebrate the sun.

Jack called during the first week of the Snap. He and his uncle would be out of town for a month working on a job they had booked in the city.

"Don't find yourself a new chauffeur while I'm gone," he said.

"I won't. Unless, of course, You-Know-Who arranges it. I don't have much control over His whims." I thought of the first time I was jerked off my feet into the air and then of Fa dragging me down under the waves in the Iona bay.

"I'll think of you while you are gone," I promised quietly… the relative anonymity of the phone made it easier to say—easier than it would have been in person where I could see his eyes, feel his body heat, and smell his scent.

We agreed to have dinner with his uncle once they were back in town, and I reluctantly hung up the phone.

The weather wasn't the only thing uncommonly still during the Snap. Dhia was also incredibly quiet, at least when it came to me. I talked to Him. I sang. I begged Him for answers, for direction. I watched for His hand to move but felt nothing. It felt as if He'd been there one day and vanished the next. My emotions were all over the map. I had so many questions, and Dhia's silence only served to make them seem more pressing, more urgent. I tried to look at Ailsa's journals, but her words flew out of my brain as quickly as I took them in. The relentless emptiness of the air made me fidgety and a little uneasy, as it did most everyone else.

I avoided Donal and Aggie and holed up in my found office in the admin building with my journal and my Bible. Unlike the words in Ailsa's journals, the words I read from scriptures seemed to stick with me. I became hungrier and hungrier for them—even the passages I didn't understand stirred in me a desire to know Dhia more. I just wanted more. The lack of His tangible voice drove me to His written words. I began to memorize passages, repeating them in the shower and while I fell asleep at night. The nights were long; and my dreams were restless, color-filled, smoke-filled confusion.

I stared often out the window of my stolen perch into the cold bright stillness and pondered. I thought a lot about Jack—not so much of himself, as the idea of him: what he represented for me. He represented my weakness, vulnerability, lack of emotional control, and my need. That scared me. I'd fought so hard not to need anyone, not to let anyone get close to my heart. Jack threatened all that I'd worked for.

I thought too of the Blues. I hadn't heard from Fa in a long time. Why? I thought she was supposed to be training me, and yet her visits were few and far between. When would I see her again? When would my next jaunt take place? It seemed so long ago! What was happening on Petra? Where would Dhia send me next? Who would I meet there?

And the SuCH group... what was that about? How did they fit in? Was I supposed to do something about them... or just pray for protection from them? I did pray for Dhia's protection every day; but with Jack out of town and not hearing from Shine or Fa, I began to feel isolated and more than a little vulnerable.

Dhia's silence continued. The space between myself and Himself seemed as still and empty as the bright clear sky. For the first twenty-four days of silent sun I heard nothing from Him. On the twenty-fifth day He spoke. I was trekking across campus from the science lab to the dorm, silently pleading with Dhia to speak with me, to say anything... even if He didn't want to supply me with answers to my questions when I heard Him say, "Hush, be still! Know that I am God." His voice was loud and even, and it startled me. I stopped suddenly, and the person walking behind me almost plowed me over.

"Please excuse me," I murmured to the girl. She glared at me and moved on. Bad day, I guess.

Be still and know that I am God, He'd said. So I obeyed. I stood still on the walkway and looked up, first into the empty sky, then at the static trees. Nothing, absolutely nothing, moved. No birds or squirrels rustled in the trees. There were no longer students milling around me. It was as if the world was entirely stationary, and I was the only one in it. Dhia taught me, then, what it meant to be still and know that He is God.

Dhia's presence rushed in to fill the space around me, just as concretely as it had in the tiny mountain healing room on Petra. One moment, I was standing in the center of the walkway. The next moment I was lying flat, facedown on the ground. My eyes were shut. His light was too bright. I could see its glow through my eyelids even with my hands pressed tight over my face. I felt power wash over me like a hundred-ton wave from my head to my toes, pressing me into the pavement. Then truth exploded in my skull, lingering like an enormous brain freeze. Beauty followed it, bringing tears to my eyes, and a sob tore at my throat. Goodness hummed in my hands, purring like a powerful but contented tiger. Then love shot up from my feet, coursing and forking every direction on hot pink lightning bolts, convening again at my heart—filling it to bursting. I'm not sure how long the experience lasted. Moments, maybe? I'm not sure I even breathed during that time. I desperately needed it to stop and simultaneously never wanted it to end. It finally did end, however; and I lay there, afraid to move, gasping for air like a fish out of water. I heard nothing. Once my breathing had returned almost to normal, I lifted my head tentatively to look around. Seeing no one, I sat up. I was somewhat surprised to see that my body had not left a permanent dent in the sidewalk. There was a distinct shadow, a faint brownish-black outline of my exact body shape on the cement. I touched my hand to it and pulled it back, reflexively. It was hot. I wondered if the outline would fade with the escaping heat.

I glanced around again and spotted a student heading my direction. I didn't want to get caught crouched beside a steaming, or smoking, outline of myself... My brain wasn't in any shape to manufacture a viable explanation for that. I stood up carefully and tested my shaky legs. Stable... though my head was spinning, and the entire world was that vivid green color that obscures your vision when you enter a dim room after having spent time playing in the brilliant-white snow. I blinked rapidly, trying to clear the afterimages and regain normal vision. I made my way slowly back to Bert. I could see normally by the time I reached the front doors, all except for one tiny sparkly spot in the vision of one eye, which didn't seem to want to clear. I blinked repeatedly, but the squiggle remained.

I called in sick to a meet-up with Aggie that evening, citing a headache as my reason. It was true enough. My sensory circuits felt overloaded, and my head had begun to throb. I stopped at the dorm kitchen and poured myself two large glasses of water from the water cooler, then returned to my room to rest and rehydrate. I lay on the bed and willed my shaky muscles to restore themselves. My feet felt disconnected. My gut felt like jelly. My fingers were numb. Out of sheer exhaustion, I fell asleep and dreamt of nothing.

I asked Dhia less questions after that. It wasn't that my questions had evaporated; they just didn't seem to matter as much anymore. Dhia was so much *more* than my questions. His holiness had been a theory before. Now it was a fact fixed in my mind and etched in my memory. I'd experienced a piece of His holy presence, and it had been more than I could bear. He had driven the truth of Himself all the way to my core, where it fused with my heart. A new sense of peace—one that didn't lift and flutter as much with my emotions remained with me—along with the curious, stubborn squiggle in my vision.

I met Aggie in the microbiology lab the next day. There was a bounce in her step and a smile on her face that I'd not seen in quite a while.

"The weird weather agrees with you, I see," I said.

"We made up," she announced with an almost-childish sideways smile.

"Ha! Suspicion confirmed. It was Donal that had your panties in a bunch."

"Panties in a bunch?" Her face drew into a question mark.

"Sorry. It's my grandma's favorite phrase. It means 'knickers twisted,' grumpy, irritated, angry, pissy…"

"Oh, I see," she said, still looking puzzled. "Yes, Donal and I didn't agree on something. We couldn't decide who was right or wrong, so we called it a draw and moved on."

"And the issue was…?"

"It was about trees, actually." She looked a little sheepish.

"Trees? You were mad at Donal for over a month because of trees?'

"It sounds a little silly, now…"

"A little?" I interrupted her.

"I don't want to go into it. It was just… our first real fight."

"What do you mean your first fight? You guys pick at each other all the time! You bicker like an old couple."

"That's no big thing, though. Everyone does that, don't they? Everyone in my family does, anyway… and everyone in his family too. This was different. It was a fight. He wouldn't back down. He hurt my feelings."

"You got it taken care of, though?"

"Yes. Definitely. Well, I think so. Actually, I don't know. We kissed, though, so I think so."

"Ew. I can't hear about that."

"You are so weird about kissing!" Aggie exclaimed. "Kissing is so natural, so human… and you are a nurse! You should be able to handle it, no problem!"

"I know. I accept it. I just don't want to think about you and Donal kissing any more than I want to hear about my parents kissing."

That reminded me of my mother, that she was gone—a fact which hadn't hit the front of my mind for a few hours. A shiver ran up my spine, but the coldness didn't stay.

"You okay?" Aggie asked, a look of concern clouding her face.

"Yeah—just thinking. I'm fine. Congratulations on getting back together."

"Thanks. Maybe we can get together, have a group meet-up, the four of us."

"Four?"

"Yeah, you, me, Donal, and your mystery guy…"

"Oh, Jack?"

"He has a name!" she exclaimed.

Several students turned to stare at her, and the professor's eyes flashed a warning shot across her bow. We both knew he only gave one warning shot. She dropped her voice, and we returned our attention to our petri dishes. I dropped a few drops of antibiotic-laden fluid from a beaker onto three different specimens and returned the petri dishes to the warmer, holding my breath until I was a safe distance away again. The odor still followed me.

"Well? If this Jack is real, then when do we get to meet him?" she whispered upon my return.

"I guess we can all get together sometime."

"Sometime?"

"Well, he's out of town right now."

She looked dubious.

"Seriously. He doesn't go to the college, remember? He works with his uncle, installing windows. They have an out-of-town job this month. But when he gets back, we will set something up."

"Do you promise?" Aggie's arms were crossed.

"I promise. Cross my heart. You work on staying friends with Donal long enough for us to get together, and I'll work on setting something up for all four of us. We went to a really neat little tea shop on Saturday, actually. I think you'd like it."

"Okay, I believe you, for now," she acquiesced. "We will see what happens."

Phew! Being under Aggie's scrutiny was enough to make me sweat. I didn't envy Donal.

"So the real date was Saturday, yes? How was it?"

"Good. Good enough for another one, at least. That's good." I felt the obnoxious red flush creeping up my neck again.

"So it's love?" she asked.

"Do you love Donal?" I asked, turning the tables on her.

"I... don't know,'" she said, flustered.

"You've known him all year. I've only known Jack a short while. If you don't know whether or not you love him, then how should I?"

"It's different with Donal. We were friends first. I don't think it's the same with you and Jack," she said. "Your brain melts, and your face turns color when you talk about him."

I knew she was at least partially right, but it wasn't something I understood or wanted to discuss. Class had ended, and it was my turn to walk away without answering. Aggie let me.

The weather was still and clear for another four days after that. The people of the town were getting ready to call in scientists; gloomy weather was their comfort zone. Stripped of their wind and rain for too long, they began to stay indoors, vigilantly watching through their windows for the return of normalcy.

"It's nae natural," I overheard a local man tell the checker at the market, shaking his head.

The checker clucked his tongue at him in sad agreement. "Sure enough. Dhia's mebbe radge at someain." He meant "mad at someone."

I didn't agree with the checker's assessment but didn't think he would welcome my argument.

On the twenty-ninth day of the Snap, as I exited the admin building rehearsing speech lines for English class, someone stepped directly in front of me on the walk. I mumbled, "Excuse me," and tried to step to the side, but the girl mimicked my steps and stood her ground. Half expecting to see Professor Mac, I looked up... directly into the clear blue angry eyes of a stranger. She was slightly shorter than me with stringy brown hair and a bright yellow blazer.

"I'm sorry, do I know you?" I asked.

"I know you, and that's enough," she snapped.

Her words sent a surge of something hot and ready from my feet to my fingertips. I stood very still.

A Dhia help me, I prayed silently.

Out of the corner of my eye, I saw a few curious students gather to stare. At least we weren't alone.

"Are you waiting for me to speak?" I finally asked the girl.

"There are better places for you than here," she whispered, taking an aggressive step toward me. I stood my ground.

The words, "And where do you suggest I go?" were on the tip of my tongue, but I caught and banished them. I didn't really want to know what her answer would be. I stared at her instead, breath caught in my throat, until she broke gaze and went on her way.

A few students, none that I knew, stepped up beside me once she disappeared inside the building.

"Hey, you okay?" a deep voice said. The voice belonged to a tall blond guy with a sparse, shaggy beard.

"Oh yeah. I'm okay," I said, noting that my voice was a little shaky. I didn't sound okay.

"You sure?" an older girl asked.

"I'm sure." My blood pressure seemed to be returning to normal, slowly. I just needed a few minutes.

"What did you do to her?" the blond guy asked.

"I have no idea. I don't know her."

"Seriously?"

"Yeah, seriously. I've never seen her before," I said, sinking to a nearby bench. The small crowd of students slowly dispersed, all but the two who'd talked to me.

"That's what evil looks like," the older girl said matter-of-factly.

I really looked at her for the first time. She was a short brunette with shabby clothing and an even shabbier backpack. Something about her reminded me of Millie.

"Evil... that's exactly what I was thinking," the blond bearded guy agreed. "I'm Baz. This is Mairi."

"Kiah, nice to meet you," I said.

"I'm not joking about the 'evil' bit," Baz reiterated. "I mean nothing against that girl, I don't know her... but there was more at stake in her eyes and her voice than a bad day. You need to be careful."

"I catch your drift," I assured him.

"Are ye a believer, then? A Christian?" Mairi asked.

Her question surprised me. People at Aodhagan didn't talk much about their personal faith.

"Uh... yes. Yes I am. Are you?"

"We are. There aren't many believers on campus. Jest a few. We 'ave prayer meetin's, if ye want to join us."

"I didn't know there was anything for Christians at this school." I was feeling steady again and aware that I needed to get to my next class.

"There's nothing official. There aren't enough of us for that. A few of us meet on the odd day to read scripture verses and pray," Baz explained, penning a phone number along with the time and date of the next meeting on a scrap of paper, which he handed it to me.

I told them I would think about joining them for a meeting if I could work it into my schedule. I still felt unsure about meeting with other believers that weren't Called. I hated feeling like I had to hide things from people. We said our good-byes. I glanced up at the admin building and saw the brown-haired girl staring down at me from the third-story window. She gave me the chills. That afternoon I spotted Jen, the newbie from the SuCH club, sitting alone in the cafeteria, dissecting a muffin. I sat my tray down beside hers and scooched in next to her.

"I'm hoping this doesn't have walnuts in it. Walnuts make my nose itch," she said in explanation of her behavior without looking up from her task.

I picked up a clean fork from my tray and joined her search.

"The sign over them said 'Butterscotch Oat,' and I don't see any lumps. I think you are in the clear," I assured her.

"Thanks. It seems silly, but I'm just allergic to everything... Oh, it's you!" she said, finally looking up at me.

"Yeah, from the club intro day, you remember me?"

"Yes, of course!" She dropped her voice. "That was weird."

"Professor Mac... with the flier, you mean?"

"Yeah, that. But the whole thing... that club..."

"What do you mean?"

Jen looked around as if to see if anyone was watching her, then scooted even closer to me.

"I went to one of the meetings, the other meetings I was telling you about—the ones with the more committed members?" She gestured over her shoulder with her thumb to indicate the "otherness" of the meeting she had attended. "It was up in the mountains. I thought it would be a bonfire with snacks and singing. Kum-ba-yah sort of stuff, you know?"

I nodded.

"Well, you had asked me if we had to swear in, to take vows...?" She waited again for me to respond, so I nodded again.

"That's what they were doing. Swearing in for something. It wasn't just a club thing, though. It was like a religion thingy."

"What kind of religious thingy?" I asked.

"I don't know, chanting, robes, weird languages... but not like church. I've been to church. It's never been like that. It felt wrong... bad or something. I don't know. I wondered if they could be witches, even... The school wouldn't put up with witches, as a club, would they?" she asked. Her eyes widened, and her brow furrowed, making her look like a troubled child.

"I don't know. I guess the college wouldn't discriminate against any religious preferences," I said.

"I guess not." Jen didn't seem reassured.

"So are you still in the club?"

"No way! Are you kidding? Daphne, Cora, and I rode up there together. Cora wanted to stay, but Daphne and I wanted to leave. So we got out of there fast... I fell over a log," she said. She pulled up the hem of her jeans to show me her impressively bruised and abraded knee.

"Ouch."

"Yeah, ouch… and creepy. Daphne and I are never going back. It will make a good story, though. When I'm older and somebody asks about the college I went to, I can tell them, 'Well, I think I met some witches, once, in the woods.' That would make a good story, right?"

"Sure. Great story," I said without much conviction.

"What about Cora?" I asked.

"Cora?"

"Yeah, Cora… the girl you went up there with?"

"Oh, she got a ride home with someone else."

"I mean, have you talked to her since you got back?"

"Well, sort of. I mean, I've seen her since then, but she acts sort of different. Like the girls in high school who are your friend one day and not the next, and you just never know why… She told me I don't take being a woman seriously enough, and she thinks it's really irresponsible that I don't respect the Earth more. She said if I respected the bond between women and the Earth I would have stayed with the club." Jen rolled her eyes. "I have no idea what that even means!"

She stared at me expectantly, as if waiting for me to shed further light on her experiences.

"I don't know either," I said. I threw my hands in the air to demonstrate just how clueless I was. I didn't think telling Jen the small bit more that I knew about the druids would be of any use. "But it sounds like you made the right choice," I said.

"Oh yeah, definitely. You don't have to tell me that!"

Jen had mentioned she had grown up in a Christian family. I felt the urge to talk about that with her, but just thinking about it made me nervous. My faith was so new and so private. I knew that discussing matters of faith was offensive to some people, and I didn't want to step on her toes. Jen didn't seem the type that was easily offended, however, and she had broached the subject first…

"You said you grew up going to church. Are you still a Christian, then?" I asked quietly.

"Oh, well, yeah, I guess so," she said, as if I'd asked her whether, having been born a human, she still claimed to be one.

"There's a little Bible study on campus. Someone gave me the information on it… I haven't been, but you could go… if you want to. Maybe take your friend Daphne?"

"There's a Bible study here? On campus?"

"I'm pretty sure it's on campus. I haven't been to it, but I can give you the info, in case you want to go." I pulled the little slip of paper Baz had given me from my bag and transferred the information into the flap of Jen's notebook, which she offered me for that purpose. I noticed doodles of hearts, animals, and flowers in the margins of the notebook.

"You are a pretty good artist," I complimented her.

"Oh. Thanks."

I needed to get to class. I stood to leave. "I have to get going."

"Me too. Maybe I'll see you around?" She looked hopeful—and so young.

"Of course."

Do I look that young and naive? I wondered as I watched her bop through the great hall cafe toward the exit doors. There was no one there to answer that question, except Dhia, and I was relatively certain that in His eyes I did seem pretty young and naive. That thought made me smile.

The next morning, after twenty-nine days of clear skies, I awoke to the sound of howling wind and rain on the rooftop. I'd never been so happy to hear a storm. Students and staff alike donned their wellies and tromped to class through the gathering puddles with glee, bracing against the wind. The dry, surprised ground had a hard time accepting the return of the water. Puddles were forming everywhere.

I had clinicals that afternoon at the nursing home. The residents were crankier than usual. They had enjoyed the intermission from the rain. The return of moisture had kicked up their rheumatism and their complaints, which made for a long, nerve-grating shift. The howling wind pushed at the carpool vehicle as it crept back to the school that night. I was crammed into the van alongside Aggie, Donal, and three other slightly wilted nursing students. Someone smelled like vomit. Someone else, or possibly that same unlucky person, smelled of body odor. As we piled out of the van, I began to fantasize about a warm shower and warm bed… until my shoulders began to buzz.

Now? I asked Dhia silently. *You have to be kidding me!*

Now, He answered. He wasn't much of a kidder.

"I'm going to get some fresh air, guys. Go on in without me," I announced, waving them towards the dorm.

"Fresh air? It's raining!" Aggie said.

"You call this rain?" I joked, hoping she'd leave off and head inside. She didn't.

"Going to see Jack?" she asked instead.

"No, he's still out of town, remember?"

"So I'll see you tomorrow?" she prompted me.

"I'm spending the weekend with my family… my great-aunt. I'll see you Monday."

Aggie's arms were crossed, and she was scowling, but she did look slightly more worried than nosy.

You need to learn to be more discreet, I told myself for the umpteenth time. *Why couldn't you just go into the dorm first and sneak out the back?*

I probably could have, but in my defense, I had been doing what Dhia said. He had said to go *now*.

"I'll see you Monday, and I'll be fit as a fiddle," I promised, patting her shoulder.

"Fit as a fiddle?" she asked. "What does that mean?"

"That means I'll be healthy and happy. No midnight diving. I promise." Childhood habit almost made me cross my fingers at that.

"Suit yourself. See you Monday," she said.

She followed the other students toward the dorm, while I followed the strong urging toward the forestry building. The rain was building, and my scrub pants were nearly soaked through. As I ducked behind a row of trees, I was yanked off my feet and into the air. I exclaimed in surprise, then looked around to see if anyone had seen or heard me. There was no one in sight. I picked up speed and height quickly, clearing the tallest trees by a good forty feet. The wind gusts were stronger than any I'd flown in before, and it scared me a little. I climbed higher above the clouds until I located a moderately dry pocket of air and followed it all the way to Iona. Once the island appeared below me, I dropped down again through the wind and rain into Shine's front yard.

Shine waited on the porch, door open, with a dry towel.

"Hi there!" She waved to me as I skidded a few feet and landed firmly on my butt in a puddle.

"I'm still working on my landings. My skills come and go." I climbed off the ground and hurried to the porch.

"I can see that," she answered.

I took the towel from her, and we went inside.

"I came straight from clinicals. I could use a shower."

"I can see that too. You can check out the bathroom then. I just repainted it." She clapped her hands in that girly fluttery excited way that didn't seem to have made it into my genes and led the way to the tiny hall bathroom. Formerly yellow the bathroom was butter yellow with hundreds of tiny pink-, purple-, and blue-painted flowers from floor to ceiling.

"You've been bored, I see…"

"No. Yes. Well, yes and no, actually. I have had some free time," she admitted. "But I prayed while I was painting. Every single flower represents a different person."

"Wow, really?"

Shine reached out and touched a blue flower a little ways off from the others, just behind the edge of the door.

"This one's yours," she said.

"It's by itself," I noted.

"For now," she said.

"What does that mean… that you aren't done painting yet?"

"I don't actually know. I started when He told me to, painted why He told me to, and I stopped when He told me too. I saved the paint in case I need it."

"I guess that makes sense. It's nice."

"Thank you. I thought so too. I'll let you shower." She admired her work for a moment longer, then dropped a dry set of clothing on the toilet before exiting.

I examined her artwork again, wondering if each of the blue flowers represented a Blue. If so, what did a pink flower represent? Many of the flowers had five petals; some had only three or four. A few had even more. Mine had seven. I located the soap, shampoo, washcloth, and shower door, memorizing the location of each before I turned off the light and stepped into the shower. I let the warm water wash off the faint odor and complaints of the sour old people and felt at peace. I reached for the soap and the shampoo... They were in exactly the places my fingers expected them to be. Shine had left me a patched pair of PJ pants and the same flowered T-shirt I'd worn the last time I'd dried off at her place. I exited the bathroom and pulled the squeaky door shut as quietly as possible behind me. Shine had turned out all the lights except for the one on the table beside the couch. She had left me a cup of tea and a note that said, "Quilts everywhere—Use whatever—See you in the morning."

She was right. There were quilts everywhere. Shine collected old quilts that no one wanted anymore—mostly from flea markets and antique shops. I chose two of them, shoved a few piles of books aside, and stretched out on the couch. The wind howled and the rain beat down on the roof, but the little house closed in like an oyster around me, and I slept fast and hard.

SMOKE

I dreamt of a foreign beach littered with beach huts and seashells and dead mollusks drying and stinking in the wind. I walked along the beach past shops that sold hot fried bananas and top-removed coconuts with questionable straws shoved into their middles. (Were they single-use straws... or collected from the trash cans, rinsed in the ocean, and reused? The verdict was out.) There were shops selling recycled fabric, locally made clothing, handmade items of little to no use, used dishes, pots, and pans... The shops were little more than lean-tos scattered along the beach. I wandered inland through a hodgepodge of wooden huts that began just behind the rows of shops. Most of the huts were open-air—tattered curtains hung where the walls should have been. Small fences surrounded some of the huts, and most were built on daises, several feet off the ground. Chickens, dogs, and a few pigs pecked at the dried mud beneath them. I climbed the steps to one of the huts, removed my shoes, placing them in a basket made expressly for that purpose, and ducked inside. A platform bed dominated the space. Also present were a table, two chairs, and a small cupboard. I was alone. I tied back the curtains opposite the bed, revealing a view of the ocean, then pulled a few fried bananas from the bag I'd brought with me into the little house and planted myself on the bed to watch the sunset. The sun lingered, longer than it should have; and a single note, played on an instrument I didn't recognize, rose from somewhere outside the hut. It was a sweet note, and I never wanted it to end, but it did, of course.

It always does. I smelled something burning. I scanned the skyline for the source of the smoke, but the source didn't present itself. Soon, the little room was as filled as an open air room could be with thick, black putrid smoke; and I was coughing, choking, sputtering.

I sat up suddenly in bed, no longer asleep, but the smoke didn't dissipate with the dream. In fact, there in Shine's living room on her saggy little couch, it was even stronger. There was a noise too like the hum of a million angry bees. It wasn't smoke at all—but a horde of demons.

"Kiah, you in here?" a voice shouted from somewhere to my left.

It sounded like Fa. I certainly hoped it was.

"I'm here."

"Start praying, loud so I can find you," Fa demanded.

I rebuked the swirling darkness in a loud clear voice, and Fa stumbled through the room toward me bearing a flashlight whose beam was all but useless in the thick black putrid air. She joined me on the couch, tucking in tight behind me, so that we sat cross-legged, back to back. Only when Fa touched me did I notice how *cold* the room was; Fa's shared body heat was welcome. The smell was just what I'd remembered from other demonic encounters: vile and sulfury, sweet and rotten... *But something's missing*, I thought. Fear. Fear was missing. In the past, when I'd been in the presence of tangible evil, I'd felt fear. But I felt no fear it in that room, at that time. Instead, I felt calm determination and an extremely heightened sense of awareness.

"Where's Shine?" I shouted above the drone of the demons.

"Oh, she's coming," Fa shouted back, sounding inexplicably amused.

We continued praying as we waited for Shine. The black cloud shifted away from us as we prayed, becoming thicker at the edges of the room than it was just around us at its center. Small orange bursts appeared here and there against the black. The stench made me gag.

"You okay?" Fa asked.

"I'm fine," I reassured her.

Just then, Shine's dim outline appeared in the doorway from the kitchen.

"By the shed blood of Jesus Christ, the Son of the Almighty God, who died on the cross, descended to hell, gained the keys to life and death, and rose again on the third day, I demand that you leave now!" she shouted.

Her voice—no longer sweet and bubbly, but authoritative and commanding—gave me goose bumps. It affected the black horde infinitely more. The horde vibrated, swirled, and began to lift slowly, like a curtain at a theater, leaving a solid clear space along the floor.

"Go to the feet of my Lord and Savior Jesus, and He will have His way with you!" Shine spat out her words, and that was all it took... The cloud turned tail and fled, with a departing growl that left my ears ringing—leaving Shine, Fa, and I in the cheerful little room.

"Well, *that* was annoying!" Shine said.

"That's one way to say," Fa said, uncurling from the couch and stretching.

"Anyone else's ears ringing?" I asked, pulling at one earlobe and trying to pop my ears by yawning.

"The ringing will go, soon," Fa said. "It's good to see you."

"I've missed you. When did you get here?" I hugged Fa impulsively. "And where are we going?"

"I got here at midnight. And we aren't going anywhere, I think. Not right now. We will wait and see."

"What was that all about?" I asked. Both Fa and Shine shrugged.

"It's getting more common, though. I'd bet my ringer washer it has something to do with that club at your school," Shine conjectured.

"You have a ringer washer?" I asked.

"I'm buying one from someone on the mainland. It's coming soon." She rubbed her hands together in expectant delight.

I thought she was probably right about the SuCH club.

"The demons were easy to dispel. God is good," Shine said.

"Yes, He is," Fa agreed. She slipped quietly to her knees and began thanking God for his protection. Shine and I followed suit. I'd felt strangely calm while the demons swirled around us, but the quiet prayer time in that room stirred something inside me that I could barely contain. The blood rushed through my veins, and it took everything I could muster to stay quiet. I prayed in Gaelic. The words I was saying felt strangely intimate, and I wanted to keep them between Dhia and myself. In my mind's eye, I was at the bloody feet of Jesus, worshipping and speaking praises, and I never wanted to leave. We eventually fell quiet and sat silently on the floor for quite a while—staring out the window at the rain. I thought of the reality of God... on Petra, on Earth... how simply *amazing* and *powerful* He truly was.

"Hungry?" Shine finally asked.

"Starved," said Fa.

"I didn't have time to make anything yet. Want to help me?" Shine asked, bouncing up off the floor and heading toward the kitchen.

"You'll have to teach me," I said. Boiling spaghetti was the extent of my cooking skills.

Fa and I followed Shine to the tiny cook space that was Fa's kitchen. I washed my hands, then took a seat on a barstool at the tall square table at the center of the room. Fa lit the antique gas stove, and Shine brought a chipped ceramic bowl of fresh raw sausage from the fridge.

"Make patties, silver dollar sized," she directed, handing me a tray to lay the completed patties on.

"So tell us," Fa said, glancing at me while she cracked eggs into another bowl.

"Me? Tell you what?" I asked.

"Fill us in," said Shine.

"On what?" I said, suddenly wary. I'd been expecting official business of some sort and was absolutely *not* prepared to be the center of the conversation. I thought of Jack and wondered if there was an unspoken rule that forbade Blues from dating.

I hope this isn't an intervention! I thought.

"Fill us in on life... things... what you have been doing...," Shine prompted.

"Okay, I'm just not sure where to start... What do you want to know?"

"Start with your time at home," Shine suggested, slicing a tomato.

Shine knew about my mother's leaving, but I told the story again, since Fa had not heard. At least, I didn't think she'd heard. They listened intently, not interrupting to give platitudes, which I appreciated.

"So she left you and your father, with no real words for you?" Fa asked.

"No words for me or for my father... She left without any explanation at all. The note on the fridge was for Dad, and she sent a postcard a few days later saying that she was well and she wouldn't write again, but it didn't even have my name on it," I explained.

And how have you handled this?" Fa asked.

"I'm not sure how to answer that. On a scale of one to ten...? I mean, at first, I felt nothing. Just cold and empty. I got a little angry a few times before I came back to school. I ransacked her closet, refused to sleep in my bed, childish stuff like that...," I admitted.

"Did those things help you?" Fa asked.

"Well, in the moment, I guess... They felt good. But no, they didn't really help anything in the long run. The only thing that really helps is talking to Dhia. It's just that sometimes. I don't know even understand how I feel well enough to tell Him about it. I just feel this weird, awful void. And then there's the dreams..."

Shine took the sausage patties from me and laid them one at a time on the hot griddle that topped the stove. The meat sizzled and filled the room with the scent of meat and herbs. "Dreams?"

"Yes, they are snippets, little more than snapshots, really... of my mother. In the first, she was standing on a beach at sunset. In the second, she was in a formal room full of flowers and oils, jotting things in French on a clipboard."

"Were these memories of yours?" Fa asked.

"No. Absolutely not." I shook my head vehemently.

"Does your mother speak French?" Shine asked.

"Yes, she does."

"And do you?"

"No."

"What do you think the dreams mean?" Fa asked.

"I don't know. I thought maybe you would know more than me. I wondered if they could be glimpses, real glimpses of my mother— of what she's actually doing."

Fa shrugged her shoulders. "Maybe. Maybe not. You should ask Him."

"I have. He hasn't answered that particular question yet." I ran my fingers through my hair and mumbled. "Maybe there's a backlog, maybe I ask altogether too many questions. There are certainly several outstanding."

Shine laughed a little at that. "He loves to hear from us, Kiah. Never fear that you talk to Him too much. He never forgets your words. He just doesn't live on the same timeline that we do. He *created* time, remember?"

"He also created me to be cognizant of time. It's hard not to be…," I complained.

The sausage was nearly done. Fa added eggs and halved tomatoes to the griddle. Shine fished a ball of fresh mozzarella from the fridge and sliced it, arranging it on three plates.

"God is never surprised," Fa said. "To remember this… is always comfort to me."

"I hadn't thought if it that way before… He's never surprised. I can trust Him…" I tucked her words into a slot in my brain entitled Things to Remember When Everything Seems to be Falling Apart.

"I may get impatient when I'm waiting for answers, but I never expect my life to be perfect. I learned that from my dad, I think. He always takes things as they come and doesn't spend a lot of time wondering why things happen or if it's fair. He moves right on to what needs to happen next. That's probably why neither of us has lost our minds over Mom."

"You are sensible in this way," Fa spoke again. "I've seen this. It's very good. So many people kick and scream and talk about how things *should* be for themselves. I always wonder… why do they think everything *should* be *good*? God never promised us that. People have the right to choose, and people often choose sin. That's the world we live in."

Fa planted herself in front of me, looked me straight in the eye, and said in a direct but gentle tone, "But it is hard, still, for to lose your mother. You must allow yourself to grieve. Maybe she is not dead, but she is gone to you, and that *is* loss to you… whether you see her again or no. Maybe even more of a loss to know she is alive, but not choosing to be with you. Do not fear to feel this, Kiah. Know how you feel, then let Dhia carry the burden for you."

A rush of pent-up anger and sadness flooded my chest. "I don't know how, Fa. I don't know how to feel about this or how to grieve."

"And you do not have to know. What good will a label do? Dhia will teach you. You only need to listen and not fight what He tells you. Let yourself feel sad when sadness comes, and angry when anger comes. And when you do not know… when you feel only a void, ask Dhia what it is that you're feeling, ask for Him to show you His truth and then His beauty and then His goodness. There is always His goodness to be found. Breathe deep, give up your unknowing, and see what He brings to you. And don't keep your jaw so tight," she instructed as she waggled her head at me and tapped my jawbone gently with her finger.

I tried to obey. Purposefully letting my jaw hang slack and breathing deeply, I prayed silently, *I need your truth, Dhia. I need your wisdom. I am overwhelmed!* Another wave of emotion related in my chest, but it was a smaller wave, and a measure of comfort came with it.

"And what about Jack?" Shine asked. She was dishing up seared tomatoes, sausage, and fried egg onto our plates. My stomach growled. The mention of Jack's name stirred emotion of an entirely different sort.

"Maybe we should sit down first," I said, not sure I could go straight from one emotionally loaded topic to another.

Shine grinned… which I took a good sign. If she was grinning, she obviously wasn't mad. If she wasn't mad, maybe I wasn't breaking any rules by dating. If I wasn't breaking any rules… well… that made things harder, in a way. It meant I'd have to decide for myself whether or not to keep seeing him. A small part of me almost hoped for an outside reason to say no. The way it felt to be with Jack… to smell him, to hear his voice; it all colluded to derail my reasoning.

An unwelcome thought popped to mind for perhaps the thousandth time. *It would be so much easier to do life alone.* I pushed the thought away… I knew, instinctively, that it wasn't of Dhia. He specifically said in the Bible that we were made to live and work and be together, not alone.

We cleared a spot at the table and sat down to eat. Fa dug right in.

"Don't most Christians pray before meals? Not that you have to, but I just thought, well… isn't that what people are supposed to do?" I asked.

"I think the only rule for when to talk to God is to do so when you have something to say. The more I love Him, the more I will speak to Him. The more I speak to Him, the more I will know and love Him. My heart has said so much to Him, all morning. Short answer? I do not always pray when I eat," Shine said. "How about you, Fa?"

Fa shrugged. "Sometimes I do. Sometimes I don't."

'Now about Jack…," Shine prompted me once again. They hadn't taken me up on my rabbit trail invitation.

"Right… Jack." Saying his name aloud made my ears pink, and I wished I could crawl under the knotted rag rug. "So Dhia sent Jack to the dorm, to fix a hole in my window."

I took a drink of milk from the glass that Shine had placed in front of me and almost spit it right back into the cup. "I think there's something wrong with your milk!"

"Oh no. Nothing's wrong with it. It's goat's milk," Shine explained.

I noticed Fa hadn't touched her own glass of milk. She knew better. Smiling as if she'd bested me, she rose from the table. "I'll get tea," she said, retrieving a pitcher of iced herbal tea from the fridge.

I coughed and spluttered a little, trying to be polite. I'd never had goat's milk before and wasn't sure I wanted to try it ever again.

"So go on. Jack fixed your window…"

I told Shine and Fa about the window, leaving out the part where I crawled pathetically across the floor on my hands and knees to peer out the window and watch his departure. I did tell them about his commitment to doing anything God asked of him and how it had all started when he had come to live with his uncle.

"So he listens to God, even when God tells him to get up and leave his warm bed in the middle of night and go without knowledge of his destination. Sound like anyone else we know?" Shine asked.

"Sounds like a Blue, to me," I said. "There are people in his family who have the Calling. Could that be why?"

"Being called to follow God is not exclusive to Blues. Perhaps Blues are called to do certain things… tend the gates, heal people on Petra… but think of how many believers there are on the Earth… What if *everyone* rose to their Calling?"

I tried to imagine what that would be like: millions of believers all listening to Dhia, simply doing whatever He set before them in His power. The mere idea of it gave me chills.

"Hearing God is a choice we *all* have," Shine continued.

"Do many people hear God the way Jack does, then?" I asked.

"No, not many do. But not many choose to try either. Not many people ask what His will is and then wait for His answers and follow His directions," Shine said. "Which makes your Jack a rare man of God."

"He's not *my* Jack," I protested.

"So are you planning to see him again?" Shine asked.

"Well, I don't know. I mean, I'd like to. I'd *really* like to." I swallowed hard, trying to quell the fluttery feeling in my chest. "I'm just not sure if it's what Dhia wants me to do. I've asked Him, and He doesn't say yes, but He doesn't say no. I thought I should maybe wait until I hear something definite from Him?"

"So you are saying that Dhia set you up on several blind dates with a man who listens to and follows God well—a rare, true man of God—and you wonder whether dating him is a good idea? God gives us choice, Kiah. I think He's given you a pretty good indication that He favors this man, and He's put him directly in your path."

"I don't think it's as simple as it sounds," I hedged. "Do you know any Blues who are married?"

Fa and Shine looked at each other, and Shine shrugged.

"I don't. But that doesn't mean there aren't any. We aren't nuns. And most of the Blues work on the Rock. There aren't many men there."

I looked at Fa. She shrugged her shoulders as well. "I don't know if any Blues are married or no. I never asked them," she said.

Of course she didn't ask them, I thought. Fa was as single-minded and forward moving as a mule with blinders.

"Okay, I *have* thought a little about what it would be like to date him, and I wonder... how would that work, exactly? I mean, what if, and that's a really big *if*, but what if I dated seriously or got married, and I was always flying off to some foreign, secret, unnamable place, getting older much faster than he was because of the amount of time I spent there... weeks on the day! How would that even work?"

"So you *have* thought about it," Shine said. I had the distinct feeling she was teasing me a little.

"Well, yeah, I thought about it, I mean... haven't you?"

Shine shook her head. No, she hadn't. She had never been in love.

"Kiah what makes you think you would age faster than him?"

"Petra time... one week there equals a week here, right? If I spend enough time here, won't I get older faster?"

"It doesn't work that way, Kiah," Fa said.

"Then how does it work?"

"God invented time. It works however He wants it to."

I thought of Cumina Shae Hedley, alive at over one hundred fifty years of age, and felt a small measure of relief.

"You're sure?"

Fa sighed and shook her head again. "God will not give me one minute more or one minute less of life than He wants for me. My life is His, in length and breadth. That is enough assurance for me. Is it enough for you?"

"It is. I just hadn't thought about it that way before," I admitted.

"Will you think about it that way now? That is the question for you."

"Yes," I promised. "I will think about it. I will pray about it. That doesn't tell me what to do about Jack, though…"

Shine shook her head. "No, it doesn't. So talk it out. Pros and cons, feelings and instincts… What are the facts?"

"Well, first, I've never dated before. This was my very first date. I never was the dating type even *before* Dhia came along and started talking to me. I certainly never considered it once I'd said yes to the Calling. I already have so much to think about, and then a *guy* comes along? It just doesn't seem like it *fits*…"

"Fits what? Your plan? Or God's?"

I thought about that for a moment. It certainly didn't fit any plan I'd made, no matter how loose. I hadn't ever thought of the possibility that, as complicated as it might seem, it fit Dhia's plan for me perfectly.

"Why in the *world* would Dhia want that as part of His plan for me?" I had my hands on my hips at that point.

"Ask Him," Fa quipped.

"I *did*! He just hasn't answered yet!"

"Then He must not be ready to tell you. Or maybe, you are not ready to hear. If God wants a man in your plan, then it will fit, better than you could know. If He does not want that for you, then some-day, you will know. Kiah, your mother taught you to think. Thinking is good, but sometimes, you cannot think enough to find the answer. Now you must learn to listen and to trust during the times when you have no answer. Maybe that's why God has this man for you? This man who listens well? What if this man is a big part of God's plan for you and you are a part of God's plan for this man? Do you think you can know better than this, today, by thinking?" Fa queried.

"No, I guess not," I said, plopping into my seat. I felt very young and unprepared for everything. Even *thinking* about thinking less, and letting things flow with Jack, was a stressful proposition. "It just surprises me. That's all. I didn't see this… guy thing… coming. I wasn't looking for it."

"And you have strong feelings for him?" Shine asked.

My eyes filled with tears, and I looked at Shine but couldn't answer.

"Are there very many things in your life that are turning out the way you expected? Does Jack surprise you more than the rest of God's plan for you?" Shine asked.

"Yes… yes!" I was adamant on that point. "Jack almost surprises me more than almost anything else, actually."

"Then you have a lot to learn about your value, about the value that God built into you." Fa wiped her hands on her towel and approaching me, placed her hands at the base of my neck just as she had above the horseshoe valley so long ago. Then she prayed. She asked Dhia to give me wisdom and peace to know what to do and to know who I was to Him and who He meant me to be to Jack.

The tears that had been knocking at the backs of my eyes arrived full force. I didn't try to stop them.

IONA ABBEY

Fa was exhibiting signs of restlessness. We'd spent the entire morning in uninterrupted conversation, with zero action to break up the social monotony, and that simply wasn't her style. There was no urgent mission to attend to, no broken bodies, no pressing needs. I wondered what she normally did in her down time, but didn't ask.

"Anyone up for a walk?" I suggested.

"Good!" Fa declared, hurrying into the living room to gather her shoes and outerwear.

"I think she means yes," Shine said.

I petitioned Shine for a pair of outdoor-worthy pants, and she produced a pair of faded baggy bell-bottom jeans.

"Shine, where did you even *find* these?" I asked her. "They could not possibly been manufactured after the year 1972."

"I'm not sure. I might have gotten them at the thrift shop." It was a safe bet.

We all donned rain ponchos and headed for the populated side of Iona via the trail that circled the northern tip of the island. The rain was a fine heavy mist that seemed to drift every direction at once. We walked in silence, Fa jogging ahead, Shine stopping to examine the undergrowth here and there. One of her jobs was to identify noxious weeds and report it to the grounds department.

"Here!" Shine shouted ahead to Fa as we neared the abbey, pointing to the nearest door.

Iona's original church building was erected in the 1200s. The buildings were expanded in the 1500s but fell into disrepair, and the ruins were passed over to a trust in the 1890s. In 1938, the modern Abbey was built. It was a beautiful stone-and-glass collection of buildings perched at the water's edge. Shine produced a set of keys so large it would have made any janitor green with envy and led us through a staff entrance and into a small break room where we left our ponchos on hooks. She led us to the main chapel. The gray weather made it dim enough inside that the light cast by the racks of votive prayer candles flickered across the walls in waves.

"Beautiful, isn't it?" Shine asked, running her hand across the rocks where the candlelight played, watching the light slip through her fingers.

"It is. You love it here?" I asked.

I do." She nodded. "It's a place built solely to honor God. It's beauty for His sake. I love it very much." Her face lit up. "Have you seen the *Book of Kells*?"

Fa shook her head. No.

"No, they don't keep it here, do they?" I asked.

"Not usually. It's kept at the library of Trinity College, in Dublin. But there was a special gathering, this past week. A group of historians met for a retreat, of sorts, and they arranged to have the book brought here, for a special viewing. It's top secret. No one else is supposed to know it's here," she whispered. "It goes back tomorrow. Do you want to see it?"

I nodded, curious. Fa decided not to join us, but to wander the abbey alone.

"I can show it to you. It really is beautiful," Shine said.

I thought of the *Book of Kells*, and its cover, which rested in Nan's attic trunk. The book cover, like my mother's disappearance, was one of the unanswered questions that itched and chafed at my consciousness when I let it, so I tried not to let it. Shine logged our presence in a visitor's register outside a locked door. The room contained a few kneeling stations for prayer, an altar in the front of the room at the base of a large ornate set of windows, and a sturdy oak table at the back of the room. On top of the table was a large locked wooden box. Shine unlocked the padlock and lifted the top off the box, revealing a tinted display case that held the *Book of Kells*.

It was a book. I don't know what I'd expected;… perhaps the ringing of bells and sighing of angels. It was intricately decorated and very old, but was, after all, just a book. The pages were yellowed vellum, calfskin. I waited for something urgent and telling inside me, something I felt connected to, something that would tell me why I had the cover; but I felt nothing.

"Beautiful, isn't it? This is the Chi Ro page. Have you heard of it?" Shine asked.

I shook my head. I hadn't.

"It's the most popular page in the book—the most intricate. You can stare at it for hours and still not see everything."

"The *Book of Kells* contains the gospels only, right? The first four books of the New Testament?" I asked.

Shine nodded. "In Latin. There are mistakes, actually. Did you know that? The monks made a few text mistakes when they scribed it. It wasn't really meant to be read, so much as it was made to be looked at and admired. It was made to impress the common people, who were mostly illiterate."

"It is impressive," I admitted.

"It is. It's been rebound multiple times over the years, sometimes well, sometimes not so well. One book binder trimmed the pages and some of the art with it. The green ink, made of a compound that doesn't get along so well with vellum, has corroded some of the pages. Overall, though, it's still amazingly intact."

"No one knows what happened to the cover?"

Shine shook her head. "There are theories, but no real leads."

Is there something You want me to see, Dhia? Something you want me to know about this book? I asked silently, but heard no answer.

Am I supposed to tell Shine about the cover? I asked. Again: silence.

We replaced the wooden lid and locked it.

"I like this room," Shine said fondly, as if referring to a favored pet chicken.

"Yeah?" The room smelled of must and dust. The windows were beautifully colored and intricate.

She nodded. "I pray here."

"It seems so formal… a little intimidating," I said.

"There's that aspect to God, though, you know? The powerful part, the part that deserves respect, the part that inspires awe. It reflects a part of Him, a part that the world wants to forget."

"I think I met up with that part of Him recently," I said, remembering my encounter with Dhia on the campus walk, the feeling of the concrete against my skin and the chalky, inescapable taste of it between my lips as I lay pressed into the walkway by His Holiness. "We had twenty-nine days of sun at Aodhagan, not one cloud in the sky. Did you hear about that?"

"Recently?"

I nodded.

"It was totally still—not even a breeze, as far as I know, during the entire twenty-nine days. It was so strange. I only mention the weather because part way through the sunny stretch, I was walking across the campus, and Dhia showed up."

"What do you mean He 'showed up'?"

"He showed up. One minute I was walking along the sidewalk, asking inane questions… basically whining. The next minute, I was flat on the ground and couldn't move. I felt Him everywhere, in my chest, my arms and legs. It was holiness that I felt the most, I think; but love too, and power, truth, beauty… I was flooded with it. I wish I could explain it better. There just aren't words… Have you ever experienced something like that?"

"Not quite like that, no. There are so many facets to His character… Even though He never changes, He is new every morning simply because there is so *much* about Him that we don't know!" Shine was grinning, thrilled at the very thought of God's greatness.

"Did it change anything?" she asked, her eyes dancing.

"Change… how?"

"I mean has anything changed, with you, since that experience? Did you learn anything new? Or have you noticed anything… different? About yourself? About what you see and hear?"

"Well, peace, for one thing. I've felt more peaceful. I had been asking Dhia so many questions, about… everything. My life, my mother, Jack… But after that, I stopped asking so much. It's seems silly to ask endless questions once I know He is so real, and so powerful, that I can barely even handle His presence. It made me feel like the kid in the back of a car on a long trip, saying, 'Are we there yet? Are we there yet?' When, really, all I really need to do is pipe down and shut up and trust Him to drive while I look out the window. Then there's the squiggle…"

"Squiggle?"

"Yeah, a squiggle in my vision, like a sparkle that won't clear. Even though I had my eyes closed, it was so bright… I think it burned a scar into my vision. Oh, and the ground under me was hot and scorched when I got up."

"Seriously?"

"And it still is. I've gone by that spot since, and there's a shadow, almost like the chalk outline at a murder scene, but brownish black. It's a serious scorch on the concrete."

"Did it burn you? How's your skin?" Shine asked.

"My skin?" I pushed up the damp sleeves of the borrowed pink sweatshirt and surveyed my arms. They looked and felt normal.

"Looks okay. How did you feel?" Shine asked.

"I felt slammed, shaky and weak, then fried, overloaded, and dehydrated for a few days. I drank a ton of water and got some extra sleep and felt better."

"Sounds about right." Shine laughed. "Remember when He showed Moses part of His butt and Moses's face glowed so bright for days that he had to cover it to avoid blinding anyone?"

"No, I don't remember that at all. That's seriously in the Bible?"

"Yes, of course it is. Just goes to show… every part of God, even His butt, is too good to handle."

Too good to handle… That summed up the experience, and Dhia, perfectly.

We left the side room, then. It was frustrating to see the Book of Kells and still feel clueless as to why I had it's cover. I was waiting for a light bulb moment… directions, instructions, purpose… something that told me what in the world or even something *outside* the world to do with it. I wondered if Dhia's silence was an elaborate lesson in patience. We met up with Fa in the cloister overlooking the courtyard. The grass in the courtyard was vivid green, still soggy, but the rain had ceased, and a few shafts of sun had pierced a hole in the cloud cover. Fa had lost her restless edge. Her focused peaceful intensity had returned. We sat on the ledge under the columns and enjoyed the smidgeon of sun.

So what are your summer plans?" Shine asked. It sounded like a leading question. There was an edge to her voice that pricked up my ears.

"To go home, I guess. Get a job if I can find one. Make some money and come back in the fall... but that's not set in stone. Do you have something else in mind?"

"Something closer, maybe. Have you thought of staying here?"

"Here as in... Iona?"

"Not necessarily. Here as in Scotland. Finding a job nearby and staying the summer, in case you're needed."

"Can't Dhia find me at home?"

"Of course He can. I've just been feeling like maybe you should be here..."

I turned to Fa. "And you? Do you feel the same way?" I asked her.

Fa nodded. "I have felt the same. It's a good option. You would be easier for me to find."

I didn't think that was necessarily completely true... Blues seemed to travel far and wide, as freely as they wanted; but I didn't press the point.

"I haven't even thought of it, but if I should be here—I'll pray about it," I conceded, noting the answering flutter in my chest. Going home for the summer, despite my mother's absence, was the easier answer. No fuss, no responsibility, no questions as to where I might stay... I hadn't actually considered anything else. Had I missed something?

"Sometimes Dhia doesn't speak directly to us, but through those around us," Fa said, as if she'd read my mind. "You should still ask Him. He will confirm for you what is the right thing to do."

"Is this why I'm here this weekend?" I asked them.

Shine, perched on the low stone wall of the courtyard, tilted her head in question and looked at me.

"Well, Dhia brought me here, and I've been waiting… waiting for the main event. The *point* of this little trip…" Fa and Shine both stared at me as if they had no idea what I was talking about.

"Rescuing, bleeding, dying, almost drowning in bays and lakes… there's usually a main event, right? So what is it? Why am I here this time? What are we here to *do*?"

Both Shine and Fa stared at me for an uncomfortably long time before Fa answered, "You are the point, Kiah. Not training you, or rescuing others, but caring for you, loving you."

"Me?" my face was getting hot and not from the feeble sunshine.

"Yes, you."

"But why me? My boy issues, my summer plans? Am I in trouble?"

"No, of course not." Shine waggled her head at me as if I was being ridiculous.

"I guess I just don't understand," I responded, unaccustomed to people wanting something *for* me rather than *from* me. It made me suspicious.

"It's okay, not to understand. Just accept it. Maybe, someday, it will become clear to you." Fa patted my hand. "You matter. Can you accept that?"

Something in me balked and bucked wildly at the idea that I mattered apart from the things I did…

"I choose to accept that," I said.

"Good," Fa said. "That's a good first step."

"And I'll stay here, for the summer."

"You asked your heart? You asked Dhia, already?" Fa asked.

"I did."

"Also good," Fa said.

We collected our belongings then and started the long walk back to Shine's cabin. Fa dove into the back bay as we passed, returning to Petra. Shine and I continued on without her. I gathered my now-clean scrubs from the drying line on Shine's covered porch and gladly returned her bell-bottoms to her.

"They remind me of my mother," I told her.

"Your mother wears bell-bottoms?"

"No not that I know of... maybe she does by now. Who knows... but I'm sure she used to wear them. She's of that age."

We were in the kitchen, and Shine poured me a cup of tea.

"She does love you, you know... your mother. Not everyone has the capacity to handle things the same way, especially when they are running from God."

"I know she loves me, in her way. The only way she can. I just wonder, sometimes, why some people have more capacity to love through adversity than others."

"Old wounds probably have something to do with it," Shine conjectured.

"Once bitten, twice shy."

My shoulders began to buzz, and for once, my stomach didn't drop through the floor.

"I should go," I said.

"Will you take the ferry?"

"No." I pointed out the kitchen window at the sky.

"Your favorite," Shine teased.

"I don't mind it so much anymore. It's getting easier," I said, and it was true. "I'm sure I'll see you soon."

"Count on it," she said, hugging me warmly.

I opened the front door and felt my body lift straight up off the porch into the sky. The ground zoomed away in a blurry rush of color, then the trees, the house, the walking trail... all reappeared in miniature below far below me when my ascent suddenly halted. I could see Shine waving at me from the porch. I waved back, then sped away, watching the island slide by beneath me. The sky was clear, and the bay appeared; the gray wind-whipped water like silvered buttercream frosting on an enormous cake. More islands, more ocean, and eventually the mainland appeared. I drifted higher as the density of homes, vehicles, and people increased below me. When campus appeared below me, I began to descend, believing Bert was my destination; but a strong urge drew me onward. I banked left, following the urge, and soon realized I was headed toward Nan's village.

I skidded to the ground just down the street and around the corner from Nan's farmhouse, startling a small herd of sheep that fled, bleating, from the corner of the field where they had been resting.

"Sorry, guys," I called after their retreating forms.

It was evening, and smoke was drifting from Nan's fireplace. I reached the porch and was checking my teeth for postflight bugs before knocking when Nan startled me by opening the door.

"I had a feelin' ye would come tonight," she said.

"You did?"

"The Lord told me." She wore a wide smug smile.

"Did He happen to tell you why?" I asked, hoping she knew more than I did.

"No, we didn't get thet far..."

Nan ushered me inside.

"I made links," she said, meaning sausage. She'd made more than sausage. There were fresh rolls, sheep's cheese, sliced fruit, and broiled potatoes as well. My mouth watered. We ate, and I tried to unwind, to relax. She wanted to hear all about my classes and friends. I even told her about Jack.

"He's a good man, then?" Nan asked, searching my face for any hint of deception.

"Yes, he's a good man. Probably better than I deserve actually."

"Nonsense. Thet's nonsense, and I hope ye ken it," Nan scoffed.

"He's a good man, Nan. I'll have you meet him," I promised.

"I trust ye, 'course... but I'll meet him happily, jest the same."

"Ye can bide here, if ye need to, fer the summer," she said.

"I thought you said you didn't know why I was here? I think you know plenty!"

"The Lord said ye'd be needing a place, and that's all I needed to hear. Ye can stay, of course. I'd be grateful of the company. Do ye have a summer job, then?"

"Uh, no. Actually, the idea of staying here the summer only occurred to me today. I guess, if I'm staying, I better look for work."

"Seems to work best, thet way." Nan poured us each a cup of after dinner tea. I took a sip.

"Nan, this isn't Scottish tea." I was surprised. The tea had a warm, earthy flavor that I recognized, but couldn't conjure a name for.

"Nae, it's Pu Erh." She pronounced the name of the tea with some degree of concentrated difficulty. "It's fermented tea, Chinese. My natural doctor told me it would lower my cholesterol," she said, waving her hand in the air again, as if her cholesterol was of no consequence. "I told 'im I'd try a cup, and I did. I liked it, so I bought some—fer the taste of it, not fer my cholesterol, mind ye. It's nae too cheap, though. Comes in little plugs, like chewing tobacco, and ye must unwrap each one before ye can make the tea," she complained.

"I can unwrap them for you, Nan, as part of my rent payment."

"It's a deal, then... and ye can help with the dishes, an' all."

I promised to do that, and more. Nan's offer of housing was another confirmation that Fa and Shine's suggestion originated with Dhia. I thanked Dhia for being so clear and tried to wrap my mind around the change in plans. I'd need to find work quickly and fly home for a week or so at the end of the quarter...

"How much of yer belongin's will ye be bringin' here?" Nan asked.

"Well, everything I have, but I don't have much... only what I brought with me on the plane ride over in September." I thought about the first day I'd arrived at Aodhagan, with Elsie and shivered. It seemed *so long* ago.

"And have ye found out more about the items from yer box? The books and the journals the personal items?"

"Some, but not as much as I'd like to."

"Maybe I can help ye with that, if ye like...," she suggested.

"Oh, I'd love that. Thank you."

The sun was setting, then, and the room was getting chilly. The sky outside the window began to spit rain.

"Will ye stay the night?" Nan asked.

It was getting late, and my shoulders weren't buzzing.

"I didn't bring anything to sleep in, but I'd like to stay," I told her.

Nan rummaged through her bathroom and her closet and produced an extra toothbrush, and an ancient floral nightgown that had belonged to her mother-in-law.

"She was fat," she said by way of explanation once I'd donned the flannel nightgown. It was meant to be floor-length, but for a very short person. It was like wearing a large horizontal pillowcase that reached just past my knees. I slept in the guest room vacated by Nan's son and daughter-in-law. She bustled about in the room, moving faster than usual, pulling linens and blankets from closets and drawers. The prospect of having a summer visitor seemed to put wind in her sails, and I wondered how lonely she got, living alone.

I left the window open a crack that night, and though I was comfortable, my mind flitted here and there uncontrollably, and I barely slept. Finally, toward midnight, I drifted off and dreamt of my mother. I didn't see through my mother's eyes, as I had in the glimpses before... Instead, I was an unseen observer in the scene. Mom sat, still as a picture, on the edge of an antique iron bed in a small neat room with frilly but formal bed linens and matching curtains. A gnarled leafless deciduous tree was visible outside the window, against the backdrop of a hazy pink sky. She was still for a while. Her purse gripped in one hand; then her other hand began to flit back and forth to the phone. Finally, she dropped her purse, caught, and clasped her errant hand inside the other, forcing it to be still and behave. A pile of luggage that I assumed was hers, sat at her feet. Her face was a blank slate, her mouth a straight line. The only clue to her state of mind was a steady stream of tears that ran down both her cheeks and dripped from her chin. An overwhelming sadness tinged the air a literal blue. She made no move to staunch the flow of tears. The glimpse lasted only a few moments.

It made me sad to see her sad. I didn't wish sadness for my mother—not that it much mattered *what* I wished for her. I wanted her to be at peace, but you can't wish peace on someone and make it so.

Sometimes peace only comes at the far end of sadness, I thought. I didn't know whether that was a new truth Dhia was showing me or something stowed deep in my heart. I knew my mother wouldn't find peace until she stopped running from Dhia. For the moment, our roles had reversed; I became the mother and she the child. Mothers put the needs of their children above their wants and preferences; they are like nurses in that way. My patient may not *want* me to put pressure on their open wound (that hurts!), but if it's what they need to stay alive, then it's what I will do. My mother needed Dhia, the very One she was running from. I couldn't make her stop running and accept Him, but I could pray for Him to remember her, to call her name: so that's what I did. I held in my mind the picture of her still form perched on the edge of the bed, and I prayed for Dhia to call her heart.

LADY OF THE HOUSE

I woke the next morning with just a few seconds of obligatory confusion as to where I was. The sadness I'd gleaned while dreaming of my mother had lifted. I shuffled into the kitchen in a pair of Nan's too-small slippers and the square flannel gown.

"I feel like Alice in Wonderland when she drinks from the bottle and outgrows her clothes," I told Nan. *Or was it "Eat Me" that enlarged Alice, and "Drink Me" that shrunk her?* I couldn't remember.

"Just eggs and tomatoes for breakfast, this mornin'," Nan declared, "with last night's links."

"Sounds perfect," I said, setting water to boil for tea.

"And get yerself ready. We are heading out for a spell."

"Out? Where?"

"Ye'll see. Bring yer rain jacket. If ye havena got one, check the front hall closet," she said, a twinkle of mischief in her eye. She had something up her sleeve, and it was plain to she loved keeping a secret.

I rummaged through the hall closet for a coat, spotting a pair of rubber boots presumably Evan's, that were large enough for my gargantuan feet.

"Can I borrow these Wellies from in here, Nan?" I asked, getting a muffled affirmative in response.

"Can you give me a hint about what I'm dressing for?" I pressed.

"Ye'll see," Na said, appearing behind me with a plate of breakfast. We ate quickly, but the doorbell still interrupted us. Nan answered it and led the elderly women, obviously a friend of hers, into the dining room.

"It's a soggy mornin'. Are ye still for it?" Nan's friend asked.

"Och, aye. If ye are," Nan replied.

"I'm Scottish, nae?" The woman grinned. She looked about Nan's age, but taller and faster moving. Her hair equal parts red and silver, stuck out at odd angles from her green head scarf. The scarf matched her eyes perfectly, a fact that I had no doubt she'd noted when she donned it.

"I'm Tearlag Xue, a friend of yer family fer a verra long time. It's a pleasure to meet ye," Tearlag said, offering her hand. Her handshake was firmer even than my own.

"It's nice to meet you too. What is your last name again?" I asked.

"Xue, pronounced 'Shoo-eh.' It's nae Scots. My last husband was Chinese."

Her last husband? I wondered, but didn't ask, how many husbands she'd had.

Tearlag settled herself in a chair, and Nan poured a cup of coffee for her. "Moira tells me ye have an interest in yer family line…"

"Um… Yes. I do, actually. Do you know something about our family history?"

Nan chuckled. "There's nae a body in these parts who knows more about the ancestry of the local families than Tearlag."

"You keep records, then?" I asked.

Tearlag tapped her temple. "It's all up here. I've had thoughts of writing it down, time and again, but it feels like a concession to age, and I'm not ready for thet jest yet. Someday, though, I might. Moira thought ye might want to ask a question or two?"

Nan nodded in Tearlag's direction, giving me the go-ahead. I knew exactly what I wanted to ask.

"Well, I wonder if you know about a woman named Ailsa. She'd be related to the Clachers in some way. I have a journal of hers. It was passed down from family members, and I wondered, well… I wondered if she was a relative? No one seems to have heard of her."

"Ailsa, ye say?" Tearlag leaned back in her chair searched her memory banks for the name.

I noticed she was wearing jeans. Elastic waist but still... not standard apparel for women her age.

"I canna say I recognize the name. But I'll think on it, and maybe somethin' will spark. Have ye a notion when she lived?"

I searched my own memory, trying to estimate an age from what I knew. "At least one hundred years ago... maybe more? The book seems that old."

"Let me think on it," she said, then slapped her hands on the table. "We've a ways to go. Let's get on the road. We can gab along the way."

We rinsed our dishes, gathered our umbrellas, donned our boots, and headed out into the rain. Nan didn't drive. She had actually· never taken her driver's test, though the family farm had given her the opportunity to operate tractors and occasionally run the farm truck through the field. Tearlag, on the other hand, drove a surprisingly sporty little Vauxhall Chevette.

"Ye have enough room?" Nan asked out of courtesy as she settled into the front passenger seat, and I crawled into the back.

"Of course," I answered, also out of courtesy, though it was tight.

The old women still didn't seem interested in divulging our destination.

Tearlag drove faster than anyone I'd ever met. I braced myself to keep from sliding back and forth across the backseat as she slalomed bikers, hikers, sheep, and dogs. Nan seemed to be handling Tearlag's driving speed quite well—was obviously used to it. Tearlag had quite an impressive memory. She seemed to know every family in the area: where they'd come from, where they'd ended up, who they'd married, where their property lines ran, and with whom they had disputes. She worked backward from the present, following branch after branch of the Clacher family tree until she reached their known ends.

"Ye ken, of course, the Lady of the House?" Tearlag asked, glancing at me in the rearview mirror. We'd reached into the past over 150 years by that time.

"No, I've never heard of her."

"She was a noble lady, thet one," she said, and Nan nodded in solemn agreement.

"Noble? I thought our family was mostly farmers, workers…"

"Och aye, they were, as was Isla Clacher… verra poor. She was born to Camran and Eubha Clacher July 26, 1820."

"You remember her *birthday*?" I asked, incredulous. I could barely remember my own birthday.

"Only because it was the day the Union Chain Bridge opened, across the River Tweed. Ye ken the one?"

I did know that bridge, actually. It still spanned the border between England and Scotland. It was still impressive that she knew the date of the opening of a bridge.

"Camran and Eubha were well respected in the community, but verra poor, as I said before. They had a son, but he died young… childhood disease of some sort. Isla was ill fer some time but survived. She was a sickly woman but had a verra good heid on her shoulders, and even as a lass, she was sought for her wisdom. Her parents died in an accident when she was nineteen, and with few options, she married a Craig… Alastair Craig if I min' correctly. He was an older man… lost a wife himself, and lived alone until they merrit. I dinna ken what type of man Craig was, but folk respected Isla. They lined up to spend a few moments in her living room, to ask her their life questions, to stow their secrets with her, and gain a piece of her mind."

"What do you mean by 'stowing their secrets with her'?" I asked.

"She listened to their darkest secrets and, so, helped them carry their burdens. She dished out wisdom, answers to their hardest problems. They paid her, in return, with whate'er they could—eggs, vegetables, trinkets, books, an' sich. Thet's how she became known as the Lady of the House. They say the secrets wore heavy on her shoulders. She lost several bairn, still in the womb. Folk blamed the sadness she swallowed in the hearin' of people's darkness, their sins. 'Course, life was hard on childbearin' women then. Losin' a child was common."

Nan nodded her head in agreement once again. The older women fell silent for a few moments, adrift in the memory of their own histories, their own hardships, their own losses.

"Isla finally bore a live child, a wee lass, when she was nearin' forty years of age. The child was sickly, though. She often stopped breathin'. Her Ma and Da blew air into her mouth to restore her. They took turns awake at night to watch o'er her. Isla stopped seeing folk at her house altogether and devoted her time to her child instead... 'course she would. She started a healin' garden and learned everythin' there was to ken about herbs and foods that cure ailments. Still, the wee lass lived only a few years."

"What happened to her?" I asked.

"Nae a body kens fer sure. They say Isla went to the garden one mornin' wi' the lass and arrived home that afternoon without her. When her man asked what happened, she said the lass was 'borne on the wings of gossamer,' and nae amount of questioning made her say anything more on the matter."

"So the child died?"

"I assume so. She was ne'er seen again. They looked fer a grave, but nain was found. If it was anyain else but Isla, there would have likely been more questions asked. Isla held her fair share of respect in the eyes of the local folk. They trusted her... assumed she buried her wee lass in a private place, and grief stopped her from sayin' where."

The hair on my arms was standing on end. *The child had disappeared.*

"What was the girl's name? The daughter?" I asked Tearlag, but Tearlag shook her head.

"I've nae notion. The child was nae as notable as her Ma. She dinna live long enough to 'ave her name remembered. After the mournin' period, Isla returned to seeing local folk, dispensing wisdom in her livin' room. Folk were happy to have the Lady back. This, here is the graveyard, though, where the Lady was laid to rest. Yer Nan thought ye might want to wander a bit, see what you can see."

"Absolutely," I said, eager to explore the graveyard, despite the rain.

"I leave ye to it, then. Yer family plot is over the rise, on the left, near the cleft of the hill. Close by is the Craig family. Ye'll have to search a bit. Moira and I will wait for ye here, I believe... unless ye fancy a walk in the rain?" she asked Nan.

Nan waved me on. "I've put my feet oan in the rain before. Go on wi'out me. Holler fer help if ye can't find what ye need."

I unfolded myself from the backseat, donned my backpack, and put up the umbrella. Two of the spokes had torn clear of their fabric constraints, but it was still moderately effective at shedding the bulk of the falling moisture. I trudged up the hill past rows and rows of mostly ancient graves. The years of steady rain had taken its toll on the older grave markers, which leaned and sagged. Some of the names were washed, almost unrecognizable.

I found the Clacher family plot in the cleft of the hill, just as Tearlag said I would. I marveled at the sheer number of Clachers planted there.

Where is the Lady of the House? I asked Dhia silently. I stood as silently as I could, listening and hoping Dhia would reply. My feet felt the urge to move, and I followed the urge farther up the hill, scanning gravestones until I came to those of Alastair and Isla Craig. A little thrill went through me. *Dhia lives, and He speaks!* It was still amazing every time.

"Thank you!" I exclaimed aloud.

Isla's stone was large and stately, grander than those around it, and bore a cross at its center. It stood beside her husband's much simpler marker. Perhaps the community had come together to honor their much beloved Lady of the House with a gravestone worthy of her status. Just behind Isla's marker was a small, pinkish, ovoid stone. Unlike those around it, it was natural and not carved from a larger block. It read,

Ailsa
Borne on the Wings of Gossamer
August 18, 1822

My chest tightened. *I found her. I found Ailsa!* I thought, though, actually, I hadn't found her. I'd found only her place in time. I was quite certain it wasn't the resting place of her remains. Ailsa was very much alive for many years past the date on that gravestone.

What happened that day in the garden? I wondered. *Was Isla Called as well? Perhaps to serve in her own community rather than on Petra?* My head swam. Each answer I found posed three more questions. The questions never ended. I struggled to dislodge a sweater, and my notebook from my backpack without getting soaked by the pouring rain. It was no use. The water was already pooling at the small of my back. I propped the umbrella over Ailsa's stone and used the sweater to mop as much moisture from the surface of it as I could. I made a crude gravestone rubbing of the words etched there, then stowed the rubbing in my satchel and dashed back to the car.

"Did ye find anythin' of interest?" Nan asked as I climbed back into the rear seat.

I nodded.

"Thet's good, then," she answered.

"Yes, thank you, thank you very much for bringing me here. I think I'll come back sometime and look around some more...," I said, struggling to staunch the emotion welling in my throat.

"Perhaps when ye aren't as likely to wash away." Tearlag clucked, peering out at the angry gray rain clouds.

I nodded, not trusting myself to speak.

Get it together, Adenauer! Pull yourself together! Or, as Nan would say, *Dinna fasch yerself!* Emotion was bubbling up and threatening to spill over I tried to identify the feelings... It felt like nostalgia, but for what? The stories weren't *my* stories. There was sadness too. Was it behalf of Isla... that she lost her child? Or for Ailsa, that she lost her mother? *Loss*—loss was definitely a part of the choking ball in my throat. It struck me as ironic that I felt so deeply for long dead women I'd never met, yet couldn't sort out my *own* feelings regarding my *own* absent mother.

Help me, Dhia, help me to know my heart, I begged silently.

I Am, He answered.

APRIL AT AODHAGAN

It was a Monday, and much of what was true a week ago just wasn't true any longer. I'm not referring here to a specific untrue thing—but the general tenet that change is the only constant. Change happens when you are looking and when you aren't looking… whether you accept it, worry about it, or reject it. You don't even have to stay conscious for the world to keep spinning. Spring didn't burst onto the scene at Aodhagan, as it did in my hometown. It snuck in, instead, under drooling gray skies that cleared only intermittently to reveal the true spring green color of the grasses and leaves. The flowers along the ground, and the blooms on the trees crept open in the gray light, then burst into color when the sun made its rare appearance. I loved those moments; I made it a point to stop and drink them in.

I signed up for a clinical glimpse on a general med-surg floor at the local hospital and was eating a hasty lunch in my room an hour or so before my shift began when I received a phone call. It was my one of the nursing professors.

"The nurse I arranged for you to follow called in sick today, Kiah. Your shift this afternoon is cancelled. I did manage to arrange an overnight shift at the Emergency Department at the city hospital, however, if you can find a ride there. It begins at 11:00 tonight and goes to 7:00 a.m. You aren't required to accept an overnight clinical shift. I can find something for you sometime next week, if you like, instead. It's your choice."

I thought about it for a moment. I had a class scheduled for 9:00 the following morning. I hated the idea of working a night shift. I loved the idea of working in the Emergency Department. Excitement won out over prudence. I also felt a little internal shove that made me wonder if Dhia had something interesting in store.

"I can make it there tonight," I said.

"You have a ride?" the professor asked.

"I'll find one."

I called Jack.

"Jack speaking," he always answered the phone that way. His voice was rougher than I remembered.

"Do you have a cold?" I asked.

"Allergies, maybe… is this Kiah?"

"Oh, yes. Sorry. It's me. You are back… in town that is. How did it go?" I asked. I was *so bad* at small talk.

"It was, work. Okay, actually, a little boring. But we got a lot done. Good job with the small talk, by the way."

"Thanks, I try."

Really, I'm calling because I, um… I need a ride. Tonight. I have a clinical. It's nothing crazy or anything… but you are the only person I know with a car, and I hoped, maybe you could take me? To the hospital? It's tonight at 11:00. Or not, that's fine too. I can find another way…"

"Are you going to let me answer?" Jack interrupted.

"Yes, of course, go ahead. I just hate asking for things."

"I can see that. You are only calling for a ride?"

"Well, sort of. I mean, I do need a ride. But I'm kind of glad to have a reason to call you too…"

"In that case, I'd be happy to give you a ride."

"Oh, good, thank you," I said, relieved.

"'But not at 11:00."

"No? Why not? Is that too late? I mean, you could take me early, I guess, and I could wait there…"

"I was thinking I would pick you up at 5:00. You would come eat with my uncle and me, and then I'll take you to your clinical later on."

"But why?" I blurted. "I mean, that's not what I mean."

"It's not?"

"No, it's not. What I mean is... yes. I'd love to eat with you and your uncle. I'd love to meet your uncle and see you."

"It's a yes, then? Five?" Jack asked.

"Five. Casual, right? At your house?"

"My uncle is always casual," Jack said.

Four o'clock rolled around, and I felt as petty and ridiculous as all the girls I always made fun of. I'd changed my clothing a purely unacceptable number of times, finally settling on jeans and a turquoise sweater since the evening was chilly. I stuffed my scrubs in my backpack along with my stethoscope and the scribbled address of the city hospital. City was the largest medical facility in the region. I still felt as much like an imposter in scrubs as I did in the uniforms on Petra. It felt like false advertising somehow. I wished I could wear a sign that said, *"Don't count on me. I'm clueless."* I suppose my student nurse pin got that point across.

Jack stepped out of his car and gathered me in a tight hug when I reached his car that night. I pressed my face into his neck and listened to the blood pound in my ears.

"Missed you," he said.

"Missed you back," I said. The odd nervous tension I'd felt even that afternoon on the phone was gone—replaced by a low electric thrill that shot back and forth between my hand and his arm, my eyes, and his. For the first time, being with him felt more good than scary. We climbed into the car and got on our way.

"I thought this was your place?" I said as Jack pulled up in from of the glass shop.

"It is. My uncle lives there." Jack pointed to a large brick building next door. The windows, along with four sets of tall arched garage doors along the street, were all cemented shut. The place looked abandoned.

We exited the vehicle, and Jack led us through the alley beside the shop to a locked gate. He unlocked it, and we shuffled through sideways to the back of the building and into a surprisingly elaborate walled garden with vines climbing in every direction. There were vegetable plants, nut trees, fruit trees, and flowers everywhere.

"This garden's been here forever. It's over an acre," Jack commented, noting my surprise.

"It's beautiful. Does your aunt keep it?" I asked.

"She used to, until she died. My uncle has kept it up ever since. The shop and this building have been in the family for years. It was originally a firehouse, but it was decommissioned years ago. My great uncle refurbished it, moved into it, and put in the garden."

"Your uncle owns this building too?"

"Yes, and the one next to that and the one next to that. Don't tell anyone, but he owns most of the town," Jack whispered.

"You are kidding!"

"No, it's been in the family for years."

If the boarded street side of the building said, "We Are Closed. Go Away," then the garden side said, "We Are Loving and Living. Come on In." The wooden windows were freshly painted goldenrod yellow, and the double entry doors were fire engine red. Ivy climbed all the way to the roof of the brick building, where someone had trimmed or trained it away from the roof. Pulling open the heavy red wooden door, I was reminded of Sam and the red door of his little stone church. It was a happy comparison. It felt like coming home.

The door opened into what used to be the back bay of the garage where the fire trucks had been kept. The brick walls and cement floor had been sealed and whitewashed, and a large fireplace dominated the far wall of the great room. Jack's uncle was nowhere to be seen.

"He'll be here shortly. He's probably getting washed up after work," Jack explained.

"He owns most of the town and still works?" I whispered as softly as I could.

"Absolutely. He wouldn't have it any other way. What he does has nothing to do with what he has and everything to do with what God asks of him," Jack explained.

To my left was a half wall that barely separated a large kitchen area from the living space, and to the right was a series of closed wooden doors. The garden wall was dominated by the original firemen's lockers. Jack's uncle used the right half of the locker space for shoes, boots, coats, gardening supplies, gloves, tools, and a myriad of other items. The left half of the lockers housed kitchen items, linens, and books.

I counted five mismatched, aging couches and a handful of chairs and rockers arranged into three separate sitting areas, each centered around its own plush rug. The sitting area near the fire seemed the most formal, though *formal* was hardly the right word for it. The other two sitting areas were smaller and perfectly arranged for reading, with lights that hung on cords in just the right places from the ceiling over each space.

Jack made a beeline for the kitchen area, and I followed him. A full pot rack hung from the ceiling over the large kitchen island where a cavernous farm sink and gas stove top floated in what seemed like an acre of concrete countertop. A mammoth chandelier hung over the rectangular walnut dining table in the eating area. Pantry cupboards lined the back wall of the kitchen, and the gorgeous set of china displayed there drew me my attention. The china was white, or at least it had been at one point. Minuscule cracks criss-crossed its surfaces and age had yellowed it. Dark blue vines and tree branches traveled across the cups, bowls, and saucers in every direction. It was a large circular serving platter, a coffeepot, and a teapot that caught my interest, however. Flying eagles ringed the coffeepots and teapots and the edges of the serving platter. Dominating the center of the serving platter was the exact same Gaelic Bible verse as I'd seen on the flying eagle medallion Sam had given me over Christmas break.

> Do you not know?
> Have you not heard?
> The Lord is the everlasting God,
> the Creator of the ends of the earth.
> He will not grow tired or weary,
> and his understanding no one can fathom.
> He gives strength to the weary
> and increases the power of the weak.

Even youths grow tired and weary,
and young men stumble and fall;
but those who wait upon the Lord
will renew their strength.
They will soar on wings like eagles;
they will run and not grow weary,
they will walk and not be faint.
Isaiah 40:28–31

I was standing on tiptoe, excitedly examining the china when Jack's uncle entered the room.

"You must be Kiah," he said in a voice that was much deeper but quieter than Jack's.

I startled noticeably.

"Yes, sorry. I was looking at your china. It's beautiful," I said.

"It is. It's been in the family for years. My name's Bran." He extended his hand toward me.

"Shouldn't I call you Mr.…" I paused, realizing I didn't know what his last name was. He didn't supply it.

"No one calls me mister. It's just Bran," he said with a note of finality.

"I'll call you Bran, then. It's nice to meet you," I acquiesced.

"Come, sit down. Jack, though I'm sure he hasn't told you, is a fabulous cook. He has a magic touch with food."

"No, he didn't tell me," I said, surprised, nudging Jack with my elbow.

Jack rolled his eyes. "Don't raise her expectations, Uncle. Her palate could be more discerning than yours."

"Doubtful," Bran said.

He led the way to the seating area in front of the fire. The firehouse was charming but uninsulated and a little chilly; the heat was welcome. Jack busied himself in the kitchen, and I sat on one of the couches across from his uncle.

"I'm a little surprised by something. Your accent. I guess I expected it to be more…"

"Scottish?" Uncle Bran finished my sentence for me.

His English was actually quite formal, British, with a touch of something else mixed in.

"Well, yes, actually. I thought you were from here, had lived here all your life."

"That's mostly true, except for the time I studied in India and Great Britain. I also spent some time in a Dutch colony in South Africa," he said, settling into his chair.

He wore a faded pair of clean khaki work pants and a shabby but freshly pressed flannel shirt. His hair was thinning only at the temples, where gray fanned out and ran in two parallel stripes across his thick dark hair toward the back of his head, somewhat like a skunk. His mustache was salt and pepper, and his eyes were astonishingly green.

"I recognize the print on your china," I blurted. I just couldn't keep it to myself; I had to ask. I rummaged in my backpack and found the silver medallion, which I'd stashed there. I'd been planning, but forgotten, to show it to Nan. I handed him the medallion and waited as he examined it.

"Seems similar, all right. Where did you find it?" Bran asked.

"In Seattle Washington."

He looked surprised. "Really?"

"Actually, a friend found it in Seattle, at an estate sale. He gave it to me as a gift. What is this print? Was it something store bought?" I asked.

"No, actually. It was custom designed. Passed down in the family for generations." Bran flipped the medallion over, examining the back of it. "It certainly seems identical, but I had no idea that any medallions were made. Is this the only one?"

"I have no idea."

"And your friend, did she say anything else about the person who owned it?"

"It was a he, a man, who gave it to me. And no, he didn't know any more than that. It was an old Irish lady who died. She lived alone in a little house on Lake Union. My friend found the medallion in a box along with a bunch of pencil stubs and paper clips."

"Hmmm, I guess we'll have to ask Dhia about that, then," Uncle Bran said, handing me my medallion.

His use of the word *Dhia*, rather than God, surprised me.

"You speak Gaelic?" I asked him.

"I do, and I heard that you do as well," Bran said, "and that you prefer to use the name Dhia, rather than God, when referring to our Lord."

"Oh, yeah? And what else have you heard?" I glanced in Jack's direction, hoping to chastise him with my expression. Jack, however, either hadn't heard me or pretended not to. He was chopping something while something else sizzled at high heat on the stovetop. It was starting to smell wonderful, and my stomach growled.

"He's told me where you are from and who your family is. And knowing that… he doesn't have to tell me that you are Called, but I assume that you are?"

"Um, yes." My heart sped up little. Somehow, saying it out loud in front of a stranger still felt forbidden. "You know about the Calling, then?"

"I do," he confirmed.

"And Blues?" I asked, fishing for the limits of his knowledge.

"I'm not familiar with that term. Jack's great-aunt had an aunt herself who was Called at a young age," he said. "They say she listened well to God, spoke of Him constantly… enough that people eventually began to ignore her. They called her crazy. One day, she announced her intention to follow God on a quest. She said her good-byes at the dinner table, then went to bed. No one took her seriously, but in the morning, they found her bed made up, and she was gone. All of her clothes and belongings were accounted for. She took nothing with her."

I shivered, making the mental comparison between her disappearance and my mother's, as different as the circumstances were: one woman running to Dhia, the other running away from Him.

"Some members of the family respected the Calling," Bran continued. "They wanted to keep the matter quiet, to respect her wishes. Some family members panicked. They thought she'd been taken by someone with ill intent, or worse, had gone completely mad and might be wandering in the woods somewhere. A search was organized, but she was never found. Finally, the part of the family that couldn't handle the circumstances and the rumors left the country. They moved to the United States."

"Jack's great-aunt included...," I surmised.

"Indeed. She told Jack stories of the Calling against the family's wishes. They called her crazy too—either because they believed she was or because they wanted to discount her tales, forget the past."

"So what do you know about the Calling?" I asked Uncle Bran.

Jack was beginning to set the table.

"Not much. I know the Lord calls people to serve Him, some of them in their own back yards, some of them abroad, and then there's those He calls for a different purpose. I'm only mildly curious past that point, however. If God wants me knowing more, He will tell me. I love the Lord. I do what He puts in front of me. I don't want more than that."

"Sounds like Jack," I said softly.

"Yes, he's a man of God," Bran said, rubbing the sides of his face with both hands as if so much talking was stressful on his jaws.

"I did set a memorial to Cumina MacBain, in the family plot... just this year. I felt prompted by the Lord to do it, and so I did. Jack can show it to you sometime, if you like."

"Cumina MacBain? Is that the woman who disappeared?"

Bran nodded.

"Around one hundred fifty years ago?" I asked.

"That sounds about right."

"Food's ready," Jack announced. Bran and I rose to join him at the table.

"Do you happen to know her full name?" I asked Bran.

"McBain... Cumina Shae MacBain," he said.

The image of her small ancient form huddled in her nursing home bed flashed in my mind; goose bumps traveled up my spine and down my arms as another puzzle piece clicked into place.

"Hey, are you okay?" Jack's concerned appeared before me.

"I'm okay," I said as reassuringly as possible.

I still needed to work on my poker face. I breathed deeply and tried to steady my nerves. Cumina Shae MacBain Hedley. First, I'd found Ailsa and, now, Shae. I considered, then quickly discarded the idea of telling Bran and Jack that I was relatively sure I'd actually met Cumina Shae, but that her name was Hedley, not MacBain, by the time she died. There seemed to be no value in the disclosure. Bran had recently felt the need to put up a memorial of her, right about the time she died. It didn't seem a coincidence.

"Shall we?" Jack said, gesturing to the food. Both Jack and his uncle were staring at me, waiting.

"Oh, sorry. I tend to drift," I said. I pulled my chair up to the table in earnest and banishing my musings to the back burner.

We started dinner with prayer. Uncle Bran, first, in Gaelic, then Jack in English. It was humbling to hear the passionate prayers of true men of God. The dinner was wild Scottish pheasant with fingerling potatoes with beets, leeks, and turnips braised in a red wine rhubarb sauce.

"I thought your uncle was kidding or at least overstating about your ability with food," I told Jack. "Where do you get your recipes?"

"I don't really use recipes," Jack said. "I just pick a few foods I really like and build on from there."

He seemed as pleased with my approval of his skills as I was with his flavor combinations.

"Who else do you cook for?" I asked.

"No one, really. I just cook when I'm here, for fun."

The dinner conversation meandered from there. Bran's business was experiencing a moderate boom. He'd begun to do custom windows for select clientele. He enjoyed the work, and his clients enjoyed his talent.

"There's nothing as satisfying as creating something uniquely beautiful with your hands," Bran said, taking a sip of his pear brandy.

We discussed my classes, the nursing program, the college itself, even the horrible seating in the great hall cafeteria. Bran and Jack both agreed that the great hall deserved something better than peeling laminate tables.

Bran had attended a local church for years. It wasn't Catholic, but it was formal and liturgical.

"I enjoy the songs and the reverence," he said, "and I think it's important to meet with other believers. The Bible tells us not to forsake meeting together, but I just don't believe that sitting in the back of a church service a few times a month is what the scriptures mean. It's not enough." Bran's voice rose in volume. "The Lord means for us to live together, as brothers and sisters… to support each other, to love Himself and each other. He makes it clear what we are to do, but people have made His words into something that they aren't. People are inclined to do that… to twist the Lord's words to fit their own small self-centered agendas." He loosened the neck of his shirt as he spoke.

"I don't mean to preach." He made it a point to lower his voice once again. "I've no right to judge the world. I'm as big a part of the problem of sin as anyone in this world, and I know it. I do believe, however, as followers of His way, that we ought to keep each other accountable to the original intent of His Word, and there aren't nearly enough believers willing to do that. Not nearly enough Christians willing to trade in their dollars and their comfort to carry the cross."

"I agree, Uncle," Jack said with conviction.

"I do too," I said honestly, "though I haven't given it as much thought as you obviously have. I'm rather new to the scriptures, new to my faith."

"Jack told me you didn't grow up in the faith," Bran said. "He says you came by it naturally, directed by the Lord Himself."

"I guess so, though I hadn't thought of it that way until recently. I thought I was strange…different from other people. When I look back now, I see God's hand in so many things I heard, saw, and experienced. It makes me wonder how often people hear directly from God and never realize it."

Bran nodded his head in earnest agreement. "I've wondered the same. I think people overlook God all the time. Jack says you see visions and hear Him speak, however. That's a special gift from Him. Most people don't hear him quite that loudly or clearly. I wonder whether you listen well because He speaks to you so clearly, or He speaks to you so clearly because you listen so well. At the very least, He has great plans for you." Bran's voice was serious, and his large green eyes were deeply sincere.

"I know He does. Sometimes that's what scares me the most," I admitted.

"Good, it should," Bran said.

My face must have registered my surprise.

"It's good to fear the Lord. Not in the sense of running and hiding, of course, but in the sense of remembering our place with Him and the place of honor He deserves to hold in our lives. It's right to fear Him absolutely, but to stand firm in the face of the world and the enemy, knowing we serve a fearsome God. The tasks He sets before you, you absolutely cannot do without Him. He fashions our lives that way, as an incomplete circuit, a large *C* with ends that can never meet so that only He Himself can complete it. Only He can make us whole. We must hold fast to Him or die alone and incomplete. People feel the lack of Him. They plug anything they find into the hole, but nothing else fits!" Bran bumped the table passionately with his fist to enunciate the last few words of his assertion.

"Was I preaching again?" he asked Jack.

"Yes, you were, but it was a sermon worth hearing, Uncle Bran. It's the truth, and it must be spoken," Jack said, wiping moisture from his eyes.

Jack and his uncle were so openly, vividly in love with Dhia, the very same Dhia that plastered me to the ground and swept me up off their feet. They had, as far as I knew, never had the same intensity of experience with Him as I'd had; and yet they were more fervent, more solidly sure of Him than I could imagine... even to the point of openly weeping at the mention of His awesome power. I felt Dhia's presence strongly in the room, almost as strongly, if not as visibly, as I had in the healing room on Petra on the day of the Stripe.

Why aren't we all this in love with Dhia? Why don't people understand how much He loves us?" I whispered, dabbing tears from my own eyes. Jack and Bran didn't answer, because honestly, there was no good answer. Sin? Deception? Brokenness? Smoke. Those were the only places to pin the blame.

"God is good," Jack declared.

"Yes, He is," I agreed.

"Yes, He is always good," echoed Bran. "Are you planning to fly home for the summer, then?"

"No, actually," I said, steadying my voice. "I'm sort of looking for a job, here in Scotland this summer. I'll be staying with my great-aunt. So if you hear of any jobs…"

I hadn't told Jack my plans to stay local for the summer. I glanced at him as I let the cat out of the bag. He looked relieved.

He'd been quiet most of the evening, and I wondered why. Perhaps he was just giving his uncle the chance to get to know me. I glanced at my watch. It was well past 9:00 p.m.

"Oh, I haven't been watching the time. What time do we need to leave in order for me to arrive at the hospital before eleven o'clock?"

"Ten o'clock would be good," Jack said. "Don't worry. I've been watching the time."

"Should we clean up, then?" I asked, pushing away from the table.

"I will do the washing up," Bran declared. "It's a first time guest tradition. The next time you come, and forever after, we all pitch in."

"I can live with that," I said. "Thank you."

"You are very welcome. It's been a pleasure. We don't have many female visitors," Bran said.

"That's true, except for the cat," Jack added.

"How do you know the cat's female?" Bran asked.

"You named it Cherry, and that's a girl's name, right? I just assumed…" Jack trailed off, suddenly unsure what gender the cat really was.

"I named it Cherry because of its color, not its gender. I'm not in the habit of staring at its underside," Bran said. "Where is it? I suppose we could check." He scanned the room for the cat.

"I don't want to know that badly," Jack said with a wave of his hand. "How about you?" he glanced at my direction.

"I can live with this particular uncertainly," I said.

"Can we count on you to come again?" Bran asked.

"Absolutely. Great food, great company. You couldn't keep me away," I answered.

Bran put his hands on Jack's shoulders and looked into his eyes. "The peace of God go with you," he said in a firm voice.

"And with you, Uncle," Jack said.

Something about the exchange moved me. It was so forthright, so sincere.

Jack and I left. We wound through the back garden to the alley and out to his car.

"Your uncle is amazing," I said once we were both in the car and on our way.

"I agree," Jack said.

"That thing he said… 'peace go with you'?"

"He says it whenever I leave. It's a blessing."

"It seems like he means it."

"Every time," he agreed.

"He loves you. I can see that."

"I love him too. He's a good man." Jack unlatched the gate, and we were back at the street.

"You didn't say much tonight," I commented.

"Oh, yeah?" he said thoughtfully. "I'm actually not much of a talker. You should see me in groups. I'm quieter than an oyster."

"Really? I didn't know that oysters made any sound at all," I said.

"They don't."

"Well, you already know my opinion of small talk," I reminded him.

"I remember. It's part of why I like you." He reached for my hand, and we made our way to the car in silence. We rode most of the way to the hospital in silence as well. Jack finally broke the silence as we pulled into the hospital parking lot.

"I'm glad you will be here this summer."

"I am too. Really glad."

"Does your reason for staying have anything to do with the Calling?" he asked.

"I'm not sure yet. I'm not hiding anything from you. I really don't know," I assured him.

"I believe you. I'm sorry, I don't mean to pry. I just get concerned, a little…"

"That I might disappear?" I finished his sentence for him.

"Everyone else seems to," he muttered, staring at his hands.

"I know. I get it. I've wondered the same thing. Honestly, Jack, I don't think that's going to happen. Look at me!" I insisted, and he did.

"I don't think I'm going to disappear. It's not the same for me."

"You might have to remind me sometimes," Jack said.

"Okay, I will, but you have to trust me too. If you don't trust me, at least trust Dhia."

Jack nodded.

"And I am looking for a job," I added.

"I'll keep my eye out. When do you need me to pick you up?"

"Seven fifteen, if that's okay with you."

"Seven fifteen it is. Have a good night." He squeezed my hand, and I climbed out of the car quickly, before I could change my mind and jump back in. I hurried into the building, willing myself not watch him drive away.

Is this what love feels like… romantic human love? I asked Dhia. There was no answer.

WRETCHED FOOT

The double glass doors slid open automatically, and the rush of air that escaped held the mixed odors of chemicals, humanity, overworked furnace, and despair. There was activity literally everywhere at once, but I comprehended little of it. Several people dashed past without looking at me. A woman in the waiting area was vomiting into a small green basin on her lap while the younger man beside her patted her back awkwardly, tilting his head away from her. There was a small boy in the corner, frozen to the edge of his chair, intently watching the action around him. His mother held a blood-soaked cloth to his forehead and looked worried. It took a few moments to recalibrate my nervous system to the strange new environment. I checked my watch and started my search for the bathroom so I could change clothes.

"Are ye boak… sick, thet is?" said a voice from the reception desk beside me. I spun around and noticed, for the first time, a pruney cupcake of a woman sitting in the chair behind the glassed wall in the reception booth. She was old, almost elderly, and dressed head to toe in lavender. Her suit would have looked professional on someone much younger, but the bows on her gray pigtails and fact that her feet didn't reach the floor made her look more like a child playing dress-up. Her name tag read "Greer."

"Um… no. I'm not sick. I'm a student, actually," I said, holding my backpack up in the air for her to see, as if she would glean some understanding of who I was from its presentation.

She cocked one eyebrow at me.

"I have to change clothes and meet Jean. Do you know where I should go?"

"I'll show ye," she said.

I winced as she hollered loudly over the wall of her cubicle to someone shuffling papers on the other side, "Watch the desk a minute!" then hopped down onto the floor and unlocked the door, leading me into the maze that was County Hospital Emergency Services. Many years before, County Services had begun its life as a birthing hospital. Then the hospital had added on and on, in layers around the original building, and then finally in grids and hallways out from there as the needs of the community grew. Emergency Services, which generated less income than any other department, inherited the oldest, most original part of the building. Greer led me through corridor after corridor, dodging gurneys and interns. I tried to memorize each turn, but there were too many distracting sights and sounds. At length, we arrived at a door marked "personnel," and Greer punched in numbers on a keypad, then held it open for me.

"There's a changing room in the back. Here's a key for a locker." She fished a key out of her pocket and handed it to me.

"It's my locker, but my things don't take up much room," she said, gesturing at her own small form. "I'm willing to share."

"Oh, thank you," I began to say, but she waved my words away.

"I'll be here through mornin', same as you, I expect?" she asked. I nodded.

"Good, I'll wait for ye now to get dressed," she chirped.

I began to protest, then thought of the maze we'd come through, and the fact that I had no idea how to find Jean. I hurried into the locker room to change. When I returned, Greer was perched on a plastic chair at one of the break room tables, eating a pastry.

"Well, then, look at ye. Ye look almost official," she said, pointing to my student name tag.

"Looks can be deceiving," I mumbled.

"Ye'll do fine. Jean is the best," Greer responded, patting me on the arm. For a moment, I wanted to grab a donut and plop down beside Geer just to bask in her air of her confidence. The moment passed quickly, however, and I was anxious to meet Jean. I didn't want to be late.

Greer led me back into the middle of the maze to the trauma bay—a group of large open rooms clustered around a central nurse's station. Nurses' Station was a truly inaccurate term for it. Medical Decision Hub/Command Central would be more apt. In the emergency department, the nurses work hand in glove with the doctors, social workers, therapists, and anyone else who happens to run by in medical garb. There were as many doctors as nurses shuffling papers and accessing computers there. The noise level in the trauma area was near cacophonous. Perhaps if I'd understood the beep, squawk, and high-pitched insistent whining of the monitors, it would have seemed more organized, less catastrophic. Maybe.

"Thet's her." Greer pointed out a petite black woman in maroon scrubs who darted back and forth in what seemed to be the busiest of the trauma bays. "Go straight to her, do whatever she says, and ye'll be fine."

I repeated Greer's words over and over in my head as I approached the room.

"Do ye need to be here?" a voice barked at me as I entered the threshold of the room. I looked up in the direction of the voice and saw a tall lanky bald man glaring directly at me.

Before I could answer, and without looking up, Jean responded to him in a loud authoritarian tone, "She's my student, John. Leave her be."

She turned to me then. "Kiah? Welcome. Find a spot at the edge, and watch for now. Keep a sharp eye."

I nodded and did as I was told. *So far, so good.*

The air in the room reeked of menthol pain rub and something rotten. The patient, barely contained on the stretcher, was quite a large man. He was barely conscious, moaning and moving his arms and legs weakly. The shabby street clothes he wore told me he had arrived quite recently. A few hospital blankets hung off him at odd angles. I counted seven people in the room, including the paramedics who'd brought him in; but as the man began to thrash and vocalize more strongly, the number quickly grew. His legs flew up off the bed as he wailed, and someone threw me a pair of gloves.

"Grab a leg," a voice advised, and I took hold of the flailing limb nearest me, just below the knee. Even through the pant leg and the blanket, I felt the intensity of the man's pain and anguish. I also had the sensation of intense heat and cold. The rotten smell intensified, almost too overwhelming, and I couldn't tell whether I smelled it with my actual nose or if my empathy was in overdrive.

"I wonder what kind of drugs this man has in his system," someone pondered aloud.

Several nurses worked at the man's left arm to install an intravenous line, but the thrashing rendered their efforts useless. Someone ordered an intramuscular sedative, and another someone dashed from the room to retrieve it. I, meanwhile, was feeling a nonsensical urgent need to remove some part of the man's clothing.

"Just do what I'm told, and I'll be fine…," that's what Greer said, and that's what I plan to do! I told Dhia silently while fighting to keep hold on the man's leg. There were four other sweaty faces pressed close to mine, doing likewise, as if we were all riding a single bucking bronco at a wacky human rodeo gone terribly awry.

Take his sock off… Now, Dhia's voice shot up through me, clear as ever. I could have ignored it but didn't. My upper body was directly over the man's foot, so I worked my hand underneath the blanket and began to remove his sock.

"What are you doing?" asked Jean, whose face happened to be hovering just left of my ear.

I didn't answer but pulled the last bit of the sock over the man's heel and slipped it off, revealing a completely black foot.

Jean muttered a French curse word under her breath, then shouted, "John, take a look!"

I leaned away from the stretcher as far as I could without losing my grip on the patient's leg, to let the doctor get a good view of the offending appendage. A nurse uncovered the patient's hip and injected a hefty dose of sedative, and the man's limbs relaxed.

"It looks like gangrene to me. How did you find it? Did you smell it?" Jean asked me.

"Basically," I said.

Once the sock and the blankets were off, everyone could smell it. The foul odor hung heavy in the room.

"That must be his reason for the menthol rub," someone conjectured.

"You are hired," John said, directing his comment to me. A few people chuckled. I wasn't sure if they were laughing at me or if I should laugh along with them.

The nurses had the IV line inserted within moments. Jean retrieved two pairs of scissors, handed me one, and began to cut at his pant leg.

"Let's see what else we can find," she said. It was a treasure hunt I didn't particularly want to go on. With the pant leg gone, we found that the black rotting skin ended just above the ankle. A pink band separated the necrotic tissue from the healthy tissue above it. The patient had fallen quiet, and things became much more orderly. We removed every stitch of clothing and found nothing else that would indicate disease, or even poor hygiene, besides the rotting foot. There were even fresh traced of deodorant on the inside of the man's T-shirt.

"How can he be mostly healthy and keep himself reasonably clean but overlook something like this?" I asked, trying not to gag at the odor.

"Denial can be a powerful thing," Jean commented, scrubbing the skin above the black foot with surgical scrub in preparation for surgery. The bottom half of the leg would need to be removed.

"Denial can be *that* strong?" I asked incredulously.

"Apparently," Jean replied.

We worked quickly and quietly and sent him off to surgery. With the patient gone, Jean sighed, stretched, and turned to wash her hands. I followed suit. She was a slight woman, with shoulder-length jet-black hair pulled back in a low ponytail. Her eyes matched her hair perfectly, and her nose was as much like a button as it possibly could be.

"So I'm Jean… or did I say that already?" she asked, scrubbing her hands vigorously.

"Yes, I think so, or maybe you didn't. Greer pointed you out."

"Are you a second-year student?"

"No. First year, actually."

I waited for the inevitable disappointed look that said *Good grief, now I'm babysitting. I hope this one doesn't faint at the sight of blood.* But Jean didn't give me that look. Instead, her eyebrows shot up in surprise.

"Really? I would not have guessed that. You have a presence that does not say 'new.'"

"I'll take that as a compliment," I said.

"As you should. Next patient?" Jean gestured to the door, then hurried from the room without waiting for me to respond. I followed. We saw seven more patients that night. The first was a toddler with second-degree soup burns down his back. We dispensed pain meds, examined him, and moved him quickly to the burn unit. Our second charge was an elderly man who broke his hip while climbing out the window of his nursing home three hours past curfew. He warranted X-rays and a trip to surgery. Our third patient was a fourteen-year-old girl with a nose ring, a raging case of herpes and her own serious case of denial. (She believed the disease was a direct result of the poor quality of toilet paper her cheap mother insisted on buying. She swore that her life would be practically perfect if her mother had never born. We didn't explain the obvious holes in either of her theories.) It was 2:00 a.m. by then, and I'd grasped the general layout of the labyrinthine unit. I even trekked to both the front desk and surgical suites unaccompanied.

Our fourth patient, a middle-aged woman, had driven herself to the ER with indigestion and the inkling that something else was "just not quite right." She was correct. Dr. Collins, who insisted everyone call him John, caught the subtle signs of a silent heart attack, ordered stat labs and an EKG, and sent her to the cath lab just in the nick of time. Around that time our fifth patient arrived. A young mother with a toxic blood alcohol level, she had had been thrown through the front windshield of the car she'd been driving. Her newborn son was found dead at the scene of the crash. She died of severe head trauma soon after her arrival at the hospital, before the staff even had time to open and use the veritable cornucopia of tools, supplies, and life-saving tactics at their disposal. No next of kin was listed. Jean finished up the required charting on that patient around 4:00 a.m. I'd managed to memorize the code for the supply room by that time, and even located the "Hole in the Head" kit with some expediency, though our patient died before we were able to make use of it. Our sixth patient, an elderly homeless woman, wheeled her wheelchair through the doors of the trauma bay at 4:15 a.m., demanding that we shower her immediately and give proper attention to the cold she had been fighting for a full twenty-three hours. We scrubbed and evaluated her, found her a fresh set of clothes, treated her for lice, and gave her a free clinic ticket that would allow her to have her diabetic-induced ulcers treated twice weekly at no cost. Our seventh patient arrived by ambulance just after 6:00 a.m. He was a sixteen-year-old type 1 diabetic, found unconscious on his bedroom floor by his mother with a blood sugar of 750, which was over seven times normal. He'd apparently decided to take a hiatus from his diabetic testing and diet, imbibe a few liters of soda, and eat an entire pizza after his parents had gone to bed.

By 7:00 a.m. my feet, back, and shoulders were aching; and my admiration of Jean's confident nursing skills had risen over the moon. Jean was a good teacher and a great nurse. She thought on her feet, spoke from a place of wisdom and humility, and moved fast—still managing to make her patients feel listened to and cared for. The busyness of the night didn't leave Jean and I much time for conversation. We worked well together, speaking in clipped sentence and pointed gestures. I spent much of our time together nodding and listening, offering my hands and feet whenever I could.

Those were the things that *did* happen. I remember them well, but it was the things that *didn't* happen that bothered me the most. I *didn't* hear from Dhia, except in regards to the foot. I *didn't* feel the call to heal. No blue light glowed beneath my fingertips to remind me that any and all healing is done by Dhia Himself. Emergency Services bore the pall of pain, fear, disappointment, and grief that night. There was no one to grieve for the woman and her son, so the staff grieved quietly for them. No one spoke of the sadness, but I saw it etched on everyone's faces. By the time the shift finally ended,

I felt as if I'd been there for years. I wasn't sure whether I'd actually impacted any of our patients' lives in a meaningful way or if their pain had only multiplied and spread. I was afraid I would carry it with me… that it might never leave me. I wondered how Jean could do the job, go home, then come back and do it again and again day after day.

Dhia! What did I miss? Wasn't there more you wanted to do for those people? I heard no answer.

"You did well tonight, Kiah. I'd be happy to take you on for a preceptorship, if you like," Jean offered at the end of the shift as we sank into a pair of plastic chairs in the staff lounge for the first time in twelve hours. My chair was cracked. I scooted to the edge of it to avoid getting pinched. Jean was far too fresh-faced for someone twice my age who'd just worked a life-sucking ER shift. It didn't seem fair. Part of me was surprised and pleased that Jean saw promise in me. Another part of me couldn't imagine ever purposefully taking her up on her offer. The patients in the ER came and went so fast I was barely able to absorb their names before they were off and gone again to the OR, CT scanner, morgue, inpatient floor, or back to the street. As amazing as Jean was at her job, I wasn't sure I wanted to have anything to do with that kind of care. That night, we had cared for people's bodies but not their hearts and only in passing. It wrung out my own heart, squeezing it until it felt dry and incapable of proper function.

"Thank you. I won't have the opportunity for a preceptorship for a few years yet, but I appreciate the offer," I said, and I did.

Greer winked at me as I dragged past her station at the front desk and toward the front door.

"So will we see ye again?" she asked.

"We will see," I responded with as much of a smile as I could muster, then returned her locker key and thanked her.

Jack's car idled in the no parking zone outside the double doors of the Emergency Department. I climbed gratefully into the passenger seat. Jack took one look at me and remarked, "Long night?"

"Yes, a very long night."

Employing the "sleep when you can" technique I'd practiced on Petra, I was unconscious with my face plastered to the side window before we left the parking lot. I slept all the way back to campus. Jack nudged me gently when we arrived at the dorm and pointed me in the direction of the front door. I mumbled a simple thanks, not trusting any other words my fatigue-muddled brain might come up with. I somehow managed to change clothes, gather my school work, and make it to classes. Don't ask me what I learned in class that day. *I do not know.*

MAY OR MAY NOT

The end of the school year is just as busy but nowhere near as enjoyable as the beginning. Unless, that is, you happen to be graduating, which I wasn't. The research work and the term papers, which had long held the glorious end of the year due date were suddenly actually due. The test grades students let slide ever so slightly at midterm loomed large and menacing. I spent most of my waking moments outside of class in my stolen office getaway—studying, hiding, and studying. There was also the issue of finding a summer job with a flexible schedule in case unexpected absences became necessary.

I guess You could say I'm on call... right, Dhia?

It had been over a month since my shift in Emergency Services. I'd thought perhaps time and sleep would have changed my outlook on emergency nursing, but it hadn't. It had instead solidified my feelings. I checked emergency nursing off my mental list of career possibilities, but with a caveat... *I'll do it if you want me to, Dhia, but You might have to shout really loudly.*

It was less than two weeks before I was set to fly home for a quick visit. I was propped up on the bed in my dorm room, cramming for a chemistry exam. I would have studied in the relative peace and quiet of my little office rather than the dorm, but I'd missed several calls from Jack. It was in the days before cell phones and my little office had no phone. Stress and lack of sleep had me cranky, and I wasn't the only one... I'd witnessed my first actual Aodhagan fist fight an hour below in the dorm hall.

The phone rang.

"Hello?"

"Hey, sweetheart." It was Dad's voice, not Jack's. I made the mental switch necessary to continue the conversation.

"Oh, hi, Dad."

"Whatcha doing?" he asked.

"Just studying. Finals are next week."

"You getting enough sleep? Eating well?" I'd noticed Dad asking more about my health and hygiene of late. I wondered whether it was something natural or if he'd read about it in a manual. *Parenting Tasks Dads Must Assume When Their Children Lose Their Mothers. Lesson 1: Ask whether they've eaten their vegetables. Lesson 2: Has your child been brushing their teeth?*

"I'm sleeping, eating, and eliminating, Dad. Just like the textbooks say I should." I sighed.

"No reason to be graphic."

"Right, sorry. I am in nursing school, you know. It tends to be somewhat graphic."

"I suppose it does. That's not actually why I'm calling, however. I have some news."

My heart raced. "Mom?"

"Oh, no. Nothing from her. Sorry, I didn't mean to make you think that. Actually, the thing is… I was thinking of moving. Not just thinking… I *am* moving, packing up the house. I have a buyer, and it's a good price. I should have told you sooner, but it all happened rather suddenly. I just… I don't think I can be here anymore. There's too much of her here… your mother, that is. I need to get clear of it, go somewhere new."

"Are you moving out of town?"

"No, not out of the area. Same job. Just a new house."

"Well, that's fine, I mean, it's a great idea, right? I totally get it. I am still planning on being there Tuesday, two weeks from now. I'm staying a week, then flying back here. Is that still okay?"

"Of course. I'll be at the airport. I have your flight information written down. I'll have everything moved by then. You'll have a room

513

in the new place, of course. It's a nice one. The house on the hill, just down the road from Mary's place, where your horse lives. It's smaller… It's yellow…"

"I'm sure it's fine, Dad," I said. It occurred to me that I might never again have a reason to see the house the house I'd called home for so long.

Was that okay with me? It felt okay. Strange, but okay.

"You're not mad, then, that I didn't ask you first?" Dad said, sounding relieved.

"No, of course not. It's not my call. The house was really Mom's thing, anyway," I reassured him.

"I thought you might feel that way. I hoped you would. You're easygoing about things that way. I admire that."

My eyes moistened. Dad wasn't prone to giving compliments, so when he did, they meant something. I cleared my throat to keep my voice from sounding husky. "So it's Tuesday, two weeks from now, at 4:00 in Seattle."

"I have it written down. I'll be there. Did you find a job yet?"

"No, not exactly. Aunt Moira is ready for me to come, though. She's looking forward to it."

"I suppose she will value the company," he said.

"I think so."

The barrel of things to say was empty. It never seemed to be terribly full.

"I'll keep packing, then. You keep studying. I'll see you soon," Dad said.

"Okay, I'll give you a call before then."

"Sounds good, love you…"

"I love you too."

I hung up the phone and sat on the bed imagining my childhood home in packing shambles. Mom always got sturdy boxes from the local liquor store for packing. She wrapped plates in paper, bulky items in bubbled plastic. I wondered if Dad was doing the same things or if he'd do it his own way now that he had the chance, not that it mattered.

The topic of packing boxes reminded me... the front desk had left a message about a package I needed to pick up. I hadn't ordered anything and wasn't expecting anything. I didn't have the *money* to order anything, even if I'd wanted to. I scooted down to the desk and found Big Bert, the resident assistant, manning the station and chewing her fingernails down past the quick. She cussed quietly at her cracked bleeding pinky finger.

"I'm here for a box. Room 17," I said.

"Ooh! Ye scairt me. I ken which room is yers, a'coorse. That's my job!" she said proudly.

"That's good. It should be easy to find the package then, right?"

For some reason, Big Bert put me on edge. My attitude suffered where nosy people were concerned. Big Bert was one of those people who constantly had her beak in everyone's soup except her own. She turned and rummaged in the tiny mail room.

"It's a big one, says fragile, and it's nae local. What is it, then?" she said, carting the box to the desk, as excited as a bomb-sniffing dog in a luggage store.

"I'm not sure, Big Be... I mean, I'm just not sure, really. I obviously haven't been opened it yet." I suddenly couldn't recall her actual name. *Molly? No. Macy?*

"Yer nae expecting anythin'?" Her face fell as her prospect of discovery dwindled.

"Well, it could be the long-burning candles I ordered," I mused, tapping my fingers on the desk.

Her eyebrows shot up, and she rose to her feet. "Now ye know the rules disallow burnin' materials of any sort in the rooms..."

"Ah! I gotcha," I interrupted her, giving her what I hoped was my most disarming smile. "I just wanted to make sure you were paying attention... Marta."

That's it... Marta. Marta, Marta, Marta. Must remember people's real names...

"Yer sure? I can get ye a current book of regulations, if ye need it." Marta looked dubious.

"I'm sure. Thank you." I tried to wrestle the box out of her hands. She let loose of it rather reluctantly.

Aggie happened by just then and joined me at the desk.

"It was nice talking to you, Marta," I said, escaping down the hall with Aggie.

The box was heavy. We closed the door, and I hefted it onto the bed.

"What is it?" Aggie asked, peering over my shoulder.

"You're as nosy as Marta," I teased. "Actually, I have no idea what it is. Grab scissors."

Aggie fished in the desk drawer and joined me box-side. "I'm surprised Big Bert didn't pry it open and try to retape it," she said.

"No way. She's too big on the rules."

The package was professionally wrapped, with a London return address that I didn't recognize. With considerable effort, we freed the contents. It was an espresso machine... brand-new, the kind with copper touches.

"You drink coffee?" Aggie asked.

"No."

"Did you order it?"

"No, of course not, why would I order it if I don't drink coffee?"

Aggie shrugged. "Not everything you do makes perfect sense, you know."

"I guess that's true."

"I'm just trying to ask the pertinent questions," she continued. "It looks expensive. If you didn't order it, then who is it from? Are you sure it's even for you?"

I suddenly wasn't sure. I checked the label. It was addressed to Kiah Avis Adenauer.

"You know, when I was younger, my father bought me a very expensive leather jacket..."

"How nice for you. What does that have to do with coffee?" Aggie interrupted.

"Let me finish! I had never even considered the possibility of owning a leather jacket, but Dad liked them. He liked them a lot, so he bought me one. I was surprised, but actually, I grew to love it. I still have it... though a sneaker wave caught me at the beach, and

I went for an unexpected swim, so the zipper's corroded. It's kind of greenish…"

"You are babbling, Kiah. What does this have to do with coffee machines?"

"Well, my dad drinks coffee."

"And?"

"And… he hasn't seen me all year, and he decided to move out of our house… He just told me. I think he feels a little guilty about moving without asking, and bad about everything being topsy-turvy, so… gift! Espresso machine. It looks like a good one, right? It says it makes amazing foam."

Aggie gave me a distinctly puzzled look. "Americans are so weird."

"I know." I sighed. "It's so true."

"I think this is a good thing." She jumped suddenly to her feet, energized by an idea.

"It is? Do you drink coffee?"

"Yes, but that's not why. It's finals week…"

"And?"

"And… people are studying. They need caffeine. There's nothing available after 10:00 p.m. on campus except the vending machines. It's supply and demand!" She grinned.

"You want to *charge* people for coffee? Like, what… a pound or something?"

"Or two pounds. People will love it. No, not love, *need*. They need us to keep them hydrated and caffeinated!"

"I think coffee is actually dehydrating. I learned that in class the other day…"

"That's not the point!" Aggie interrupted me. She had a wild look in her eye, and I wondered if the finals week psychosis myth was, perhaps, not a myth after all.

"Don't you think that might be frowned upon by the local sheriff?" I rolled my eyes. We both knew I meant Marta.

Just then something slid under the door. It was a folded copy of the dorm hall rules and regulations.

"Ha! See what I mean?" I retrieved the booklet from under the doorway.

"What is it?" Aggie asked.

"Cannon Hall Rules and Regulations. It's from Big Bert."

"You are joking, right?"

I explained to Aggie the conversation I'd had with Marta at the desk.

"She doesn't take a joke well, apparently," I concluded.

"Is there anything in there about selling coffee out of your dorm room?" Aggie asked.

"Let's not look. That way, we can plead ignorance."

"Good plan." Aggie dumped the rule book into the trash bin.

"I'd thought Aggie was kidding or at least exaggerating about selling coffee to our peers. She wasn't. We couldn't advertise, so Aggie spread the word organically, letting secrecy add to the appeal. The flavor options we offered: vanilla. Sales the first night were light, but customer numbers increased as word spread. We averaged fifteen customers per night before we shut down our covert coffee operation for the summer. As promised, the machine did indeed make great foam.

Jack didn't call the night I received the espresso machine. Our weekday schedules were less than compatible. We played phone tag all week. It was Friday morning before my phone rang in my presence again. I answered it.

"Hello?"

"Hello, I can't believe I caught you. You are alive!" It was Jack.

"Alive, barely," I confirmed.

"You studying?"

"No. I was, but I finished. If I try to cram another thought in my brain right now, I think it might leak," I whined.

"I have the perfect idea. How about I kidnap you and we go somewhere? No studying, no deep thinking, just eating and drinking and maybe a little talking."

"When?"

"Now."

"Where are you?"

"Five minutes away. I delivered… something, and I can be there in five to pick you up."

"I have no money. Perhaps we could drop the eating and drinking part?"

"No dice. I'm too hungry, and I'm gainfully employed. I insist on paying for you… or at least eating alone while you watch me, if you are too stubborn to let me pay."

We'd had petty arguments about that before.

"I'm too hungry and tired to argue."

"It's settled then. I'll see you in five?"

"See you in five," I agreed. My pulse rate still increased a good 35 percent whenever seeing Jack in person was imminent. We went to the Bing Song teahouse again; it was one of Jack's favorite places. A small blue turtle with a Chinese symbol on his red shell was depicted on the sign over the entrance door to the restaurant. The owner caught me studying the sign.

"I am Li Bing." She pointed to herself, looking proud. "My husband is Song, and so… Bing Song. *My name is first,*" she whispered, "because it sounds best this way. For the Chinese, turtle means 'long life.' Tea can make your life better like this." She winked at me, then walked down the hallway into the atrium, and we followed her.

Ask her if she needs help, came Dhia's prompting from inside me.

With what? I wondered, not immediately understanding what He meant.

Work.

Seriously? I balked. *Just straight out ask if I can work here?*

The owner seated us, then disappeared behind a newly planted stand of bamboo into the kitchen. I'd hesitated too long and lost my chance to obey quickly.

"So did you find a job yet?" Jack asked as we perused the menus.

"No. Not yet. Finding part-time employment in a college town is like looking for a needle in a needle-free haystack when you have hay fever."

"Fun, then…" He chuckled.

"Exactly."

Bing returned to take our orders.

"Any chance you are looking for someone to work here, part-time, over the summer?" I asked immediately, wanting to make up for stalling.

She blinked at me. "You need work?"

"Yes, actually."

"You know how to cook?"

"No."

"You know how to make tea?"

"Well, sort of, with teabags." I hedged.

Bing furrowed her brow, dubious of my methodology.

"You know how to *not* break dish?"

"That, I could handle… probably," I said.

"Does not sound promising, but honest," Bing said. She pinched the back of my arm just a little, as if testing me for something… It was my turn to doubt her methodology.

"I do need help. My husband likes to do plants more than dishes, lately." She rolled her eyes and pointed at the climbing ivy that hung above our heads. "I could give you a try."

"Seriously? I mean, that would be great. Thank you! I will be done with school and available in three weeks, so…"

"You just leave me a phone number and call me when you are ready. Learn names of tea, please. This is necessary," she instructed.

I gave her my information, and she took our orders.

"I guess this *was* a good idea. Thank you for inviting me," I said, breathing a sigh of relief.

"Did you thank Him?" Jack asked me.

"Dhia? No, not yet, I guess."

"There are no coincidences," he reminded me.

"That's true. I'm learning that. Did we talk about that before? Because I've been thinking that exact thing."

"No. But it's true," Jack said.

Thank You, Dhia, I prayed silently, and I meant it.

What do you see? I heard Dhia ask me.

I looked at Jack. *Goodness.* When I looked at Jack, I saw more goodness than I'd seen in almost anyone I'd ever met, Blues included.

"What?" Jack asked. "You have a funny look on your face."

"I'm feeling grateful, I guess. And old man told me to take note when I felt grateful, and I've been trying to do that. I guess I'm grateful for you." My neck flushed red. I wasn't used to talking so frankly.

"I feel the same," Jack said. He brushed my fingers with his hand, sending goose bumps all the way to my scalp.

TAKE WING

They were hundreds of people, each going somewhere—brushing past each other without really looking or seeing one another. If I hadn't been hanging bat-like from the roof of the train station, I probably wouldn't have noticed her either. She weaved purposefully through the crowd. Her hair seemed lighter than I remembered it, almost colorless. She wore a professional pantsuit. She entered a tunnel, and I squinted to see the numbers on the platform; but in dreams, as in visions, squinting doesn't improve eyesight. I followed her into the lighted tunnel, down a flight of steps, and onto another platform where she boarded a train. I could smell her perfume; she'd changed brands. It wasn't a scent I recognized. I tried to call out to her, but she didn't respond. I stood on the platform and screamed her first name through the windows of the train, but no one heard me. I was invisible. The train left, and I was alone on the platform. I heard a loud pounding noise, and the platform faded from view. I woke up and crawled out of bed. The odors of mildew, exhaust, and my mother's strange perfume still clinging to my nose. I snorted, trying to get rid of them. I opened the door and found Aggie and Big Bert standing just outside. A few more curious heads peeked from open doorways down the hall.

"Yes?" I said, wondering what I'd missed out on.

"Are you okay?" Aggie asked. Her worried expression mimicked that of all the other faces peering in my direction.

"Perfectly okay, why?"

"It's 3:00 a.m., and yer screamin' like yer bein' murdered!" Big Bert exclaimed.

"Oh, no… really?" I asked, feeling the red flush creep up my neck again. "Screaming?"

Aggie nodded in confirmation.

"I'm so sorry. I had no idea. I was dreaming… I'm sorry. Really. I'm fine." I tried to smile reassuringly.

The faces in the doorways changed from concerned to irritated. "So not murdered, just crazy," someone murmured.

"I got it from here," Aggie told Big Bert. She stepped into the room and tried to close the door. Big Bert's foot was in the way.

"Yer sure?" she demanded.

"If she screams again, I'll slap her silly," Aggie promised. "It's finals week… Everyone loses it sometimes." That seemed to satisfy Big Bert. Muttering under her breath, she pulled her foot from the doorway, and Aggie eased it closed.

"I'm so embarrassed," I told Aggie, sinking down onto the bed.

"You actually sounded as if you might be dying. What kind of dream were you having?"

"Someone was leaving, and I was calling out after them. Loudly, apparently."

"That's it?"

"Yep, that's it. Cross my heart," I promised.

"What is 'cross my heart'?" Aggie asked.

"It just means a promise. It means I promise you, I'm fine. I'm tired, Aggie. It's the end of the year. I'm having weird dreams… I'm fine, okay? No worries. No major issues.

"Okay." Aggie sighed. "But I'm staying here tonight."

I started to protest, but Aggie put her finger in the air. "I'm tired too, Kiah. No arguing."

Aggie began to pull extra blankets from the closet and lay them out on the floor.

"Okay," I acquiesced, "but you sleep on the bed."

"You have a final at 8:00 a.m.?" Aggie asked.

"Yes."

"I finished my last final today. I don't need the sleep as much."

Aggie turned the lamp off and muttered something about crazy Americans under her breath. Once again, I had to agree. I did feel a little crazy. And guilty. I crawled into bed and fell asleep, but not quickly and not deeply. Closing my eyes, I fought the sensation of free fall. Fa, Shine, my mother, Aggie, Jack, Millie, Aaron... all marched around in the storage area of my brain while I fell. They sifted through my personal file drawers, emptying their contents onto the floor. Mother was looking for evidence that could be used against me. Aggie followed my mother, demanding to know who I really was; she got the cold shoulder. (*If you get anything out of her, Aggie, let me know. I'm very curious myself.*) Fa hunted for apples but disappointed, found only mangoes. Jack searched for candor, Shine for compassion. Millie dredged for proof that I was still, in fact, *me*. Aaron, the man I'd left at the village on Petra, wanted his life back. He searched for files with his name on them. Finding nothing, he cried and crumpled to the floor. I couldn't comfort him. I woke from the dream again and again, trying to shake it off, but it stubbornly returned, replaying. Finally, just after dawn, I gave up on sleep. I slipped to the floor quietly so as not to disturb Aggie, who had rolled tightly into a ball of blankets in the corner. Not even her head poked out. I dropped to my knees beside the bed. The questions I usually kept at bay scrambled to be addressed.

A Dhia, what if I'm not who they think I am? What if I can't do this... whatever it is that You want me to do? What if I'm not enough? I need You, Dhia. You come before me. You come behind me. You hem me in on my left and my right. You guard my heart. Please guide my steps, every one of them! I want to know Your voice. I want to see You move. Teach me. Teach me to trust You with all my heart. I don't see what You see. Help me see with Your eyes. You are the alpha and the omega.—the One who saves. You are the Creator. You are both the beginning and the end, and I rest in You. I rest in You. I rest in You.

The fear lifted. I felt able to get up off my knees and do the next thing. It was still early. I gathered clothing as quietly as possible, jotted a thank-you note for Aggie, and snuck out to the shower. The campus was slowly emptying of students. Those who'd finished their exams emanated relief. Those who still had a test or two to go sported the dogged determination of marathon runners in their last mile. There was an air of resignation too. Whether we'd done our best or our worst… whether we had gotten straight As, barely scraped by, or landed somewhere in between, as most of us do… it was ending. The records were being inked—a fact that the faculty members were just as pleased with as the students were. I wrote my last exam, finishing early, and dropped the completed test packet onto the desk in front of the professor.

"Last one?" she asked.

"Yes."

"Feels good to be done, doesn't it?" she said, winking as if we were old pals. The prospect of summer freedom seemed to have loosened her up. It was the first time she'd said anything to me of a personal nature.

"Sure, I guess so. Have a good summer," I told her… though, when I thought about it, I didn't feel the least bit done. Restless. School was over, and I should have felt free and relaxed, but a profound sense of restlessness was setting in. The coming summer didn't hold for me the promise of a *break*. Something was coming. I didn't know whether to run toward it with open arms or squeeze my eyes shut and duck for cover.

I didn't hurry back to the dorm. Jack was due to pick me up in a few hours and deliver me to the airport in time to catch the red-eye to Seattle. I'd already packed my room and didn't relish the prospect of waiting for hours on the front step, watching students leave. I walked the scenic route back to Bert. It was too warm for a jacket, but not warm enough for shirt sleeves. I tied my sweatshirt around my waist and purposefully dawdled. I found the stretch of sidewalk that bore my scorched outline. It was still there, though the sun and rain had faded it. I traced it with my finger and since no one was around, laid face-up on the sidewalk. Closing my eyes, I tried to remember precisely how Dhia's presence had felt.

I just want to know You, Dhia. I want to know You. I feel like I haven't even begun, I prayed silently.

"Comfortable?" I heard a loud, close voice say.

My heart skipped a beat, and my eyes flew open. Aggie's face hung above mine.

"What in the world are you doing?" she asked.

"Taking a break." I was inordinately pleased with my ability to provide a quick plausible answer. "I just finished my last test. Jack's coming in a few hours, and I have nothing to do until then. I feel like I haven't stopped moving since September. So… I'm taking a break. Join me?"

"Join you?" Aggie said. Her eyebrows disappeared into her hairline. "Lie on the ground? Seriously?"

"Yes, on the ground. Come on. What's the worst that could happen?"

Aggie sighed and joined me, using her jacket as a pillow.

"You are crazy, you know," she informed me.

"I know. But you are lying on the sidewalk beside me for absolutely no reason. What does that make you? Besides, it's nice, isn't it?"

"I guess so… maybe a little unorthodox." Aggie crossed her legs and settled in, enjoying herself more than she wanted to let on.

"So what are you doing here, *really*?" she asked.

"Really…? I was praying."

"Praying?"

"Yes, praying."

"I didn't know you were religious. What kind of religion?"

"I don't know if I'm religious, exactly. I'm Christian. Are you?"

"Well… I'm Hungarian," she said, giving me a knowing glance… Only, I didn't know.

I shrugged my shoulders and looked clueless.

"Most Hungarians are Catholic," Aggie explained. "And I was born in Esztergom. It's kind of a holy city."

"So do you pray?" I asked her.

"Not as much as I should, probably. Praying makes me feel guilty," she said.

That surprised me. "Why?"

"Sin… rules… all of that… I haven't gone to confession in years." Aggie winced.

"So? I've never been to confession at all. Is that what you think of God? That He's all about counting your sins so he can beat you over the head with them?" I asked her.

"Well… yes. He's good, and I'm not, right? At least not nearly as good as I should be. If you heard the things I think in my head! Besides, Donal's not a Catholic. Neither was my last boyfriend, and even if they were… we haven't exactly been angels."

"I don't think God's like that, Aggie. I mean, I think He's *holy*, but I don't think He's all about you making people dwell on every bad thing they've ever done. I don't think He's all about reminding everyone of how much better He is than they are."

"What do you think God's about, then?"

It was the first time anyone had asked me that question. It was also the first conversation in which I felt like I knew *more* than someone else about the nature of Dhia. I felt ill-equipped to answer.

"Well, *love* is my first thought. When I pray, I know He loves me. I feel it in *here*." I thumped my chest with my forefinger. "And *truth*, I think He's about *truth*… letting people know the truth of who He is and what He's done for us. He paid the price for us, Aggie. He gives us Grace. He's about grace. Goodness and beauty too… He's all those things. He's why I live," I said. I felt a tear slide down my cheek, but I didn't bother to wipe it away.

"Wow. I didn't know you felt that way about God," Aggie said. She scooted a little farther away so she could see my face properly. "I didn't know *anyone* felt that way about God. This matters to you a lot, yes?"

"It does."

"Well, you keep surprising me," Aggie said. She scooted closer to me again and patted my hand.

Class let out in the building just behind us, and students began to fill the sidewalk. Most people skirted us, avoiding eye contact. A few people glared. Aggie and I started out giggling, then dissolved into outright laughter.

"Maybe we should go…," I suggested, gasping for breath. Aggie nodded her agreement, and we helped each other up. Aggie didn't seem to notice the faded scorch marks on the path, and I certainly didn't point them out. Someone honked as we approached the parking lot near the dorm.

"That's my ride," Aggie said. "I'm flying home today."

We said good-bye, and I headed to my dorm room. Most of the doors up and down the hall were braced open, and the sad little rooms stood empty. The aromas of living filled the halls: spilled-food smells that clung to the carpet, mold and mildew from water leaks, shampoos, lotions, potions and hairsprays, sweat, popcorn, the faint contraband odor of cigarette smoke. The air felt different than usual. I couldn't wait to leave. I plunked down on the naked bed beside my suitcases. I'd collected more junk than I thought I had over the course of the school year. Jack had promised to take a few boxes of blankets, trinkets and clothing to Nan's house for me the following day. I smiled, thinking of the interrogation that awaited him when he arrived on Nan's porch with my belongings. I wondered if I should warn him.

The telephone rang.

"Hello?"

"Hello, are you ready to come home?"

It was Dad. I didn't have the heart to tell him that I didn't feel like home was home anymore.

"I'm almost on my way. My ride comes in a few." I hadn't told him about Jack, just yet. I wasn't exactly sure how. It seemed like a face-to-face sort of conversation to have. "Thanks for the coffeemaker, though. We put it to good use... We made and sold late-night lattes to students studying for exams."

"What coffeemaker?"

"The espresso machine. The one you sent last week," I reminded him.

"I know nothing about a coffee machine. Where did you get it?"

My stomach sank. "It came to my dorm room, in a huge box... from England."

"Last week? Are you sure it was for you?"

"Yes, it had my name on it and everything. You really don't know anything about it?"

"Not a thing. I promise," he said. We both fell silent, and I wondered if he was thinking what I was thinking. *Did Mom send it?*

"I don't know what to tell you, kiddo. Maybe you have a secret admirer. I do have something else to tell you, though. Something that came up today..." His voice trailed off, and I could tell he was searching for the right words. My stomach dropped even further.

"About Mom?"

"Well, yeah. I didn't find her or anything... It's not that. But we were packing up your room today. Gary and I... we found something."

"What kind of something?"

"A letter. It's addressed to you."

I suddenly felt as if I might vomit. I rolled quickly to the side of the bed, almost dropping the phone in the process.

"Are you there?" Dad asked.

"Yeah, I'm here. Was the letter under the pillow, just under the bedspread?" I asked.

It was Dad's turn to be surprised. "Yeah, yeah it was. You knew about it?"

"No, of course not. It's just... when I was little, Mom and I used to leave notes there for each other. It was like a game... It's been such a long time, though. I never thought to look there..."

"Of course you didn't. Well, I have it here. It's sealed. Do you want me to read it to you, or...?"

"No. No, thank you. I'll read it when I get there."

"You sure?"

"I'm sure. Really sure. It's waited this long. It can wait another day," I said. *What could it say? What could it possibly say?* I couldn't even imagine, but I *really* couldn't imagine trying to process the message, no matter what it was, on an airplane full of strangers.

Dad stayed silent.

"You can read it yourself... if you want to, Dad. I mean, that's fine with me, if you are curious..."

"Oh no. It's not for me, honey. I really don't want to read it. I just... I didn't tell you Mom had left until you got home, and I didn't tell about the move until after the decision was made. I thought I should give you a heads-up this time," he said.

Dad was trying hard, *so* hard to do the right thing.

"Well, thank you. I'll read it when I get there."

"You're sure?"

"Absolutely sure." My palms sweated and my heart raced.

"Are you okay?" he asked.

"Oh, yeah. I'm fine. You okay?"

"I'm fine. Just fine. Almost everything is out of the house. There will be boxes everywhere, at the new place…"

"That's okay. I can't wait to see it. I have to go, Dad. My ride will be here any minute. I'll see you soon."

"Okay, be safe. I love you," he said softly.

"I love you too."

I hung up and rested my forehead in my shaking hands. My mother hadn't walked off into the sunset without a word. She'd penned a letter to me and left it in a place she probably thought I'd check.

How would I know to check that, Mom? I'm not five anymore! Of course, chastising her in my mind did no one any good. She wasn't there to listen, and that was the bottom line, really… the whole entire point. The existence of the letter, whatever it said, didn't change the fact that she simply wasn't there.

I glanced at the espresso machine in the corner. I hadn't really wanted the thing in the first place. Now I really wanted *not* to have it.

"Dhia, you have to help me, help me focus! Please help me understand. Help me dump the questions and hang on to You. Help me find You in this. I don't understand…"

"Nothing ever surprises me." Dhia's voice was so clear and impossibly resonant that I sprang to my feet and looked around. I saw nothing.

"I know, Dhia, but it surprises *me!*"

"I know. Trust me," He said.

A warm sensation spread over the nape of my neck, as if a large hand rested there. It felt so real that I ran my fingers from shoulder to shoulder, looking for a physical source for the warmth but found none. The warmth remained.

"I trust You," I whispered. "I trust You."

Somehow, despite the letter, despite all the uncertainties that surrounded me, I felt peace. The peace settled my breathing, my heart rate, and my nervous stomach. I shut my eyes, and an image hung in my mind. It was the stone cottage on Petra. For the first time since I'd left it, I really let myself think about it. I wanted very much to be there. I also knew absolutely and without any concrete reason that I soon *would* be there.

"Thank you, Dhia." A knock sounded at the door. I knew it would be Jack. I hesitated for a moment before answering, savoring the moment with Dhia. Then it was time to go.

ABOUT THE AUTHOR

Kiah Cross is a wife and mother of six who lives just outside Portland, Oregon. She works as a nurse both at home and abroad in a not-for-profit capacity. See www.kiahcross.com for more about the author as well as a collection of letters, sketches and photographs that pertain to but are not found in this book.